TRAPPED!

Button, button, who's got the button? Bailey turned in a slow circle. She could almost hear Lacey panting. She'd run in the same direction, however wildly it seemed she'd been going.

She had to be somewhere about, and close. Maybe . . . Bailey slid her palm along the wall in front of her, looking for a crack or unfastened panel. Somewhere about here . . .

The wall clicked.

Bailey blinked as it suddenly swung open into darkness in front of her, and at the same time, something swung into the back of her, knocking her through!

She went headlong into nothingness, and the wall solidly thudded into place behind her.

"I think," said Bailey quietly, standing very still, "I found that secret passage."

And worse, as she strained her magickal senses, it was blacked out, warded, against any kind of magic whatsoever.

She was trapped, with no way for anyone to hear her!

Also by
EMILY DRAKE

The Magickers

The Curse of Arkady

The Dragon Guard

The Gate of Bones

www.magickers.com

THE GATE OF BONES

THE MAGICKERS #4

EMILY DRAKE

DAW BOOKS, INC.

DONALD A. WOLLHEIM, FOUNDER

375 Hudson Street, New York, NY 10014

**ELIZABETH R. WOLLHEIM
SHEILA E. GILBERT
PUBLISHERS**

www.dawbooks.com

First paperback printing, September 2005
1 2 3 4 5 6 7 8 9 10

DAW TRADEMARK REGISTERED
U.S. PAT. OFF. AND FOREIGN COUNTRIES
—MARCA REGISTRADA
HECHO EN U.S.A.

PRINTED IN THE U.S.A.

I'd like to dedicate this book to friends and family who have enriched our lives tremendously.

Wayne Allen
A tall, lanky and self-made man whose hard work and thirst for knowledge continues well into his nineties. A man who never fails to share his insight and advice, with sincere thanks.

Uncle Sam Stein
Another self-made man whose hard work is exceeded only by his generous heart and inventive mind. May we toast your one hundredth!

Bernard Couch
A plain-spoken gentleman who brings light to our home every time he crosses the doorstep, with sincere gratitude for the pleasure of knowing him.

Larry Stone
A gentle giant with a sense of humor exceeded only by his sense of fair play. Thanks for the opportunities he's bestowed upon our family.

To Alexander, Tyler Jo, and Adrian
With a thank you for being young readers and magical people yourselves!

And to my mother Barbara and my aunt Criss, for sharing with me their love of books, reading and adventure. You shall both be greatly missed and your memories treasured.

Contents

1	Night Raid	*1*
2	Dark Roads	*9*
3	Sparklies	*17*
4	Planners and Dreamers	*26*
5	The Beginning	*35*
6	Alarms and Other Considerations	*43*
7	Wills and Ways	*48*
8	Mud	*57*
9	Crystal Shields	*64*
10	Mulberry Bush	*72*
11	Sticks and Stones	83
12	Wind Beneath My Wings	*91*
13	Button, Button	*101*
14	Chutes and Ladders	*107*
15	Plans and Plans Gone Awry	*115*
16	Swinging Gate	*119*
17	Ouchified	*124*
18	Journals	*131*
19	Words and More Words	*145*
20	Threats	*154*
21	Happy Birthday, Happy Birthday— Happy Birthday!	*160*
22	Narian Nights	*173*

23	More Nights	184
24	Ghostwalking	197
25	Myths of Time	207
26	Oops	215
27	Chains	224
28	Tightrope	231
29	Chaos and Order	238
30	Planning	246
31	Sting Like a Bee	252
32	Power!	261
33	Aftershock	272
34	No, Henry!	281
35	Gate of Dread	288
36	Aunt Freyah	296
37	Isabella's Fury	306
38	Who's Been Sleeping in My Coffin?	310
39	Webs	319
40	Sanctuary	325
41	Hunting	334
42	Desperate Times	343
43	Desperate Measures	348
44	Frying Pans and Fire	359
45	Pearls of Wisdom	366
46	Face-to-Face	373
47	Dragons and Dungeons	377
48	A Helping Hand	383
49	Stuck on You	390
50	The Decision	401

Night Raid

A FULL HUNTER'S MOON rose over the fields and forest of Avenha, its golden shine almost as clear as the sun through the cloak of night. Avenha itself slept, the villagers weary from days of busy harvesting and storing for the coming winter. Signs all around them had warned of a long, harsh season awaiting them. Like villages all over, they prepared as well as they could. Now, as the moon rode the evening sky, the hunters it had been named for were out to catch those unwary creatures who grazed under its brilliant light. Newly harvested fields brought them all in: deer, boar, hill sheep. The next weeks would be spent curing meat and tanning hides as the days of autumn trekked toward winter.

Renart shifted uneasily at the chieftain's gate, trying to stretch his long legs without disturbing the others as he sat silently. He did not know why he'd been summoned and wondered if he was finally back in favor. He rubbed his hands together, the tattoos dappling the curve of his thumb and index finger marking him as a member of the Trader Guild. All he'd ever done was what he'd been born and trained to do, barter and trade.

Except he'd chosen invaders to do it with.

But how could he not? They'd seemed so harmless, so confused when they'd first arrived. Defenseless, even. Renart had rarely been more wrong. Of course, there were those who later understood his attraction to them. The new arrivals did seem somewhat out of the mists of tall tales, people who'd just awakened to the world. Yet the others who'd followed them had none of the helpless charm of the first group. He'd made friends with invaders. Traded with them. Given them knowledge and supplies through which they survived . . . and some of them survived well enough to hunt down his own people. Renart couldn't blame any of the chieftains who had later refused to deal with him when the Trader Guild pulled his license and demoted him to the lowly position of clerk for his mistakes. No, even if there hadn't been trouble, he could see the problems he'd caused. He'd established trade with a new people, without the consent of his own master and guild. Now, he realized, it looked like a shameless grab for power on his part. It hadn't been, though, it had been done out of curiosity and pity. He'd testified to that, over and over. Surely, they would eventually realize the truth, and he would regain their trust.

Surely? He stared at his shoes, odd things, invader things . . . *sneakers* he was told they were called. Certainly, their strange soles made walking very quiet. He wore them like a badge of honor despite all the trouble they had caused him. He didn't think he was truly wrong for what he'd done. He could never have predicted that the invaders would be the same people, yet two distinctly different groups. Like good and evil, two sides of the same coin.

Torches at the gate burned low. In the chieftain's hut, glowing coals were banked against the growing chill of the night, and a hooded lantern cast little illumination beyond its immediate circle. The chieftain sat on a sagging hide chair, his legs folded comfortably, the dappling of the tattoos across his cheekbones and forehead that marked his line and position little more than shadows in the room. He tapped a pipe against the stones banking the coals, and tiny sparks flew out. Renart gathered his wits about him.

A guardsman stirred in the gatehouse. "How much longer do we wait?"

"Night after night," Mantor answered. "Until the trap is sprung."

"And if they do not come?"

"Then our ambassadors have greatly misunderstood our new guests. But I think not. And I think our wait will end tonight. What do you think, Renart?"

The young trader flushed. "I—I wonder both how I can help and why you called me. Chieftain Mantor, there is no one better than you at what you do, but . . ." Renart shuddered in memory. "The Dark Hand is unstoppable. They use sorcery. I can only advise one way to meet that."

"Good thoughts. I need a scribe to help my daughter with the warehouse records. As for it being you, specifically, well . . ." He paused for a long moment. "I do not wear the tattoos of chieftain because I am a good painter, eh? I look at people and judge them. At seasons and harvests, I judge them. I think you deserve a second chance." Chieftain Mantor looked across the tiny flames licking up now and then from the red-hot coals, gazing at his daughter, her faced marked the same as his, as she took notes on the conversation, her hands busy with ink and paper. Her eyes were better than his in the dim light.

Another man stirred in the gatehouse. "What if we've misjudged?"

"I do not think we have. We know of the laziness of these invaders and the outlaws they have gathered to them. We know the other villages they have hit, just as the harvests have been laid down for store. Shall we wait for the Holy One to return as Warlord, or protect ourselves with the skill he passed down to us? I vote we fight." The chieftain's attention returned to rest on the questioner. "Nervous or eager, Flameg?"

"Both. Waiting is never easy." Flameg shifted his burly frame, and wood creaked under him as he moved. He stilled immediately. They had wanted to draw no attention. No one knew they waited. No one knew a snare had been laid. His hand brushed across his longbow.

"Do not even think it." Mantor traded looks with his head guardsman.

"No." Flameg nodded. "I will think it, but not act it. The council has agreed with your guidance, and for that matter so do I, but—" He had no time to finish his sentence. A call sounded from the gatewalk, and even that could barely be heard over the low rumble, the sound of hoofbeats approaching.

Many hoofbeats.

The group got to their feet. Trader Renart had said little, his wiry frame wrapped in a tartan cloak against the chill of the autumn night, his hair in a mouse's nest of disarray, his eyes still sleepy from a hastily caught nap. He was not a fighter, not like the chieftain and Flameg or even the chieftain's heir and daughter, Pyra. His tattoo marks sprinkled the backs of his hand and his clever fingers, like a craftsman. Once he was back in the graces of his guild, and far in the future when he became a master trader, he'd gain a single dot at his temple, to indicate his knowledge and experience. Flameg's markings were across his powerful shoulders, not to be seen unless he took off his tunic. Renart flexed his hands now. He wondered again if he should have regretted it, those first tentative trades, especially with the second group, who his keen senses soon told him were vastly different from the first people he'd met. Yet he'd not hesitated to barter and trade with them. Not until they'd caught and tortured him. They were mortal enemies, these Magickers and Dark Hand, and it had been his ill luck to discover them both.

Did they bring war with them, war such as only the Warlord had once fought? His far-flung kingdom now lived in peace, in cities and villages across the lands, ruled only by councils which took the Warlord's words from the writings of his time, and from the words and visions of his Holy Spirit now. Even the Warlord's fortresses were now little more than dry, rotting piles of wood, barely more than a wall here, a guard tower there. He was neither a warrior or a counselor who heard the spirit, but he was a trader and scribe. So, as the others prepared, he reached out to Pyra.

He took the paper and ink from Pyra, and the leather pouch she tossed to him, as she drew her curved cutlass to join her father. Trying not to show the tremor that ran through him, he stowed the writing instruments and implements, and then slung the pouch over his shoulder. The rumbling thunder grew louder until it broke into hoofbeats. Unmistakably, it roared into the noise of horsemen charging down the valley toward Avenha's gates.

Mantor gave a quick nod and a grunt of satisfaction. "They come. Now the trap awaits." He crooked a finger. "Follow me."

Orange flame trailed down the hill as the riders swept through the night, torches in the hands of the outriders. Renart held his breath. He had heard the tales, and hoped them exaggerations, but he knew now they were not. He turned his gaze away. He had not brought them to his world, but had he helped them thrive? Barely more than three dozen at first, they'd attracted the lazy and outlawed who would rather steal than work themselves. He looked at a charge of nearly fifty riders, and it took his breath away.

In a cloud of smoke and dust and chaff from the newly shorn fields, the raiders swept up to the barred gates, barely slowing. Riders at the front threw up gloved hands. Crystal gems grasped in their palms caught the gleaming light of the Hunter's Moon and threw it back at the wooden gates. Gemstones flared, emitting great bolts of power. Lightning cracked, and the air stank of scorched wood as the gates exploded into fiery splinters.

Above and to the side, the chieftain's gatewalk

trembled, and Mantor cursed under his breath. Renart looked quickly at him. Had he thought the gates would hold against sorcery? His guardsman caught the chieftain's elbow. "Now?"

Mantor shook his head. At his flank, Pyra's face paled, but she kept her stance at the ready. "Not yet," Mantor answered quietly. "Not yet."

Renart kept his balance, his strange shoes gripping the narrow wooden gatewalk with ease, but he hardly noticed. Below, riders swept into the town, hammering down doors and heading with precision toward the longhouses where the food stores were kept. It made him ill to watch. Despite the carefully laid plans of the chieftain, a door was suddenly flung open and a shouting man ran out. He brandished his scythe, sharp and hooked, and his square body blocked the narrow street. Then he sank with a cry of pain, an arrow buried in his thigh, and the raiders rode over him without a second thought.

"Stubborn man," grunted Mantor. "He wouldn't leave and let me handle these raiders. They'll pay for that, even so."

Pyra let out a muffled sound. Renart watched her put her wrist to her mouth, stifling her emotion. Chieftains had to be made of stern stuff. Her free hand tightened about her cutlass, her wrist like a mask over the expression on her face. Renart thought for a fleeting moment he'd never seen anyone more fierce or beautiful.

"It won't work," said Flameg.

"We shall see." Mantor pulled his own longbow off his shoulder and nocked a wicked-looking black arrow. His body blocked them all into the shadows of the gatehouse. His dark eyes narrowed as he looked down into the village that was the trust of his guardianship.

Renart found himself breathing again, shallow, quiet inhalations. The raiders raced to a storehouse and, with shouts and gestures, surrounded it. Six men dismounted and gathered up a battering ram, taking aim at the stout double doors. Wood groaned and then cracked, but stood up to the assault.

"Enough!" A woman's voice split the air. Curbing her mount with a strong pull on the reins, she kneed the others aside and raised her gloved hand. In it, the crystal gleamed. A ray of power blazed from it, her horse rearing under her in fright, as the warehouse door shattered. She pivoted her horse around, her great skirts swirling about her and covering the animal. With a look of disdain, she lifted her hand, and again Lightning swept out of her palm. The remains of the door blew apart in splinters that caught fire and drifted through the air in orange curls.

"We can't fight blades against Lightning fire."

"Not this way, no." Mantor lowered his longbow. He pulled back into the shadows even farther, drawing all of them with him. "Take Pyra and go, Flameg."

"Chieftain—"

"There is nothing you can do here, now, tonight. Take her and go."

The guardsman's mouth clamped shut, his lips thinning in protest, but he lowered his head and then made a fist of obedience, bringing it to his shoulder. Pyra threw a kiss at her father, before scampering after Flameg as he swung down from the gatewalk and the two disappeared. Renart tried to watch her leave, but the hidden gate worked all too well, and she was gone without a trace.

Mantor hissed.

Shouts of anger rose, and the warehouse shook as the horsemen pounded inside and . . . and discovered the structure was empty. Torches dipped and flared, and wood crackled up into reluctant, smoky flame, for the wood had been green, on purpose. Eventually, it would burn, but slowly.

Mantor had left them an empty village to ransack. Only a few stubborn old men had refused to go, and one of them now lay dead in the street. The chieftain ground his teeth angrily. Renart heard him murmur something to the Warlord under his breath.

In fury, the raiders bashed down stores, homes, guild houses, the other two empty storehouses, and burned all they could, looting what few goods had been left behind. They destroyed everything they touched.

Empty, Avenha had been, but not unlivable. Now, it was. Renart sighed, then choked as smoke filled his nostrils, his throat. His eyes watered fiercely. With screams of hatred and anger, the horsemen swept back to the gate, and milled about, shaking their hands and throwing the last of their torches on the broken walls of Avenha. Then, with the horses crying in pain as spurs and whips lashed their sides, the raiders thundered back into the night.

They waited until only the noise of the fire could be heard, then Mantor stirred. He swung down from the gatewalk, and held up his hand to help Renart.

Once outside, trotting across a newly harvested field, heading for the hillside caves where he had sent his people, Mantor said, "You were right. They're unstoppable, this Dark Hand. You were also right about how we must fight them." Under the Hunter's Moon, Chieftain Mantor halted and put his hand on Renart's shoulder. The trader suppressed a shiver, suddenly realizing just why the chieftain had brought him to Avenha that night.

"Send for the Magickers."

2

Dark Roads

MORE USED TO RIDING in a caravan than on a horse, Renart took the night road cautiously, following a ribbon of trampled and rutted dirt that seemed ominously dark despite the Hunter's Moon at his back. He needed speed, but riding at night called for caution lest he lame or lose the horse altogether and be stranded on foot. On foot, he would never get to the Magickers before the cold of the mountain passes got to him.

He wondered if his suspension would get worse for seeking them out again, without his guild's direction. But then, how could it? The chieftain had sent him, and who would argue with Mantor, a leader of Avenha as well as a councillor of the Holy Spirit? If one who followed the Warlord in all ways of his life told him to do something, Renart was bound by the laws of the land to do it.

If it brought him trouble this time, he'd bear it. Or perhaps he would become a wanderer, one of those itinerant workers who always seemed unwelcome wherever they traveled, beyond laws and civilization. He didn't think the wanderers had a good peddler among their groups; he could probably teach them quite a bit and learn a bit himself. He could travel

9

again, then, something his ink-stained hands and mind longed to do. Being a clerk for the warehouses was *not* what he had in mind when someone said "Trader." Not in the least.

Then again, he was traveling, his saddle-sore legs reminded him, and riding on a very dark road. The only good thing about it was that he could tell it clearly led away from the direction in which the raiders had ridden. Renart murmured a word of thanks to the Warlord's Holy Spirit for that happiness. He had no idea if the spirit of that long-ago warrior heard him or not, but the lands had lived long and in prosperity after his death, due to the strength of the Spirit he left behind to keep it so. The councils prayed to him and received answers, or so they claimed, and they also had written volumes well stocked in libraries everywhere of the sage advice the Warlord had given while he was still alive. Yet, even the old Warlord had been quiet about this latest menace in his countries. Did he sleep? And if he did, would what Renart was about to undertake wake him?

The countries he would leave behind him, the Warlord had explained, were like a chain of clasped hands, an impenetrable wall of spirit and knowledge that could hold back any foe . . . as long as it remembered it was a chain composed of many and acting for the good of many but never at the expense of a few unless so willed and offered in sacrifice. Simple enough. It had kept them safe for centuries, once the living Warlord had turned back the enemies from across the great sea. It was said it was not only his might that had turned back those enemies, but a massive plague, and many worried that those times could return. Yet the Spirit of the Warlord seemed to keep them safe.

Now, Renart wondered, how the Warlord's words would stand against these strange enemies from much, much farther away than that. With thoughts weighing heavily on his mind and his eyelids, he traveled the dark road slowly into the night, finding no answer and only the immediate danger of being a fool alone on this journey. He hoped morning would find him safe and well along his way.

As the night's darkness thinned and even the light of the moon paled before the dawn, Renart swung down off his horse, and found a good place to pasture it for a bit of rest and grazing. He squatted in the damp grass and debated on making a fire for warmth, but the thought of night raiders still about made up his mind for him. Why take chances?

He stretched gingerly, feeling muscles protest being on horseback for so long, and the scarred welts from his torture also protested, although with far less pain than he'd ever hoped. It was something he tried not to think about, knowing that he could have been beaten far worse than he was, and that the healing ointment applied by Tomaz Crowfeather's deft hands could have helped far less than it did. That Magicker was an elder, one with a great sense for the land and its beasts, and had a presence about him that had reassured Renart from the first time he'd spied him. Tomaz had remarked at the time, that the beating was not too bad, and that Renart was lucky. The Dark Hand had ways of knowing whether he spoke truth or not, in answer to their questions, and if he held back. They must have decided early on that Renart knew little.

And so he had, then. The questions Isabella and the quietly menacing Jonnard had put to him, between blows, made no sense. Were there other Gates? How often was the Gate opened? Who came through? How had Haven gathered people? And more . . . more that, despite the beatings, he could never have answered. They'd finally thrown him out on the road in disgust, where he'd made it back to his little peddler's cart, crawled onto it, and let the old horse draw him where it would. Luckily, it had taken him to Iron Mountain.

Until then, he'd not realized that the two groups of newcomers were like night and day; although the Hand had made him a bit uneasy at first, they'd concealed their true nature with guile. He hadn't seen much of the Magickers since then, for upon returning to his home city of Naria, his master discovered Renart's healing condition and the Trader Guild put him through a verbal inquisition to which he *did* know the answers, and he'd had his ranking and license taken from him while they discussed his actions. How naive he'd been, he realized now, not seeing that his actions had made many traders uneasy, as a grab for power and influence. He'd only seen it as a charity.

Renart rubbed his hands together. He should have brought gloves, he knew that. It was autumn now and the nights and even days would grow damper, colder, and any trader knew how important it was to be prepared while out on the road. It was just that he'd been clerking in warehouses for weeks now and hadn't thought about being on the road again. He wondered if Chieftain Mantor would be able to influence the councillors as he promised he would. Oh, to be established again, doing what he loved. . . .

He'd get a firsthand sight of how the academy was coming along, and how the wanderers he'd sent there were working out, as well. Wanderers were a strange people, outcast by most towns and villages for their refusal to accept rule by the councils and the Warlord's Holy Spirit. No Spirit, they claimed, no matter how powerful and influential in this life, could help being tainted by evils on the spiritual side, and therefore was not trustworthy in a Spirit life. Never mind that the Warlord had proven Himself time and again. They refused to accept him, and so the rest of Haven refused to accept the wanderers.

Still, a people had to live, did they not? They were not harmful, just strange. Strange and often poor and bedraggled, as if punished for their beliefs. Perhaps they had been. Renart closed his eyes a moment in thought.

He awoke with the sun's rays striking his face, the morning fog completely gone from the meadowland, and his horse still cropping grass contentedly. He leaped to his feet, let out a groan as his whole body began to ache, and quickly made ready to ride again.

To save Avenha and the other peoples he had grown to love, and to redeem himself. Traders got few chances to be heroic, and this was his! To ride! He snapped the reins and his horse raced forward on the road.

"Trent, if you don't stop asking for stuff, I am never going to get Henry Gated out of here." Jason sat cross-legged on the top floor of the academy, his face shadowed by a corner beam, but nothing could quite hide the intensity that gleamed out of him. The power that he would use to open a Gate between two worlds already hummed through his body, in preparation for being loosed.

Tall and wiry Trent stopped in mid-sentence, and swung around to look at Jason, his fingers still clenching a handful of white paper. His jaw worked as if the words couldn't quite come out, then he said, "Don't you get it, Jason? You, Henry?" He turned toward Henry, who also sat with an apologetic expression over his round face, black hair unruly, and caught in mid-yawn. Henry put his hand over his mouth as heat flooded his face.

The long summer and mild autumn so far had turned the boys lean, grown them tall as they had hit that time of life when boys became men, almost overnight it seemed. Only Henry wore clothes like they'd all worn when they first came to Haven, but that was because he was going back. Back for supplies and news and to reassure families at home that the Magickers were doing fine, and Haven was indeed a Haven. Henry, the ambassador between two worlds and showing diplomatic grace, would not mention the growing menace of the Dark Hand. He scrubbed his face now and widened his round eyes, then put his glasses back on.

"I am listening," he vowed.

"Well, good. Because you need to. This stuff is important." Trent tapped his papers. "I need these books or articles, Henry. Anything you can pull out of a used bookstore or off the Internet, okay? Because Haven is full of people almost like us, but not us, and these myths . . . these tales they tell . . . hold the answer to their beginnings. I need as much research done as you can manage. Now, I know what Gavan and Tomaz told you to do is more important, I'm just asking for a little help here." It went without saying that the wishes of the elder Magickers, the headmaster and the beastmaster, would rule all of Henry's actions.

Henry reached out and took the lists. "I'll do it," he said confidently.

"Good." Jason stood. "Are we settled, then? I can Gate now, but after the day's work, I'll be too tired to do it. So I need to get Henry out of here now, and get the passage closed again before the Hand senses anything."

Trent made a gesture which had as much to do with the music that always seemed to be thrumming inside him as it had to do with what he and Jason and Henry were talking about. "Look . . . remember we talked about the Gordian knot and Alexander the Great? The wise men and prophets said only someone who could undo the knot would fulfill their prophecy about a great ruler . . . and Alexander, instead of trying to untie the knot, just took up his sword and sliced through it."

"Yeah." The list of things needed crackled a bit as Henry folded it carefully and put it in his pocket.

"That's a myth. The reality is that the Gordian knot was most likely a complicated political arrangement of alliances and religions that opposed anyone who would unite that part of the world. Rather than deal with them and get caught up in their politics and bribery and self-interest, Alexander just took his armies and conquered them. That was the sword slicing through the knot, see? So . . . we hear things from the wanderers and Renart and others, and somewhere in the myths we're hearing is a little bit of truth about Haven."

"Right."

Trent rolled his eyes and threw up his hands. "No one listens!"

"We all listen. And you're right. But what we have to do now is get the academy built before the rains start, and then winter hits us. If for no other reason than we need a way to keep our butts warm and dry. Then, when that's done, we can sit around a desk and talk about your theories. On long winter nights it might even be a fun thing to do." Jason stood, folding his arms, and tilting his head at Trent.

Trent's mouth snapped shut and he settled for a mild punch to Jason's shoulder. The other boy rocked back with a soft grunt, still grinning.

"Hey! Don't punch the Gatekeeper. I have a date to go home!" Henry scrambled to his feet, gathering up his empty backpack. He'd bring it back brimming with items all the exiled Magickers had requested. Foremost on his list seemed to be chocolate, requested by Bailey and Ting.

"I'll look for you in a week's time," Jason promised.

"Just remember, time is different here than there."

"Right. Which is why I won't just open the Gate. You're going to have to tell me if you're ready yet. I think we can touch thoughts that long. Don't give me big explanations—just a 'yeah, let's go, or no, see me next week,' got it?"

Henry's head bobbed. "Got it."

"Good." Jason gripped his friend's shoulder. "Say hi to everyone for us, right?"

"First on all my lists." Henry took a deep breath. "Okay. I'm ready."

Trent turned his back on them, his face creased with a kind of sorrow, and Jason knew he was thinking of his father, left behind and sorely missed. Jason filled his hands with his crystals and gripped them tightly. With a deep breath, he opened his mind, and found that essence which was the Dragon Gate, and swung it open. He literally tossed Henry through it, and slammed it shut, hoping that the Dark Hand had not sensed the abrupt flow of energies.

He stood for a long moment, feeling the surge of great power running through him, and ebbing away, as though it sank into the very floorboards of the unfinished building about him, as if the academy grounded him. Then his heart did a double beat, and he inhaled again, and his crystals stilled in his hands.

Trent waited another moment before saying gruffly, "C'mon. We've got a lot to do today."

"Always," Jason agreed. He looked up at the sky. "Maybe a roof in a few more days?"

"Maybe. Although I think I'd rather have hot water."

Jason snorted. "What do you think I am? A magician?"

Trent tackled him and they wrestled with laughs and snorts and grunts until the sound of shouting for them drew them apart and into a long day of hard work.

3

Sparklies

WAKING MEANT more than just prying the eyes open. It also meant finding the nerve to stick one's arms out from under the covers into the cold morning air and then putting one's bare feet on chilly wooden planks. So Bailey eased out of her warm cocoon of a bed gingerly, her face all screwed up in an expression of intensity as she woke and then dashed to the cupboard, flinging clothes every which way till she found the warmest combo she could find and dove in headfirst. Once dressed and with her feet shoved into a pair of fleece-lined boots, she could work on the niceties of dressing . . . like ties and belts and tucking in her blouse. She turned around, pulling on her lacings, to see Ting's brown eyes peering over the tops of her blankets with amusement sparkling in their depths.

"It's cold," muttered Bailey.

"And likely to get much colder!" Ting agreed. "Do you realize we might get snow?"

While snow had sounded like the epitome of winter fun in sunny Southern California, here . . . far away and someplace strange . . . it sounded . . . well . . . *cold*.

"I dunno," answered Bailey dubiously.

"You'll love it! We'll have the chimneys working

17

by then, and this place will heat up. Gavan and Tomaz promised."

Bailey arched her back and looked at the wooden structure encompassing them, and their sleeping room just a small part, one day to be a classroom. Iron Mountain Academy (IMA wizard school, she added mentally) was no longer a dream, it was nearly a reality. One without a top floor and roof and indoor plumbing, as of yet. "First," she commented, "we have to finish building it."

"Not on an empty stomach!" Ting threw herself out of bed then, scrambling for her clothes in much the same hurried fashion as her best friend. Bailey would have crawled back into her still warm blankets to wait, but her boots hadn't been cleaned, and she had no intention of pulling them off just to sit on her cot. So she paced back and forth until the vibration of her boot heels set off an irritated chattering in the corner. A small whiskered mouse face poked out of a wooden barrel that had once been a nail keg but had now been appropriated for her home. As if also anticipating the return of the Ice Age, the little pack rat had promptly filled it with as many scraps of paper and fabric as she could find and drag in for her nesting.

Bailey squatted down and put her hand out, palm up. "Morning, Lacey."

The little creature stopped chittering, put her paws to her whiskers for a quick scrub, then hopped into the hand. Bailey swept her up and deposited her in her bodice pocket as Ting gave one last brush through her gleaming blue-black hair.

They looked at one another and said, in unison and emphatically, "Breakfast!"

As they headed down the inner, spiraling stair, they could hear the sounds of others who were already awake and about. Workmen's voices rang through the air, along with the thump of hammers and the noise of handsaws. The smell of a wood-burning fire as well as cooking food filled the air, while a thin fog curled away from the ground. Breakfast was always served in the outdoor camp, to feed the wanderers who helped with the construction, for Gavan and Bailey's mother Rebecca couldn't help but take pity for the thin, tense faces of those who'd come to help build the academy.

The hardest part of leaving home and coming to Haven was trying to understand the new people they eventually met.

Quiet and wary and seemingly shy, it had been months before they'd actually met anyone face-to-face—and that first one had been Renart, the young trader who'd bartered items with them from the shadows. Some days they'd find a shirt folded up on a rock, for which they left small things of their own, the next they'd find a basket of eggs. Eventually, one day, Rebecca had been startled to find Renart himself, sitting cross-legged, awaiting them, his six-fingered hands folded in his lap, his eyes bright with curiosity, with a new sack of trade offerings at his side. They taught him to shake hands and he taught them how to "sketch a bow." Gavan and Tomaz painstakingly made "Talker" crystals, crystals that they had imbued with a kind of translating ability, and they'd shared their first words with the native of a new world the Magickers had, basically, invaded.

Rebecca Landau turned from a great pot, hung on a cooking rod, and waved her spoon in the air. Bailey beamed at her mother in pride. "Who'd have thunk," she whispered to Ting, "that someone who hates camping would be doing so well in Haven?"

Indeed, Rebecca glowed. Or maybe it was just reflected heat from the campfire which kept her cauldron of oatmeal bubbling. One tiny streak of charcoal etched the side of her face and Bailey grinned, wondering if she should tell her mom or not. Old, naturally, and a mom, of course, but Rebecca still looked slender and pretty, her light brown hair pulled back from her face in French braids, and her long skirt swirling down to sweep the ground. Yup, old Mom looked pretty good in Haven gear.

Over the hubbub of the workmen, Madame Qi's imperious voice could be heard, and the thump of her bamboo cane. "Shoulders straight, arms out, eyes closed . . . I want you to breathe deep!"

Ting's mouth opened in a soft laugh at her grandmother's drill sergeant tone. She nudged Bailey. "She's got them at it already."

"Our turn will come tonight," Bailey groaned. She was still sore after yesterday's exercises.

"It's good for you," Ting protested.

"So is cod liver oil, but that tastes like tuna fish gone bad, very, very bad, and you don't see me taking it!" Bailey wrinkled her nose, freckles dancing.

"Oh, you shush." Ting put up her hand and ran to the small, wrinkled Chinese woman who held a line of young men at her command with nothing more than the crack of her voice.

Bailey veered away to the campfire. "Need help, Mom?"

"No, no. Qi and I got everything going this morning." Rebecca pulled at her shirtsleeves, then dished out a bowl of steaming oatmeal, or what passed for oatmeal, and gave it to Bailey. "I have a little bit of brown sugar and raisins saved aside for you . . ."

"Wow!" She beamed at her mom. "Is Henry going to bring back more?"

"If he has the money. It's difficult for him and his family . . ."

Bailey sat on a stump, wooden spoon in hand. Actually, it was more like a miniature pancake turner than a spoon. Someday she'd have to explain the concept of spoon bowls to a Havenite and see what they could come up with. "Being an ambassador between two worlds isn't all it's cut out to be, huh?"

"One could say that." Rebecca frowned. "He's also worried about being watched."

"Ummm." Bailey nodded slowly. No wonder Henry's visits between were getting more and more unreliable. Watched! That could ruin everything . . . She carefully sprinkled only a few pinches of brown sugar over her hot cereal, and doled out half a dozen raisins or so. The idea of rationing had been with them since day one, but sometimes it was hard. Still, it was far, far better than living in a world which now promised to hunt them down like dogs and then observe them like laboratory rats.

Bailey stirred her oatmeal thoughtfully. Lacey gave a hopeful squeak from her pocket, so Bailey dipped in a fingertip and then offered a dollop of the creamy cereal to the pack rat who delicately nibbled it away.

Ting came over, got her own bowl and slid in next to Bailey saying, "Move your big rump," with a wicked grin on her face. Bailey moved over with a roll of her eyes. They ate quickly while the heated breakfast could still warm their insides, and that was a good thing because a commotion broke out among the boys.

"Stefan," said Madame Qi firmly, standing ramrod stiff, her cane outstretched in her hands. "You must try."

"I tell ya, this isn't working for me. It isn't. It's like . . . it's like trying to make a silk whatever out of a bear-skin." Big, square Stefan frowned, his face grimacing in frustration. He punctuated his remark with a wave of a beefy arm, leaving the quad and coming over to the campfire. "Ready for breakfast," he said with a grunt. Effort and emotion reddened his face as he grabbed up a bowl and waved it near Rebecca.

"Stefan, you are not dismissed."

He grunted again. "Yeah, I am. 'Cause I *quit.*" He waved his bowl again, and Rebecca hesitated, looking toward Madame Qi.

Her bamboo cane slashed the air like a sword. "Stefan, you must train both your mind and your body."

With a roll of his shoulders, he turned his back on her. "It's not working."

For a moment, Madame Qi looked like what she sometimes was . . . a very aged, small Chinese woman, with great concern written across her wrinkled features. Then she straightened and the weakness fled, even as Ting drew in her breath and held it. "Think on it, Stefan. I will be here when you are ready." She turned her attention back to the others who were jumping up and down in the cold morning air, trying to keep their bodies warm and limber. Her voice cracked out instructions and the three still in a line bent to follow.

Rebecca spooned out a hefty dish of oatmeal but said nothing to Stefan who took his meal and retreated around the corner of the building to eat alone.

Ting sighed then.

"Do you think she's afraid of him?" Bailey eyed the corner of the building where Stef had disappeared.

"Maybe. More likely, she just doesn't want to provoke the bear coming out. Every time it does, he loses more and more control, unless he wills it, you know?"

Bailey nodded. She stood with her empty bowl and dropped it into a second cauldron of bubbling hot water, readying the dishes for a good cleansing. Before she could offer her services for cleanup, another hubbub of voices roses, this time from the wanderers who were grouped together, voices rising, arms waving, and then they swarmed on Gavan Rainwater, the Magicker on whose shoulders many burdens were carried.

Gavan listened a moment, his cape swirling about his young, strong body, his dark blond hair curled to his shoulders, his wolfhead cane sheathed by his side the way some might carry a sword, and when he turned about in answer to the protests, his piercing blue eyes fastened on Bailey.

Uh-oh, she thought, even as she wondered what she could have done this time.

Gavan moved toward them with a dramatic swing of his long cape, wanderers in his wake, their babble diminishing to a quiet murmur. He stopped by the outdoor kitchen fire. "It seems we have a thief."

"Thief?"

Everyone stopped in their routine then, whether it was cooking, eating, or dancing to Madame Qi's barked instructions, and looked at the headmaster.

The wanderers stayed at Gavan's heels, their eyes wide with curiosity, their wandering status tattooed in a single dot over their right eyebrow, their six-fingered hands shoved in as they crossed their arms over their chests. The headmaster nodded solemnly, then pointed his cane at Bailey.

"M—me?" squeaked Bailey.

"One of the Lantern crystals is missing. Dokr here has checked everyone, and among his tents. The crystal isn't crucial till afternoon falls, but their work depends on illumination. It seems most likely, Miss Landau, that you know the perpetrator of the crime. You were visiting their camp yesterday, I believe?"

"But . . . but . . ." She stared helplessly at Gavan. She had no need for a Lantern crystal, she could focus the light into her own any time she concentrated. What, then . . .

Gavan raised his eyebrows and stared into her face. She felt as if she should know the answer, and had no idea. Why would he think she'd stolen . . . ?

Lacey poked her head out curiously. The little pack rat saw the gang of people nearby and gave off a mousy squeak of fear, diving back into Bailey's pocket.

"Oh . . . no," breathed Bailey. "Lacey!" She bowed to Gavan and the workmen. "I'm so . . . so sorry. Sparklies, you know? Let me go check her nest."

Gavan's mouth twitched as he tried to maintain a stern expression and nodded his permission.

Oh, that Lacey! How she'd even gotten into their tents . . . it must have been when she and her mom had gone through yesterday, distributing apples to the children. Good thing Gavan had remembered! Bailey took the stairs to her room in great leaps and then picked the nail keg up off the floor and dumped out its contents onto a tabletop. The nest came tumbling out, mats of fabric and tissue and pack rat treasures. Sure enough, a bright citrine crystal rolled out from the other clumps of useless broken bits of this and that.

"Thief!"

Lacey chittered from the depths of her bodice pocket, as Bailey swept up the crystal. She ran downstairs, breathless, and put it into Gavan's hand.

The Magicker made a show of it, examining the gemstone, concentrating on it, letting its brilliance rain through his fingers as he cupped it closely, then solemnly returning it to Dokr.

"My apologies, Foreman. The little beast knows only that it is pretty, and not that it is part of your hard-earned wages."

Dokr clicked his heels as he bowed, accepting back the Lantern crystal. "Master, we who are poor know the value of many things thought useless to others. With these, we can work when and where we please, and our craft is our only way to keep our families secure."

The Talker crystal at Gavan's belt flared slightly as it translated the words almost effortlessly, although Bailey sometimes wondered if that was really what was said. Dokr didn't seem the flowery or overly diplomatic type, to her. But grateful, yes. She dipped a curtsy at him, adding her own apology. Without the workmen, the academy would never be finished before winter storms made building impossible.

Gavan nodded at her, turning away, and dropping his hand on Dokr's shoulder. "Perhaps, for your trouble and dedication, we could add, oh . . . six more Lanterns to your end wages? You can do that, can't you, Ting?"

Ting shifted her weight and frowned in thought, her almond eyes slanting a little. "Six would be difficult. I think I could manage three, however. Would three be all right?"

Dokr lit up like one of the crystals he coveted. "Oh, master, mistress, that would make us wealthy indeed! Blessings on you!" He turned to his men and added a few more sentences, and they all scattered to their jobs once more, their drawn faces now happy.

Gavan nodded in approval at Ting and crooked a

finger at Bailey. "Next time," he said, "keep an eye on that pet of yours. We can't afford to lose the construction crew!" His laugh belied his scolding words as he sauntered off.

"Win some and lose some," Ting said, as Bailey sagged in relief. Her gaze indicated the sullen Stefan who'd come out to listen a moment, before isolating himself again.

"Yeah." Bailey rubbed her nose. Who said coming to a brand-new world was going to be easy?

Planners and Dreamers

"PSSSST! TING, are you awake?"

A silence followed, then a sleepy answer came from the darkness of the room. "Do you mean . . . lately? Or now?"

"Now."

"No." The response came accompanied by the rustle of blankets and the squeak of the uneasy sleeping cot as Ting burrowed back into its depths.

That was silly. Of course she was awake if she was talking. Bailey tried again. "Ting?"

A pink shimmering answered her as Ting stretched out one hand and touched a fingertip to a crystal lying in the night between them; at her touch it began to glow with a soft radiance that lit the whole room. "Bailey," said Ting, sitting up, pushing her long dark hair from her eyes, and smiling slightly, her almond-shaped eyes tilting a little more. "What is it?"

Their voices echoed slightly in the room, because it was huge, and nearly empty, a big bare wooden dorm room meant to hold a class of students someday in the near future. Now it held only the two of them, two spindly cots, and an assortment of three-legged stools that they used for tables and dressing stands and whatever other use they could be put to. One even held a few things washed out and draped over its upside-down position, as a drying rack. The three-legged stools had been constructed by hand, from rough branches of wood they found, and Bailey was proud of them, primitive as they were. Things were not in Haven as they'd been at home.

This was their home now, more than home, their sanctuary. It was the place they'd come to, escaping discovery and more persecution in their own world, and both girls felt more than a little like pilgrims come to the new lands. Magick was reality, and reality had morphed into another world altogether, a world with new peoples and places, hopes and dreams.

"I can't sleep."

"I noticed. Why not?"

"I keep thinking about tomorrow. Where we can go, what we might find."

"The great search for chocolate," noted Ting, her face lighting with amusement.

"Why not?" Bailey bobbed her head in agreement. Her sun-tinged golden-brown hair fell in soft waves to her shoulders. Normally she wore it pulled back in a ponytail that danced with every lively move she made. "Tomaz has found wild turkeys . . . horses . . . we don't know what's wandered across Gates in the past. Cacao trees could be growing somewhere!"

Ting grinned. "We can only hope."

"Always."

"Think you can find a pizza tree?"

Bailey made a sound of pleasure. "Don't make me hungry. I don't want to get caught trying to get a midnight snack."

"As if the boys don't go into the kitchen at least once a night." Ting looped her slender arms about her knees. "What would you do if we did find cacao trees?"

"Oh, Henry has orders to bring back to me every-thing he can find on the Internet about growing cacao and making it into chocolate!" Bailey made a little face. "And, of course, we'd have to plant sugar beets for sugar."

"Renart would love that. Sugar beets would be something he could trade anywhere!"

"He'd make a fortune on them." A solemn expression crossed Bailey's face as she considered their first friend in Haven, the six-fingered trader who'd risked much to barter with them, and found trouble for doing it. He'd approached her mother first from the shadows, leaving food and clothing for barter, and it had been months before they even met him face-to-face. It seemed as if he had sensed how different they were from him. Yet, as he'd put it more than once, they were all the same in souls. He'd suffered for his deeds, though, shut out by his own people. "If the Trader Guild ever gives him back his license to trade. Do you ever think what it means for us to be here and changing this world?"

"Every day, Bailey. Every day."

"We couldn't have made it without Renart." Bailey pulled her blankets closer about her, aware that the room had grown chilly as night steeped heavy and close about them and the half finished building. She took a shivery breath. "I've got this map."

Ting smiled. "So that's it. I knew you had something you've been hiding every day, for weeks. Is that what made you think about chocolate?"

Bailey shook her head slightly. "Not exactly. I mean, yes and no . . . Henry can bring back chocolate chips, but what if I run out? No. There's other things that have to be here. I've been reading it and looking it over, and this is where I'd like to go tomorrow. I can't wait any longer. Well, today," she amended, looking at their shuttered window. She pulled a scroll from under her pillow and unrolled it beside the glowing crystal. She tapped it. "Here."

Ting peered at it. The trader's hand markings and scratchings were impossible for her to decipher, but she knew Bailey had been working at it for weeks. It wasn't so much a different language barrier, as that traders used guild-taught secret marks on their maps, often hiding their findings from outsiders. Secret routes to caches of spices, furs, precious metals were meant to stay secret. But Bailey, like Renart and her mother Rebecca, had a nose for other curiosities. The richness of the world did not rest in gold or diamonds. Ting smiled at her. "I'll go," she said. "I still don't know where or for what, though! You know I can't read that."

Bailey let out her breath. "Actually . . . I think these are unicorns. I'm not sure, but . . . it seems like it."

"Unicorns! Bailey, that's not possible."

"Think about it! Really think about it. See, this is our world." Bailey took out her crystal. At her touch, it lit softly, with a violet glow. She picked up Ting's crystal and moved them close. "And this is Haven. Now we know they're the same, but not the same. Some *when*, they separated. But they still touch in places, for moments." Gently, she clicked the two crystals together. Their glows seemed to merge into a third, hazy glow. "Look what's crossed over! We know that happens. Jason has his dragon—"

"Actually," corrected Ting, "I think the dragon has him. If it is a real dragon." She paused thoughtfully. "Sometimes I think it's just a mass of energy, and a dragon is the way it appears to us, you know?"

Bailey didn't know. She had only the barest idea of what Ting was saying. She frowned. "People have crossed over. And dogs. And horses. And other things."

"The people here have six fingers."

"Well . . . that is odd, I'll admit, but Anne Boleyn had six fingers. Some people do!"

"And have been called witches because of it, but that's something different altogether. Maybe it's just a genetic thing that happened and stayed." Ting hugged her knees tighter. "But unicorns. What if that's just some wild rumor, some trap set by the Dark Hand to get us to go wandering?"

"What if it isn't? What if it could help your grandmother and . . . and everyone else?"

"My grandmother is doing fine here."

"I know that. I know she looks stronger, but it's cancer, Ting. You don't know what we can do to fight it here."

Ting pulled on a strand of her blue-black hair. "She won't go back. She says she can feel the bones of the earth here, and it strengthens her. I can't make her go back."

Bailey leaned forward intently, her hands full of the glowing crystals that cast a dancing light through the entire room. "What if what she feels are unicorn bones?"

The two girls sat in a long silence. Then Ting said, "How did you get permission to go look?"

"I told them I thought I could find chickens, wild chickens. From what Renart told me, anyway, there might actually be. And we could use a steady supply of good eggs, rather than just what we can steal from the nests around here." They were careful about what they took, not wanting to diminish the natural population around the academy grounds.

"True! Oh, yum . . . scrambled eggs with cheese! That sounds even better than unicorns, at the moment." Ting shivered hopefully. She lay down, and as if in answer to her growing quiet again, the light from her crystal began to dim as Bailey set it back down on the stool between their cots. "But sleep first, right?"

"All right," Bailey agreed, if somewhat reluctantly. She rolled her scroll map and tied it before stowing it back under her pillow. "Sleep sounds good. But not as good as chocolate," she added firmly, before diving into the depths of her blankets. She smiled as she pulled her covers tightly about her. Ting thought her a bit crazed about the unicorns, but she was willing to go for the adventure anyway. That's what friends were about. And maybe they'd find something wonderful.

Three floors upstairs, a deeper voice with a growly under rumble to it, stated, "Rich. I'm hungry."

Another squeaky cot shuddered in the nighttime as its occupant rolled over with a groan. "Stef. Man. You're *always* hungry."

"I can't help it. I'm eating for two here."

"The way that bear cub side of you is growing, I'd say you were eating for a whole flock of bears. Flock? Herd? What do you call a bunch of bears?"

"Other than hungry? I dunno."

The two boys lapsed back into silence. It sounded almost as if Rich's heavy breathing verged on the edge of a mild snore when Stefan said, again, "Rich. I'm *starving* here."

A sigh. Then a crystal flared white, sending the room into near daylight brilliance as Rich sat up. "All right, all right," he muttered, combing his fingers through his wild red hair which stood up at every angle. "Let's go get you something to eat."

"Thanks, Rich!" said Stefan happily, as if it had been Rich's suggestion all along. He heaved himself to his feet, all stocky and square and looking not unlike the bear he morphed into when he willed it and often when he did not. His stomach growled as if seconding the wisdom of Rich's suggestion.

Downstairs, they found a wheel of cheese and pulled it out of cold storage, along with a slender knife, and a loaf of bread, and sat eating simple sandwiches. Rich had one, eaten slowly and deliberately, after cutting off the crusts and making sure nothing was out of order. Stefan gobbled down four big-fisted sandwiches before letting out a contented sigh that turned into a belch, and reaching for one last slice of cheese, without the bread, declaring he was full. He frowned a bit then, golden-brown brows knotting between his blue eyes.

"I miss FireAnn."

"So do we all." Rich had his heels up on the rough kitchen table and immediately dropped his feet to the floor as if the fiery Magicker with the thick Irish brogue might come in and berate him for his manners.

"She could cook anything," mourned Stef.

"She still can. She's just not with us, that's all. Jonnard and his crew dare not touch her. Or Eleanora. Especially," Rich added darkly, "Eleanora."

Both boys lapsed into silence at the thought of the young and beautiful Eleanora, stricken by the sudden aging that mysteriously hit users of Magick and who had been sent into a coma so she would not age. Then her sleeping body had been stolen by Jonnard and his followers of darkness to keep her hostage, along with FireAnn. Rich wrapped up the remains of the wheel of cheese almost fiercely. To his relief, there was a great deal left. He knew that they had to manage their rations and yet Stefan always seemed to be hungry, always seemed to be needing more than his share.

"Things," Stef said, "aren't always what they seem."

Rich straightened up the table and cleaned the cheese knife. "No? What was with you and Madame Qi today?"

He shook his head. "I can't study her way. I try, but I feel like I have to fight it. I do try, Rich."

"I hope so. I mean, they're just trying to help you." Rich stopped eating for a moment, and watched his friend's face. "We can't have you breaking into your bearskin at the drop of a hat. It's hard on you, and all of us."

"I know," he said heavily. "But her way isn't working. So . . . well, I haven't given up."

"No?"

"No." Stef's heavy voice sounded even deeper than usual and more firm. "I'm going out scouting tomorrow."

"On free day? I thought you'd sleep or something."

Stef shook his head. "No. Scouting. And then lessons."

Rich put his hand on the back of a chair. "Lessons? In what?" He blinked.

"I've been learning how to swing a sword."

"You what?"

"Yup." Stef colored slightly but with pride. The warmth flooded his big, square face.

"You're kidding me? And you go where to learn that?"

"Renart's town. There's a lass. . . a girl. . . there. Her father's the swordsmith. She's giving me lessons whenever I can get there. And, hmmm." Stef cleared his throat. "She's pretty. She thinks I'm . . . well . . . they've heard of other shapeshifters, skinwalkers, see? She thinks I'm heroic. Someone who could be a great warrior, you know?"

"Well. I'll be." Rich sat down, and looked at his friend. "That's great, Stef! But don't be taking this hero thing too seriously yet. You have to learn what you're doing! You could cut off a toe or something until you know, you know?"

"I know," rumbled Stefan glumly. "Bear doesn't take to lessons well, but we're trying."

"So, it's better than Madame Qi's way?"

"Much better. Bear wants to fight, not flow like a river. Or something like that."

"And she's pretty."

"Yup!" Stef brightened again.

"Wow." Rich considered his friend. Stef was not a rocket scientist, but he had good common sense, except when the bear had control of him body and soul, and . . . well, he guessed they were all growing up. Stef was as big now as most college fullbacks. The Magick seemed to bring growing spurts to all of them. "That's great," Rich added. "Really great."

"It's nothing much." Stef looked closely at him. "Don't go making it out more than it is. I just like her, that's all, and the bear doesn't scare her."

"And she's pretty."

He grinned foolishly. "That doesn't hurt either."

"Anyone else know?"

"Gavan knows I go. I Crystal there and back. He watches, makes sure I do it right, so I don't get lost. He promised not to tease or anything."

Rich crossed his heart. "I won't tell anyone."

"Good. Come with me tomorrow, then?"

"Gee. Well. I . . . hmmm. Swords aren't for me, Stef."

"I know. Go to the market, look at the herbs and stuff, scout around. You might hear something I don't." Stef folded his great hands, faint scars across the knuckles from years of playing football. He leaned forward. "There has to be word of 'em, somewhere, Rich."

Rich thought a moment. While he wasn't into mingling with strange crowds . . . who knew what germs and fevers they carried . . . still, the allure of new herbs and intriguing gossip drew him. He nodded his head. "All right, then. Tomorrow we go adventuring!"

Stefan beamed. He lumbered to his feet. "Now," he announced, "I'm sleepy!" He made his way to the back stair without waiting, and Rich scurried to catch up, crystal in hand, lighting their way.

And still the night wore on uneasily.

5

The Beginning

JASON KNEW HE WAS dreaming. He moved through it as though striding through real life, yet knowing he wasn't and unable to break the dream and awaken. It gripped him like a tiger with steel-trap teeth. He walked through a fortress or castle, its stone walls leaning in on him, his footsteps hammering on the floors and the hairs on his arms standing up as nervousness ran through his body. He did not know the place, but it felt as if it knew him and had been waiting.

He walked alone, but he was a Magicker and knew he was no longer ever truly alone except, perhaps, in his dreams. Somewhere nearby his friends slept . . . Ting, Rich, Stefan, Bailey, Trent, and Henry, although Henry slept in another world that night, off on a mission for them all. Somewhere, farther off, his enemies slept as well. Hopefully. Things Magickal were far more mysterious and dangerous than even he had ever dreamed.

Everyone dreamed, of course. Some remembered their nights and some did not, and he usually did not worry about his except that, once in a blue moon, his dreams were achingly clear. This was such a time. Jason would have awakened, rolled over, punched his pillow, and ignored it if he could. Where he slept now was not the comfort of his old bed, and what he used for a pillow probably wouldn't take punching very kindly, and the fact that he dreamed in spite of it all told him it was important. Maybe he was a Prophet instead of a Gatekeeper. So, with both fear and curiosity, he continued to walk into the dream.

A pair of immense wooden doors, lashed together with black leather and ornate bronze nails, loomed at the end of the stone passage. With no idea of what he would face beyond them, dread filled him. Jason raised his hands in readiness to push them open, and found his fingers clutching his crystals, one in each hand . . . the lavender crystal in his left and his gold and blue accented crystal in his right. No dream yet had been so real. He could feel the faceted edges of the gems cutting into his palms. Should he wake or should he stay? What faced him behind those doors? He thought he'd made the decision to go forward and find out, but now he found himself hesitating yet again. Wake up! Or could he?

The doors creaked open, swinging inward before he even touched them. The thought struck him that, gripped by the dream or not, he should take the chance to turn back. It was, after all . . . only a dream. Wasn't it? But curiosity prickled at him, as much as fear, and so he took a deep breath. After all, he'd seen a great many strange things since he'd become a Magicker. Jason marched into a great hall; a group of people swung around to face him, the clamor of talk dropping into a low murmur, a ripple of acknowledgment rolling toward him. The cavernous room, with its elaborate stone arches, seemed like the interior of some great, aged castle or fortress—except that it wasn't. Aged that is. It looked fairly new, the stone raw and clean rather than worn and stained with time.

Someone stamped an iron staff onto the stone floor with a harsh ringing sound. The man stood tall and straight under his sweeping robes, the staff of black iron firmly in his grip, and nearly as tall as he was. The noise cut into his ears and Jason suppressed a grimace.

"The accused is here. Court is convened!"

He knew he shouldn't have gone in. Panic tingled through him for a moment, like a lightning strike. Just as quickly, it left him. He was, obviously, the accused, for he was the only one who'd just arrived. Jason lifted his chin, sizing up the crowd of strangers as he used to check out an opposing soccer team. A good defense or a good offense depended on knowing and understanding what and who he faced.

"Accused of what?" he sang out, and his voice carried just as strongly as he hoped it would. There were lapses these days when it would fail him at the oddest times, sending Bailey and Ting into fits of giggles and Trent looking the other way, clearing his own unpredictable throat and drumming his fingers to a music track only Trent could hear.

Jason squared his shoulders as the men facing him broke away from their groups and sat down in stern-looking wooden chairs. He did not assume they were human, not as he was, for they did not come from the world he'd come from, although he was now a part of their world. They were dressed much as he was now, in clothing he'd come to know as Haven garb, jerkins and tunics and short coats, pants tucked into leather boots and so on, with formal looking robes over that. Bailey referred to it as styles from the Princess Bride Shop of the Realms.

One man raised his hand, and the murmuring ceased entirely, all gazes drawn to Jason. Jason looked back at the man, his white hair braided back neatly, his chin beard neatly clipped, his dark eyes with a slant that resembled Ting's Chinese ancestral features, and his six-fingered hand lowered to rest on his knee. So like and yet unlike.

"You are accused, Jason Adrian, of bringing war and death to Haven."

The words fell into silence, and then the fellows

sitting around the speaker burst into talk again, agitated and overriding each other in bursts of sound. This was it, then, what he knew had to come, and what he'd feared. Condemnation for his actions. And yet, was it fair? Was it at all fair? Words tried to bubble out, all at once, so he kept a lid on all of them until he could sort through them and choose the right ones. What did they expect him to say? Did any of them really want to bother listening to his story of how and why they arrived?

What would he answer? What could he? "I am the Gatekeeper," he agreed slowly, "who opened the Dragon Gate to Haven."

"Plead you guilty, then?"

He hadn't said that! Jason shifted uneasily before the assembly. How unfair could they be? He wondered if he were indeed dreaming or if he saw something that awaited him in the future.

Finally, he said, "If death never existed here before, if war never existed here before, then, yes."

"You mince words like a cook chopping for a stew. You deny your actions?"

"People do different things for different reasons. Do the reasons matter to any of you?"

The assemblage turned to stare at the white-haired man, as if he alone had a voice and could speak for them. He shook his head, his eyes creasing in a sad expression. "Not in this court, I fear."

"But sometimes things happen because they have to, because bad as they are, worse things would happen if something else were done. . . ."

"It makes no excuse, Jason Adrian. Are you guilty or not?"

Jason bit the inside of his cheek to stop his words, and to create a different kind of pain than the guilt he felt. Oh, yes, he'd opened the Gate to his enemies as well as his friends, and he could never deny that. And he would never find peace in himself until the day when he found a way to drive Jonnard and the Dark Hand out of Haven, or died trying. He wouldn't lie. "I don't deny what I did, but you must understand—"

"We do not have to understand anything!"

"But you do. You have to try to . . . I didn't know anyone was here. I had no idea there were people and villages and problems. My Gate didn't show me that, I didn't know!"

"And if you had known?"

Jason tried to meet the other's piercing gaze, unflinching. It was the toughest stare down he'd ever done, besides the dragon.

"I would have asked," Jason said.

"Do you think that would have made a difference? Giving us a choice?"

It would have made a difference to *him*. Having a choice seemed to be a great and wonderful thing. Like in being asked if he'd wanted to be born a Magicker, or losing both his parents, or being yanked out of his own world, or . . . the list went on too long. This was beginning to sound like a debate class in high school. Did choice make a thing less evil because it chose to be evil? Not Jonnard. Not the Dark Hand! "It would have made it easier on all of us," Jason said. "We could have been ready."

"There was nothing to be made ready for," the judge told him, "till you brought disaster amongst us."

With a deep breath, he raised his arm. The iron staff struck the flooring again, and rang like a bell throughout the immense room. The sound stabbed through his ears, making Jason wince. "The accused accepts the charges!"

Jason made a stammering sound and stopped, before he could feel any more idiotic and guilty under their stare. He managed a deep breath. "Then," he said, a lot more evenly than he felt, "since you're so determined to have me guilty . . . what are you going to do with me?"

"Not just you, Jason Adrian. All of you. The Magickers."

"Oh, no. Huh-uh. You brought just one of us here

for trial, and that was me, and no one else. I'm the Gatekeeper, anyway. So . . . what are you going to do about it?"

"You insist on standing alone?"

"You're not going to try the others without their being here! That's bogus! Where's the justice in that?"

"The justice in that," said the white-haired man quietly, "lies in the oath all Magickers swear to one another. But it is you, and you alone, who puts that oath aside now. So be it." He inclined his head, deep in thought for a moment, both hands wrapped about the staff.

For a very long, cold moment, Jason had the feeling that he'd just failed some sort of test. But he couldn't think how he could have done that, or what else he might have said. Nor did he think it was very fair that he was being given the sense of all this *after* it was a done deal! Where was the fairness in that? But it was a dream, he told himself, just a dream, and when he thought about it later, it would make about as much sense as a certain young lady falling down a white rabbit's hole into a tea party.

"This is serious business," the judge finally said. He wrapped and unwrapped his hands about his staff. "Remember you this."

It was as if he'd just read Jason's thoughts. . . . Jason took a deep breath, then swallowed, and nodded. Serious business. He'd keep that in mind, for later.

Their gazes locked. "Guilt being undeniable, then, the punishment is mine to give. I charge you with undoing what you have wrought."

That was the trap, then. From the frying pan into the fire. "I can't take them back," Jason said. "Not my friends. It's too dangerous to go back. You don't understand what our world would do to us for our Magick. As for Jonnard and the others, I'll do what I can." He tightened his left hand into a fist, gripping his crystal so tightly it slashed into his skin. "I'll either send them back or make it so they can't do any harm here."

"The undoing is your punishment. No more, no less."

"But I can't do that."

"You stand, Jason Adrian, with a foot in each world. To undo what you have done, you must choose!"

"Choose?" He stared back at the other in disbelief, feeling his jaw drop slightly. What did choice have to do with any of this? It had already been made . . . did they think he could back up time? What did they expect of him? Did they make fun of him because he hadn't given them any choices?

"Choose!" The white-haired man raised a hand and chopped it through the air, and at his signal, the staff rang out sharply yet again. This time, the stone floor cracked under its impact. A huge line began to open up, and then widen, snaking its way toward Jason, spreading between his feet and zigzagging onward. Jason looked down.

The rift began to yawn, a chasm opening up, and he was straddling it. A mist began to swirl about each booted foot and he would have moved, but he could not. He seemed rooted in place. And the chasm widened and deepened until he could see that he would soon fall in, and indeed, the whole room would collapse into its unseen depths. Perhaps even all of Haven might be swallowed up.

"You must choose, Jason Adrian." The white-haired man waved to his fellows and, cautiously skirting the doom that was splitting the hall, they began to leave. "Or you will destroy both worlds in which you stand."

"Wait!" Jason struggled to raise feet that felt as if they'd grown roots and anchored themselves into the stone, even as they pulled apart, and his position grew worse and worse. "It's not just my world, it's yours, too. Things can't just rest on me!"

They passed him relentlessly, just out of reach, until the last man stood next to him, the white-haired judge. "Do you see your dilemma?" he asked Jason, softly.

"I can't do what you want. Don't *you* see? What's past is past. All I can do is change things that may happen."

The judge shook his head slowly, the creases about his eyes deepening them into even sadder folds. He bowed deeply, turned on his heel, and followed the others out of the great room.

The doors slammed shut. "Wait!"

His voice bellowed, echoing, in the hall. Below, the chasm growled as if it had a voice as well, earth and stone groaning in movement as the crack deepened. And he couldn't do anything about it!

He grasped his crystals tightly, feeling the Magick surge through them. "Help, trouble, danger!" he cried, and the crystals sang with his need, his last and only chance. *Alarm! Warn the Magickers! Alarm!*

Darkness yawned under him. The edges of the abyss crumbled, and he began to fall. He looked down into the crevice and saw orange flame and heat rising to meet him as if he'd opened the gates of hell itself. Then it rushed toward him with a roar, and he realized he looked down into the mouth of a dragon. Eyes glared up at him as the snout snapped shut and massive black claws gripped him, snatching him up. The beast winged out of the abyss, Jason tight in its hold. Pain pinched him even as the icy nothingness of the void tried to reach out and swallow him. The dragon had him and would not give him up. Its claws tightened without mercy.

6

Alarms and Other Considerations

ANGRY DRAGONS make the sound of a hundred hissing teakettles, Jason had a moment to think. Maybe a thousand, but then, that would be a Bailey exaggeration. A hundred would be sufficient, all whistling at eardrum-piercing sound and strength. The pain of the claws hooked around him, and the shrill of the hissing woke him from his dream, for once and for all. Cold night wind shrieked past his ears till his nose turned icy cold. For good measure, the dragon shook him once, as they soared out over the Iron Mountains, leaving the framework of Iron Mountain Academy and the work camp of the Magickers in tiny relief below them.

He was awake now, well and truly, and what good did it do him? One of the biggest, most dire beasts he could dream of had him in its grip.

Unceremoniously, the dragon swooped low over a plateau, barely visible in the near dawn sky, and baited its wings as it settled to land, dropping Jason in a heap.

Jason rolled and got to his feet, dusting himself off. Plucked both from a dream and a sound sleep, he was nonetheless suddenly wide awake, as the dragon lowered its immense snout to look at him.

43

"Do I look angry?"

Steam boiled off his orange-red scales like steam off one of those teakettles Jason had been thinking about, and firelight danced deep in his amber eyes. Smoke curled out of his sooty nostrils in a slow, deliberate flow.

"Do I look sleepy?" Jason shot back, trying to comb his fingers through his hair.‘

"What would I know of sleep, with the nightmares of Gatekeepers keeping me awake day and night?" the dragon grumbled back, his voice deep in his chest and sounding rather like a freight train laboring uphill. He settled next to Jason and wrapped his long tail about him rather like a blanket against the still chilly night.

"Truce?" Jason asked.

"Truce," the dragon rumbled. They paused for a very long moment, watching the edge of dawn flirting with the deep of the autumn night, with the Hunter's Moon still riding high in the sky. It would no doubt be there till nearly midday, Jason decided.

He'd been asleep on the seventh floor of the now distant Iron Mountain Academy, the unfinished but final floor, awaiting beams and roofing, but a rather fine place to sleep. A solid floor underneath, the only roof that of the sky . . . he and Trent enjoyed it. He wondered what Trent would make of waking up and finding him gone. Or if he'd even seen the dragon snatch him up. Trent slept deeply, whatever troubles he gathered during the day usually banished by nightfall.

"Deep thoughts," said the dragon, flexing a paw and then stretching it out, to curl his talons gently about Jason's body. Jason sat back into the embrace of a deadly yet oddly comfortable chair. There was a brilliant dark blue sky overhead framing the dragon's orange-red form, and soft, sweet grass under Jason's legs, and yet there was nothing peaceful about Haven this morning. He wondered that grass grew so far up in the mountains, and decided that when the frosts hit, the grass would probably die off for the winter. His sanctuary, and far removed from the world he'd grown up in, and yet he could not find what he looked for.

"I was thinking," he said slowly, his voice catching up with a mind that had, indeed, been sunk in thoughts as deep as the ocean, "that it seems to be awfully easy to start a war, and impossibly hard to stop one."

A vibration rolled through the dragon's body, warming it, and Jason felt the amusement in the beast. "And this revelation just occurred to you?"

Jason scrubbed his hand through his hair again. It was growing, and he needed a haircut, he realized, and the family barber was . . . what, a whole world away? He wondered if any of them, exiled as they were, had bothered to bring scissors. Maybe Trent or Henry could invent them.

As for family . . . he hadn't any, not really, except his stepmother and his stepfather, his own parents having died, but his world, he realized, had been his family. And now that was gone. He'd given it up, fleeing willingly to this world of Haven to which he'd opened a magical Gate, and it seemed that his action, like so many others, had been taken without much thought to the consequences. Like scissors being left behind. And hamburgers. Computers. Television. Laws and lawmakers. Soccer. Or as Bailey would add, her freckled face quirked in a longing smile, *chocolate*.

The dragon, he realized, was waiting.

"I guess I never thought about it that much. I mean, we're always fighting about something at home, terrible fights that go on for generations and people do what they can to stop them, but there always seemed to be . . . I dunno . . . hope." He sighed at that.

"And you've no hope here?"

"Not yet." He would have scratched his nose, but he realized he'd been fidgeting, and the dragon talon chair that wrapped about his lean form could grow impatient with him. "It's my fault for drawing Jonnard and the Dark Hand after us, and I've got to do something about it. I didn't know who else shared Haven, but I've brought in something terrible, and I'm the one who has to deal with it." The realization that he had personal enemies who would stop at nothing had finally sunk in.

Another hot rumbling passed through the dragon's scaled body, and Jason realized the creature was laughing noiselessly. The dragon lowered his immense muzzle to Jason and eyed him with one of his great, glowing eyes.

"Then let me make your acquaintance," he said. "It is an honor, if dubious, to meet the young man who single-handedly invented war and conflict."

Jason pushed at the dragon's nose, turning the muzzle a little away from him. "You know what I mean!"

"And you know what I mean. You're no more responsible for war than I am for rain. Nor are you culpable for Jonnard's actions. I agree that you must find a way to deal with him, and soon, or he and Isabella will cause much misery here in Haven. Yes." The dragon's gaze deepened a moment, and he lifted his head and looked off over the Iron Mountains ringing the valley, as if he could see very, very far away. "Misery and death, and more."

Jason didn't want to think how anything could be more than death. A shiver danced its way down his arms. "What should I do?"

"Sometimes, the best and hardest thing to do is . . . wait."

"Wait? I can't wait—"

"There are other fates in play besides yours, Jason. I did say it might be the hardest thing to do."

Jason shook his head. Every day meant the Hand grew bolder and stronger, and the towns and villages about Haven suffered. He didn't know what he could or should do, but he did know he couldn't wait much longer to do something. "No other advice?"

"Don't you mean, no better advice?"

A blush heated his face. "Kinda, I guess."

The dragon belched a puff of smoke, its version of a snorting laugh. Jason waved the cloud away from his face, coughing. Now Bailey was going to complain till he bathed! Nothing worse than a nonsmoker around a dragon-smoked person. Before Jason could venture much else, alarms began to sound, faintly heard up on their plateau but heard all the same, just as he'd felt in his dreams.

Jason jumped to his feet. Before he could grasp his crystal and focus on returning, the dragon shoved his nose between Jason's knees, dumping him back onto his neck, even as the beast ran forward and launched himself off the mountaintop.

Alarms. Death, and other things, Jason thought, as he wildly grabbed for a hold on the scaly neck and they descended at breakneck speed down into the valley.

7

Wills and Ways

BAILEY WOKE to noise, rolling over in her cot as Ting groaned. "There have got to be quieter ways to wake up," her friend said. Horns wailed and howled like the famed hound of the Baskervilles.

Bailey rubbed her face. It seemed like she had just closed her eyes. She stared at the rough ceiling of the sixth-floor east wing dorms, marveling for a moment that there *was* a ceiling overhead, and feeling a bit of chill in the air. "Is the sun even up?"

"I don't know," answered Ting sulkily. She stood, and began to braid her long black hair away from her face. "I will rise, but I won't shine!" She reached for her clothes, folded in a neat pile on a three-legged stool in the corner. Bailey's things hung in a helter-skelter fashion from a hook on the wall. Well, three hooks, actually . . . and one had slipped down to rest across her boots. As she reached for her blouse, it stirred and the little kangaroo rat, the pack rat Lacey, poked her whiskery face out curiously.

Above them, the roof sounded like a pack of goats stampeding over them. "Boys are up," she commented, as she laced her tunic and pulled her boots on.

Bailey dressed quickly, her pulse beginning to race.

"This is serious," she said. "I think there's real trouble." She could feel an uneasiness dancing in the air. "You don't suppose they found out about my map. . . ."

Ting nodded. "Me, too." She rubbed her fingertips across the crystal charmed-bracelet she wore. The gems woke at her touch, gleaming softly with all the colors of the rainbow. The two looked at each other. "They wouldn't sound the alarms for that. They'd just pull us in and lecture our hides off."

"True!" Bailey wrinkled her nose and tried to lighten the mood. "I can't decide if we look good, or if we look like refugees from an old Renaissance Faire." She tugged on the hem of her blouse.

Ting nudged her. "We look good!" She sprinted for the staircase. Bailey was hot on her heels, Lacey tucked securely in a pocket of her bodice, chittering as they raced downstairs. The clattering of their hard-soled boots seemed a dim echo of the thundering of the boys across their ceiling, but all emerged, at the same time, into the yard of the Iron Mountain Academy where Gavan Rainwater and Tomaz Crowfeather awaited them.

Tomaz still dressed as the modern Navajo he was, but Gavan had reverted to the clothes of the age he knew best, breeches and boots, vested shirt, and flowing cape. He had been trained in magic in the golden years of the true Renaissance, even though a magical war had ripped him out of time and sent him forward to the twenty-first century. Now he'd returned. Somewhat. None of them were quite sure *what* the world of Haven was, or could be, or had been, except that Jason had found safety for them there. Yet it was neither safe nor their home, really.

The wooden-framed building that would be their academy and home was still far from finished, yet enough had been built to provide shelter that thundered with the running footsteps of the others. It had been built in two wings, like a giant V against the rust-colored Iron Mountains, and only its seventh and final floor gaped open, unfinished and unroofed. The wanderers who labored on it would return soon, to get the job finished before the autumn rains started. Then, Gavan had more plans for the academy, before winter's cloak flung itself over all of them, but pride etched his face as he looked at the structure and the teens tumbling out of it.

Only Jason didn't appear. Stef came thudding down the back stairs last, shrugging his vest into place. He never wore shirts anymore and only the last few days had he even started, reluctantly, to wear a vest over his fuzzy-haired chest. His great feet stayed, mostly, in thickly strapped sandals. He looked almost as furry in his human shape as he did in his bearskin shape when he changed, and a summer of sun had tanned him a rich golden-brown all over. Rich was the only one of them to have stayed in his original clothes. The others had either grown or just worn their regular world clothes to bits. Rich had stayed in beige cargo pants and a sleeveless sweat top, but he wore a deeply pocketed tunic over it.

Trent looked almost piratelike, having hit a growth spurt which made him taller once again than Jason. His hair had darkened to a sandy brown, and he wore it in a single braid at the back of his head. He stayed in his jeans, but their length had shrunk and shrunk on him till they hit nearly mid-calf. His ankle boots were cuffed under the bells of his pants, and Bailey always fought the urge to say "arrrr!" when she saw him.

She didn't expect Henry; he was on one of his brief trips back to their own world, the only one of them who could slip back and forth without causing much of a stir. She could only pray he'd bring some chocolate back with him although there were so many important things they needed. Her mother and Ting's grandmother leaned out of a second-story window, watching. They waved but stayed up in what would one day be real classrooms, keeping an eye on the horizon. It was Magickers who gathered anxiously about Gavan and Tomaz, young Magickers, in answer to the alarms at dawn.

And that was not all. A weary, lathered horse carrying a bedraggled rider stood there, Gavan's hand on the bridle and Tomaz murmuring soft words to the animal who looked as if he could drop in his tracks. As the rider unfurled his dirty cloak, and the sun brightened from dawn into daylight, Bailey could see his face.

"Renart!"

"Indeed," said Tomaz gently. "It has been long, my friend, since you've visited." He took Gavan's hand from the animal's harness and pressed the reins into Bailey's fingers, as he helped Renart swing down. "He needs walking, Bailey, slow and sure."

"But . . . but . . ." The leathers felt cold and stiff in her hand from the night weather, and the horse snuffled at her mildly. She didn't want to miss the excitement, and shifted from foot to foot.

"Here," Tomaz said, "would be fine. In small circles. You'll not miss a word." He winked at her, the expression deepening the creases in his own southwestern-marked face. With a blush, she began to lead the tired horse about.

"I think I broke his wind," Renart managed, his own voice hoarse and cracked.

"No. You used him hard, but these mountain horses of yours are sturdy. The question is: why?" Gavan brushed his hair from his piercingly blue eyes, and peered at the Haven trader.

"Dire need, and I was sent here."

"After being forbidden to see us and having your Trader Guild license pulled?" Gavan folded his arms and sat down on the step of the academy. He gestured for silence as the boys ranged around.

The alarms blew one last, quavering call, clarion trumpets in the wind, and Jason appeared from the mountainside of the academy, looking disheveled and wind rumpled, and smelling of hot metals like copper and brass. He always smelled like that, Bailey thought, when he'd been with the dragon. His hair had streaked light blond from the summer in the wilderness, and he had made a headband out of his old blue-and-white soccer shirt, to keep it pulled back. Pants of dark indigo dye were tucked into his boots, and he wore a long-sleeved white shirt under a matching indigo vest. He spent a moment tidying himself up, before flashing a sheepish grin at Gavan who muttered something about dragons and alarms.

And Bailey thought it had been Renart who'd set off all the noise! She pondered the skies behind the Iron Mountains but saw no sign of the beast, except for the massive stone gate carved in its likeness leading into the mountain and nowhere, unless Magick opened it. Yet its presence had set off the elaborate warding system the elder Magickers had ranged about the valley.

Renart's horse, exhausted as it was, tossed its head, letting out an anxious whinny as it rolled white-rimmed eyes at Jason. The dragon scent put it near the end of its endurance and it trembled. Bailey put her hand to its soft nose, and spoke gently, her voice unconsciously imitating that of Tomaz.

Renart collapsed on the step beside Gavan. The boys said nothing, but grouped together, waiting. Rich, ever on the alert for illness of any kind, fished through a large hide pouch he wore over his shoulder, and drew out a small bottle, and a cup. He half-filled the battered cup and handed it over. "That will help," he said.

"Many thanks, young Magicker," the trader said, grasping it and pulling it close with his six-fingered hands.

Rich blushed to the roots of his fiery red hair. "Any time!"

Gavan waited till Renart had emptied the cup. Then he coaxed the story from the trader. "Our success here came from you, my friend, from those early days of bartering and trading that kept us going. You were blamed and banished for that, and we owe you much. You say you were sent here? Or are you risking further punishment for coming? And what drove you so hard?"

Renart took a deep breath, the color coming back to his face. "Sent," he said quietly. "By Chieftain Mantor, of Avenha."

Gavan's brows arched. His deep blue eyes lost the last smudge of sleepiness at the trader's words, and he sat back, awaiting the rest of Renart's explanation, keen interest crossing his face.

"I was asked to attend the Hunter's Moon," Renart continued. "Surprised, since few talk to me, and I lost my guild status with my license."

Trent made a noise of outrage, but Renart gestured, dismissing the tall boy's indignation. "It's all right. It's temporary, and like the tides, a trader's life is full of highs and lows. We all expect it. I would not have done any differently, even knowing that. You were outlanders and most intriguing." Renart paused, smiling faintly, as if remembering. He plowed ahead again. "At any rate, I could not refuse Mantor. He's a shrewd man and holds much power, not only within his lands of Avenha but in many neighboring areas. His word even carries to the high steppes and the capital. If he traffics with me, others will follow. So I went. Mantor was expecting raiders."

"Ah," murmured Tomaz. He hooked his thumbs in his silver disk belt, the conchas gleaming like small, hammered suns, a work of his homeland. "And did they show?"

"They did. They were displeased at the decoy storerooms Mantor set up, and avoided the catching pits he had dug in the surrounding streets and fields, and used their crystal lightning to smash gates and set the walls on fire. They vowed to be back, and take their vengeance for his trickery."

"And that's the good news," commented Jason dryly.

"Almost. Even better, after the many times I suggested it, it was he who said . . . 'Send for the Magickers.' "

Big, burly Stefan stomped back and forth behind Rich. He grunted. "Fight fire with fire."

"Just so." Renart nodded at the boy who could, and often did, change into the bear he was coming to resemble more and more.

It was Tomaz who voiced the comment, "We were all branded as enemies. Does this signal a change of mind?"

"I believe it does. And with it, a change of fortunes for us all. He's a proud man, the chieftain, but smart. You have to go. You have to."

Bailey watched Jason who paled as Gavan said, "We are not proud of the countrymen who followed us through the Gate, Renart. I don't know what we can do to help, but help we will. Understand, though, that Jonnard and his Dark Hand have hostages of ours . . ." Gavan paused and breathed slowly, as if fighting for words or to contain something within, "And our hands are tied on many levels."

"This is a breakthrough," Renart protested. "You must go. Not for me, but for yourselves. If you intend to stay here and finish your school and live your lives, then you have to be accepted. Otherwise, you have traded one prison for another, my friends."

"How many raiders?"

"A goodly number. I think I counted fifty or so. There are more. I've heard of two groups that size hitting the winter stores. She gathers them every week . . . there are always those who find working the land too hard, and taking from others easier. They flock to her side, this Isabella and her son."

The Magickers looked at one another, remembering Isabella as one of their own, once . . . tall, haughty, in sweeping gowns and jewels, and with unbridled ambition. In the centuries following the magical split that set the Dark Hand against those who followed Gavan and his leader, Gregory, she had worked both sides, building her fortune and holding herself timeless and aloof, or so it had seemed. She had a depth to her powers they could only guess at, and an evil will to keep going. "She and Jonnard are building a kingdom," Tomaz said slowly, and no one argued against that.

Gavan stirred restlessly but said nothing, his expression one of intense thoughts.

"I'll go." Jason spoke up.

Trent traded looks with him evenly, before adding, "If Jason goes, I go."

"There are masters here, and students. There is little wisdom in division." Tomaz paused, as if he thought to say more, and instead dropped back into silence. Jason lifted his chin but also held his silence.

Renart wrung his hands. "It's not just an opportunity for me. These are my people. We cannot stand against the winter if we are stripped bare." He stared at his six-fingered hands, knuckles white.

"We will go." Gavan stood. "Bailey with me. Boys with me. Tomaz, stay with the others. Make sure that Jonnard has not thought we would rush off and leave this place unattended."

Ting frowned. She hid her disappointment, like her hands, in the pockets of her long skirt and would not look at Bailey. Gavan traded looks with Tomaz, and then reached out to Ting.

"I need you here," he said, "because of your rapport with Bailey. If anything happens, it'll be easiest and quickest for you to draw us back, through Crystal."

"Oh," said Ting. "Oh!" Then she brightened, her eyes widening with the realization of his words. She would anchor for Bailey as Bailey would anchor for her.

Bailey began to walk about again, the trader's horse smelling of sweat and heat and bruised heather from its run over the hills. It seemed to be breathing a little easier, although its gait was far from easy. She shot a sidelong glance at Ting, a little upset about her own plans for exploring being delayed, but this seemed far more important. Ting nodded back at her, eyes crinkling in understanding.

Renart looked at his mount. "Should I ask how we're going to get there?"

Gavan took his wolfhead cane from the staff harness at his back, and leaned on it, the great diamond crystal in its jaws winking in the morning light. "Now, Renart," he said easily. "How did you think?"

Renart swallowed. "I had hoped . . . not that way."

"We've few horses here, certainly not enough for all of us. As long as you can picture part of Avenha for us, and hold it, we can get there." Gavin rubbed his palm over his crystal focus in the wolf's jaws. "Everyone going, link up." He waited till Bailey passed the horse's reins back to Tomaz and linked arms between Jason and Trent.

"The one thing you absolutely must remember, Renart, is that as much as we may wish to fight the Dark Hand, as much as it is our will to do so . . ." Gavan frowned. "We may not have a way." He cleared his throat. "But we will answer the call!"

Renart swallowed tightly again. He linked an arm through the crook of Gavan's elbow.

"Now think of Avenha," Gavan ordered, "something you can see no matter what, and hold to it, tightly."

The Stars help him, Renart tried to think of something else but all he could concentrate on was the lovely face of Pyra. His stomach lurched and there was a whistling in his ears as they winked out of *then* and went somewhere *else*.

8

Mud

SO THE SEVEN of them appeared abruptly in the sleeping quarters of the chieftain's daughter of the prosperous and important holding of Avenha. Bailey reflected that there was nothing like an actual demonstration to learn a good defensive kick and put-down hold, although Renart's red, bulging face indicated that Pyra's reaction was more than a mere demonstration as he squirmed in discomfort under her foot. And, as far as alarms went, Pyra's and her sisters' screams more than equaled any of the wailing windhorns from the Iron Mountain Academy. When all was said and done (and much was, in the confusion), their arrival was met with a great deal of fuss.

Bailey stared at the wiry chieftain's daughter with unabashed admiration. "That was some move."

"Like it? I'll teach you later. Every woman should know how to defend herself," Pyra said frankly. Her cheeks had flushed a bit, and her dark eyes flashed with an inner amusement, as she glanced over at Renart who had finally recovered some composure but wouldn't look back at them.

"That," answered Bailey, "would be terrific!"

"Good. When Chieftain Mantor has spoken, and matters have been handled, I will meet up with you

and show you a few of my tricks." Her solemn words
did not chase the hilarity from her eyes as she turned
away then, and began to bring order to the shambles
of her tent, which had nearly caved in around them
during the tussle. All of Avenha's city proper had
been sent into the hillside with its many caves, and
tents dotted the hill about the caves as well, for additional housing while the night raiders were expected.

Wrapped in the shreds of his dignity, Renart escorted them all out, as the booming voice of Chieftain
Mantor could be heard. He'd been one of the first to
respond to the brawl in his daughters' tent, had taken
a quick survey, and left when he was certain things
were under control. He sat on horseback now, a small
herd of similar mounts crowded around him, shaking
their heads in the early morning, chomping their bits
and stamping their feathered legs on the dewy ground.

"Dibs on the gold one with the white face," Bailey said.

The ruler of Avenha turned his gaze on her, a slow
smile creasing his face. "Because of the pretty color,
outlander?" His hands opened and closed on the
many lead reins bunched in his hold.

Bailey leaned back a little, unsure of what was really
being asked of her, yet instinctively knowing there was
much more to the chieftain's question than there appeared to be. When in doubt, the truth seemed best.
Still, she picked her way through her answer, much as
one of these sturdy horses might pick its way across
uncertain terrain. "I have a sense, a Talent, for animals. It's pretty, yes, but more than that . . . I can
feel a soundness in its legs, a curiosity but not fear of
us, and a pride in its . . . well, how it carries a rider.
How it performs." Bailey stammered to a halt, and
stood nibbling on the corner of her lip. She cupped
her crystal pendant, her focus, and let its well-being
flood her.

Mantor stared at her closely for a long moment,
then nodded. "A useful Talent." He sorted out the

gold's reins and passed them to Bailey. "Anyone else have this . . . dibs?"

No one else had the Talent Bailey did, but it seemed unlikely that the chieftain would have brought ill-suited mounts for the expedition they had planned. The only clear choice was the large, broad-backed bay which seemed destined to carry Stef's bulky weight. Everyone else just shrugged and took whatever horse Mantor assigned to them.

Once up, Renart looked a lot more composed. He flushed deeply when Pyra appeared at her tent flap and gave a wave which could have been directed at any of them, and almost lost his seat when his horse sidestepped suddenly. He grabbed for its mane with both hands, and suffered the snickers with grace. Mantor leveled his consideration on Renart. Finally, he said, "A trader would be an asset to the family line."

That remark made Renart blush even deeper and Mantor swung his horse about and into a trot before the flustered man could stammer out a reply of any kind. His garbled words were lost in the thunder of hoofbeats as the horses broke into a trot, following their leader.

True to her Talent, Bailey had chosen well. The gold moved with steadiness and a smooth gait that made it easy for her to sit the saddle, although she had rarely had a chance to go riding. Southern California, a world and a lifetime away, with its bustling, ever growing cities, had few stables left, and riding had become more and more the hobby of those with time and money to burn. She had neither.

The others rode much as she did, with flapping arms, legs ramrod stiff in their stirrups, trying to maintain as comfortable a seat as possible. Mantor moved among them, giving hints, reaching out and adjusting lanky frames when he felt like it. Trent rode as he walked through life, as though he heard an inner music and moved to it. His horse seemed to trot to the same rocking beat. Stef didn't ride his horse so

much as conquer it, and Rich seemed about to fall off
at any given minute, his attention far more on the
plants dotting the ground about them. It was only a
matter of time, Bailey thought, till he dove into those
selfsame plants nose first. Only Gavan showed any
horse sense at all, settling into his saddle, his cape
flowing like a stormy ocean behind him. Of course,
he'd probably been on a horse or in a carriage far
more than any of them. Bailey watched him, thinking
of the times he'd come from. All of the older Magickers had adapted quickly. But was Haven almost
like home for him—or just as eerily strange as she
found it?

By late morning, her bottom was sore, her stomach
and her pack rat were reminding her noisily that they
hadn't had breakfast, and she was pondering bringing
all those subjects into public knowledge when they came
to the top of a rocky crag and Mantor halted his horse.

"Down there," he said. "Although they're making
no attempt to hide their whereabouts." He crossed his
wrists, resting them on the pommel of his saddle and
looked down into a valley crisscrossed with darkness.
"That was an old fortress belonging to a warlord who
died of a terrible disease, so his troops abandoned it
many years ago. They have gone in, rebuilt much of
it, added new outbuildings, most of it for barracks and
stabling. To attack them directly would be to risk
much, especially with their sorcery."

Gavan dismounted. He tapped Trent on the knee.
"What do you see?"

Trent stood in his stirrups. Bailey gazed at Trent.
He couldn't work Magick but he could see it, and that
was more than they could, because the working of it
seemed to blind them to subtle underlying traps and
strands. It wasn't a Talent exactly. . . . He shaded his
eyes as he stared across the encampment of the Dark
Hand, and then nodded to Gavan. "There are ward
lines everywhere, that's the shadowing you see. Add
that to the sentries positioned about, and they're
armed to the teeth for trouble."

"Which we won't give them today." Gavan smothered a faint sigh. He pulled his staff free and ran his hand over the crystal diamond in the wolfhead. It flared, then clouded.

Stef grunted. He scrubbed a thick hand over his brushy golden-brown hair. "I came to fight," he said flatly.

"We all did," Rich told him.

"No," Jason put in. "That's stupid, Stefan . . . did your football team ever go to a game without some scouting first? Think about it."

Stefan made a face, then dropped into sullen silence.

"Nothing yet. At least we know where they are, and that they're confident about being able to hold it. That will make a big difference on how we approach things." Gavan twitched, his feelings transmitted almost instantly down the reins to his horse, and his mount sidestepped quickly with a nervous snort.

"Then what are we going to do?" Rich, his face paler than ever, even under the Haven sun, stared at the headmaster.

Trent jabbed a thumb down toward the valley. "Figure out how to get a lot closer without getting tangled in that web." He stretched in his stirrups, surveying the dark weaving, an intense look on his face as if memorizing it. "I think it can be done," he finally finished.

"Good lad." Gavan swung his horse about to face Renart and Mantor. "Eleanora and FireAnn are down there." He stared gloomily into the encampment. "You understand, Chieftain Mantor, that they hold hostages of ours."

"As I am certain you understand that their raids threaten the lives of many people."

"Winters have never been easy to survive."

Mantor's horse stomped a hoof as if reflecting his rider's mood. The chieftain looked from Gavan to Renart who stayed remarkably silent now, though his fine brown eyebrows seemed knotted in protest. "All of you—" and Mantor gestured across the band of them and down across the valley fortress. "Are interlopers here, bringing much with you that is new, strange . . . and evil. We sift for the good, as we sift through our grain, sorting the wheat from the chaff. Many have voiced that all of you are alike, but I say . . ." And Mantor paused a moment. He cleared his throat. "I say that you are no different from any men, that you must be judged one at a time." His six-fingered hand flexed on the reins, and his horse tossed his head. "Renart and I agree in this. It has led to Renart losing his license, and the respect of many. All of you know better than we do, what needs to be faced down there, and what the cost of that will be." Mantor leveled his gaze at Gavan. "Are you telling me that you will not help us?"

"No." Gavan shook his head emphatically. "I'm saying, right now, they have a knife to our throat." He smiled, grimly. "We have to figure out how to blunt the blade before it cuts. But, there is no denying, we intend to fight what we're responsible for, and now we know where they are . . . and what we're facing. Magickers, mark this valley. We'll be back." He swung up then, and with a sharp kick, sent his mount back down the crag the way they had come, in a rattle of loose pebbles and stones.

Mantor let out a primal sound, but whether of agreement or disgust, no one could be sure. He wheeled his horse about to plunge after Gavan. With a sigh, Renart kicked his horse into a trot. Bailey's horse turned to follow without the slightest tug on the reins from her to signal it, and the boys' mounts did the same. Halfway down the crag, her horse veered off the trail and picked its way to the left, down what she could only describe as a goat's trail. She tugged on the reins, but it swung its head back determinedly, and she finally let it go. At the hill's bottom, though, she could not spot the others, only a faint dust cloud from their passing.

"Uh-oh," said Bailey quietly. She pulled on the

reins and kicked her horse in the flanks, putting it into
a trot in what she could only hope was the right direction. A rustling came from the brush behind her, and
she turned in the saddle, expecting to see Stefan or
Rich trailing.

Something did indeed trail after her. Brush crackled
and pebbles flew from its headlong passage. Jaws carried low, hide of black-streaked silver, ears pricked
and eyes catching the sun with a glint of green, a
wolfjackal ran after her, mouth curled in a vicious
snarl. Neither wolf nor jackal but the worst of both,
she'd seen enough to fear them. They'd savaged Jason
once. He still bore the scars on his left hand, and she
hated to count the near escapes she'd had! Bailey
leaned low over her horse, and kicked harder. "Where
there's one, there's more," she cried out, urging the
animal. "We're in trouble."

The horse didn't seem to catch the scent of the wolfjackal, but broke into a shambling run as the beast let
out a long, quavering howl and was answered by three
more close by. The horse let out a shivery whinny of
fear muted by the thunder of its hooves. "Big trouble," shouted Bailey, as she took up the ends of her
reins and tried to snap them against her horse's shoulders. Memories of old cowboy movies spurred her,
and her shout seemed to inspire the horse. It laid its
ears back, stretched out its neck and pushed into a
run, sprinting low across the rough countryside.
"Faster!"

The tough little horse was built for mountains and
walking all day, not running. It had speed but precious
little, and she could tell from its panting that it
couldn't run much farther or faster.

Bailey grasped her crystal in desperation, and
twisted in her saddle. She pulled back on the rein,
bringing her horse around in a circle, slowing it. Her
crystal warmed in her hand. She had plans in her future, and she wasn't going to let anything or anyone
stop her from them.

Time to make a stand!

9

Crystal Shields

BAILEY RUBBED her amethyst gem, its answering warmth filling her hands. It wasn't her power, but a focus for it, and she bent her head in concentration to conjure up what she wanted. A Shield of light and energy between her and the enemy. *Think, Bailey, think!* A shimmering leaped into the air and, like a bubble, seemed to settle about them. Her horse whickered anxiously, its golden flanks lathered from the hard run. It stamped in fear as the Shield surrounded it, but it settled under her hold. *Arrooooo! Aroooooo-ah!* Their throats full of noise, the pack of wolfjackals crested the hill and raced toward them. Five in all, from shadow gray to dun to coal-black, their eyes blazed down at her. Their throats swelled with growls and yips. Bailey swallowed. Was she making a mistake trying to put up a Shield here . . . or taking the only chance she had, alone?

She rubbed her crystal a second time, in hopes of sending out a Beacon, a shard of power to alert the others. The Shield dimmed. Her hand shook, and she narrowed her eyes. *Concentrate.* But her mind strayed as the wolfjackals charged at them, their howling broken only by heated snarls, and she dared not look up from her gemstone to see how close they really were. The Shield would hold. Now she needed a Beacon!

She would have dropped her crystal if it had not been cleverly trapped and hanging from its chain. As it was, it bounced out of her grip and dangled for a second before she caught it back up again. Lacey chittered nervously at her from her bodice pocket, and Bailey could only mutter, "Quiet, I'm thinking!" back at the little pack rat.

She clutched her amethyst tightly, feeling its edges bruising her fingers. It felt warm now, but she knew well its cold panes and facets, the geometric precision of its inner secrets. She had trapped herself inside the crystal once, and if Jason had not rescued her . . . an icy shiver ran through Bailey at the thought. She nearly dropped her amethyst again. *Don't think! Don't fear it—just focus!* Her horse shifted under her, putting its ears flat back and baring its teeth, ready to fight. Bailey drew its reins tighter, fearing now that even if she could hold the Shield, the horse might charge through it, breaking the Magick. The way her crystal fought her now, or she fought it, she might not have the strength to put up a new one. Even now, her body shook as though she lifted a tremendous weight.

Bailey bit her lip. Hold on . . . just hold on! Someone was bound to notice the energy surge in this small dell. Someone was bound to notice that her endless chatter had stopped . . . weren't they?

The wolfjackals ranged about her. They began to circle. She could smell the strong odor of their heated bodies. Curved ivory teeth cradled lolling red tongues that dripped with eagerness to taste them. Bailey snugged her legs deep into the saddle's stirrups and wondered if they might yet have to try outrunning the beasts. Her horse had caught its breath, and now stomped defiantly as the lupines circled. One of the wolfjackals bumped another, and they snapped and snarled at each other, their harsh cries shattering in the air. The pack leader turned to face her, head on, eyes glowing, ruff silvery about its neck as it stared boldly, unafraid.

No normal animal meets a human gaze like that.

Bailey hefted her crystal a little higher, and the Shield wall shimmered, growing a bit stronger. Tomaz had worked with a wolfjackal pack, accepted by them somewhat, claiming that they were chaos torn free, but their natures were neutral. They sought Magick's overflow, but Bailey felt here and now that they were evil. Pure, vicious evil. She didn't know how the elder Magicker could think otherwise!

And if anyone doubted her, they could trade places with her *right now,* and watch the wolfjackals grin as they imagined her sliding down their gullets for an afternoon snack!

Her horse shivered as if sharing the same thought. Lacey gave up chittering at her and dove headfirst into the depths of the bodice's pocket, with not even her black tufted tail hanging out. "Coward," muttered Bailey. Not that she blamed the little creature one bit.

A wolfjackal lunged at them. The Shield exploded in fiery purple-and-red sparks where it hit. It shrieked in fear and pain, rolling away, paws scrambling in the dirt. It cowered low, glaring at her, and then growled deep in its throat. The Shield healed itself immediately, and Bailey let out a low sigh of relief. It had held. It would hold . . . though for how long, she could not be sure.

She could see them thinking. The pack leader paced about her, its legs moving in the easy swinging gait of a wolf, and it touched muzzles with each of its pack, even the injured one. Then a second wolfjackal drew close. It did not charge as the first attacker had but rather swiped a paw.

The Shield crackled and spat, sparks flying again, but to a lesser degree. Then, slower than the first time, it healed itself where the wolfjackal had torn an opening.

Bailey blinked. Did they see that, too? Did they sense it or know what it could mean? She'd never seen a crystal's Shield gape open like that, or heal back. In all the times she'd had to use a Shield, it had never, ever, behaved like that. Anything could dart through those tears. Anything. . . .

The wolfjackals pulled back, circled, eyeing her closely. She could feel the strain in her arm as though she held a great weight in her hand, the crystal warm enough to nearly burn. She tried to splinter off a thought to Jason, Gavan, anyone, everyone, but the crystal resisted her as if it needed all her power for the Shield and nothing else mattered. As if it were too weak to channel any other magic. Or as if she were too weak . . .

The wolfjackals sank into a crouch, haunches tensing. Her horse stamped and rolled the bit in its teeth. They were thinking beasts. Had they reasoned out what she feared? Or worse . . . had they somehow *read* her thoughts? She had animal sense. Maybe she could push them away. She settled in her saddle, digging her heels in, bracing herself, and opened her mind to see if she could touch them as she often did Lacey. It wouldn't, couldn't, be pleasant, but she had to try.

For a moment, she felt nothing. She relaxed back on the mountain pony, feeling its flanks heaving under the saddle blanket as it fought both its tiredness and its fear of the beasts crouched before them. She could feel the burn of air in its lungs . . . but no, no, she was touching the horse, not the wolfjackals. Bailey wrenched her thoughts away from the beast she rode to the beasts who faced them.

Her hands shook. She felt tired, so very tired. She didn't know if she could even hold onto her crystal another moment . . . her eyelids fluttered. No! No! She shoved back, and the leader of the pack opened his jaws in a huge, wolfish laugh at her.

She hadn't touched them, but he had touched *her*.

Bailey shrank back as if burned and almost threw her crystal with the jolt of her feelings. She clamped a lid down on her fear quickly, and held on with everything she had. A searing caress along the edge of her thoughts, and she almost thought she heard "Mag-ickersssss cubling." But she couldn't have. Wolfjackals could not speak. Could they?

What was it the one wolfjackal had said to Jason? *You are mine.* Bailey swallowed tightly. She wasn't about to become a shaggy snack if she could help it! She might be here till night fell and hell froze over, but she would keep that Shield up.

Jaws snapping at air, the pack leader slashed a wolfish snarl at her, as if in answer. Heart sinking, Bailey clenched her crystal and felt its angles cut into her skin. Looking down, she saw that its purple color had bleached away to nearly silver white. Fool! Why couldn't she have remembered the Avenha outcamp well enough to Crystal back? She'd never tried Crys-taling anything as large as a small horse, but how could that be different from a gaggle of Magickers? But she didn't dare try it without a clear inner picture of her destination, and that she did not have.

What she did have was Ting and her mother, and the bare bones beginning of the Iron Mountain Acad-emy, much farther away. There, there was her haven. Distance shouldn't really matter, the theory of crystal teleportation was merely the folding of distance. But it did matter, at least to one as young and newly trained as she. She knew that. This time, though, it couldn't. Bailey cupped both hands tightly about her amethyst. Home, she thought. Channel all her will to bring them safely home. . . .

The crystal flared in her hands with icy cold light. Not the warmth of power, but a deep cold chill that frightened Bailey to her very bones. She felt a brief touch of Ting, a jolt of surprise and a gut-wrenching kick as if repelled, and then . . . nothing.

The crystal made a noise as if fracturing deep inside.

No! Oh, no, not that! Bailey let her power go, felt it drain immediately as if barely held there, and the Shield shimmered down to mere sparks before restor-ing itself, slowly. She dropped her eyes to her hands, examined the crystal quickly before leveling her gaze back at the pack. She narrowed her eyes, willing herself to maintain a steely gaze as if that, and that alone, would keep them from her. Her amethyst seemed whole. She had to believe that it would continue to hold her focus. Without that belief, she had no defense left.

Nor enough power left to try it again, last chance or not. No, their last chance would rest on the mortal power of the little horse to try to outrun the pack when it broke through her faltering Shield.

And it would. If not on this leap, then on the next, or the one after. Bailey knew it in her bones.

Two sprang as one. The first yowled in pain as the Shield threw it back amid a shower of hissing sparks, the power of it dancing about the wolfjackal's fur like bits of fire. The second leaped low, and pierced the tear in the Shield. Bailey's horse squealed. It whirled about and lashed out, hooves striking the wolfjackal solidly. A howl of pain cut abruptly in two, and the limp body sailed through the air, landing outside the Shield's shimmer, and lay still.

The pack leader nosed it, and made a low growling sound as if to promise revenge for the fallen. Bailey curbed her pony to bring it about, to face the enemy again. Magick or not, they wouldn't be easy to pull down! She sat straighter in her saddle.

"Well. Well, well. The little Magicker has teeth. And more."

She hadn't heard a sound, nor had the wolfjackals, but with low growls, they slunk back, curling back and forth among one another, snarling. Bailey twisted in her saddle and saw Jonnard of the Dark Hand watching her from horseback, a faint smile twisting his pale face. Dark cloth and a darker cape, seemingly wrought of shadow, wrapped him from head to toe, revealing only his face and hands. His horse, an immense steed of the deepest midnight color, stood far taller than her own rugged mountain horse. It arched its neck, and an unseen hand or wind stirred its mane and unfurled its tail like a silken coal-black banner. Leave it to

Jonnard to ride only the finest horseflesh he could find
in Haven.

"Oh, yes," he added. "It is true that the female
blooms sooner than the male, is it not? And look at
you. You make Eleanora look so . . . old."

"Get out of here." His words, though she didn't
quite understand them, still brought an angry flush to
her face. He was taunting her, that she knew. Well,
she wasn't helpless. Yet. She'd show him that! Her
hand clenched her crystal so tightly she thought its
one sharp edge might draw blood.

He quirked a finger at her. "How long do you think
that Shield will hold? Or . . . that crystal?" He smiled
at her, without humor in his eyes. What did linger in
his eyes was something she didn't recognize, but it
made her afraid. "Let me take you from this peril,
Bailey. Rescue you, if you will."

"It will hold long enough," Bailey shot back at him.

Jonnard gestured at the wolfjackal pack, and sent
them racing away, after a short snapping disagreement
from the leader. They left their dead pack mate behind them. Moments after they were gone from view,
a green fog boiled up from the ground about the wolfjackal body, and as it leeched away, thinning, the car-
cass disappeared with it. The tiny vale seemed deadly
quiet, with only the snort of his warhorse and the
quieting pant of her sturdy pony.

Jonnard considered her. "I could take you to . . .
join . . . Eleanora and FireAnn."

Bailey lifted her chin. "You could *try*."

Jon laughed. "You've grown, Bailey. Not as tall as
Jason or Trent, but . . . aye, you've grown." He leaned
forward in his saddle and his fine dark horse paced
forward proudly. "Not enough to withstand me."

"Maybe not, but I bet I could put a big dent in that
ego of yours."

"Or die trying, I imagine." He reined his horse to
a prancing stop. "What can I do to convince you to
visit with me? Just a while? We haven't talked in
many a month, yet I remember mornings at camp. Do

you still rise in the morning, Bailey, as bright and sunny as the dawn?"

She felt flustered. He was up to something, but she had no idea what. Jonnard had tricks within tricks. "I wouldn't go anywhere with the likes of you."

"No? How sad. And here I had hopes you'd put me on your dance card. And you so charmingly unaware of your . . . charms." He paused suddenly, quirking his head, as though aware of something else. His tone changed abruptly. "Then I shall simply give your regards to the lovely ladies already guesting with me." He flicked his reins, and his horse threw his head up, about to bolt into movement.

"They'd better be safe!" Bailey called out, even as he put his heels to the dark horse. A cloud of dust and turf was all the answer she got as Jonnard raced from view, back the way the wolfjackals had fled, and she had no time to wonder why, as a thunder of hooves from the other direction told her the lost had finally been found.

Bailey lowered her aching arm in relief, and let the shield go, its purple sheen flooding back into her amethyst, its color returning a bit. Like her, it looked exhausted and nearly bled of every morsel of strength. Lacey climbed out of her pocket, and onto her shoulder, where she wove her tiny claws firmly into the fabric and took up a determined perch.

"Oh . . . now you make a showing," Bailey said to her fondly, and tilted her head to rub her cheek against the small bit of fluff. Lacey chittered back. She looked up at Gavan and Jason and the others as the small herd of horsemen surrounded her, and she said, "It's about time."

10

Mulberry Bush

JONNARD STRIPPED off his riding gloves as he strode up the crude stairwell toward the chambers his mother had claimed as her own. He could smell the aroma of her perfume before he even arrived at the doorway and threw the door open, and her scent washed over him even more heavily, a wave of roses and jasmine and something darker, more mysterious than mere flowers. Perhaps nightshade, he thought. Perhaps something even more deadly. He smiled faintly to himself as he stepped inside her apartments. So different from Bailey who used no wiles yet beguiled.

Isabella sat at a writing desk, her dark vermilion gown almost completely enveloping the chair, her graceful neck bent forward as she perused the many volumes stacked upon the desktop. Thin, spidery spectacles rode the bridge of her strong, prominent nose, the delicacy of the one setting off the harshness of the other. The hammered satin of her deep red gown made faint rustling noises as she turned a page and said, without looking at him, "Teasing Gregory's lot, were you?"

"Assessing them." Jonnard tucked his gloves away in his cape, and took up a perch on a tall stool not too close and not too far from her writing desk. His mother looked at him then, a careful nonexpression on her imperious face. If anyone, he thought, had the strength to rule this motley world, it would be her . . . or himself. Then he revised his estimation. He was not ready for the discipline of ruling . . . yet.

"Assessing," repeated Isabella. Her voice still held the faint trace of a French accent, that country in which she had hidden and lived for many many decades. It added to her charm. She closed the book she was reading, taking care to place a pewter bookmark in it first. "I was wondering when they would take the bait we've been laying so carefully." She removed her spectacles carefully, folding the bows, and putting them down on top of a stack of other books. "Have you looked in on our guests to see if anything untoward has occurred?"

"Not yet. I came to you first."

"I see." Her legs moved, the satin dress sounding again with its music of the fabric, and he guessed she probably crossed her legs beneath its skirts. "Tell me what transpired."

"The wards told me we had trespassers. I saddled up to take a closer look. The impulsive one, Bailey, had already separated from the others." Jonnard made a gesture with one hand. "I sent the pack out to keep her cut off and hold her."

"And what, if anything, did you learn?"

"That they have not yet learned what we know." Jonnard smiled with that.

"Good. It's to our advantage, obviously. Anything else?"

"She or her pony killed one of the pack, so I will have to make amends there." That brought a frown to his face, which evaporated quickly. Things happen, and he was not particularly worried or inconvenienced by the loss of a wolfjackal, but he would have to compensate the pack, a trivial nuisance. "As for the others, they saw what you wanted them to see, and I would say from Bailey's state of mind, that you've accomplished what you wanted."

"Did I?" Isabella's mouth twitched slightly. She moved her hands, so that they formed a blockade. "Jon, when is a gate not a gate?"

He looked at her quizzically. "I . . . I don't know."

She looked down at her hands. "When it is a wall." She then flexed her hands, opening them as if they were the aforementioned gate. "He has us locked in. What I want, is that Gate open and free-swinging, so that we can move back and forth at will. I thought I sensed a trembling in that force the other day, but nothing I could pinpoint. But if we could move as we need, Jonnard, then both worlds would indeed be open to us. I would be warm again, and lodged in comfort. . . ." Her gaze became distant, as if she looked into her past, or perhaps another world. She stirred after a moment. "We can use the one, and rule the other, but not until we have a Gatekeeper."

He could sense that her energy seemed down. "He has us bottled up and he is the cork."

Isabella nodded to Jonnard. He made a fist, then turned it, so he could view the strength of the cords across the back of his hand and wrist, the width of his knuckles. "I will break him, Mother. He will either open that Gate for us as you need it, or there will be another Gatekeeper to take his place."

"Can you do that, do you think?"

He could feel the answer blaze deep in his eyes before he put it into words. "I can, and will."

"Good." Isabella stretched out her hand, picked up her spectacles once more, and retrieved her book. "See that you do."

He hesitated a moment, then said, "Perhaps you should draw a bit from the Leucators. You need your strength."

Isabella looked at him over her glasses. "I am fine."

Corrected, he bowed. Dismissed, Jonnard stood, leaving his mother to her study, and went to visit the hostages. Housed in another, quieter wing, with far fewer amenities, he felt a chill brought in with the wind that seemed to know how to wriggle its way through the wooden structure. If they were to stay, he would see plastering invented. Along with indoor plumbing. Jonnard brushed the hair from his forehead before stepping into the guard's hallway, and sketching a gesture at them that he wanted entry.

The two relaxed their vigilance. They were hard men, from a time in the past, when death was both more frequent and less objectionable than it was in current times. He'd instructed them in just enough magic to keep the wards about the prison rooms safe, to open and close them, and nothing more. They had enough Talent for that, little more, nor did they have ambitions for anything more. They knew that would sign their death warrant, for Jonnard kept his Magick close, and they had been chosen for their duty because of their loyalty and their deep suspicion of anything enchanted. Devil's work, they called it, and they did it only to keep the greater Devils . . . those two women . . . locked safely away.

He passed through the first threshold, coming to a locked and barred door to which he held the key in a small leather pouch cinched tightly to his belt. He fetched it out and unlocked the crude brass lock, hearing the tumblers grind as he did so. Then he set aside the lock, moved the bar it secured, and put his shoulder to the door. The weight of the door alone would deter most women from escape. But, as the power of his own mother often reminded him, a Magicker woman was not an ordinary woman.

As he stepped in, an herb-scented mist greeted him. He sneezed and waved the steam away with one hand, raising his eyebrows at the seated woman and the woman standing by her, waving a towel over a basin of steaming water.

"Another cure-all, FireAnn?" Jonnard asked, with more than a touch of mockery in his tone.

"Whatever it takes," the red-haired woman replied tartly, "to get rid of a pestilence like yerself."

Jon grinned in spite of his anger, and leaned against the doorjamb. "She takes good care of you, Eleanora, but are you sure she isn't dosing you to death?"

The seated woman lifted her face to him. She had been beautiful, once, but now care lined porcelain skin with deepening wrinkles, and silver streaked her lustrous brunette hair. "Even over this smell, I could catch your stench, Jonnard. Been rolling with the wolfjackals again?" Her voice, still low and pleasant, nevertheless held a stinging tone.

"Wolfjackals make excellent household pets. Perhaps I should send one or two up to bunk with you." His grin widened as FireAnn shrank back a little, in spite of herself. "How delightful to come and trade barbs with you. Too bad it will end someday. Not today, of course. Your men rode up to the gates, and looked, and left."

"Left?" Before he could see the expression on Eleanora's face, FireAnn whisked the towel over her charge's head and shoved the basin under her nose, and the only response he could read to his word was that of a muffled sneeze from under the towel. But he could see the surprise on FireAnn's face before she turned away and continued fussing over Eleanora, the redhead's hands swollen and distorted with the painful symptoms of acute arthritis. Their time in Haven had not been kind to them, nor had he intended it to be.

Magick was not a renewable source, despite what they had been taught by Gregory. It did not flow in every being or in every living thing about them. It could not be tapped or restored, unless from another Magicker, and that only with great difficulty. It came from one source, from within themselves and when they burned it out, that was it. It could be banked, like a smoldering fire, or stoked till the blaze reached the skies, but when all the timber was burned, it was nothing more than ashes, and these two women were part of a movement that squandered the precious commodity that gave them superiority. He could not forgive them that.

If they but knew it, they would thank him for cutting off their use of their Magick now, saving it for the years to come. But of course, his mother's and his work on the fortress hadn't damped all magic use, not entirely. He could smell it here in these rooms. Fire-Ann, no doubt, using that part of her that came from her background in herbcraft and witchology, and healing. There was Magick in every move she made on behalf of her charge although very little now, yet some seeped in. She could help it no more than he could. He wondered if Eleanora even knew or, if knowing, was grateful. He doubted it. She would believe, as she had been erroneously tutored by her father, that Magick renewed itself, like wind, air, water. . . .

Jon's face settled into a grimmer expression. He steepled his fingers, watching FireAnn carefully. She looked the Irish witch, with her fiery hair all in curls, captured but not tamed by the kerchief she always wore, and her dress with its over apron of many pockets. Even with her back now to him, he could see the stiffness in her posture, the sign of her hatred for him. He made no attempt to hide the disdain he felt for them either.

"Yes, left. No rescue being plotted today, I fear." He paused, after drawing his words out, then added, "Oh, forgive me. I did not mean to put a damper on the news."

"You meant exactly such a thing, you little shit," Eleanora muttered, her voice muffled by the towel about her head. "I hope to be around when someone wipes that smirk off your face."

"I hope you will be around. Alas, you seem to grow ever weaker, even with the tender care of FireAnn."

A loud, less muffled curse answered him. FireAnn removed the towel as she turned about, and both women stared at him with venomous hatred.

Jonnard returned their stares. "Don't blame me," he stated, "if your training has been erroneous these many years and now you suffer the consequences."

"Consequences?" Eleanora's mouth twisted as if

she fought not to hiss the word at him. "Your mother is a parasite and those Leucators . . . those *parasitic constructs* . . . are what takes the life from me breath by breath and gives it to her."

He straightened, with a yawn. "Fun time is over. You would do well to remember you are here by Isabella's sufferance, and should be accordingly grateful."

"Grateful?" FireAnn spat on the wooden floor. "You sided with a viper, lad. Take care it doesn't bite you in the ass as well!"

Eleanora reached out a slender hand, trying to keep it from trembling, as she laid it on the other's arm. "FireAnn," she cautioned.

"Yes, FireAnn, you should listen." He started to turn away, but bitter words brought him abruptly about face again as FireAnn cried out, "Oh, yes, fine advice from the son who murdered his father for his mother's sake."

"You know little of us, I see, for all the time you've spent here." Jon drew his chin up. "My father was burned out, done, and he would rather have died than have lived a day without Magick coursing in his veins. I did him a kindness, like putting an old, crippled dog to sleep. He knew that, and she and I know that."

"I'm certain you tell yourself that on nights when you cannot sleep." Eleanora looked into his face, and held her gaze firm.

He smiled again, coldly. "I sleep quite well, thank you. Let us pray you do."

He slammed the huge door into place at his exit, using strength from outside his own body to do it, feeling the very timber shake at his touch as he dropped and then locked the bar down.

Fool! He'd let them get to him, after all.

Who would have guessed that there were days when he missed his father Brennard keenly? Who would have guessed?

Jon tossed the key in his pouch and tied it away again, and left the prison wing.

*   *   *

Gavan frowned at Bailey. "At this point, I doubt I need to say how dangerous that was."

"I was trying to keep up." Bailey shifted her weight from one foot to the other, patted her pony's neck, and tried to look contrite but didn't quite succeed. "It's not my fault you guys went off and left me."

His rainwater eyes darkened to a stormy blue, and his mouth opened to drop a scathing reply when Trent called out, "She's right—it wasn't her fault. Look here," and he traced a line along the hillside only he seemed to see. "This was laid here, and it's only Bailey's luck she's the one who was misled by it."

Gavan's mouth snapped shut. He traded a look with Jason, who said quietly, "What is it you see, Trent? We can't see it."

"Ah. Well," and he snapped his fingers. "It's like a fence, a low one. Probably the horse sensed it and just started trotting alongside it, not willing to cross it. It's not a real barrier, more like a . . ." He frowned and drummed his hand on his thigh. "More like a nudge. It's fading now, even as we speak."

"So, someone would have been singled out, regardless, if they ran into it."

Renart shuddered. His hands went white-knuckled on his reins. Gavan thumped his shoulder. "Not meant for you, my friend. One of us."

"I've seen the wolfjackals," the young trader said tightly. "I didn't like it."

And he must not have, to be so blunt, Jason thought. He nodded. "It isn't a deadly trap, or it would have been."

Bailey tilted her head at him, and made a scoffing sound.

"Sure, you defended yourself, I'm not saying *that*. I'm saying, he probably wanted another captive, if anything. So you foiled that plan." Gavan regarded her. "But what did he say to you?"

She shrugged. She'd already recounted most of the

conversation. "That I was blooming and made Eleanora look old. Something about being on my dance
card."

Gavan frowned. Renart coughed and looked at the
ground, studying something there he found fascinating. The boys stared at her. Then Jason said, "Well . . .
he is right."

"Nah." Rich shook his head, and traded a glance
at Stef. "You think?"

"It's Bailey," Stef protested loudly.

"Right. It's Bailey."

Jason watched her a moment longer before saying,
"But Bailey has always been kinda . . . ." He muttered
something as he kicked his pony in the ribs and trotted
off across the terrain.

"What did he say? What?" Bailey looked around.

No one answered. Then Renart gave a little bow
and said, "I believe, little miss, he said beautiful. I
could be mistaken, though."

Bailey tossed her head, ponytail flying, a pleased
look on her face as she turned away.

Gavan twitched in his saddle. He looked over the
horizon. "That settles that," he muttered.

"Settles what?"

"Everyone mount up. I'm going to knock on their
door, rather hard, before we leave." Gavan swung his
wolfhead cane out, and tucked it under one arm, like
a lance or spear, as he put his heels to his horse's
flanks and the beast galloped forward with a tiny
squeal of eagerness.

"What are you doing?" Rich called out.

Gavan looked over his shoulder, his cloak flowing
about him. "There are times when you have to let a
snake know that you know it is a snake." He caught
up with Jason and cried, "Follow me!"

"Oh, boy!" grunted Stefan, and thumped his sandals
on his sturdy pony's sides. The horse grunted, too,
before breaking into a spine-jolting trot after Gavan.
One by one, they wheeled around to follow. They
crested the hill in a line, ready to follow Gavan in

whatever he planned, but he reined up hard and looked down, then pointed a hand across at Renart.

"Are we at the right spot?"

The trader had come chugging up the terrain last and reined to a weary halt, his face pale. He blinked at Gavan, unthinking for a moment, then looked down across the valley and shock dawned across his face.

"They're gone. It's . . . it's empty."

An evening wind had arisen, growing autumn cold as it swept over them, and down into the valley, where the broken ruins of an old wooden fort lay abandoned.

Gavan's jaw tightened, then he said slowly, "We saw it less than an hour ago. They couldn't have pulled out in an hour. Even with crystals. That would have been a massive operation, and we'd have *felt* it, if nothing else."

"They can't be gone."

Trent stood in the stirrups of his saddle, as if he could gain a sight the others couldn't, his gaze sweeping the valley. He said nothing.

"Don't bother," Gavan said harshly. "Your Talent is to see Magick where the rest of us cannot. Not to see what isn't there at all." He looked at Renart. "Are there other forts in the area? Any at all . . . within a week's ride, say?"

Renart thought hard, then nodded slowly. "At least two, I'd say. This is a boundary here, of the Warlord's old kingdom. There would be ruins of fortifications across its old borders. There was no need to keep the forts, because now we have the Holy Spirit to protect us."

Gavan ignored the last of Renart's information. He made a chopping gesture at the valley. "Then we saw a projection. A trap, far more elaborate than that set for Bailey. It's a good thing we didn't ride into it." Gavan pivoted his horse around. "They've grown strong. Far too strong." He put his horse into a slow canter, back the way they had come, as the sun showed signs of lowering toward evenfall.

Trent shook his head and caught Jason by the elbow

as their horses jostled close. "It's *there*," he said quietly.

Jason looked back. "Think so?"

"I know so."

"But then . . . how . . . why?"

Trent shook his head. "He wouldn't believe me. Even you aren't quite sure. That's some Talent I have, isn't it?" He bit his last words off bitterly, shoved his boots into his stirrups, and rode off, leaving Jason alone for a moment on the hillside.

There or not . . . if Jonnard and the Dark Hand had accomplished anything, it was to make them all doubt themselves a bit. Jason frowned heavily before turning for home.

11

Sticks and Stones

AFTER AN APPEAL from both Rich and Stef when they turned in their mounts to the Avenha strongholding, Gavan let the boys Crystal on their own to Naria, the town where Stefan had found a weaponmaster. Gavan defended his decision by commenting, "Stef is more than a shapechanger, he's a berserker, and that energy has to go somewhere. Better he should use it in the training arena rather than pacing about us restlessly. He'll come home tired and bruised and happy, and Rich will keep him from trouble."

Trent's hand twitched, drumming thin air, but he merely shrugged. Bailey gave Renart a hug which made Lacey squeak indignantly from her bodice pocket and the laughter broke the tension a little. Jason rubbed the back of his neck in relief, not liking the unhappiness shadowing his friend's eyes.

Not to be believed . . . he knew how that felt. Or rather, not being able to walk in the truth of his own life. That was what he'd left. Trent still struggled with it. Admitting he had no Magick, that his crystal was dead and stayed dead . . . had been hard. But in that admission to everyone around him, Trent had also discovered he did have Talent. Just an obscure and difficult one to understand, let alone train. He could see what they did, or the trails, the remnants of it. He could see just what it was he lacked. A blessing and a curse, as he'd often told Jason.

Jason understood that well. He put his hand on Trent's shoulder, and gripped it, waiting for Gavan to draw the rest of their group together for Crystaling back to the academy grounds. It was dark, and late, and a chill wind had risen with a hint of fog to come later. This was a land of seasons, and discovery, and danger.

"What do you think Gavan meant by berserker?" Bailey asked, as the headmaster lingered for a moment to talk to the chieftain and his daughter, and Renart. Their hushed voices and turned backs shut out the younger Magickers, and she had joined the boys with a toss of her ponytail in protest.

"A berserker is a warrior." Trent shrugged. "He uses his anger to fuel his fighting, lets nothing get in his way. Old legends had them turning into bears and other large creatures. Maybe it wasn't legend."

"You think?"

"It's a possibility," Jason told her. "Maybe it only happened once or twice, but the witnesses remembered and related it, and hundreds of years later, we think of them as folktales. But now we have Stef. So maybe."

Bailey stroked Lacey's head thoughtfully, looking over the hill and caveside encampment of Avenha. Campfires dotted the area like smoldering orange eyes, and the smell of woodsmoke stung their noses. The actual city below lay shrouded in darkness, still abandoned for the moment. "I just can't . . . you know . . . I can't imagine Stefan killing anyone."

"None of us can, but it may come down to it. I don't think Jonnard is going to give up Eleanora for anything less."

"No. I guess not." She let out a soft sigh.

"Out of the frying pan, into the fire, huh?" Jason kidded her softly.

Bailey nibbled on the corner of her mouth before

nodding slowly. "Sometimes it feels like it." She became very quiet as Gavan broke off talking, and moved to rejoin them. He linked them all together with his large hands, and murmured in a voice only Jason could hear, "Work with me," as he brought up his wolfhead cane, and the crystal in its jaws glowed. Jason added his Talent to Gavan's, and the crystal flared like a newly minted silver coin. A stomach-jolting swoop, and then they were home.

Bailey shook herself. Lacey let out a rattle of scolding clutters before diving nose first into her pocket and refusing to come back out, apparently upset by the teleportation.

Trent's stomach growled, as they all dusted themselves off. "Dinner," he said emphatically.

"Washing first, we all smell like horses." Gavan cuffed his charge lightly and sent them off to the primitive wash stands built by the waterfall off the Iron Mountain. The cold water may have made them smell better, but they all stood shivering as they regrouped to make their way to the kitchens.

Warmth and light from the rooms flooded over them, however, along with the rich aroma of stew and freshly baked bread. Ting and Bailey's mother Rebecca busily set steaming bowls on the table while Ting's grandmother sat with her snapping dark eyes, and watched all of them. She had brewed tea and the kettle sat in front of her, with its row of cups; she would serve them once they all sat.

So dinner went, as it had been going for months, familiar and yet different, and Trent ate as if famished, and made a sandwich out of thick bread slices with stew ladled between them, to take back to his room for "later on." No one said anything, but Jason grinned. The only one in the group who could outeat Trent was working off his bearlike aggressions elsewhere that night.

And the difference between the two was that one could see Stefan bulking up over the months, but Trent stayed wiry thin as always. After dinner, the boys cleaned while Ting and Bailey dashed upstairs "to talk" and Rebecca and Madame Qi went out to the lecture hall to talk and work on darning clothes at their leisure.

Gavan disappeared to find Tomaz; the other hadn't shown up for dinner, but they could all feel his presence about, and that left Trent and Jason elbow-to-elbow at the great tubs for cleaning up.

"Did you mean what you said?"

Trent looked at him. He thought for a moment, then twitched one shoulder. "Sometimes I do, sometimes I don't. I mean, how do you handle the pressure of being a Gatekeeper? Hard as you study, you can't turn that on and off, right?"

"True. But that's not the point. It's that you thought Gavan wouldn't listen to you. That he wouldn't think you told the truth."

"He wouldn't have. And maybe he's right . . ." Trent paused, scrubbing bag in hand, elbow-deep in the foaming tub. "Maybe it was an illusionary trap, laid by the Dark Hand. But I don't think so. What we saw was there, and it's still there, only he can't sense it. And you can't. And no one else could but me. And I've got no Talent, virtually, so, how can I be right?"

"But if you are, you are," answered Jason flatly.

"It's that black and white? Look, Jason. Nothing in life is that black and white. Nothing."

"Some things are. I trust you."

"But if I were wrong a lot, you wouldn't. I might have been wrong about the old fort, but I don't think so." Trent rubbed at his nose, leaving a soap bubble on it. It left a glistening spot as it popped.

"We should go back, then."

"After what happened to Bailey, I don't think so. Not just the two of us."

Jason finished up his stack of crockery and slid it carefully into the rinsing tub. "You need to talk to Gavan."

"You think so?"

He nodded. "Don't you think so?"

"I suppose you're right." Trent slowly finished his own stack of crockery, before adding, "I think I'll talk to Madame Qi first."

Jason smiled a little. Ting's grandmother had a kind of no-nonsense philosophy that was welcome to them all, which she sometimes thumped into place with her bamboo cane, and sometimes slipped into their heads with just a wink of her dark eyes. Either way, Qi was old and very, very learned, and her strain of Magick went deep in her blood, although she was untrained by Magicker standards. "Good idea." If anyone could get past Trent's wariness, she could.

They raced each other then, through the last of the kitchen cleanup before tumbling outside to check the perimeter wards and stargaze and see if they could find Tomaz before bedtime. They were successful in all.

Ting pulled Bailey into their room quickly and shut the door before hugging her so hard that Lacey had no choice but to climb out of her pocket with a squeak and clamber onto Bailey's shoulder as if in fear of being crushed.

"I thought you weren't coming back!" Ting paused as the words tumbled out of her and she stood breathless for a moment. "I felt your touch, a tug and then . . . oh, Bailey. All my crystals went dark!"

"What?" Bailey blinked at her in astonishment.

"Every one of them. I couldn't find you. I knew you were trying to get back somehow. I went frantic. And Grandmother couldn't help and I was afraid to let anyone else know. My crystals!" Ting flung her slender hands in the air, where they made movements like lost, startled birds.

"But . . . but . . ."

"No, wait, that's not all. I heard the wolfjackals howling." Ting sat down then, gazing up at Bailey, her eyes intent. "I knew they weren't around here. I was so frightened for you. I knew you were trapped, Bailey! What happened? Tell me everything!"

Bailey sat down. She pried Lacey off her shoulder, and put her down where the tiny pack rat scampered across the wooden flooring, looking for interesting and sparkling bits of treasure. Distracted, both girls watched as the clever creature found something and skittered into the corner, climbed into her cage, and stowed it away.

"So that's where my barrette went," muttered Ting. "Such a troublemaker."

"I'll fetch it out later," Bailey promised. She sat back, clasping her arms about her knees as she folded her legs under her on the cot. "We Crystaled to Avenha. The whole city is in retreat, up in the hills and caves behind it. I guess years ago, they wintered there during really hard times or attack or something. Renart got us horses and we rode out to an old fortress where they said the raiders camped."

"Was it the Dark Hand?"

"Oh, yes. As if there were any doubt." Bailey let out a tiny snort. "A long ride, though. I think my legs are going to fall off by tomorrow morning. Something odd about the fort, but I'll tell you that later. Gavan looked it over, and then turned around. We thought we were going to, well . . . I dunno . . . attack or something, but he didn't."

"He can't."

"Still. We rode all the way out there."

"Maybe he was hoping to get a trace of Eleanora."

"Maybe. He should have. We were close enough, but I don't know." Bailey frowned, trying to remember. "If he did, he didn't show a sign of it. We turned back then, noting to Renart that we couldn't do anything now, but that we *would*. I think he understood that. And I got lost heading back."

"Lost! Oh, no."

Bailey nodded at Ting. "That's when the wolfjackals hit. They galloped over the low hills and surrounded me. It's like I couldn't decide what to do first, and I tried to do it all at once, Shield, reach you, Crystal back, Beacon Gavan and Jason—and only the shield held. Everything else I couldn't do. I know I get flustered sometimes, but . . . it was scary, Ting. Really, really scary."

"I know," said Ting quietly. She reached her hand out and grasped Bailey's wrist. "I was so frightened."

"They circled closer and closer. My little horse kicked one of 'em to pieces. I didn't know how much longer I could hold out, and then he showed up."

"Gavan? Jason?"

Bailey shook her head, ponytail bobbing vigorously. "Jonnard!"

"No!" Ting's eyes widened. "That snake!"

"He laughed at me. I don't know how I managed, I kept the Shield up and finally, someone felt the energy, and I could hear the hoofbeats pounding over the hill. He could, too, so he talked some trash and then rode off as fast as he could."

"Wow."

"Then Gavan got mad. So we went back to the fort. I don't know what he was going to do, but he was going to do something . . . and the fort wasn't there! Not a sign of it. Just old ruins. Before, it had buildings and wagons and we could see the raiders training, working. Now, nothing. As though it had all been a bad dream."

"That couldn't be."

"No, it couldn't." Bailey leaned back and stretched her tired legs gingerly. "Gavan said it had been a trap, some kind of illusion, he thought. I don't know. If that's true, then they're strong. Very, very strong." She shook herself, as if shaking off an unspoken thought. "Jason and Trent were muttering at each other the whole time, so something is going on. I just don't know what."

"Bailey," said Ting softly. "My crystals finally started coming back, but it took hours. And I'm thinking . . . I'm thinking that the power here is very strange. I think we get depleted easier and recover a lot slower. Maybe don't recover at all, if we're not careful."

"You think so?"

"I think when you reached out for me, you drew on me. I know I felt this surge, and then everything went dark. I don't think you meant to, but if you hadn't, you might not have kept that Shield up. And it could explain a lot of things."

"Such as?"

Ting flipped her long dark hair over her shoulders. "Why the building is taking so long. They're pacing themselves. They can feel the power drain, too, but they're not telling us that. You know they don't tell us a lot of stuff."

"True. But this is serious, then!"

"Very serious. The internal structure of this whole academy is laced with Magick, for one reason or another. To protect against fire and rot, and to ward against other Magicks. It has to be difficult to do, and they're going slowly because they have no choice."

"Then Eleanora's time could be . . . running out."

Ting nodded, and both girls fell silent.

After a long moment, Bailey said, "Well. This makes it a whole new ball game, doesn't it?"

"What do you mean?"

"If we're weaker, they're weaker. And if they're not, then we need to find out why. You and I, my girl, have some experiments to run. When we have some more answers, then we can tell Gavan and Tomaz what we've discovered. I think you're right. We don't have much time!"

Wind Beneath My Wings

JASON WOKE WITH THE certainty that something was wrong. He rolled over in his cot, smothering a groan from sore muscles that had been used to ride a barrel-bellied short horse all day, and put his face back in his pillow. In a way, he welcomed the soreness. He used to ache all over after a bruising soccer game, and it was a way of reminding him he'd done something fun and great at the same time. He'd have to get the Havenites together in soccer teams as soon as he could figure out how to make good balls. The rest of the game would be fairly easy to re-create, and he thought they'd take to it. Maybe even the wanderers could put together a team to compete as they went from town to town, gaining acceptance on a level no one could predict or prevent. Athletics had a way of bringing people together.

But those thoughts didn't smooth down the hairs on the back of his neck. Jason peeked to the side and saw, in the early morning darkness, Trent sitting bolt upright on his cot, eyes squeezed tightly shut, his body gyrating and jerking as he performed what Jason could only call "air drums," his hands and arms beating out rhythms on an unseen drum and cymbal set. His head bobbed in time to a hard rocking beat that Jason could all but hear himself as he watched. Jason sat up slowly to face his friend, who seemed to have no idea of time or place, so lost was he in his song. Trent's mute musical performance grew in fervor until suddenly he stopped, drained, and just sat, his hands on his knees, breathing as hard as if he'd been on stage for a driving drum solo.

His eyes opened slowly to find Jason watching him.

"I'd ask what that was," Jason told him, "but I think I know."

Trent lifted his chin. "Sometimes you feel like you've gotta do something."

"And sometimes it feels like you can't do anything right."

Trent shrugged then. "Look, I can't blame Gavan or Tomaz or any of them. I faked all of you guys out for a long time. So who says I'm not faking now?" He fetched his crystal out, his opaque, dead-looking crystal. "They should have known it when I picked this one out. Everyone else's is transparent, or nearly so. You can't focus your energy into something you can't see into." He tucked it away. "We might as well both be useless."

That time at summer camp near the still blue waters of Lake Wannameecha, when they'd been called to picnic tables, their tops covered with trays of glittering gems and crystals, and told to pick a crystal, seemed incredibly long ago, although it had only been a few years. His life had changed immeasurably since that time, as had Trent's. Jason pointed at his friend.

"I think the whole point is that you see differently than we do. That crystal was on the table with all the others because, like all the others, it had something. It offered a conduit the elders could sense, even if they couldn't understand it. Our crystals are chosen just like we are, even if they never find a user to bond to. They're just gems, after all. Even if most of us can't see or feel what you do, we can tell your Talent is there, and growing. Yesterday was a fluke. Gavan wasn't thinking about you or any of us. He was trying to find Eleanora and couldn't."

"So in a stable of racehorses, even a pack mule has value?"

"I didn't say that! And you're no mule, even if you're as backassward as one, sometimes."

Trent gestured through the air before dropping his hand back on his leg, and beginning to tap out the unheard rhythm again. "Look, I appreciate the effort. I do, really. But you're not me, and you wouldn't understand. I know you're trying, but you're not me."

"That's right. I'm not. I know that I couldn't be myself without you around. Look at you. Really look. You kept almost everyone fooled for months about your Talent. You're so damn smart, none of us knew any different, and if we wanted to know anything, if we didn't understand anything about the myths and power behind magic and all the new stuff we were learning, there you were with an answer. How much cooler is that?"

"Almost anyone," Trent said somberly, "is better off than I am. Look at you."

"You want to know the worst part about being me?" Jason said suddenly.

"Worst part? How can there be a worst part? You're the golden Magicker, Jason. You're the Gate-keeper." Trent looked at him sideways, then swung around to face him, his fingers still moving in a drum-beat on his leg to the music only he could hear.

Jason shrugged. "It's only good because no one else is, right now, but no one can show me what to do either. Yet that's not it. I don't mean being a Magicker, I mean being *me.*"

Something flickered in Trent's eyes. "You mean, like being an orphan?"

"Yeah, like that."

"It never seems to worry you. Look at your stepparents. Joanna is great, and McIntire is way cool. They let you come here, they made things easy."

"But they're like that to anybody, Trent. The dirtiest, mangiest stray cat could wander in, and they'd clean it up, and bathe it, and feed it royally, and then find the best home in the world for it . . . and it's like . . . it's like I was never any different to them."

"You can't mean that! Of course you're different."

Jason shook his head. "Maybe, but I never felt it. I can't say it, exactly. Joanna never talks about my dad, you know? It's almost as if he never existed, or she never wants to say anything imperfect about him. So I don't know what he was, and I'm forgetting what I knew. I'm forgetting my dad. My mom was already forgotten, except in a dream now and then." He looked away for a moment, and swallowed hard. "So I'm growing up, and I feel like I'm never quite part of anything, you know? But I get along, and it could be a lot worse. They treated me well. I didn't have to live in a cupboard under the stairs or anything—but I never know quite who I'm supposed to be. Suddenly, I find out I have a temper—"

"You? A temper?" Trent wrinkled his nose in disbelief.

"I am being serious here. I wake up at night, with my fists clenched, and I'm so mad I'm just sweating it out, and my teeth hurt 'cause I'm biting down so hard on it. That angry."

"Wow." Trent shifted. "Is it at me or something?"

Jason shook his head. "It's at myself. Maybe someone else sometimes, but it's like finding out you have a volcano inside of you. I feel like I'm going to explode with all this anger and I can't go to Joanna and say, did my dad have a temper? And if he did, what did he do about it? Did he go walk it out or did he sit in front of the TV set for hours and punch the remote, or did he yell and scream at someone? 'Cause she would never tell me. She has this code about making sure I have this perfect impression about my dad, and all it does is make him a nonperson, like he never existed. But he did, and it's the warts I need to know about, it's the . . . the wrinkles that make him real!"

"Did you ever tell her that?"

"I tried. Once. It was right after I overheard something." Jason paused. He scratched the corner of his eye. "McIntire had said something I wasn't meant to hear. Something that made it sound as if my dad had been drinking the night of the car crash. That maybe, once in a while, he did that. I tried to ask her. She wouldn't say a word about what McIntire had spilled, just told me, 'Jason, don't worry about anything, you'll be fine.' But I'm not. I want to know. At the same time, I don't dare be less than perfect either. How would she deal with me then? How badly would I disappoint her? Would she look at me and compare me with this loser she never talked to me about? I felt like I couldn't breathe sometimes."

"Jeez." Trent let his breath out slowly. "I think she just wanted to make things smoother for you. Losing your mom so young, and then your dad, too, I think she is always worried about how hard it is for you."

Jason nodded slowly. "Like the stray that doesn't have a family, or not a real one, anyway."

"Cut that out! We're your family!" Trent's expression blazed.

The corner of Jason's mouth twitched. "Exactly. So when I say to you, don't take it so badly, you know what I mean."

Trent blinked slowly, then a smile crept over his face. "Did you walk me into that?"

"Like Bailey into a wall." Jason nodded again, firmly. He stood up. "Anyway, you're coming with me."

"Where?"

"Somewhere," Jason said firmly, "you've never been before."

He left a note for Gavan about missing the morning of the workday, that he and Trent had work to do. Then they grabbed some food from the kitchen pantry before the sun had begun to crack open the sky, and Jason took Trent climbing up one of the easier slopes of the Iron Mountains. They scaled it slowly at first, muscles awakening and stretching, and then warming even as the sun warmed their backs as it dispersed the clouds of night. They emerged on a wide, flat plateau.

Trent cast his gaze about.

"Looks like a plane could land here."

"That's about the size of it." Jason stepped back, took a deep breath, and opened his mind, sending out an appeal he was not even positive would be answered. He was not sure what would happen.

A cloud drifted through the brilliantly blue sky, a sky that looked as if it had been washed clean just for today's appearance, and the sun dimmed for a moment. Before he could look around, sound rushed at him, and a keening shriek not unlike that of an eagle, only this came from a fire-rimmed throat coated in shimmering orange-red scales that looked as if they had just been pulled from a heated forge.

The dragon circled lazily once or twice before diving sharply and swooping down on them. Trent stood absolutely still as though not wanting to attract anything by movement. He'd seen the dragon a few times, but there was no way anyone could be nonchalant about its appearance, awesome and demanding. The dragon curled his talons under him, taking on the appearance of a rather large cat, and looked down with huge lanternlike eyes.

"Greetings, young Magickers. Note that I said Magickers and not appetizers." The dragon rumbled at himself in amusement.

"Always nice to hear," Jason responded. He took a few steps and leaned in, and scratched the scales just under the curve of the reptile's jaw, being careful not to ruffle the edges. Not only could he hurt the dragon, but the edges were sharp enough to slice through his fingertips, quite painfully. "I never ask, but I must today. Trent and I have some scouting to do and I wondered if you'd take us."

"Two hearty lads on my back?" The dragon managed to raise a ridge of scales over one eye, much like an eyebrow. His long, spiny whiskers quivered as well, but he did not sound insulted.

"If you would allow it."

"What sort of scouting?" Both spoke at once, Trent's higher voice underscored by the low rumbling of the dragon.

"Anywhere you want to take us." He had hopes, of course, where he wanted to go but knew if the dragon agreed to carry them anywhere, it would be where the dragon wanted to go. And, truthfully, flying anywhere on dragonback would be glorious.

"Get on and hold tightly then. Have a soft belt, do you?" The dragon tilted his triangular face curiously at Jason.

"Two," answered Jason softly, pulling them from the inside of his vest. He kept one on him at all times and had stuffed the second one in before hauling Trent out the academy doors. He looped them about the dragon's neck and mounted quickly, then put an arm out to help Trent up. "Mind the scale edges. They're sharp and if you dislodge them, he gets sore. Use the belt to hold onto, and watch me."

Trent took a deep breath before grabbing Jason's forearm and leaping up. He settled behind Jason and secured himself within the looping belt, leaning over once or twice to see how Jason did it.

"Everyone set?"

Jason could feel the dragon's voice rumbling throughout his body, vibrating against his calves. "Looks like it."

"Good, good! A fine, brisk day for flying!" The last roared out as the dragon broke into a run and launched himself with a bellow off the edge of the plateau into the bright blue sky. For a dizzying moment, it felt as if the whole world fell away from under them. Trent gasped in Jason's ear, echoing Jason's moment of stomach-dropping sensation. Then the dragon's wings beat strongly, one, twice, thrice, and they caught a current stream and soared along it, climbing slowly but steadily.

They banked, and below them could see the small dale where the academy and the Dragon Gate lay, and the small encampment. Trent pointed as they wheeled over it, the dragon's body heat warming them from the inside out, it seemed, even as the cool morning air whipped past them.

Trent let out a yip of sheer joy as they skimmed the Iron Mountains, and the small corner of Haven that they knew fell away. Even Jason had never seen this part from dragonback, as the dragon generally kept to the valley and dale of their refuge. But it seemed as if the dragon knew his mind today, his wings dipping into the air and pushing them farther and farther over the unknown. Indigo and silver rivers crossed below them like lacy ribbons. Dark green forests looked impenetrable. Small roads cut across the terrain in determined manner, linking one small patch of community to another, marked by their quiltlike squares of fields and groves with a town square in the center. Trent bumped Jason's shoulder with his chin.

"Look at that," he said, his voice snatched out of his mouth, the words whipping away almost before Jason could hear him. Trent pointed. "See the Magick. I can. It follows that edge of the area. It's as if it were a river of its own."

"You'd see more on the ground, though, right?"

"Sure. Like energy lines. But that. That's one massive band of power, for me to see it up here!"

Jason tried to note its position and wondered if it had anything to do with the old Warlord's spirit presence and the forts that had made up his border, but he couldn't see well enough to know if there were more ruins about or not. The dragon seemed to be carrying them high enough to remain unnoticed, even if their noses and ears and fingers felt like they might freeze off!

"Hold on!" the dragon commanded.

Jason laced his numbing hands deeper into the woven belt. Trent did the same, his body stiffening behind Jason in apprehension.

With a defiant bellow, the dragon did a wheel and roll, and came across an immense lake, his belly barely clearing the surface even as Jason let out a dizzy groan and Trent a whoop of excitement.

"Did you feel that? Out of nowhere, from the clouds to the water!"

The dragon extended a taloned paw, slicing through the water, and coming up with a handful of large, wiggling fish. He swallowed his meal in one gulp and belched contentedly, before turning about on a wing tip and launching himself skyward again.

It felt like riding a rocket. Up, up, up, straining, straining, straining, till he thought his eyes might pop out, and then the beast leveled off again, and a loud vibration thrummed through their bodies. The dragon, it seemed, was humming in contentment.

"Sushi does a body good," Trent laughed in his ear.

Jason grinned at that, then, his stomach settling down from the loop-the-loops. Trent had more of a Talent for dragon riding than he did! Or at least, the stomach.

They slowly circled back toward the Iron Mountains and although the ride seemed too short, Jason found himself shivering, the only warm parts of him wherever he was in contact with the dragon's body. When they landed, both boys slid off and leaned against the beast for a moment, shaking and laughing and grinning.

The dragon tented his wing about them. "Enjoy that, did you?"

"That was great! That was . . . incredible!" Trent's nose was bright red with the cold, and joy sparkled in his eyes.

"Thank you," Jason managed. He quickly untied the soft belts from the dragon's neck and stowed them away inside his shirt and vest, then ran his hands over the creature, careful to ensure that he had not damaged the scales or leathery skin in any way. The dragon purred a moment as Jason stroked and massaged him.

Then he cocked an eye at Trent. "Seeing power?"

"I was, yes."

"Do you look for it?"

"Ummm." Trent thought about it. "I guess not. It's either there, or it isn't, right?"

"Not always," the dragon said, his voice booming deep in his chest. "But it is best not to search for the hidden powers. They are that way for a reason, and many are unpleasant to deal with. You see the brightest, and that is best for you, I think."

"I'll take that as a positive, then." Trent hugged himself a moment, and the momentary hesitation caused by the dragon's words fled his expression, replaced by exuberance. "Man, that was great!"

"Good. You can stay up here all day and talk about it, but me . . . I think I'm going back down where it's warm, even if I have to work for it!"

Trent grinned at him. He found the trail they'd hiked up and disappeared over the edge. Jason ducked out from under dragon wing to follow, but found himself stopped by one obsidian claw.

"Watch him," the dragon said. "He sees too much and knows too little."

Jason bit his lip, then nodded. "Okay. I'll remember that."

The dragon inclined his head. "And next time, bring warmer clothing." He laughed, his hot breath washing over Jason, as he drew his foot back, freeing the Gatekeeper.

"You'd better believe it!" Jason threw one arm about the dragon's snout, hugging him, and then he hurried to catch up with Trent.

If there was still a hot breakfast waiting down below, he wanted to be sure he got his share.

13

Button, Button

BAILEY PLUCKED Lacey out of her pocket, rubbing her thumb over the sleepy rodent's head. If Lacey could have snored, she would have, as the pack rat's eyelids reluctantly fluttered open. "Time to work," she crooned softly. Lacey nicked her tufted tail, catlike, as if answering and then gave a half chirp.

"Must be hard on her," Ting offered, leaning over to pet the small creature herself. "She's nocturnal by nature, but we keep her up all day."

"Don't fool yourself! She does a lot of sleeping in my pocket." Bailey flashed a grin. "Besides, keeping her awake during the day means *we* sleep better at night. She does a lot of rattling around otherwise."

Ting wrinkled her nose. That was too true. Because the pack rat was more than a pet, Bailey kept her close, but the tiny rodent's nighttime habits of rambling, searching, nesting, bug hunting and so forth made sleeping really difficult for others. She gave Lacey one last head rub between Bailey's fingers and said, "Put her to work, then! I need my sleep." She leaned over and picked up a small basket of glowing crystals, each one imbued with energy that Gavan Rainwater and others had flooded into it, each one able to do a variety of small enchantments. Some of them she could read easily if she tried, others were too intricate and powerful for her to decipher. Ting would like nothing better than to sit down and sort through the tiny gems, pondering each of them and its inner mysteries, but she knew that would be frowned upon. If the elder Magickers had wanted her to know, they'd have told her. Still . . . she ran her fingers through the basket's contents, letting the crystals rain through her slender touch. She trailed after Bailey as they climbed into the inner workings of the unfinished academy wing.

Their footsteps echoed in the hollow rooms of the building. Bailey knelt down, placing Lacey on the floor. She held her hand out to Ting, who gave her a crystal. "White ones in the ceiling ducts," she repeated, although they'd been doing this for days.

"Right." Bailey handed the small crystal to the pack rat who took it eagerly with a chitter and promptly stuffed it in a cheek pouch, then sat and cleaned her whiskers as if she hadn't a hidden treasure on her. She fed her several more before sitting cross-legged on the floor, closing her eyes, and reaching for Lacey's thoughts.

Whiskers. Dirty and dusty, must groom. Lacey sat, combing her paw through her long, silky whiskers with pride. Beautiful whiskers, and useful, too! Bailey gave the creature's thoughts in her head a little nudge. Treasures must be placed on rafters and in ventilation ducts, in nooks and crannies all over and then *left* there, unnested. Lacey flipped her tail in irritation at such unpack ratlike behavior. Gathered, yes, and put away for safety!

Bailey nudged her thoughts again. "No cookies," she muttered aloud and Ting muffled a giggle at that. Bailey opened one eye to stare at Ting. "She's being stubborn."

"Imagine that." Ting hid her grin behind one slender hand.

Bailey shut her eyes again. Tomaz wouldn't approve of this way to work with the beast, but she found it easier. When Lacey moved, she dashed and hopped around so quickly, that Bailey got motion-sick trying to look through two pairs of eyes. This way, she could concentrate on the pack rat's movements without feeling like she was going to hurl doing it. That, of course, made her less in charge but more in tune with the animal. Sometimes she wondered if Tomaz Crowfeather knew what he asked of her, but then remembered him with all his crows and ravens about him, and knew he knew exactly what he was trying to teach and ask of her. He could brush thoughts with almost any animal, if he tried. She wondered if her Talent would someday be as great as his. She shivered at the thought. There were many animals she had no desire to share with! Starting with wolfjackals and working her way down to cockroaches!

Lacey dashed off with a squeak. The thought of cockroaches had pushed her into action. As much as they made Bailey shudder, they made Lacey hungry. Crunchy and good to eat. Not as good as cookies (what was?), but almost. This building had a disturbing lack of such good things to nibble on, although crickets could be found now and then. It was not the season for crickets as evenings got cold, but they would be back in the spring. Lacey scrambled up beams and dove nose first into the heating ducts. She found a good niche for the crystal in her cheek, took it out and placed it. Sniffing for insect goodies and not finding them, she dashed deeper and deeper into the ducts, placing crystals whenever Bailey poked at her to do so, until her cheek pouches had emptied. Luckily, she found a lazy, sleepy cricket and munched it down before scrambling out of the ducts and returning to Bailey's outstretched hand.

Bailey had just pinched off a piece of oatmeal cookie, more health food than cookie, but the pack rat didn't care. Bailey opened her eyes as the whiskery face nuzzled all her fingers thoroughly, mopping up every possible bit of crumb.

Ting ran her hand through the basket again. Not

many crystals remained for placement. "I could do this," she said, voicing her thoughts aloud.

"All of them?"

"Well, not all, but most! And I can tell that Gavan has enchanted some of these a couple of times, as if he didn't get them strong enough the first time."

"Why?"

Ting shrugged. "No idea. Unless he's just doing too much. Which is why I said, I could do this. We can help, you know, more than they let us."

Bailey looked about. "We have been helping! We've built almost this entire academy." She stood, dusting her fingers off on her breeches. "I want to know where the secret passages are."

"Secret passages?"

"Sure! Don't you think they're in here? I'm willing to bet they are. For escaping and hiding."

"They built them when we weren't looking?"

"Something like that." Bailey made a soft fist and tapped experimentally on a wall, listening. She moved a few paces down and tapped again.

Ting watched her for long moments, then said, "Well, far be it from me to suggest that if I had a creature who could wiggle inside almost any passage-way to look . . ."

Bailey shot her a glance. "Use Lacey?"

Ting shrugged.

"She knows the inner ways well enough, but she's not smart enough to know if it's a regular passage or a secret one, you know?"

"But you are."

"Of course! Now, give me some more crystals and let's move a room over."

Ting picked up her basket with a soft laugh, and shadowed Bailey to the next lecture hall.

Bailey waited for Lacey to fill her cheek pouches with a few crystals, then put her down and directed her scampering off. She sat down cross-legged again, shoulder to shoulder with Ting, feeling her senses reel again as Lacey ran across flooring, ducked into an opening, and then scaled the inner walls to the ventilation passageways. A darkness covered her eyesight for a moment, then cleared as Lacey's own acute sight adjusted, although it was the sense of smell which enveloped her. The wood had keen smells to it, and the nails another, and the bracketing and fixtures another. She could see how animals saw the world in a kaleidoscope of patterns that humans did not. It used to muddle her terribly when she first felt Lacey's thoughts, but now she knew how to both embrace and filter it. Of course, there was a part of her that vigorously rejected the idea of hunting down crunchy crickets, or rolling along colorful balls of lint if found for a wonderful pocket of nesting material in a corner, or any number of things that flitted through the pack rat's small mind.

It took most of her concentration to keep Lacey moving and placing the crystals where the diagrams she and Ting studied indicated they should be. One, two, three crystals from Lacey's cheek pouches, laid in a mitred crevice or put atop a beam, from which the rodent jumped and swung about like an acrobat.

Then Lacey took out the last crystal. A stray bit of light hit it from a crack through the joints, and the gem piece dazzled in her paw. Bailey felt the flash of emotion in the beast. Pretty!

And Lacey was off, dashing away through the vents and along the beams, crystal in her mouth and hoarding in her thoughts. Nudging her back to her job lost its possibility. The rodent flung herself into headlong flight and disobedience.

Bailey leaped to her feet. "She's off!" she cried to Ting.

"What?"

"She's stolen the crystal. I've lost her completely." Bailey pulled Ting to her feet. "You go that way. I'll go this!" And she dashed off as well. Ting picked up her basket before running in the other direction, not a clue in her head as how to find one tiny pack rat in one huge, rambling, unfinished building.

Bailey ran till she was out of breath, upstairs and down, and skidded to a halt, her heart thumping in her chest. This was ridiculous! And most of the panting and excitement she felt came from Lacey, through the barest of connections, as the little furball tried to run and hide.

"Poor thing," Bailey muttered to herself. "She knows she's been bad, but she can't help it!" She stood for a moment. If she were a pack rat, where would she go?

Button, button, who's got the button? Bailey turned in a slow circle. She could almost hear Lacey panting. She'd run in the same direction, however wildly it seemed she'd been going.

She had to be somewhere about, and close. Maybe . . . Bailey slid her palm along the wall in front of her, looking for a crack or unfastened panel. Somewhere about here . . .

The wall clicked.

Bailey blinked as it suddenly swung open into darkness in front of her, and at the same time, something swung into the back of her, knocking her through!

She went headlong into nothingness, and the wall solidly thudded into place behind her.

"I think," said Bailey quietly, standing very still, "I found that secret passage."

And worse, as she strained her magickal senses, it was blacked out, warded, against any kind of magic whatsoever.

She was trapped, with no way for anyone to hear her!

14

Chutes and Ladders

BAILEY DISAPPEARED from Ting's thoughts as abruptly as a door slamming shut. She skidded to a halt in a corridor, putting her hand to the wall, and listening. She wondered for a moment if it was her, if she'd suddenly gone deaf or something, because everything about her seemed to stop as well. Then she realized. No Bailey. No best friend of her life. Even when Bailey wasn't cheerfully chattering about something, she put out this vibration, this lively electricity that let Ting know she was awake and about somewhere. Now a void stretched across Ting's life. She hadn't felt anything like it since . . . well, since the last time Bailey had disappeared! Then, new to crystals and focusing, Bailey had projected herself inside her amethyst and it had taken days and days for them to find her, because she'd managed to toggle time itself, as well. Leave it to Bailey to get lost in a way no one else could!

And then there was now. Ting rubbed her arms which suddenly danced with goose bumps. "Bailey?" she called softly, even though they had run in opposite directions. In the new empty corridor, even her quiet call echoed a little.

If not Bailey, then, what about Lacey?

She hadn't the Talent Bailey had, for sure, but she knew Lacey almost as well! Ting wrapped slender fingers about the crystal cage on her bracelet and sent her thoughts casting about for the stubborn, fleeing little furball. She felt nothing at first and concentrated harder. Something feathered against her thoughts before rushing off. Lacey! Ting went after that brushing presence before losing it entirely.

Whatever rabbit hole Bailey had fallen down, Lacey hadn't. That much, she knew.

Ting sighed. What should she do now? Get Gavan? Hope that Bailey would get unlost any moment? She leaned against the wall, trying to think. How serious could this be? Did she just lose track of Bailey or was Bailey really and truly *lost* somewhere and somewhen again? And . . . could it have anything to do with Jonnard?

This last worry sent cold chills through her, making the goose bumps dance even harder, and Ting shivered all through her slender form. She had better find Gavan, and now. Grasping her crystal to find her direction within the walls of the academy, she set her focus on the headmaster, and let her crystal lead the way.

Bailey caught her lower lip in her teeth and tried to think, for a moment, where she could possibly be. That gave her pause, for—d'oh—where else could she be? Trouble was, as nobody knew better than she did, she could be almost *anywhere*.

In the blanketing darkness, her eyes slowly adjusted, and she reached out for thoughts of Ting or her naughty little Lacey and found . . . nothing. It was as if nothing existed but herself and this space beyond the revolving wall. Surely, if she ducked her head and took a step or two, she'd run into the Three Stooges or *Dumb and Dumber* or *someone* as stupid as she was!

"No, no," she said to herself, happy to hear her voice if nothing else. "Think of it as charmed, not

stupid. Serendipity! Look what I fell into, Watson."
Bailey took another deep, steadying breath. She
slipped one foot ahead cautiously, almost swearing she
could feel a slant in the floor, stepping ahead slowly
in case everything should drop out from under her.
Nowhere in her thoughts could she sense Lacey in her
frenzy to hide the sparkly she'd stolen, or even Ting,
who was usually buzzing about somewhere close to
Bailey's mind, even when they were separated by
great distances.

This did not bode well.

"All's well that bodes well?" Bailey muttered to
herself, as she inched cautiously through the dark
room. She raised her voice a bit. "Hello? Ting? Anyone here?"

Her voice sounded dead and muffled. Bailey brushed
her fingers across her crystal and tried to awaken it, but
something took the Magick out of the very air, and
nothing happened. It couldn't be, but it was. She cupped
her amethyst tightly. It still warmed to her and yet not
a thought, not a bit of Magick could she send through
or take from it. She was well and truly lost, and trapped,
by everything she could tell.

"Okay." Bailey inhaled slowly. "What goes up,
must come down . . ." If the wall had swung in, there
must be a way to get it to swing back out. All she
had to do was find the tripping mechanism. That
meant she had to find the wall and search every splinter of it. Moving as cautiously and slowly across the
floor as if she wore ice skates on a skating rink, Bailey
slid and glided back to a wall. She ran her palms over
it. Smooth, polished paneling, with no end and no beginning. She thought another moment.

Kicking off one boot, she pushed it up against the
base, to mark where she began her search, for as her
eyes got used to the near total darkness, she could see
a little but not much more, and the wall looked endless. She didn't want to be searching the same area
over and over. And as for places taller than she could
reach . . . Bailey tilted her head back and looked up

the wall at the shadowed ceiling . . . she'd have to hope that whoever wanted to get out hadn't put the levers out of reach!

She knocked, thumped, and rubbed every inch of wall she could touch from her outstretched arms down to the tip of her toes . . . one booted, one in a sock, down the room she inched. A snail would have made faster progress, she told herself, but then, would a snail have gotten itself into this predicament? She didn't think so!

Down the long, dim corridor she went without success until she found herself in a corner. She moved across the end panel to the other wall and thought of marking it with the second boot, then thought again. After all, it was a corner! How many corners could there be in this room? She started off again, swearing that her fingertips were beginning to get blisters as she stroked and poked every square inch of the very odd room. Then, just when she had decided to give up and take a nap, she found something. A small inlay of wood that wiggled a bit.

"Eureka!" Bailey readied to do whatever she had to, to open, turn, poke, and prod it.

"Okay," Gavan said patiently, his clear blue eyes fixed on Ting, his brows furrowed as he tried to understand. "Take it a little slower, and someone explain to me what you mean by 'Off the radar,' please. Am I to understand that Bailey is missing?"

Rich shifted his weight, his tool belt slung low on his hip, but the pockets of his belt, crudely stitched and put together, held herbs and bandages and ointments, not tools. "Bailey missing? Oh, that's new! What's the likelihood of that, hmmm? She was only missing . . . what, twenty-four hours ago?"

Ting wrinkled her nose at him. "Stop it. Yes, she's missing."

Stef had sat down on a tree stump, and he crossed his thick arms over his chest. "How lost can she be?

I mean, it's what, a seven-story building with two wings?"

"I mean she's lost, Stefan, really, really lost."

"As in off the radar," Gavan said quizzically, watching her face. "What did you mean by that?"

Ting looked at him, and could no longer hide the stricken feeling inside her. "As in, I can't feel her at all. She's gone."

"Mmmmm. You're usually connected a bit, then?"

"Always. Aren't we . . . supposed to be?" A little defiantly, Ting brushed a soft wing of black hair from her eye.

Gavan smiled gently. "We had hoped, but one never knows. It is a camaraderie some of us never feel, and some of us feel almost instantly." He put his hand out and patted Ting. "And, as Stef so aptly put it, how far could she have gone?"

"Then you don't think it's Jonnard or anything?"

He shook his head vigorously. "Not with the wards we have set about. We'd have heard an intrusion, believe me. No, it's more likely to be . . ." Gavan paused, and then a thought seemed to cross his mind. His mouth twitched. "Yes, I think I know just where Bailey might be."

"Where's that?"

"Where the most trouble is. I can only hope she didn't pull *that* lever . . ." Gavin motioned to Rich and Stefan. "I want you two up and down the north wing, and we'll take the south. Crystal me if you find any sign of her, or that pesky little rodent of hers." He swung around, his cloak swirling like a great wing about them. "Ting, come with me, and hurry. I have a suspicion. I just hope we can find her in time!" Concern colored his words.

A broken nail and long minutes later, Bailey figured out how to pry out the end of the small piece of wood. It took not one but three different pressure points, pressed in exactly the right combination, to pop it out of place. That, she found out quite by accident, and by listening carefully. She could hear clicks when she pressed on one corner or the other, but nothing seemed to loosen the inlay properly. It was rather like half unlocking a door with a key.

She found a wooden ring secured into the space behind it. It had a metallic feel to it, as if it might be bronze or an alloy, but it was definitely circular and big enough for her to curl two fingers into. A ring which she then pulled out. It seemed to snap into place. Bailey thought a moment, then twisted it. A noise of tumblers turning and inner workings working and other ominous sounds followed immediately. With a *whoosh!* the floor under her disappeared. Bailey let out a shriek and dropped into space.

The whole building rumbled. Timbers shivered and groaned, and the stairs vibrated heavily underfoot. Ting immediately thought of an earthquake, having grown up in an area where the earth moving was a fact of life. But they weren't anywhere near the San Andreas fault! "What is that?"

"That," said Gavan grimly, "is what I feared." He abruptly switched directions, from heading upstairs, to thundering down. Ting flew along in his wake, the stairs booming around them like cannon fire. They flung headlong down, down, down, as Ting wondered if the academy had a dungeon hidden somewhere (and if so, why?) and then they burst into the vast root cellar storage room where her grandmother and Rebecca were preparing shelves and barrels to store goods in, and Qi was patiently saying, "This dust will keep ants and most other insects out, very old but very good remedy," as she sprinkled a whitish powder around the edges of the room.

Both women looked up in surprise. "Ting!" Rebecca's eyes widened. "Is something wrong?"

Gavan took them both by the elbows, saying, "Move *here* NOW," and looking up with a face creased in great worry.

"Yeeeeoooooowwwww" echoed all about them, descending out of the ceiling, and with the shriek, a corner of the ceiling opened up and Bailey slid through, landing with an unceremonious thump and grunt where her mother and Ting's grandmother had just been standing.

Gavan nodded his head. "I think I need to work on the landing site a bit." He extended his hand to Bailey. "Congratulations, lass, I think you've broken the all-time Magicker curiosity mark."

Bailey sat up, coughing, the wind knocked out of her, and blinked. Finally she managed, "What was that?"

"That, if what happened is what I think happened, was my panic room, where all sounds and Magick are nullified in case of extreme attack, and my escape chute." Gavan stood patiently, waiting for her to grasp his hand. "I had planned a field trip there when everything was worked out, but you seemed to have jumped the schedule."

"Bailey, hon, are you all right?" Rebecca grabbed her daughter by the shoulders and stood her up, then began dusting her off. Any answer Bailey might have made was interrupted by an outraged piping and as they all looked up, a tiny ball of fur fell out of the ceiling chute and into Bailey's quick-thinking grasp.

Lacey let out an aggrieved sneeze and promptly hid her face in her paws. "Troublemaker," Bailey said affectionately, looking down at the pack rat, not seeing much the same look on her mother's face as she looked at her daughter.

"All's well, then. I'd better call off the boys before someone else stumbles onto something."

Bailey rounded on Ting. "See? I told you!"

The headmaster stopped abruptly in the root cellar doorway, and looked back over his shoulder. "Told her what?"

Both girls smiled innocently and chimed together, "Oh, nothing."

"I can only imagine." Gavan made a gesture that trailed sparks through the air as he left. Words lingered behind. "That should also help keep the cellar free of insects." The sparks rained down upon the ground and lay twinkling, dewlike for a moment, before being absorbed.

15

Plans and Plans Gone Awry

WHAT YOU'VE TOLD me about the wolfjackals saddens but does not surprise me," Tomaz Crowfeather said heavily. He squatted by a ward fire, warming his thick hands carefully, the fire's light adding much depth to his already time-carved face. Gavan sat on one of the three-legged stools the children . . . no, not children anymore, he corrected himself . . . delighted in making. The day's ride had tired him more than it should, and he chided himself for that, as well. To go and then do nothing chafed at him like a badly fitting and overly starched shirt. He wanted to pull and then rip the other day away from him, but could not.

"I didn't think the Dark Hand was making use of them anymore."

"They are torn from Chaos and have a need to return to it. Can you think of any force more chaotic than that which Jonnard and Isabella use? No?" Tomaz nodded to himself as if answering his own question when he heard nothing from Gavan. "So. They will go where they must just as we go to fire for warmth, regardless of its danger. We, however, know how to control fire. Usually." He stood, and hooked a thumb in the loop of his hammered silver belt. The conchas, the round disks of metal from which it was made, rattled faintly at his touch. "Do you condemn them for that?"

"Condemn, no, but I'd gladly corral them if I could. I think somehow the Dark Hand feeds off them as well."

Tomaz raised a squared eyebrow. "In addition to the Leucators?"

"Just a theory. One I was hoping you could solve."

Tomaz grunted. "I was, as well." He reached for a crude poker and stirred the ward fire up a bit, watching the shower of orange sparks shoot upward hike fireworks, and sputter out. "What else bothers you?"

Gavan halted in mid gesture of rubbing his eyes. He dropped his hand. "Shows, does it?"

Tomaz shrugged. "We know each other well."

"I couldn't *feel* her, Tomaz. If she was there, and she should have been, both her and FireAnn, I couldn't feel her! I had no lingering touch, no sense, no . . . hope."

"Yet you went back and found the fortress a decoy, did you not?"

"So it seemed."

"So you told Renart and the boys."

"I hadn't the strength left to try and pierce the curtain if it had been hidden. So I decided it was an illusion, and I think it is. I think Isabella has taken the actual workings of her little garrison and laid it over the ruins of a similar one, in a ruse to hide their location. Eleanora forgive me if I'm wrong." Gavan looked away from the firelight, into the night.

"How does that explain Jonnard cornering Bailey?"

"That's the question, isn't it? How does that explain that? He could have sensed someone tripping the trap's perimeter and come to take a look. He's capable of Crystaling for long distances, I should think."

"But why would he? Unless he were already in the region."

"Damnit!" Gavan's left hand gripped his cane tightly. "I don't know! I don't know."

Tomaz looked at him almost mildly and raised his

index finger. "We have to remember that things are often more simple than they seem. If not, they would have attacked us before now and driven us off, or even killed us. They cannot do it any more than we can attack them as long as they're holding hostages. The question is . . . what is holding *them* back?"

Gavan shook his head wearily. Then he raised his head, brushing his hair from his eyes and locking his gaze onto Tomaz. "That's it! We have a Gatekeeper. They don't."

Tomaz nodded. "I should imagine that's it. It always has been. Brennard and then Jon have been after Jason from the very beginning. After Fizziwig, too, although poor Fizzi hadn't the skill to open many Gates or keep them open. They killed Fizziwig in their haste. But Jason. Jason has a great deal of ability he hasn't called on yet."

"In other words," Gavan said dryly, "Isabella has no intention of staying bottled up here on Haven."

"I don't think she does."

"Neither would I, if I wanted to be an empress, I suppose. Well, that's it then. Jon came after his trap was sprung, hoping to find Jason. He did not. He caught Bailey instead. He retreated as soon as he discovered that. So. We keep Jason as far from them as we can."

"Even so far as to send him back home?"

They traded looks. Gavan shook his head slowly. "Let's hope it doesn't come to that. Going home for Jason could be even deadlier than having Isabella get her hands on him. She will value the Magick in him. Back home, they'd tear him apart trying to figure out how he ticked."

"Then," commented Tomaz, "we know what we have to do."

"Aye. But no idea how in hell we're going to manage it." Gavan laughed at himself, and the humor did not reach his blue eyes. "The improbable just became more impossible."

Tomaz dropped his hand on his friend's shoulder.

"We'll accomplish it one step at a time. It will be like skirting quicksand. We'll need to plan each step carefully."

"Jason won't go to them easily, if at all."

"Not for himself. So we must watch the others carefully. I suggest you get Stefan and Rich back to the academy tomorrow, and keep them here. Isabella is a cold one, but it won't take long for her to realize that Jason's great vulnerability lies not in himself, but in his friends."

"Done." Gavan stood up, leaning slightly on his cane. Its support felt comforting, and worse, necessary. He was exhausted, he thought. "Shall we tell them?"

"Not quite yet. I want to find out a bit more about our wolfjackals first. If you permit it, I think I need to visit Khalil and talk with him."

Khalil had stayed in their world, where he'd always been, lost in the deserts of what was now known as Dubai. His estates were hidden and yet substantial, and his Talents as well. But he was a Magicker, and an ally, and Tomaz was probably right in seeking him out.

Every time Jason opened the Gate, the world of Haven trembled. Isabella and Jon would feel it. Let them feel it! He thought. Let them wonder what it is we're doing. They'll think it an attack on them, somehow, as if all worlds revolve about them.

Sometimes, they did.

16

Swinging Gates

ISABELLA STUDIED her journals, with a growing irritation buzzing around her, rather like an irritating fly. But she could see nothing as she glanced up. She took a moment to extend her senses about her, wondering what the problem could be, and then a sharp knock at her door interrupted the investigation. She frowned, and rubbed at the bridge of her strong nose. A good, imperious nose, at that.

"Come in."

Tormun, one of her head guardsmen, came in, smelling of the barracks and whatever else such men smelled of, his thumb tucked into his heavy weapons belt, and an apologetic look on his rough face. "I . . . I beg pardon, madame, but . . . well, downstairs . . . the chains are rattling. It's spooking the men, madame."

"Spooking them? Are they men or nervous beasts?" Isabella let out a tiny snort of disdain and got to her feet with an immense rustling of her vast gown. "They know what the sound is."

"That doesn't make 'em any easier about it, madame. That's not why I'm here, though. I just thought you would want to be aware. Those t'ings are restless, mighty restless."

"Perhaps I should send some of the men down to keep them company?"

Tormun went white. He stiffened, rather than taking a step back, and his body hunched as though in disagreement with his mind about what action to take. Then he got out, "If it pleases you, madame."

"It does not. Those *things* as you call them are powerful sorceries, not to be trifled with. I am grateful you alerted me to the problem. I shall attend to it." Isabella scooped up a heavy ring of keys at the corner of her desk and swept past Tormun at the doorway, the hem of her gown catching for a moment on his boots and then drawing free.

It wouldn't do to let the guardsman see her concern, but she had no more real understanding of her constructs than most people did. She made them, they flourished to some extent, she fed off them, and they continued to flourish or they died. She descended into the far basement levels of the fortress, found the cumbersome key to the padlock, and entered the dark realm where she kept her Leucators imprisoned.

Most of them were on their feet, pale faces gleaming in the Lantern light she viewed them by. Their shackled ankles and wrists shook in agitation, as they moved, paced, within the tiny confines of each individual prison. Restless, indeed. But why?

She knew their faces as she passed by them. Some had decayed to absolute ghoulishness, but she knew them. Old friends, old associates, an old Magicker . . . one or two more old husbands. A Leucator had been created, with a bit of stolen soul and flesh, as a hound. It would not rest till its twin, the rightful living being, was found and it was reunited. Unfortunately, like many hounds, it had a tendency to destroy its prey when caught. Leucators, early on, had been decreed to be used only in desperate, desperate need, and never to be made lightly.

Isabella would not be where she was if she had followed rules. She had discovered a far better use for Leucators in her experimentation with their creating.

They could, when fed off of carefully, maintain the reserve of Magick within her, and extend her own life greatly. She was one of the few who had survived the magic duel between Brennard and Gregory the Gray without being stunned into a centuries-long coma, or thrown forward through the ages. She had lived the entire time, and lived long, and thanks to her efforts, many of those who were alive now, owed their continued existence to her.

She did not expect them to thank her. In fact, she had already been condemned for it. Isabella grasped the hem of her gown, skirting her way through the whining golems carefully, searching, looking for the core of the unrest. It was true that she had plundered the assets of many, with no one to stop her, and she'd built a fortune doing so. She'd also spent a fortune cocooning those in comas, making crypts to shelter their slumbering bodies, hiring watchers, bribing their families to bear what could only be called witchcraft. In some cases, she'd moved the bodies altogether, knowing if she did not, there would never be peace.

Had she done it to save the Magickers? Not really. It was more in the line of further experimentation. What had magic done to them? When would it wear off? Had it cleansed them of all Talent, or preserved it . . . and why?

Everything was useful to know. And those in slumber rarely knew that they contributed to her Leucators, or that she fed off their state in many ways. It was all in line with Antoine Brennard's beliefs that Magick was not renewable, that when it burned out, it was gone, and so it must be used carefully, weighed out miserly, stolen from others if necessary to avoid harming oneself . . . when magic was gone, it was gone. Gregory had argued that Magick was a Talent for harvesting and bending the natural powers abundant all about them. One could lose the Talent to fear, fatigue, illness, death, but if one knew oneself, it could be renewed. Perhaps not overnight, if greatly taxed, but inevitably, like great tides of the vast oceans, Magick existed and always would. So far, it appeared Brennard was correct. At least, that was Isabella's belief and it had helped her to prosper.

A ghoul hissed at her, as her crystal's Lantern light fell across it. It had been working at the manacles about its wrists, nearly had its slender limbs freed, blood slick on its skin and aiding in the escape effort, as it tried to slide loose. Isabella drew herself up, and studied the Leucator of Eleanora.

"Now," she said quietly, "that won't do. You injure yourself and her . . ." Isabella gazed up, where her captive, no doubt, was equally restless. "You'll have your time, my pet, I promise you." She stretched out her free hand and stroked the lanky brunette strands of the Leucator's hair. It hissed again, shrinking away from her, chains rattling fiercely as it tugged sharply over and over, trying to free itself. The mere nearness of Eleanora's presence obviously tortured it. Isabella wanted to draw from it, but she could feel the weakness in it, and knew that she dared not. As for the other Leucators in the dungeon, most were even weaker. They should be recovering from her tapping of them, but they were not. The raids had drawn much from her, and her resources were growing unreliable, for reasons she did not yet understand. Isabella withdrew her hand. Not tonight. Perhaps in a day or two.

Instead, Isabella veiled a mild calming spell over it and watched it sink down to its knees, then into a cross-legged pose, hunched over as its breathing deepened and it fell into slumber. She smiled thinly. "I promise you, little Leucator, your hunt will be successful before this is all over."

She made her way back through, the Leucators subsiding into silence as she did, as if the Eleanora duplicate had been the instigator of all their unhappiness, and perhaps it had. Isabella did not feel the shimmering wave of unleashed energy till she stood at the threshold, stepping out.

It hit her. Rolled over and immersed her, a wave of

unmistakable power, and it caught her for a moment, blinding her.

Somewhere, a Gate opened. She could feel the mighty breath the world took in and the even mightier exhalation as it swung back and forth. Isabella knotted her fists. That Gate! Hers. The one she needed and rightfully should have power over. That Gate. That damned Gate the boy had opened.

Isabella closed her eyes against the shiver of power dancing along her skin with sparklike touches. This, this likely had brought the Leucators to their feet. They could sense great Magicks. She opened her eyes slowly, renewed in her determination that a Gate-keeper would be hers.

She turned and left the dungeon.

Jon's head jerked back as he awoke from an unintended nap in his room, his boot heel falling to the floor with a thump from the chair seat he'd propped it on. Books and papers in his lap shifted abruptly, and he grabbed for them, even as he felt the ripple of power. He frowned. Jason was opening and then slamming shut the Dragon Gate, a wash of power reaching him like a ripple effect. Yet, the touch was unmistakable, almost a taunt. In fact, Jon thought, as he stood slowly and gathered himself, it was a taunt. The Magicker wanted him to know he had the power, and had used it, and done it so quickly they couldn't act on it. Jon gritted his teeth together. It was an intentional slap in the face, warranted perhaps by his encounter with Bailey.

Jon brushed his hair from his face, and paced his quarters. There had to be a way he could rein Jason Adrian in . . . and then a thought occurred to him. A smile slowly spread over his face. He'd have to think it through, and put it to paper before he suggested it to Isabella, but yes . . . yes, he might have a way to bend the Gatekeeper to their needs.

Yes, indeed.

17

Ouchified

HENRY FOUND the best way to let his mother know he was home, without kicking up a huge fuss, was just to show up for the next planned meal, as if he'd never been away. So he grabbed his baby sister out of the playpen, took her into the kitchen, and slid into his usual place at the table for lunch. The toddler didn't seem to have grown too much since he last saw her, and after a frowning look as if reassuring herself as to his identity, she settled in his arms and resumed banging her handful of plastic keys against the edge of the table and babbling in a language only she knew.

Time flowed differently between home and Haven. He could see that most decidedly every time he came home and looked at his siblings. The toddler grew in leaps and bounds, but then most children did . . . still, he could see it in her. His other brothers and sisters seemed to lag behind, but he himself . . . Well, it was apparent that he was growing faster than anyone except his baby sister.

Henry hugged her, glad that she'd decided she knew him as the same old familiar big brother who did most of the babysitting for her . . . when he was around. He couldn't help being a little sad at missing her, something that even the mysteries of Magick couldn't quite offset.

He was more than happy going back and forth, though. He nudged the empty backpack at his feet, and listened to the rustle of paper inside it. Lists, and more lists, of things he was to get. The oddest things were the sets of sewing and embroidery needles, but both Rebecca Landau and Madame Qi had been very insistent. These, he'd been told, are the best bartering kits . . . high quality needles of stainless steel absolutely do not exist in Haven and probably never will. Consider them as priceless as gold or diamond gems, and bring back as many packets of them as you can!

Maybe his mother would make more sense of it when she took him shopping. The needles, at least, were relatively cheap. Trent's needs might cost money and would definitely eat up his time. Research, research, research! As for what Gavan and Tomaz had asked him for, he was nearly clueless. They had pressed their scraps of paper into the palm of his hand at the last instant, and he wondered if he were meant to keep his efforts secret. Probably, he should. Seemed best. Better safe than sorry, and all that—

"Henry!" A blur swooped down on him, smelling of soap and lavender water, and hugged him tightly, and he grinned ear to ear with happiness.

"Mom!" He hugged her back.

"I wish I'd known! I'd have baked cookies."

He rocked in her arms and his toddler sister, sandwiched between them, let out a coo of squished happiness. "I'll be here a while, so you've got time."

"Really?"

He nodded. "Probably four or five days, from the looks of it. We've shopping to do, and I've got to look some stuff up."

His mother loosed him, and sat down. She'd highlighted her hair with tints of ginger blonde since he was last home, and she looked good, if tired. Laura Squibb was what everyone else would probably call a beautiful woman, although Joanna McIntire was, without a doubt, the prettiest of all the moms, as slender as a feather, with short fluffy blonde hair that was never out of place. Joanna didn't look a bit like Jason and that was because she was Jason's stepmom, and of course Jason didn't look like the big bulldozer of a man, McIntire himself, because that was his stepfather and Jason was basically an orphan being raised by two strangers. But at least they were two nice strangers.

Now, Henry didn't look like his mom but when you saw Robert Squibb, you'd know right away whose son Henry was. They both had the same thick, wavy brown hair and round face, and need for glasses, and a slightly bemused look on their faces as they contemplated the many things going on around them. His dad could wear contacts but didn't, and Henry couldn't, so the glasses stayed perched on his nose. No, sir, there was no doubt Henry was Robert Squibb's son. Although, last time he looked, there were two or three graying hairs in the sideburns on either side of Robert's oval face.

Laura took her daughter from Henry's lap. "What kind of shopping?"

"Food and seeds and . . . sewing needles." Henry shook his head as if baffled at the last.

"Oh, good!" Her face brightened. "I thought those would go over well."

"You did?" He blinked at her and adjusted his glasses.

"Oh, yes. Good needles would be worth a great deal in preindustrial times. Why, a set used to be a valuable part of a dowry centuries ago." She winked at him. "Women know these things."

"Who'da figured," Henry muttered, as she got up and briskly began to set a lunch, leftovers from dinner, which looked to be plump, juicy pot roast sandwiches, chilled applesauce, and a few other good things. He brightened. He wondered if needles went over well, how good would some decent pots and pans go? Of course, they'd be a lot heavier and bigger to drag around. Maybe he'd best leave things alone, till he was asked for them.

Instead, he wrapped his hands around a sandwich full of steaming beef and managed a smile at his mom before chowing down.

Jason reeled back, his limbs gone weak and his mind buzzing as he released the energy and firmly shut the Dragon Gate after Tomaz. The scenery spun around him and he had a wild thought that he was going to pass out; then the moment slithered past him, and the ground felt firmer under his feet. What the heck? All he'd done was open and shut the Gate. Twice in one week, true, but Henry had been a lot earlier. He had used far more energy than needed this time, and he clenched one hand because of it, knowing he'd wanted to shove the fact down Jon's throat that he'd opened the Gate and the Dark Hand could do nothing about it. The backwash of weakness was just revenge for that, he thought, and he put a hand out to steady himself.

A sharp splinter sank into his palm, and he yelped. The pain brought him back instantly, as he hopped on one foot, holding his hand, and trying gingerly to pinch the long sharp offender out. The thing was nearly two inches long and half of it was buried in the meat of his hand. Jason pulled it out as Gavan eyed him.

"Academy bit you?"

"Feels like it!" Jason shook the splinter and dropped it, then stomped on it. The other laughed softly. Jason sucked at the fiery wound, feeling the sting subside. "Man," he muttered, as the pain ebbed slowly, and the tiredness hit him again.

"Tired?"

He nodded.

"Off to bed with you, then. You've done a full day's work and then some." Gavan paused. "You let a lot of energy wash out with that last Gate."

Jason felt his defiance spring up again, and he

ducked his head, wondering if it could be seen in his eyes. "Still a little hard to know exactly how much push it's going to take to open the Gates and close them, you know?"

"And sometimes, it's fun to kick a little dirt at the bad guys."

Jason's gaze shot up. Gavan was watching him with a kind of curious, deliberate nonexpression on his face. "I don't want him messing with Bailey."

"Of course not. None of us do." Gavan looked away then, out into the night, and the faint wrinkles at the corners of his eyes pinched slightly, as if in pain, and Jason wondered if he thought of Eleanora. Of course, he was thinking of her. They all did, and would, till they got her safely back!

Gavan shifted his weight. "All the same, Jason. We cannot give them more power over us than they already have, do you understand?"

"He won't touch her!"

"Let's make sure he doesn't. But you can't do it by expending your power just when you might need it most." Gavan dropped his hand on Jason's shoulder. "Don't forget, lad, I've seen you play soccer. I know what a competitive spirit you have. I know it hurts to hang back, to deliberately let the enemy underestimate you all the time, but in this case—we've no choice. It has to be that way. They already have a good inkling of your abilities, I don't want them to know any more about you. Understand?"

Jason met those hard blue eyes unflinchingly. "I'll do what I have to."

"As you always have." Gavan smiled quickly. "I couldn't ask for more from you, but this time I am. Lay low, Jason. Learn about yourself each day, and do it quietly, because right now we can't afford to attract more attention from the Dark Hand than we already have."

"Why don't you go after Eleanora?"

"Oh, I will. First, I need to see what they can be

up to. There are wheels within wheels, I think. If I go charging in, and get taken myself, what happens to the academy? To all of you? I'm not the only one who can take care of you, but each loss weakens our chance of succeeding, of having what we want and need for Magickers yet to be found and trained. So, I wait. But don't think it doesn't stab at me, like a mortal wound." Gavan took a deep breath. "When I left her with Fire Ann, I thought there wasn't anyone better I could leave her with, unless it was Tomaz. FireAnn, you see, has a prodigious Talent few are aware of, and it's not for cooking and herbs. Her Talent is Fire."

Jason let his breath out slowly. "Wow."

"Yes: And she's a bit afraid of it, and very, very careful. Too careful, it seems, or they would never have been captured, but Fire is a very dangerous element to go throwing about, eh? I think she hesitated and in that weak moment, they got her. Otherwise . . ." Gavan's voice trailed off. "Otherwise it could have been a totally different outcome."

"So why are you hesitating now?"

"Because I must. Because we need a plan to get in *and* a plan to get out. If we cannot get out, then there is no sense in going at all. It will take all of our strengths, and weaknesses, before this is over." Gavan squeezed his shoulder lightly. "Now go and get some sleep. I need you and Trent up early in the morning. I want Trent to review the wardings we've set into the frame. We need a roof, and soon, and it looks like the wanderers will be ready to start on it in about two days."

Jason nodded. Walking away, it took all of his strength to keep his legs straight and moving; they felt as if they had turned into wet noodles. Sleep sounded wonderful. More wonderful even than chocolate, although he didn't have the craving for it that Bailey did.

His hand still hurt a bit, but as he climbed the stairs

to his open air bed, he realized that nothing must hurt as deeply as Gavan knowing he had failed to protect Eleanora.

Nothing could hurt that badly.

Nothing.

Journals

STEF WOKE SORE, BRUISED, and happy. His stomach rumbled the moment he rolled over on the floor, blankets shifting and knotting around him. His stomach had probably been rumbling before he really woke, he thought, as he kneaded his belly. He ate a lot, and sometimes it embarrassed him. He wasn't a fat guy, but he knew he was no slim jim like Rich either. Trouble was, his body seemed to have to feed both him and the bear which was no longer a cub but nearly full grown, as he was himself. If he'd stayed in football—oh, man. Stef's face cracked a grin at that thought. He'd have other players peeing in their pants at the thought of going up against him!

He got up, trailing rumpled blankets like a second skin. Rich was still asleep, curled peacefully on one of the small, rush mats the healer Kektl had left down for them. During the night, Stef could see he'd managed to toss and turn halfway across the floor of the small drying shed the healer of Naria used for a guest room. He didn't mind. Kektl was good to them, always happy to see Stef, and had the use of a bathing area off the hot mineral waters for which the great trading city of Naria was famous. All Stef knew was that a good, hot soak after the sword work was very, very

welcome. Beryl, the swordsmith's daughter, fought
hard and taught hard, and he had great purple welts
where her wooden sword had struck him through his
defenses. But he didn't mind.

He also had a spot, right below his right cheekbone,
where she'd given him a kiss for doing well and out
of happiness he'd come to visit her. That hadn't left
a bruise, but he could feel it burning his skin all the
same.

Stef pulled his blankets off, folded them neatly, and
cleaned up his part of the shed. Then he set off to the
bathing pool to clean up again for breaking fast with
Kektl who seemed to be already up and cooking, a
variety of tempting odors drifting through the air. No
wonder his stomach growled! He scrubbed himself
again, and pulled a shirt on, then his vest, for this was
a city town and his going bare-skinned under his vest
wasn't proper. It also hid the purple welts. Stef
grinned as he pawed at his hair and headed toward
the healer's croft.

Rich, to his surprise, already sat cross-legged at the
healer's table, ladling out hot tea into wooden cups.
The two broke off their conversation about the merits
of steam-infused herb therapy and bad coughs as Stef
sat down. There was something Japanese about the
way Kektl ate and lived, he realized. Low tables, sitting on the floor, sleeping on mats. He wondered
about the things Trent was always talking about—who
the Havenites were and how they got there. Stef
wasn't normally philosophical and as his stomach
growled again, he gave up the idea for a big trencher
of eggs and shredded meat, and dove in.

Kektl grinned, then turned back to Rich. "As I was
saying, that is part of the legend of our hot pools, I
think. The steam naturally loosens many ills of the
lungs."

Rich nodded. He shoved a wooden cup of tea over
to Stef as he picked up his own, to sip at the rich,
flavorful drink. Not quite like home, but close enough
to make him happy. After a long, wonderfully warm-

ing swallow, he opened his mouth to add to the discussion again, when he felt a tingling along his skin. With a frown, Rich set his cup down. He stood and bowed to Kektl. "I thank you for having us, but I think we're being called back."

"Oh?" Kektl was a tall, sticklike man, with a spiky brush of gray-brown hair that stuck out in every direction despite his frequent efforts to comb it down. His eyebrows were an echo of the hair and now wiggled in puzzlement.

Rich tugged at Stefan's arm. "Come on, I think Gavan is coming after us."

"Mmmpf?" Stef swallowed a mouthful hastily, shoveled another one in, and got to his feet reluctantly. He bowed to Kektl even as Rich pulled him out the croft doorway.

Gavan appeared in a shimmering aura of color, his cape swirling about him, then settling about his ankles. Bruise marks under his eyes showed that he had not had much sleep. "Time to go," he said, holding out his free hand.

"But . . ."

"No time to argue. Rich, make your Talker crystal a present to your host, and we must be off."

Rich pulled the crystal from his belt loop and hurried back to where Kektl stood at the doorway. He rubbed the tiny crystal, set in a nice metal cage of Ting's making, and pressed it into Kektl's hands. "A good luck stone," he said. "It will help with the dialects of all your visitors."

The healer smiled broadly. "Rich! Many, many thanks. Sometimes it is all I can do to figure out what hurts them!"

"I know." Rich folded the man's long-fingered hands about the jewelry. "It won't last forever, but I should be back with a new one before it wears out. Thank you for having us."

The man bent stiffly at the waist. "Any time, young healer. Return soon with your ideas. I enjoy talking with you."

Pleasure at the compliment flooded Rich's face with warmth. A master healer finding value in his training? Wow! He broke away as Gavan cleared his throat impatiently. They linked arms and left in a whoosh and a stomach-unsettling haste and landed to a growl of Stefan's unhappiness.

"Whaddaya mean I can't go back?"

"Not for a while, Stef, I am sorry. The training is good for you, I won't argue that—"

"Then I'm goin'! And you can't stop me."

"I can if I must, but I don't want to have to use force. Trust me on this, Stefan. This goes beyond you all the way to the Dark Hand. I can't leave you and the others out there, where they can get to you."

Stef's face had gone dark red, and he clenched both hands into white-knuckled fists. "I'd like to see them try!"

"Trust me," Gavan repeated again, his voice thinning a little, and his gaze darted to Rich.

Rich put his hand on Stef's well-muscled forearm. "Stef . . ."

He shoved Rich away. "I'll go back when I want to."

"It's not about you, Stef, or Beryl." Rich shifted his weight and touched his friend again. "Am I right?"

"Very right. We think the Dark Hand means to get Jason any way they can. They almost had Bailey. They'll go after any of you. That, with Eleanora and FireAnn already hostage . . . well, that would break me." Gavan sat down abruptly. "I can only take so much." The crystal in the wolfhead cane flickered, as if affected by his mood.

Stef let out a low grumble. Then he sighed. "All right. For now." He pushed away Rich's hand and strode off toward the academy larder, intent now on finishing an interrupted breakfast.

Rich hesitated a moment. "It's that bad?" he asked softly.

Gavan gave him a nod. "It could be. So we need to be cautious."

"We need to get Eleanora and FireAnn back."

"Aye. And that, too. I'm working on it." Gavan stood heavily, leaning on his cane.

Something about that bothered Rich, but he shut his mouth instead and went in search of the kitchens himself, for he'd had almost no breakfast at all, and there seemed to be a very long day ahead of them.

Gavan watched them leave. He realized, like yet another weary burden settling on his shoulders, that they were not the boys he'd welcomed to summer camp just a few years ago. These were young men. Still awkward, still gangly, still growing into their own, but he no longer looked down on them . . . they met his gaze straight across or, in one or two cases, Gavan had to look up to see into their eyes. They had grown, all of them. It was that time of their lives when they did. He smiled ruefully. It seemed like only yesterday he'd been such a new-made man, coming into his own as a Magicker and falling in love with Eleanora, the head Magicker's daughter. What a time that had been. She'd scarcely noticed him, for she'd been older, and wiser, and had many suitors to choose from, if she had been interested. Devoted to her father Gregory and to the schooling of their Talents, she had never seemed very interested in courting.

And then had come that day, after losing everything, and fighting to gain it back, step by step, when she'd looked at him, and slid her hand into his, and he'd realized he'd finally caught up to her. Or perhaps she'd waited for him. No matter. Their hearts were finally in step.

Now, though. Now he could not tell if hers still beat or not. He closed his eyes tightly. If this were true, he could not wait to go after her. As soon as Tomaz came back from his investigation of the wolfjackals, they would have to strike. The Dark Hand would hold him at bay no longer. The day was upon them. Trent woke with a hum, as he usually did, although that day's melody held a slightly mournful note which he changed as soon as he recognized the melancholy. He

missed his father, but knew that with the adventure
he had dived into, his father would be upset if he did
not go after it with all he had. So he would. Then, he
would go home and tell Frank Callahan of the won-
ders of another world where Jason talked with dragons and he . . . he could see Magick. Not as good as
working it, to be sure, but he could see the miracles
others worked around him, something that, till they
got to Haven he didn't realize only he could do. He'd
seen it from time to time before that, but never realized it was nearly impossible for the Magickers to see
what they were actually doing. Jason might gesture at
an object to move it, but only Trent could see the
colored wave of energy moving through the air and
affecting the rock or whatever it might be. It was cool
beyond words. He thought his dad would appreciate
that.

The problem was in finding the words to describe
it. Words didn't fit. Music did. Maybe something composed by John Williams, like for the *Star Wars* movies,
or *Indiana Jones*. Something that built and built and
became a stirring crescendo of music as the magic hit
and its force shattered everywhere, doing its will.
Maybe that.

Trent drummed his fingers against the washbasin as
he cleaned up his face and made an effort to scrub at
his teeth. He wondered if Gavan would send them all
home now and then for dental exams and cleanings.
He ran his tongue over a rough filling. Maybe even . . .
ugh . . . something more.

Jason let out a soft groan as Trent tossed dirty water
over the side of the building wall, and refilled the
basin for him. From the mussed condition of the cot,
Trent guessed that Jason had had a fitful night. He'd
gone to bed glowering over something which he
wouldn't discuss.

Looking over the side of the unfinished floor, the
chill of the morning hit him. As much as he liked
sleeping on the top floor of the Academy and seeing
the tips of the Iron Mountains and the sharply blue

sky, Trent didn't relish the idea that soon he would be waking up to a face full of rain if the roof didn't get put on. Trent grinned at that thought. He broke into a hummed rendition of "Singin' in the Rain" as he waved at Jason and hit the stairs to get a warm piece of toast or coffee or something before doing the work Gavan had assigned them. Jason would soon follow him down, making notes as Trent did the survey.

Dokr had left the wanderers' camp early, and sat squatting by the cook fire, a heavy mug of his own brew in his hand. He nodded respectfully at Trent. Regardless of the boys' age, the wanderers seemed to have this innate courtesy and, since the building had begun, Trent felt they had earned it even more. The wanderers were building the academy, of that there was no doubt, but all of the Magickers had thrown their backs and their will into it, and although clumsy at first, soon they'd become sure at following the building plan and helping. Even Ting could miter a board to be jointed neatly, and Stef used his bearish strength in putting huge beams into place that might take the muscles of three other men.

Dokr motioned to the academy. "You checking the frame again today?"

Trent nodded. Madame Qi was already up, her wrinkled face a little pinched as if the foggy morning hurt her aging joints, but she deftly drew him a cup of oolong tea. With a wink, she palmed a bit of sugar and sweetened it for him. Trent flashed her back a thankful grin.

"Always checking the framework," he said to Dokr. "Not for your craftsmanship, but for the alignment with the energies and stars."

The Havenite acknowledged his words with a sage nod of his own head. The two groups had not discussed Magick. Gavan thought it prudent not to, and Trent agreed. The wanderers were outcasts even among their own people, but why add to their burden by making them work with Magick they might con-

sider devilry? The wanderers reminded Trent of someone back home. Not Gypsies, though, although they
had that nomadic quality. They were not carefree and
colorful in the least. No, not Gypsies . . . perhaps . . .
he blew on his tea and drank it. Puritans! If the Puritans had become homeless followers of the road, they
would be like Haven's wanderers!

Pleased with himself, Trent was still humming
"Turn, Turn, Turn" by the Byrds when Jason showed
up, grabbed a hunk of corn bread and a slate and
motioned to him that he was ready.

Trailing corn bread crumbs, the two went over the
building from the buried basement and foundations
upward, going over the old warding as always to make
sure it held, before going onto the new. Trent could
see the lines of energy laid into the wood and stone
as clearly as if they'd been drawn by Day-Glo mark-
ers, and often marveled that Jason couldn't. But Jason
could sense them, and their strength, so he used both
his own Talents and his note taking, to double-check
Trent's work. So far, in all the weeks they'd been
doing this, they'd only found one failed ward. Trent
wasn't sure how Gavan and the elders did what they
did, but he knew the outcome was to keep the wood
sound against termites and dry rot and other effects
of time, to keep it fireproofed, and to provide a thin
layer of magickal protection against outside harm, and
to prevent the magic used inside from leaking out. It
wasn't strong enough to hold against an all-out attack,
but it would discourage almost anyone from ordinary
sabotage and trifling. And, from what Trent gathered,
no one could magickally eavesdrop on those inside
either. Not unless one knew the frequency.

He'd tried to explain that to Jason. The warding
Gavan guided into place was like a broadband radio
wave. It sealed Magick on all those frequencies. But
there was still leakage above and below the normal
band of frequencies. He couldn't quite put together
what he saw and heard, though. Either it was sealed
or it wasn't.

Trent pointed at the new workings. "Looking good," he said. "As far as it goes."

"Are you on that again? Gavan knows this isn't a foolproof fortress, we don't have the resources, but he thinks it's guarded pretty well."

"Oh, it is, it is." Trent pondered. "I guess it doesn't really matter, most people can't see what I do. I doubt the Dark Hand will see the problem with it either. But it's there all the same."

Jason shook his head. He finished sketching the addition, and indicating where the warding lay, according to Trent's pointing finger, and how strong it was. "Either it is or it isn't."

"Jason, my man, the world isn't black and white. Neither is Magick." He pursed his lips. "It's like . . . like dog whistles! Just because you can't hear the frequency doesn't mean a dog can't."

His friend raised an eyebrow, then stopped as the analogy hit him. "Dog whistles," he repeated.

"Exactly."

"And you think Magick works on frequencies like that."

"From what I've seen, it does. I mean, I feel magick differently than you do, and it's hard to explain, but that does it. Imagine, too, Jason, that there are colors and sounds I can't see or hear. Maybe your dragon can, though."

Jason finished sketching in the ward lines as Trent had outlined them to him. "Interesting idea. So you think this place is protected well enough for the average Magick user."

"Oh, yeah, sure. It's just not as impregnable as Gavan seems to think it is."

"That could be very important some day. I'll talk to him about it. Later, though, I think. He was up early bringing Stef and Rich back, and everyone seems a little edgy."

"You caught that, too?" Both had been conspicuous by their absence. Now, as they worked, and could see off the upper floor wings, Stef was visible working the big, two-man saw with some of Dokr's men, and his grunts could be heard drifting upward. He seemed to be full of angry energy, which they both felt like a buzz of bees shaken out of a beehive. Stef was no one to be around in that temper because the bear could erupt, and no one but Rich was certain what that bear might do.

Jason lowered his slate. "We're done up here."

Trent held up a finger. "Not quite. I want to look at the chimney shaft again."

"Thought we caught that?"

"Yesterday, not today. They added some more rocks and mortar and a new vent to it."

Jason nodded and trailed after him. Trent caught the new stonework immediately, with its spidery net of runework throughout it, and gave his approval after showing Jason the ley lines of the warding. Jason sketched it quickly, and held it up for Trent to view.

"That's it." Trent wet his lips. "I think second breakfast, and then back to work?" He gave his friend an appealing look, which wasn't necessary because neither had really had a first breakfast.

"Sounds good to me." Jason folded his sketches carefully into the slate cover and trotted down the staircase to Gavan's office where he dropped the slate on a pile of similar slates. Then the two raced each other for "second breakfast."

It was not foggy when Jon awoke, but a black-frost wind had swept over the fortress grounds as he dressed and ate quickly, after first giving the order for a mount to be groomed and saddled for him. He penned a note to Isabella that he was riding out to check the Mirroring at the fortress site before leaving. He had other reasons, of course, that he did not wish his dear mother to know. She was not the maternal type in many senses; she had abandoned him as a baby on Brennard's doorstep and not bothered to introduce herself as his mother till he was nearly eleven, but she had her qualities and he could see many of them in himself, like it or not.

She did not need to know that what he really sought at the other fortress site, the one near Avenha, was the essence of Bailey's short visit there. He wondered if he could still taste, smell, touch it. He rode off the grounds of their home fort to a secluded glen where he would Crystal the remainder of the way. The icy ground crunched under the horse's hooves, smelling of winter, and his breath frosted on the morning air. Forget fall; winter seemed nearly here. Avenha, farther south and lower in the hills, would be much more amenable to his spirits.

The horse shivered as he Crystaled them through, and shook his head nervously, not liking the teleportation, but he had been schooled by Jon for this, and so bore it. As he kicked the animal into a canter, the difference in weather and terrain enveloped them. Grass was still green here, although not the lush grass of spring and summer, and fog dewed it in heavy drops. They splashed through the morning dew like riding through a brook, and the horse whickered as he stretched out into a canter.

Jon did not rein him up until they reached the hollow where he had had Bailey trapped. Then he stretched in his saddle and looked about, letting his senses fill the air as the horse put his head down to greedily crop up the last summer grass.

Oh, yes. He could feel her. Much as when, walking into a room where Isabella sat, he was overwhelmed by musk and jasmine, he could smell and taste Bailey. She was different, though—cleaner, lighter, a fragrance as much of crisp lemon and apples as well as heavier roses—and her touch lingered on the air like something fine and wonderful. It did not leave behind a feeling of dread.

Jon let out a small sigh. He did not want Bailey in his thoughts. She was the enemy, a waster of Talent, a . . . a . . . he let his thoughts go for lack of focus on what she was, exactly. She was a problem if he kept her in his mind.

He picked up the reins after a few moments, moving his horse away from the patch of grass and guiding him over the knolls and down toward the fortress ruins where they had a Mirroring spell set to make it look as though this were their place of operation.

It triggered, faintly, for him, but then it was not meant to impress him, just the locals and any Magickers who might run across it. It had done its work admirably. Jon smiled widely as he rode the perimeter of the grounds. He'd suggested it and Isabella had implemented it, and it only took the efforts of two or three of their Leucators to keep the spell empowered. Thus, it did not drain them unduly, and he calculated it would stay as set for at least several years. He checked the areas where they had discreetly buried prisms, to make sure nothing had been disturbed and nothing had. Evidently, Gavan had kept his group far from the actual grounds, and had not pierced the illusion.

Riding past the guard tower for a second time, sweeping the area with his senses, trying to touch the hot spots of magick here and there, he caught something. Something out of place and intensely different.

Jon reined to a halt. His horse bowed his neck, and shifted uneasily, as if feeling his rider's tension.

What did he feel? Where did it come from? And why?

He turned the horse slowly about, casting. Had he felt anything, even?

No . . . no, there it was! He and the horse now faced it dead center. He looked at a corner post of the guardhouse, one of the only really solid posts left in the fortress. Jon eyed it a moment. Then he swung down and approached it, whatever it was, cautiously.

The closer he got, the stronger it got, until it burned at his mind like a brand, and a tear stung the corner of his eye in spite of himself, for it was Antoine Brennard he felt, his father. His father whose ashes now sat in a gold-and-silver casket at the corner of Isabella's writing desk. His father who had fought to bring them this far, and then failed, whose final contribution was for Jon to drain the remaining bits of his Magick so that he and Isabella could survive.

He did not think anyone else would feel this Magick. It was as though it were pointed at him, and him alone. Perhaps even Isabella would not notice it, though he doubted that.

Jon reached out a gloved hand, at the base of the post and began to dig at the ground. It crumbled under his fingers, surprising him, for this piece of the structure was solid. But this one spot crumbled and gave way, and under it, about a foot into the soil, was a leather trunk. Small, as if a jewelry box or some such, and burned into the top of it . . . his father's initials and magickal sigil.

Jon's breath hissed through his teeth. He wrestled the item out of the ground and sat down abruptly, trunk in his lap. There he opened it and found two slim journals, musty smelling but intact.

He sat, his palm hovering over them. His father had been there before. Obviously. He couldn't have been, but he had. If he had been there, what Gatekeeper had sent him through, past the Dragon Guard?

Jon opened the top journal carefully, listening to pages crackle faintly, but they held, and words struck him.

Here, by my own will and Talent, I walk through a new world.

Jon shut the book. Brennard had opened a Gate! Something he hadn't done often, or he wouldn't have sought Fizziwig and Jason so hard or intensely, but . . . the Talent had been in his blood.

Jon scrambled to his feet, closing the trunk tightly. This would require more examination, and authentication. He dared not let Isabella know any of it till he was sure.

If she'd hunted Jason for his Gatekeeping, she would have no compunction about draining Jonnard dry for his. If he had any such ability.

He was not ready to be so used, by Isabella or anyone else but himself.

Hugging the journals to his rib cage and hidden by his shadow-dark cloak, Jon mounted his horse and headed for home.

19

Words and More Words

MIDAFTERNOON, the sweat poured off Jason and Trent. Despite beginning in a chilly morning, the autumn sun seemed determined to show that it still could pack a punch. Hard work didn't hurt either, so when they finally took a break to share a bucket of cold water and some apples, Trent stared at Jason curiously over his apple core.

"Give it up. Something's bothering you."

Jason shrugged. "A little bit of everything. I don't like the feeling of having my hands tied, and I don't like the idea of Jon stalking Bailey. I know we can't do anything, but that doesn't mean I'm happy about it."

"Why can't we do anything? I mean, from a certain standpoint, not much else can happen. I truly doubt they would harm Eleanora and FireAnn any more than they already have . . . so what have we got to lose?"

"It's more than that."

Trent stood up and lobbed his apple core as far as he could throw it, muscles honed by American baseball rippling across his back and shoulders as he did so. The debris went sailing and disappeared into a fringe of woods where some birds or rodents would no doubt happily peck it to bits. He was surprised to see some of the wanderer children dart after it, diving into the forest as if he'd thrown a gold nugget out there. Jason watched over his shoulder.

"What're they doing?"

Jason thought a moment, then said, "Seeds. They're gathering the seeds."

"They're not allowed to have land for growing, I thought."

"They're already outlaws. Crops mean survival. I couldn't blame them for breaking one more law." Jason looked a few more minutes, then crunched down on the last of his own apple. He waited till one or two of the children emerged, then tossed his apple core to them. With a flash of teeth and a smile, it was caught neatly and tucked away. "Can you imagine," he said to Trent, "a place where seeds have to be stolen? It's this whole warlord thing."

Trent sat down and looped his arms about his knees. Looking like nothing more than a pirate, he sounded more like a schoolteacher as he began to talk. "It seems unlikely to us, but look at it this way . . . we had a great warlord too, sounds pretty much like their old guy. Only ours was named Chi'in and he built the Great Wall of China and united all those provinces into a country named China, after him. We don't know why he had those terra-cotta statues made of all his armies and buried, but suppose it was to . . . I dunno . . . guard and protect his empire? Is that any different than what this guy did?"

"Leaving a good deal of yourself behind as a Spirit would be a little hard for the average person to do." Jason wiped the apple juice off his fingers. He paused at the crescent-shaped scar at the back of his left hand. Thin, healed, barely more than a line now, it still ached sometimes when it had no reason to. His life was not like others, he remembered. It hadn't been since he discovered he was a Magicker. He rubbed the mark made by a wolfjackal as if testing it for sensitivity now. Nothing.

"Don't make me compare this warlord to a dragon," said Trent, his eyebrow going up in a mock threat.

"Don't even go there." Jason threw his handkerchief at the other. "Seriously, what we know almost makes me wonder if these are alternate worlds. As if there was a big split. What if the warlords are the same guy?"

"Not likely. No one here really has an Asian cast to their looks. More Eastern European, but not even that, really. I've thought about it, though. Some of the reference material I asked Henry to find for me goes over that. If there was a split between our worlds, there are three or four different times I think it might have occurred."

"You're serious?"

Trent's head bobbed. "I want to know. Don't you?"

"I don't think it's a mystery we can solve in a few weeks or even a few years. Creation mythology is like . . . like a lifetime of work."

"Mythology is more than just words, though, Jason. There's a kernel of truth inside every one, even if the centuries of storytelling wrap around it. Like the Spirit here. It's not just words that his spirit stays and protects them. They believe it, and although we haven't seen it, there are strong signs now and then that indicate it *is* doing just that."

"But a Spirit? How could that even be?"

"I don't know. It's more than tales, though, we know that. It could even be watching us, trying to decide what to do about us."

"It'll take more than words, then. And it looks like you're going to be awfully busy. I've not run across a Havenite who didn't have days' worth of stories to spin."

"Everyone has to have a hobby!" Trent bounded to his feet then, throwing Jason's handkerchief back at him. "I hear 'em yelling. Break time is over."

Jason picked up their water bucket and ladles and trotted after Trent, more thoughts crowding his mind. The mysteries Trent brought up were interesting, but not as immediate as his own problem. He'd brought the Dark Hand to Haven. He needed to either find a way to send them back, harmless, or find a way to fight them here. Either sounded nearly impossible. If Gavan hesitated, what chance did Jason have?

But then, he had something Gavan didn't. He had nothing to lose. The Dark Hand did not, yet, hold anything dear to him that would stop him. If he went in, it would be up to the others behind him, Gavan, Trent, and the rest to get Eleanora back safely. His only targets would be Isabella and Jon and those despicable Leucators. Maybe dividing would be the only way they could conquer their enemies.

Heavy in thought, Jason hardly noticed the weight of the lumber he was being tossed and told to hammer in place as the afternoon wore on.

Despite the shimmering ribbon of water that was the Gulf of Arabia, Tomaz could feel the desert heat and dryness with every breath he took, even as the sun sank into a glowing red sunset. On the fringe of the great metropolis of Dubai, skyscrapers and city lights at his back, he could almost feel the likeness to his own Arizona sands as he walked down the street, hearing the soft call of foreign voices to one another. He found the tea shop he had been told to go to, and stepped inside.

No need to announce he was a stranger there. His looks, his clothes, spoke for him. Unlike Dubai itself, where every person seemed foreign and where the city teemed with those who came from all over the world to trade and make deals and even just visit, in this outskirts suburb, he stood out.

The owner came to greet him, with a nod and smile, and pointed Tomaz to a curtained alcove. Inside, as the drapes were lowered behind him, to shut him away from curious eyes in the small shop, he found nothing luxurious, just a basic wooden café table and a few nicely upholstered chairs. In moments, the owner returned, carrying a tray and cups and the alcove filled with the smell of hot tea, steaming milk, cinnamon, and honey. He set it down and left before Tomaz could ask him where Khalil was or when he would be expected.

The draperies stirred again when a young woman entered, her face modestly veiled and her body hidden in slender robes. She put a tray of sweets and cookies on the small tabletop and gave him a smile that even the veil could not quite hide before darting out. Reminded for a moment of Ting, Tomaz chuckled and poured himself a drink and tried to decide which of the pastries he might sample.

The curtains fluttered with a hint of evening breeze, and Khalil came in, wearing desert robes as he usually did, and with a broad smile upon his face. He clasped Tomaz's hand tightly before sitting down. "My friend, it is good to see you even though I trust you are not here just with good news." Briskly, he fixed his own cup of tea, adding milk and cinnamon and honey in good measure before stirring it and sitting back, dark eyes watching Tomaz keenly.

"Good to see you as well. Not all the news is bad. We have the academy almost finished. I would say that when spring breaks in Haven, we can take students."

"Truly? That is wonderful!" Khalil's eyes gleamed with his joy. He drank his tea cautiously, careful to keep his neatly trimmed beard from catching drips. He looked at the desserts. "All are excellent here, made by my friend's wife. From not too sweet, this one . . . to brimming with taste, these." His hand swept over the food indicating as he recommended. "I have students, of course, who are eager to see Haven, and to have classes as we'd hoped." He put his cup down. "And Eleanora?"

Tomaz quirked his head slightly. "What do your senses tell of Eleanora?" It had been Khalil's Talent that put her to sleep for a while, and perhaps still, kept the dramatic effects of aging from ravaging her. None of the Magickers knew what caused it, or what could remedy it, but they'd seen several of their own die from it. It might even be a side effect of Magick itself.

Khalil considered that. "I barely sense her at all. I think she has thrown off most of the effects of my warding her. But she lives still, if that is what you are asking."

He breathed out in relief and realized he had been holding his breath, waiting for Khalil's answer. It was, indeed, based on Gavan's fear.

Khalil nodded. "Then that answers another of my questions. You have not recovered her and FireAnn yet. A hostage situation is a very nasty knot to unravel."

"It colors most of what we try to do in Haven, every day. It is like walking a tightrope." Tomaz broke off long enough to choose a small pastry and devour it. Its flavor filled his mouth with almonds, honey, and butter, and perhaps a tang of exotic spices for which he had no name. His tongue warmed happily with the tastes. Not a man for desserts, he still appreciated the goodness. Perhaps he would try to order a tray or two to take back with him, for the children. He thought of the dancing excitement in Bailey's and Ting's eyes if he could.

"How can I help?"

"By telling what you will of wolfjackals. Our friends seem to be using them in some way again, and although I do not think the wolfjackals an enemy, I do think they may be a most unfortunate pawn in the hands of Brennard's lot."

Khalil let out a long sigh and sat back in his wooden chair, stretching his long legs out in front of him. "It's come to that, then."

"Some secrets are not meant to be kept."

Khalil tapped his hand on his cup. Unlike many Magickers who were scholars more than craftsmen, Khalil was weathered, his hands callused. He worked hard in his desert stronghold, in many ways. His face was much like that of the desert hawk, and his senses just as keen. Tomaz held his silence, knowing that if it was going to be broken, it would be by Khalil.

Moments stretched. Then Khalil nodded, as if reaching an agreement within himself. "I will tell you this, which you know already. Wolfjackals are not of any world you and I walk. They are bound to Chaos and they seek it when it's unleashed, hoping to go back to the lands from which they were torn. Magick worked by us and the Dark Hand unleashes Chaos. It draws them. They feed on it, and in the case of Brennard's people, they have formed an alliance. None of them have succeeded in returning, but still they hope. They feed and yet are not fed. They are more than spirits, less than actual flesh. They are intelligent, to a degree, like wolves, and they are merciless in that the only way they know to get home is to take what they can."

"The Dark Hand offers them hope."

"The Dark Hand offers them Chaos, and in that is hope. We seek a balance, so we have less to offer them, knowingly. But—" And with this Khalil stared darkly into Tomaz's eyes. "We have a Gatekeeper."

"I won't dangle Jason as bait for wolfjackals or anyone else."

Khalil shook his head vigorously. "Not as bait, as hope. It's their only option, I think, to return. When he's trained enough, he should be able to sense their home and find the Gate to it. It may take decades, however, and they are bestial enough that tomorrow is too far away. They cannot plan for decades."

"So what have we to offer them?"

"Nothing, unless you think as they do, as wolves do. Fresh meat today, security tonight, a new hunt tomorrow. We can deal with them as Brennard's lot does. Offer them Chaos, Tomaz, and you'll bring them to you. Once brought to you, you can gradually show them that tomorrows do exist, and they can afford to wait."

"Tame a wolfjackal?"

"You ran with their packs once. If anyone can do it, you can."

Tomaz gave a short laugh. "They tolerated me. I think I amused them."

"Make no mistake on this." Khalil leaned forward, his expression intense. "They don't have to tolerate anyone. They smelled the power in you, like a predator smells the blood running just below the skin. They couldn't find a use for you, nor you for them, but the tie is still there. You can find a way to communicate with them, and help them. Or . . ." He paused.

"Or?"

"The Dark Hand will destroy them utterly, to their advantage."

"How so?" Tomaz picked up his cup again and found it had cooled as they talked.

"Think of the wolfjackals as a reservoir of Chaos. They hold it within themselves. They are storing the extra they can glean from our Magick workings, and they are made of it, to some extent. They are like a walking bomb, Tomaz. If Isabella can but figure out how to ignite them, she will. Does she think of doing it?" Khalil stood, gathering his desert robes about him. "If I think of it, what would keep her from thinking of it?"

With that, the Magicker left, the draperies of the alcove shivering as if a great wind had passed through them, leaving Tomaz with cup in hand and an iciness in his heart as though a knife had been plunged into him. Only words had been spoken, but what words!

Jon did not find time till nearly the end of daylight to retire and look over the journals. He had them hidden in a corner of his room with a ward on them, subtle, because anything stronger would attract Isabella's attention instead of turning it away, the opposite of what he needed. This was a dislike-and-ignore warding, and anyone touching it off would veer away from the items, rather like a disagreeable pair of stinky socks. He lit a candle rather than open his room's shutters, and pulled out the books. Both had been filled from cover to cover with his father's writing. It would be difficult reading, for all that he knew his father's hand, because this had been written as it would have been hundreds of years ago, with different lettering, and flowery script, and even different spelling. He was not hundreds of years old, but he had had practice reading such documents. His father had tutored him on old, handwritten treatises on magic and the makeup of the world.

In those years, he hadn't known who his mother was. She didn't try to seek him out till he was nearly eleven years old and she had done so secretly then, telling him his father must not know. He hadn't particularly wanted a mother, but Isabella was no ordinary mother. Tall and strong and carrying herself like nobility, she was more powerful than most men. It was the power that attracted him. It came from her intellect and force of will as well as her mastery of her own Magick. That, to him, had been like nectar to a bee. To have two in his life carrying power that could only be imagined by most, and to have both offer to him the same power . . . ah, yes. Irresistible.

Still, in their relationships with him, and later in their renewed relationship with each other, much remained unsaid and a mystery.

A little afraid and much disturbed, Jonnard opened the journal that appeared to be the oldest. Antoine Brennard had to have been in Haven, but when . . . and why and how? And would the answer be unlocked with mere words? Pages crackled as he turned them carefully.

Threats

HENRY SAT AT THE MONITOR, staring so intently he forgot to blink for long minutes until
finally his eyes began to sting. He rubbed his eyes
then, and ordered a printout. Trent would whoop
when he saw this article, he thought, and quickly tip-
tapped a few keys to go to another reference source
that the search engine had recommended. Most
sources had little information, but he'd spent many of
the last days dutifully printing out every scrap. What
he thought unimportant might mean something very
different to Trent.

The used bookstore had only yielded one prize, a
tattered and very old book named *Little Known
Myths*. He'd swooped down on that one and carefully
wrapped it up and tied it with string, as it honestly
looked like it might fall apart into two hundred ragged
pages at any moment. It had cost less than a dollar so
that wasn't the point; the point was he thought Trent
would really really think the book was cool. He
wanted to at least get it back to Haven in one piece,
and what happened from there would definitely not
be his fault. Not that anyone would blame him. Henry
had a habit of blaming himself. His Talent so difficult
to control and erratic, and after having had Jon suck

a lot of it away and having gone without for nearly a year . . . he shuddered. He'd given up Magicking once; he had no intention of being forced to do it again. So, unlike the others, he stammered and stuttered his way through his lessons, a step forward cautiously was better than two steps forward and a disaster backward.

No way did he want to go through any of that again. Henry inhaled, leaned forward, and sifted through the various sentences coming up on the monitor. As if panning for gold nuggets, he tossed out the sites he'd already visited, and the ones that really didn't have anything to do with the subject although they'd come up anyway . . . how did that always happen? He didn't know, but it did . . . he smiled grimly and found two more web sites that would be worth hitting for Trent. Then home and chores. Strange. He didn't mind doing chores for the few days when he was home.

The library light flickered behind him. Henry glanced up, frowning. He pushed his glasses back into place, and then squirmed about in his chair. He had an eerie feeling for a moment that someone looked over his shoulder. The back of his neck itched, so he rubbed it briskly. Two more web sites and then home, for sure!

Both had little or nothing which seemed of interest to him, but he printed everything out anyway. He added a few quick commands to delete the history of his search engine then slid his card out of the charge slot to end his session. Gathering everything up and storing it away in his backpack, he had almost finished clearing the area when shadow fell across him again. Henry glanced up, and a tall man leaned over, smiling.

It was the vice principal from his old school. "Mr. Winchell!"

"Well, Henry Squibb. I thought that might be you. I am pleased you remember me." The man smiled. He had a face that wrinkled easily, and his expression fell into the many lines and almost disappeared. "Still doing home schooling?"

"Yes, sir. My brother has the computer tied up for

a project, so I have to use the library." Also, he didn't want evidence on the family computer's hard drive as to what he'd been researching. Here, it would just sink into the overall picture of all the research everyone was doing and hopefully not be noticed.

"I see. Doing well, are you?"

Henry tried not to fidget under the man's long stare. "Grades seem to be okay." Having Winchell watch him reminded him of a discussion he'd once had with Jason over Jason's dragon: you argue with the dragon, thinking that he is wrong, and the dragon thinks you are dinner. Did Winchell think he was dinner? There was a reason none of the Magickers were still in school, and strangely curious men like this one headed the list.

"We were all disappointed you did not go on to the high school. We thought you were science team material."

Yes, that was it. The educator definitely looked at him as if he might be dinner. Or at least fodder for the very prestigious and hard-working science team. "M . . . maybe someday," Henry managed.

"Good, good! Well, then, give my regards to your mother and father. I look forward to your siblings entering middle school. All hard working, I trust."

"Yup." And none of the others were Magickers, thank goodness. At least, none that he knew of. He reached out and pulled his backpack up. "I need to go."

"Yes, of course." Winchell watched as he stood and shouldered the bag. "I take it your friends are doing all right, as well?"

"F . . . friends?"

"So many of you dropped out at once and went to home schooling, yet you all seemed to know one another." Winchell drew a little closer, his brows sharpening. His smile had completely disappeared into the wrinkled mask of his face.

"I don't know how their grades are, but I see 'em, sometimes."

"Yes, yes. Well, you know, the educational system tracks them. We feel responsible, at home or at school. You might let them know that." Winchell touched his shoulder lightly before moving away, and Henry gave off a little shudder as he did.

He scurried out of the library, got his bike, and headed for home, thoughts in a whirl. What had Winchell meant by that? He didn't know. It didn't sound good. Maybe his mom could decipher it. Adults sometimes spoke in riddles and sometimes they meant exactly what they said.

He didn't think it had been good.

After the dinner hour, when he was left to himself again, Jon put his journals away, still no closer to understanding why his father had been in Haven hundreds of years ago, nor why he had left the journals to be found only by one with Talent such as himself, although the how of Antoine Brennard's coming seemed to be emerging, page by page. It was that how which drew Jonnard in now. Was there a hidden Talent running through the veins of father and son? It was not as if he could ask Isabella; her knowledge of Antoine was even less than his own. No, if anyone had the key to the working of Antoine's mind, it was himself. Or perhaps Gregory the Gray, the lost mentor of most Magickers alive today. Teacher, guide, nemesis, who had been so wrong in his perception of magic and had lost his life for it.

Impatiently, Jon pushed away from his reading desk. His heels scarred the rough flooring as he did so, and the crystal hanging from the chain on his waist warmed to an angry glow so hot it burned through the cloth of his trousers.

Dropping a hand to it in defense to shield himself, he felt Isabella's irate and frantic call vibrating through the crystal. Jon surged to his feet. The chair tumbled over from his abrupt movement and fell clattering on its side to the floor, but he was already out the door, running, as it did so. The sense of Isabella amid the Leucators hung in his mind like the loud, ringing echo of an alarm bell, so it was that way he ran.

Thundering down the stairs in haste, he burst through the dungeon's innermost doors, skidding to a stop just short of running down Isabella who stood, her throat contorted in an angry, stifled wail, her hands knotted in the sapphire silk of her sweeping dress, her face contorted in fury.

"What is it?"

She pointed with a knotted fist. "There." She turned her face away, her tall body rigid.

Two Leucators lay limp upon the floor, looking more like sun-dried raisins than the golem twins of people she'd known and re-created. Jon's heart thumped at adrenaline-driven speed that slowed as he looked upon the sight. Drained, drained beyond all usefulness and recovery. How could she? Not dead, but as good as, and with a sweep of his hand and a guttural word, bloody light shining out of his crystal, he brought their lives to an end. It was not so much a mercy killing as a necessity because the other Leucators would catch and amplify their pitiful state, and Jon enjoyed a quiet night's sleep, which would be nearly impossible if they started shrieking.

He took a step back, as weakness from the Magick working hit him hard, and his heart slowed to a crawl. He backed to the doorway and let it support him for a moment. With a growl, Isabella swept her fist back and the two bodies went up in a crackle of white flame, then turned to ash, in a matter of minutes.

She put her chin up then and looked at him.

"Isabella." His voice sounded weak, so he paused and took a breath, and forced it deeper. "How could you do that?"

"Me? Me? You think I did that?" The white of her face flushed with a different anger. "How dare you! What makes you think I'd be that kind of fool?"

He would have taken a step back in self-defense, but it was not wise to show weakness in front of her.

Instead, he narrowed his eyes. "You didn't drain them . . . but if not you, who did?"

"Nor did I think you were raised to be a fool." Isabella swept past him at the door's threshold, her hems brushing him. "I don't know who did it." She pushed her hands into her hair, pulling it back from her face and then twisting it into a thick knot at the back of her neck. "It could only be one of them, and how they managed a draw from here, or at this distance, I do not know. But it means they have learned that Magick here drains, and drains permanently, and they are just as desperate as we are."

She thought one of Gavan's Magickers had done that? He looked at the two ashy-oily spots of residue on the dungeon floor, shackles lying empty. No. He shook his head. "I don't think so."

"Or them above." Isabella tilted her head to shoot an accusatory glance at the fortress overhead.

"If they could have done such a thing, they would have escaped us long ago."

"Find an answer, then, whelp, and quit arguing with me. It was done, and it's up to you to find out how."

He could have back traced the power drain, perhaps, if she hadn't been so quick to flash burn the bodies. He ground his teeth on his own sharp reply. She was tired, more so every day, and her anger flared often.

He put his hand out, palm up. "I will not only find out who and how, but I will bring you new reserves."

Isabella paused for a very long moment then, and the fear in her eyes drained slowly, to be replaced by a sparkle. "Will you, indeed?"

"You know I will." He waited.

Finally, she placed her hand in his. "I believe you will. The answers you seek, Jonnard, may well cement our position in ruling this world, as well as others."

The same thought had occurred to him. He let her lean on him as he escorted her upstairs. More mysteries to solve, and this one most urgently.

Happy Birthday, Happy Birthday—Happy Birthday!

THE ROOF IS DONE! The roof is done!" Bailey's and Ting's voices rang out in unison as they raced through the building and down the back stairs to the makeshift lumberyard where the others stood with the downstairs crew of wanderers, intent on making siding, window framing, and shutters. They skidded to a halt, Bailey's ponytailed hair bouncing as it echoed her excitement.

"At last," breathed Rich. He gave a huge, lopsided grin, and paused, his shirtsleeves rolled up in spite of the fog which seemed to hang over the Iron Mountains that day. Stef thumped him in the ribs, grunted, and indicated the piece of siding he was shaping and sanding as if to say there was plenty of work left to do. Dokr and his workmen winked at each other behind Stefan's back, nodding in agreement.

Gavan, however, stood quietly. He flexed his shoulders with a weary sigh and looked at the girls with a tiny tilt to the corner of his mouth. "That is good news indeed. Looks like we should have a celebration in a few days. Dokr, we'll be done on the exterior . . . when?"

The head wanderer paused in contemplation, then

counted out on his hand, six fingers wiggling. "Four days at the most, barring rain. Then two weeks on the interior, finishing, but rain will not stop us there. In good time we must hurry, though, for we must get to our winter camps soon."

"A good job, then." Gavan smiled at him. "A very good job. We had hoped to just get half built before bad weather hit, and here we are, nearly finished." He wiped his forehead with the back of his hand. "Jason, think you can bring everyone home tomorrow for a party?"

Jason had paused, working in a team with Trent on storm shutter sets, his hand filled with nails and a hammer. "Should be able to. I imagine they're listening for me."

Trent reached over to pluck a few nails and tapped them into his framework while Ting and Bailey let out another shout of excitement.

"All right, then, I declare the day after tomorrow a free day."

Stef grumbled something under his breath and went back to work as if disinterested. Gavan raised an eyebrow and watched the well-muscled Magicker wrestle his siding onto the worktables as Stef seemed to ignore him further.

Rich shrugged in apology. "It's not a free day if he can't go where he wants," the redhead offered.

"Ah." Gavan tucked the crystals he'd been working with away in the inside pocket of his cape. Faint purplish bruise marks of fatigue underscored his eyes as he then took a handkerchief and polished the Herkimer diamond in the jaws of his wolfhead cane, before looking up at Rich. "Perhaps we can arrange a field trip—if Tomaz accompanies you? He'll be back then. It's not that I want to stop the lessons altogether, but we can't keep everyone safe if we're all scattered."

"A chaperone?" Rich looked interested.

"I don't need a stinking chaperone." Stef straightened up, gripping his shaper so tightly his knuckles showed white against his deeply tanned skin.

Something flickered in Gavan's eyes, but he responded mildly, "Not so much that, I have business in Naria that Tomaz could be doing. But he'd be within distance for help if anyone needed him. Then you all could head back for the celebration."

"You're not kidding?"

"No," Gavan shook his head slowly at Stef. "I'm not kidding. You've worked hard, all of you, and you deserve a break. Madame Qi has talked to me on your behalf, as well. She reminded me that not all must walk the same Path to be on a good Road. Or something Confucian like that."

A wide grin slowly spread across Stefan's face, and it was like the sun had broken through the cloud and fog hanging over the Iron Mountains and the tiny valley. His mouth worked for a moment, then he said, "Thank you," before bending back to his work, this time with an enthusiasm that matched his brute strength. Wood shavings curled up and flew to the ground at his feet in fine, feathery onion skins.

Rich flashed Gavan a thankful look, before tending to his carpentry as well. In moments, the air filled again with the sound of saws, hammers, and the noise of wood being shaped to finish the academy, accompanied by soft singing from Ting and Bailey and punctuated by an occasional squeak from Lacey as she ran around underfoot, helpfully finding lost nails and other shiny bits of interest.

Henry laced his backpacks shut tightly, pausing for a look of pride at their bulging sides. He had a hiking backpack for each shoulder! In addition, he had huge burlap bags of staples requested by the cooks—rice, beans, flour and more—and a few additional surprises like thermal blankets and winter items knitted by his mom and older sister that ought to make everyone very happy as well as warmer. He'd tied them together, as anything on him or being held by him would go through the Gate when he went. The trick, he'd discovered, was to hitch everything together tightly.

As long as he had a firm grip on the ropes, the Gate seemed to consider it as part of him, and Jason could pull him through. They'd discovered that the first time or two he'd made a trip back for provisions, and left bundles on the floor about him, and had to wait weeks before he could return and get the rest.

He ticked off the items on his mental list. Books and notes for Trent. Letters from all the families for everyone. Chocolate for Ting and Bailey, and everyone else, really. The sewing items. Food in bulk. Recent newspapers, photocopied and condensed for those interested in the world they'd left behind. He'd gotten everything they wanted and more, feeling slightly heroic about his own efforts. He'd even found some things for the wanderers, an assortment of items Gavan had quietly told him might make some nice rewards for the crew for the work they'd done on the academy. Nothing that would be terribly out of place on Haven but things that might make their lot a bit easier. A warmth filled him at the anticipation of his friends going through his many sacks of goodies. A few days ago, he was reluctant to think about going back to Haven, now he could hardly wait. It was as though he'd had his fill of being home, and needed to go back where he was more than a son, he was a Magicker.

More than that, he and his parents had discussed the schooling issue. No trouble had yet reared its ugly head, but the warning Winchell had given hung over them all. No one wanted any questions being asked that would lead to trouble for the families. The sooner he got back to tell Gavan and Tomaz and the others, to figure out what might happen and how to head it off, the sooner he'd be happy.

Downstairs, he could smell something delicious in the oven. All he needed now, was a sending from Jason to let him know a Gate would be opening soon. He scratched his head. A faint feeling of being watched over his shoulder made him twirl on one heel to find . . . no one looking into his room.

Henry frowned. He swept a searching gaze over the corners of his room, so familiar and yet now strange in some ways. It seemed the academy, even with its roughness and unfinished quality, felt more and more like home to him. Maybe that was why he felt uneasy in his old room now, as if he didn't belong there and someone might be watching him. The back of his neck felt all creepy crawly and he knew it wasn't Jason. Jason had never felt like some kind of squirmy bug that ought to be brushed off and *squished* as soon as possible.

Henry shifted uneasily and looked about again, finding nothing as he figured he would. He'd had that trouble once before when Jonnard had been Linked with him and he hadn't even known it, but that link was severed at the great battle of opening the Dragon Gate, freeing him. Things were different now and a lot better. When he'd found out that Jon could spy through him, he'd nearly died of the humiliation. He'd been a traitor and not even known about it until far too late! Stuff like that shouldn't happen to anyone.

Nerves. He was getting nerves. If he didn't stop it, pretty soon he'd be as jumpy as fidgety old Rich! That would be pretty fidgety. Rich, with all his allergies and his hypochondria, could be darn difficult to be around sometimes. The first few months in Haven, Rich had them all in stitches over his imagined ailments about the new foods and herbs and, well, nearly everything that existed in the other world. Much to his own surprise, Rich seemed much healthier in Haven Still, that didn't keep him from fussing like some old lady over everything. Henry imagined himself getting all twitchy. That made him laugh at himself, if a little sheepishly, before heading downstairs.

"Mom!" he called out, thumping down the steps. "What smells so good?"

The smell of vanilla and sugar permeated the air about him as he sat, nearly drowsing at his writing desk, and the aroma sank into the pounding of his temples. It refreshed him, filling his senses with a hint of an idyllic youth he himself had never had, Jon rifted his chin. His attempts to back trace the drainer of the Leucators had failed, time and again, but this attempt . . . hmmm . . . yes, interesting. Just when his failure seemed deepest and darkest and most bitter to report to Isabella, this sweetness had enveloped him.

He'd done it almost idly, not thinking it would ever be revived, but it seemed Henry Squibb had come within his range again. Jon decided to follow up on a tentative sensing of someone or something and had not been sure it was Squibb, but now he knew for a certainty that he had a hold on the round-faced Magicker once again. It did not solve the problem of the Leucators, but it might hold other possibilities of its own, and at least he felt somewhat reassured at his abilities. The defeat of one problem was softened a little by unexpected success here.

Jon smiled at the pleasantness of the contact. Squibb seemed to be at home, as the warmth of a kitchen and bakery goods filled Jonnard's senses. How like Squibb to be surrounded by . . . what was it? Cupcakes? Something of the sort. He decided not to grasp for a better understanding. The link between them stayed fuzzy and indistinct and although Jon knew he could sharpen it, he did not wish to do so. That might alert Henry as to the return of his soul to Jonnard's hold.

And that would be a tragedy. So many delightful things could be accomplished with Henry within his grasp again.

Jon sat up to rest his elbows on his desk. Should he tell Isabella of this accomplishment? Not yet, perhaps. Things should fall into place a little more, he decided. A world of possibilities could open up. He closed his eyes and let his mind drift into the vanilla-scented world of Henry Squibb where he sat and ate something sweet and iced, and worried with his mother over school, and if the authorities were trying to track down the whereabouts of the other Magickers. Henry worried, it seemed, that attention was being drawn to the Magickers who had fled to Haven. Bureaucrats and red tape could be very damaging.

Oh, yes. That could be something *very* useful. Trouble brewing at home could make Jason Adrian very vulnerable.

Looking asleep but with his scheming mind very wide awake, Jonnard leaned his chin on his hands and enjoyed spying. His reverie jarred to a halt moments later as Isabella called out for him, her voice sharp with command. He collected himself before finding her in what she called the audience room. The Havenite mercenary called Fremmler stood at the far end of the room, his hat in one hand. He dressed a little finer than others of his ilk, could read and write skillfully and had the ability to talk a duck out of its feathers, but Jonnard trusted him no more than any of the other mercenaries despite his education. Perhaps it was the scarred and obliterated tattooing across his hand, signifying the loss of his Trade Guild status and honor.

Isabella gestured to Jonnard to sit, and so he did.

"I have asked Fremmler to join us for a few moments as I have an assignment for him."

"Indeed." Jonnard looked the man over quickly. Fremmler was one of the many disgruntled outlaws who'd joined them fast enough when given the opportunity to raid the society he'd been forced away from. He seemed no more aware of what Isabella wanted from him than Jon was. Jon steepled his fingers and eyed his mother, unsure of what she had in mind.

"We have an abundance of stores, and it is my understanding that many villages here about are a bit short, despite the bountiful harvest. Therefore, I am preparing to send Fremmler to the city to broker sales to those in need."

Fremmler's heavy jaw dropped in undisguised surprise.

Jon laughed. "Mother dear, that takes balls indeed, to sell them back what we have stolen from them."

Isabella smiled tightly at him. "We cannot live by grain alone. Why let it spoil if they need it? Fremmler here was a trader in good standing not too long ago." Her sharp gaze resettled on him. "I take it you still have contacts in the guild?"

"A few." He cleared his throat. "Milady, I am no longer a trader."

"You are my trader if I say you are. If they want stores, it's you they'll have to deal with. Is that understood?"

"Understood, indeed. How long have I to make the deals you want? And how do I get your acceptance of the terms I negotiate?" Fremmler quickly dropped his roughness and slid into the smooth, assured role he'd been born and educated to fill.

"I'll make arrangements for you to communicate, have no fear of that." Isabella tapped a citrine crystal shard lying on a nearby table. It glittered and shifted under her touch.

Fremmler looked a bit wary, but bowed again.

"Don't worry," said Jon with a huge grin. "That one won't cast Lightning."

"Good. Very good." And Fremmler looked a bit happier.

"As to what I want . . ." Isabella leaned forward and began to rattle off what she considered acceptable amounts to buy and deliver the shipments of goods she was willing to sell, while Jon sat and watched his mother with undisguised amusement and admiration. When she had finished and dismissed Fremmler with his crystal, she waited until the audience room door shut firmly and the sound of retreating footfalls disappeared entirely.

"You will, of course, follow and ensure his . . . safety," Isabella murmured.

Jon nodded as he stood. The prospect of getting out of the fortress for a bit beckoned welcomingly to him, and there were a few things in his father's journals he could now investigate without her questioning his journey to Naria.

Isabella raised her chin. "As for the other . . ."

"I have found a small thread, a faint contact, that I am trailing, Mother. In a few days, interrupted by this task, I shall have a most satisfactory answer for you."

She put her hand up and touched his cheek fleetingly. "Excellent. Most excellent."

He nodded as he took his leave for the evening. Her fingers on his skin had been as cold as ice.

Jason found Tomaz standing on a desert hill in Arizona, his arms outstretched to a setting sun although he'd sent him through to Dubai on the Gulf of Arabia, it seemed his Magicker elder had wandered far on his own. As he touched, and brought him through, the two crows on his forearms bated their wings and cawed harshly at him. He startled at the birds.

"Tomaz, I'm sorry! Let me send them back."

"No, no. They wished to accompany me. This is Midnight, and his mate, Snowheart." Tomaz bent a finger to the second crow and rubbed her chest where a tiny white blaze of feathers marked her. He raised both arms, sending the crows into the air, where they spread their wings and circled high in the Haven sky. Tomaz nodded, as if satisfied, then turned to Jason and grasped his arm in greeting. "Good work, as always."

Touching Tomaz filled him with a brief surge of energy, refreshing after the tiredness which had been haunting him lately. He let the warmth surge through him gratefully.

"Henry back yet?"

Jason shook his head. "I'm having a little trouble reaching him. I'll rest and try again in a bit. Gavan wants everyone home. The roof is done, and we're celebrating."

"Indeed! That is good news. Come with me and we'll find Gavan."

His knees almost felt too wobbly to walk, but Jason swallowed that down, and found that he felt better

with every step he took, stretching his legs to keep up
with Tomaz as they crossed the vale. Early morning's
bright sunlight bathed them, giving a lie to the time
of year, and the Iron Mountains stood in rusty, jagged
relief behind the academy. Overhead, the two crows
dove at them, cawing in what seemed to be avian
humor as they swooped low, barely clearing their
heads. Tomaz waved them off with a string of Navajo
in a jovial voice.

Jason found Ting and Bailey trying to string loops
of netted crystal shards about the trees close to the
outdoor kitchens, in spite of the fact the sun shone
brightly. He reached up and tied the strands at the
branches each pointed him to, although both often
talked at once, confusing everyone, till they finally got
the job finished and both girls sat down laughing and
shoving at each other. Lacey ran up with a squeak,
dropped something in Bailey's lap and scampered off
again. Jason watched the little pack rat disappear into
the undergrowth with a flip of her tufted tail.

"Aren't you afraid she's going to wander off?"

Bailey shook her head. "Not anymore. We have this
rapport, now, and she feels I'm her home. I do worry
that something might snap her up, though. She's not
as nocturnal as she used to be, and thank goodness
for that. I worry about owls!"

"She will be fine," Tomaz reassured, hugging both
girls in one embrace and making them laugh even
harder, before wandering off in search of Gavan who
was evidently taking another ward check with Trent
about the academy.

Ting took a deep breath, waggled a finger, and all
her tiny crystal shards lit up. The trees sparkled with
a dancing light effect. "Oooooh!" breathed Bailey. "It
looks even better than we thought it would."

Ting leaned back, her face paling. She looked at
Bailey, then gave a tiny shake of her head, and Bailey
grew quiet.

Jason realized something between them had just
gone unsaid, and he wondered what it was, but if they

wanted him to know, it *would* have been said. He reached up and tightened one last bit of light strand. "Stef and Rich ready to go to Naria?"

"Gavan put that off till this evening, but he said they could stay over. Stef thought that was great, he gets two lessons that way, it seems. Anyway, we're about ready, just waiting for Henry."

"Then," stated Jason, "I'd better get him." With a wave, he went off to the small, quiet glade in the valley where he could concentrate best, often talked to the Dragon about things, and could be alone to do what he needed to do. Sitting on the small boulder and finding it pleasantly warmed by the sun, he crossed his legs and composed himself, and thought about Henry and the Dragon Gate carved into the side of the Iron Mountain. Henry with his pleasant face, usually smiling behind his glasses unless he was looking befuddled over the effect of some Magick he'd just tried that had gone wrong, Henry with his ability to talk tech and Magick with the best of them, Henry who ranked among the best of best friends and who loved his family wholeheartedly. . . .

He caught the sense of him then, a glow of welcome, followed by a tinge of sadness as Henry felt his touch and no doubt began shouting his good-byes to his family. There came that moment when, like looking into a pool of water, he could feel himself looking at someone/something *else,* then that solidified into looking at Henry, all trussed up like a pack mule and hanging onto a chain of packages and burlap sacks, with one free hand to hold out to Jason. He grabbed Henry's hand as he swung the energies of the Dragon Gate open wide. He could feel the power surge of both worlds, like an immense tidal wave coming in, even as the other came in as well, both meeting with a tremendous clash and the archway of those energies a doorway through which he pulled Henry back to Haven.

Henry fell on him with a grunt and the weight of a collapsing grocery store. Jason slid off his boulder onto the soft, browning autumn grass, surrounded by cargo of every imaginable size, shape, and weight, and prayed nothing was heavy enough to break bones.

He sat up carefully, reaching out to right Henry who appeared about to disappear forever among his own bundles. "Good grief. Now I know what a ton of bricks feels like. Did you bring the kitchen sink back, too?"

"I brought back anything anyone could ever want or even think of!" Henry said proudly, if a bit out of breath, as he got to his knees, then clambered to his feet. "No kitchen sink, though, 'cause Gavan says we won't have real indoor plumbing for a while. He doesn't want to interfere with the natural technological growth of Haven."

"Right." Jason dusted himself off as he stood and stepped around the tangle of knotted ropes that linked Henry to all his cargo. He had to grin, he couldn't help it, Henry had managed to bring back package after package of . . . well, he couldn't begin to guess what it all was. *Stuff.*

Two pink rectangular boxes tied together with string dangled from his left wrist and smelled delightfully like . . . like . . . Jason reached for them.

"Ah-ah!" Henry cried and danced away from him. "That's a surprise."

"This whole mess is a surprise."

"Well, this is surprise-er," Henry declared. He let out a whoop then as the sound of running feet descended on them, and an academy of Magickers fell on both of them. "Mind the boxes!" Henry yelled just before the welcoming crowd overwhelmed him.

"This," declared Ting proudly, "is courtesy of Laura Squibb, Henry's mom, who remembered that Jason's birthday is right about now, give or take a few days."

Everyone gathered close, their mouths beginning to water at the smell of the goodies inside, their plates and napkins in hand, waiting.

"And so," Bailey finished up, waving a cake knife about, as she stood over the big opened pink boxes, one proudly displaying a vanilla cake with fine gold-and-green balloons and sprinkles all over and a second chocolate cake with marshmallow crystals all over it, "in honor not only of Jason's thirteenth birthday but in view of the fact that he is growing as if he's raced through fourteen and straight into fifteen . . . Happy Birthday, Happy Birthday—and Happy Birthday!"

A resounding cheer echoed around the academy as Bailey began to slice up the cakes and serve everyone eagerly lining up for their share.

22

Narian Nights

SO, THEN TRENT SAYS, for about the fifth time, 'Did anyone else notice that the trading capital is called Naria, almost like the mystic country Narnia from the C. S. Lewis books?' and Stefan growls at him, 'Yes, and if you point that out one more time and I don't get to go, you're going to spend the rest of your days here twisted up like a pretzel and thrown in the bottom of some wardrobe.' " Jason laughed as he licked some frosting off his already incredibly sticky fingers, and the Dragon let out an appreciative chuff of white smoke, not quite a laugh, more like a little chuckle, but that was all right.

"And this Narnia. A dangerous place?"

"Always, and steeped in wonder. Trent's point, of course, was that he thinks the writer C. S. Lewis might have somehow peeked into *here* and used his visits as a basis for his books, but I think that's far-fetched, and even if he had, it wouldn't have anything to do with Stefan. Nor did the books mention anything Like the people and places we've met."

"I see." The dragon took another dainty nibble off his huge slab of birthday cake and tried to ignore Jason's sidelong glances as if he might still be a bit hungry. In fact, he cupped his taloned paw about the plate

173

and slid it a bit closer to his chest, hoarding it. "And then what did you all do?"

"Oh, we goofed off. Trent and I got into our favorite sword fight, from the pirates movie—ah—play that we love . . . there's a bit . . ." Jason jumped to his feet, picking up a long branch from the ground to brandish like a sword. "One guy is the honest young hero, and the other is the pirate Captain Jack Sparrow, who is a bit crazy and very sneaky. So they're fighting away, and it's a good fight. Our hero is a very good swordsman, but Sparrow seems to be a bit better, and a little surprised by his opponent. Anyway, the hero doesn't like pirates and is trying to bring Jack to justice and Jack is trying to escape, but doesn't really want to hurt the hero. So it goes like this—" And Jason acted out the swordplay bits he'd memorized, his muscles stretching in forms taught him by Madame Qi and his own efforts. "Then Sparrow does this, which is totally punk, and he has the hero up against the blade, and the hero says, 'Cheating!' and Sparrow looks at him, and shrugs and says, 'Pirate!' which of course he is, meaning that naturally he'll lie and cheat, that's what pirates *do* so it's not really cheating, it should be expected . . . and the two guys kinda look at each other, shrug and grin, and go back to fighting." Jason laughed as he dropped his willowy stick and plopped back on the ground.

"You admire this pirate?"

"Yes and no. He's very smart and he tricks everyone, so I couldn't live like that, but it's his wits that keep him alive. And, in the end, he helps everyone out."

The dragon's forked tongue flickered out and he took another small nibble of the cake. "Seems you admire him a bit, though."

"I think Trent does more than I do, but, really, he's just a character in a movie . . . ah, play." Jason leaned back, lacing his fingers behind his head. "I think he's interesting. He makes a point of teaching that: one—not everyone is really what we expect them to be, so you shouldn't be labeling them; but at the same time, two—if they have a certain nature, you can't be expecting them to be anything else."

"Ah." The dragon let out a soft, rumbling purr which might be because of what Jason had just voiced, or might be because of the velvety goodness now melting in his mouth. "Still . . ." and he paused to roll his tongue about his large mouth, savoring the bite of cake. "A play is more than just entertainment, it often has life truths buried in it. You seem to be pondering a few in this favorite of yours."

"In a way. It proves there are good and bad people in all walks of life, and you have to look at each person separately, you know? You can't just lump 'em together and say, everyone who wears a hat is evil or something like that. Then, too, it says something about the basic soul of a person. We have a fable about that . . . it goes something like this." Jason stopped. "Do you know what scorpions are?"

The dragon dipped his head. "I have met them in my travels. Nasssty creatures."

"Exactly. Well, spring rains have been heavy and every place is flooding and the only safety for this group of animals is to get to high ground, but to do it, they must swim a river. Most of the animals make it, after a struggle, and the strong, agile fox helps many by taking them over on his back. Finally, all that's left is the fox and a scorpion. The scorpion has been pleading for help, but none of the other animals would take it over. The fox is his only chance and he begs the fox to swim him over. 'Don't do it,' the fox's friends advise him from the other side of the river, but the scorpion says, 'Don't listen to them. I promise not to sting you and I want to live!' After a few moments' hesitation, with the river rising higher and higher, the fox agrees, for it is a smart but helpful beast. So the scorpion hops on and they dive into the water. The river is raging and the fox is nearly exhausted as he swims close to the other side. Suddenly, the scorpion lashes his tail out and stings him . . .

once! Twice! Thrice! And the fox feels the poison burn through him, and begins to die, sinking into the waters. 'Why, oh why,' he cries to the scorpion. 'Now we shall both die.' And as the river takes them, the scorpion says, 'But it is my nature to sting and you knew that, foolish fox.' " Jason looked up at the sky as it darkened toward night. Somewhere below, Tomaz was escorting Rich and Stefan to Naria, and everyone was preparing for nightfall.

"A wise man who wrote that play."

"Very. It reminds me of Isabella and Jonnard."

The dragon rumbled lowly. "Ah. Now I have some sense of the train of your thoughts."

"Do you?"

"Your enemies bother you."

He nodded slowly. "I guess they do. I think I'm fairly certain of their natures, though."

"The problem then becomes . . ."

Jason unlaced his hands and sat up, looking intently at his draconian friend. "I think it's me I'm unsure of."

"Part of the infinite process of living, for many people." The dragon flipped his tail barb slightly. "It is a worthy pursuit to know oneself, one that many fear to understand and most never quite achieve."

"I think I need to know the answer a lot quicker than that," Jason said dryly.

"As long as you understand the answer is flexible. Perhaps not flexible but . . . evolving. Yes. The answer evolves as you do. Sometimes for better and sometimes for worse."

"That makes sense." Jason got to his feet.

"You don't seem comforted by it, though."

"Not yet." He smiled slowly. "I'll let you know."

"Do that." The dragon let his spiny face whiskers rattle as he drew his head down and nudged Jason slightly. "Again, thank you for the cake."

"Welcome. I'm glad you enjoyed it."

"Very much so, though it is not the sort of thing I would normally eat. I much prefer a nice charbroiled haunch of red meat, but it is good. As for the other quandary in your life, I might suggest patience. I have been called very patient by my colleagues. I can stalk prey for a very, very long time before I decide to attack."

Jason shifted uneasily. "I'm not sure knowing that makes me feel better."

The dragon laughed then, a real rumbling, thundering laugh, finishing in a spout of steam out his nostrils. "I am not stalking *you,* dear boy! But if I were, you wouldn't know it." The dragon dropped one scaled eyelid in a slow wink that unnerved Jason altogether.

He fished out his crystal and cupped it. "I think it is definitely time to go," he told the dragon and before they could exchange another word, he had Crystaled himself to the academy grounds. Jason let out a soft sigh of relief. He didn't want his friend reading any more of his thoughts that night, particularly the ones where he had almost decided he would have to break his vows of being a Guardian for Haven. It was *not* in his nature to lie.

Renart stretched his back and flexed his hands as he reached to light another lantern, the shadows in his office cubby growing darker and the papers he scribed on getting a bit harder to read. As the wick took and flared, and he positioned the lantern, the office glowed brighter. He took stock of his work. Only, what . . . three more journals to copy and his work in here would be finished. For the month, anyway, when caravans would bring in their goods and their own ledgers. He might, yes, he might actually be able to wheedle a small five or six days to himself, which would give him ample time to visit Avenha and take a look at its rebuilding and, with any luck at all, see Pyra again as well. Although she hadn't invited him as a suitor, neither had she thrown him out, and he hoped he sensed a certain liking on her part. Upon his return to the Trader Guild's offices and warehouse, it seemed Mantor had spoken well of him, for his load had lightened

a bit and the other traders were no longer so openly
disdainful. Perhaps his days of being disbarred were
drawing to a close!

He flexed his fingers yet again, as he reached for a
new pen. In the muted corridor beyond, the hustle
and bustle of the junior clerks and the trading ambassadors had grown quiet, for it was the dinner hour,
and many had gone to the inns, or the sumptuous
dining room for esteemed higher traders at the other
side of the guild offices. Being more eager to finish
his work for the night and remain ahead of the pace,
Renart had elected to skip his own dinner, and the
interruptions of the others as well.

Downstairs, he could hear the chime at the guild's
front door. The lobby noise often did not filter up to
him, but it being so quiet now . . . Renart paused a
moment to eavesdrop as a young apprentice scampered to the door and, panting faintly, pulled it open
with a small squeak of its huge bronze hinges.

"Trader Fremmler here, to speak to the Trader
Guild masters with an offering."

Renart dropped his pen on the desk and grabbed it
before its newly inked nib point could splatter ink
everywhere on his neat ledger pages. Fremmler! That
blackheart? The man had been cast out for life! What
could he be doing here? Even if he hadn't known of
Fremmler before, his own exploits had been thrown
into his face as if he were following in the man's cor-
rupt footsteps. According to the guild, Fremmler's
trading habits had been as bad as murder. Yet he
sounded as if he were proposing a trade!

Renart got to his feet slowly, well aware that the
lumber joints in the massive, old building tended to
creak with every movement. Yet, this was information
he had to hear and if the apprentice did his job, he
would lead Fremmler into the small antechamber for
audiences and summon a master trader, one of the
Guild Leaders, to talk to him. It would be up to the
master to throw Fremmler out, or summon town

guards to jail him for his audacity. Either way, Renart itched with curiosity to know what was going on.

He slipped off his boots and crept in stockinged feet to the small storage cupboard down the hall, where paper, ledgers, pens, nibs, ink, and the Spirit knew what else were stored by the shelf full, closed the door, and lay down on the floor. Here, he'd learned as a young apprentice himself, here things could often be heard through the flooring of what transpired in that antechamber. Sure enough, he heard the young-ling downstairs usher Fremmler in, offer him a drink against the dust of his travels, and ask him to have a seat while he announced Fremmler's arrival. Moments passed but not many. Renart fought to keep the dust from irritating his nose. He scrubbed at his nostrils twice against persistent tickles.

Heavy boot steps announced the arrival of not one, but two trade ministers! The moment the first spoke, Renart knew which two it had to be, the Guild leader and his assistant. One Renart thought well of, as he'd served him several years as an apprentice, but the old gent, Shmor, he thought of warily. Shmor had all the power, and it was he who'd demanded Renart's dis-barment. Now Renart realized it was because his ac-tions had left Shmor out of the exchange and powerless over the Magickers. Renart took a long, slow breath and pressed his ear closer to hear all the better as Shmor made noises of outrage at the un-wanted guest.

"Fremmler! Your presence was never to darken the Guild offices again. Must I summon the guards?"

"Shmor, Gammen." Fremmler sounded composed, even a bit amused. "I may no longer be a trader in standing with your guild, but I am here, nonetheless, representing a deal."

"Deal? Deal? What position are you in to offer a deal? You are disbarred!" Shmor's gravelly voice rat-tled and vibrated through the very timber of the floor Renart lay upon listening.

Gammen coughed. It was the dry cough of his many lectures, a sound Renart smiled at in memory. "It would be wise, Fremmler, if you left now. Otherwise, there are consequences. Your tattoos are branded and your standing dismissed."

"I am well aware of the consequences. However, I represent a party who could care less about the Trader Guild and its petty rules. I have a deal. Listen or not. There is always the smugglers' market where one can make a profit." Shoe leather squeaked, as if Fremmler pivoted on one heel to walk away.

Another cough. "We are all well versed in your acquaintance with the thieves' market. So, considering the stake, why have you come to us first?"

Renart smiled. Leave it to Gammen to cut to the chase ahead of Shmor who might talk in circles for days as if negotiating a great treaty and trying to leave the details so vague that no one but he would quite understand all the ramifications. No, Gammen was direct.

"My Principal requested that I come here first."

"Then you are handling the interests of another. Why would they choose an outcast to deal for them?"

"Do they not know better, you mean?" Fremmler let out a snorting laugh. "They know very well what they do."

Shmor let out a grumbling sound and ended up saying, "I would hear this deal, then. But make it quick, for you tread on very thin ice."

"The deal is this . . . we have goods to sell, food-stuffs, against the coming winter. Grains, cured meats, the usual gourds and fruits that can be laid down in cellars. We know that some of your towns and villages have meager stores due to misfortunes." Fremmler sounded intensely bored.

A dust curl seemed to be inching Renart's way and he shifted to pull a fine linen handkerchief out of his pocket and lay it over his face. A sneeze now would nearly be fatal.

"It seems your Principal is well versed in our needs."

Shmor let out another grumble, overriding whatever else Gammen might have been saying, at least to Renart's hearing. "Let us dispense with whatever pretense to pleasantries we might throw at each other. Who is your Principal?"

"Such a disclosure is not always required."

"In this case it is."

Gammen coughed faintly. If his old teacher said something under it, again Renart could not catch it.

"Lady Isabella of the Dark Hand," answered Fremmler to Shmor's challenge.

"Outrage!"

Gammen coughed in earnest, as if choking on his words, and for long moments, Renart could hear nothing clear or of any worth. He got to his feet reluctantly. Whether they dealt with him or not, he knew now what Fremmler wanted. What brass the woman had, to steal from them, and then sell the goods back. Yet it would be bought. It had to be. Their people needed their harvest against the oncoming hard seasons.

Back in his tiny office, he pulled on his boots, thinking. He'd send word to the Magickers of this new ploy. There was nothing that could be done and it would likely not win Isabella any new allies other than the outlaws she'd already drawn to her side. But it might. Yes, with enough cunning, it could be twisted, and Shmor probably would not stop the rumors for it would look just as bad for the traders to be dealing with what amounted to blackmailers. No, Shmor would want as good a light as he could cast on it. He might even say that he'd found a generous benefactor who agreed to help them in their time of need. The common people would never know the difference.

Renart frowned. He'd tell Pyra, too, and Mantor, of course, and the chieftain would, no doubt, have ideas of his own.

Renart stood up quietly, easing both feet deeper into his boots. He had much to do after hours tonight, and here he'd hoped for a good rest! Sitting down, he dove into the account ledgers once more, copying with a swift but legible hand, his mind scarcely taking in the task he did.

Oil in his lantern had sputtered more than once, signaling being close to having burned out when he finally put down his pen, swept away the used nibs into a small cup where they would be repaired or given to schoolchildren for their lessons, and closed the drawer on his paper. The hubbub of returning diners had come and gone and he was nearly the only person still in the building, or at least the only one working. Master traders might still sit in the back, in the lounge, partaking of a good brandy and chatting in front of the fireplace, mulling over Fremmler's latest audacity and the signs of a harsh winter headed their way. Some might even be talking of philosophy and the Spirit, and others might be snoring quietly, their day finished.

Downstairs the chime rang again as Renart stood, reaching for his cloak, and settling it about his shoulders, then put out his lanterns. If Fremmler's showing up hadn't been strange enough, now here was another visitor at an extremely late hour. He gathered his scribe case and trotted down the hall to the stairs. He was thinking of ducking out the back way just as the apprentice of the hour came round the corner and then gave a relieved smile.

"Renart! So you *are* still here! You have a guest."

"Me? The name?"

"Oh. Oh." Flustered, the apprentice bowed in apology. "Tomaz Crowfeather is waiting to see you."

Tomaz! Another bold surprise, but convenient. "Good," answered Renart. He renewed his grip on his scribe's case and made his way to the front door, where Tomaz stood haloed by the light of the sconces and the fading moon.

"Well met!" cried Renart and reached out for the

other's hand. "Have you business here or have you come just to see me?"

"You, I think," answered Tomaz slowly, as if considering his words before saying them.

"Good. I feel the need of a hot meal and a good drink, and I have things to discuss with you. Many things."

"Hmmmm. Perhaps it is fortunate I stopped, then. Lead the way." But Tomaz seemed a bit preoccupied, and looked around the shadowed street a moment before catching up with Renart.

He touched Renart's wrist lightly, and whispered in a voice the trader almost did not catch. "Did you know Jonnard was hereabouts, and watching the guild?"

Renart shook his head quickly.

"Then it is indeed fortunate I am here. Find a quiet inn, with private corners, will you?"

And so what Renart had thought to be an early evening now looked as if it would be a long, and startling, night.

23

More Night

RENART SCARCELY DARED utter a word till he found a curtained alcove at The Turkey's Wing, and sat down with Tomaz, the heavy drapery certain to muffle whatever they said. Tomaz took a crystal out of a vest pocket and laid it on the scarred wooden table, spoke a word, and a dull orange glow flowed out of it and mingled with the light from the oil sconces on the wall.

"We won't be heard," the Magicker told him.

Renart nodded, feeling nervous but trying not to show it. "If you saw Jonnard, then surely he saw you."

"I doubt it. I take precautions when traveling here. Our welcome is still uncertain." Tomaz gave a smile that was barely more than a faint curve of his mouth, but his eyes warmed. "Why were you not surprised? Alarmed, but not surprised."

"I was leaving work and knew I would have to contact one of you as soon as I could. Isabella sent a disbarred trader, an outlaw named Fremmler, to the guild early tonight. He came with a deal. She intends to sell back much of what they've stolen, it seems."

Tomaz let out a low grunt. He traced a knife mark cut into the wood of the table under his hand. "Enterprising of her."

"Very. She might even turn it into good propaganda, if people never understand she stole the goods in the first place. Without those stores, there are villages who will suffer terrible deprivations this winter. It will cost them to buy it back, but it is better than facing starvation." Renart shrugged off his cloak onto the back of his chair, and waited as the serving lad brought a tray in with the food and drinks they'd ordered at the counter. The meat pies smelled good and their gravies poured out through the crust onto the plates, and the bread loaf was warm as if just pulled from the oven. He took a mug of Narian tea and pulled it to him. "Is that why Jonnard was here, do you think? Isabella not quite trusting Fremmler to set up everything to her specifications?"

"That's the most likely explanation."

"Do you intend to stop it?"

Tomaz shook his head. "If I would stop anything, it would be the raiding. It would be a fool's attempt to stop a trade deal, however. Wheels within wheels and all that." He traced the knife mark again.

"If you didn't know about Jonnard, why are you here?"

"I'm escorting some of the younger Magickers on a town trip, and I thought I would stop in to see you." Tomaz leaned forward. "I have need of an old map, a copy. It doesn't have to be the artifact itself, but a reliable copy."

"What map?"

"One that shows the fortresses along the boundary of the old kingdom."

Renart's heart relaxed enough to give a normal beat. At least he wasn't being asked for the impossible, dangerous, or unwise. He lifted his spoon and made a vent in the crust of his pie, letting delicious smelling steam gush out. "I can give that to you tonight. I'd have to return to the guild house, though."

"Tomorrow morning, then. Best not to give Jonnard a reason to wonder at your comings and goings any more than he does. I am certain he remembers your dealings with us."

Renart shivered at the memory. He nodded. "All right, then. I can procure what you need early . . . but how to get it to you?"

"Where are the closest windows to your workplace?"

"Windows?" Renart had to think on that. He *was* on an outer wall, as well as the corridor. He swept his memory over the area. No, no, nothing so cheerful as a window . . . wait. Yes! A small oval near the ceiling, almost hidden by the overstuffed set of bookcases. It was hardly bigger than his head, however. "Small one," he answered.

"Show me."

Renart traced the remembered outline with his hand.

"Good. Open it for a bit of morning sun when you get into your office. Get the chart, roll it up. I'll have my crow there within fifteen marks of your entering the building."

"Crow?"

Tomaz nodded. "Make sure the chart is protected, their claws can be hard on paper."

"All right. Give me thirty marks, in case I have to trace a rendering first. The map I feel you want should have copies, but if not, I'll have to make one."

"Done." Tomaz took up his own spoon and began to chop the golden-brown crust down into the meat and its gravy, and for a long time neither said anything as they ate, and enjoyed, and thought difficult thoughts. When they both had pushed away their plates, he said, "I have places to go yet."

"Sleep for me, with much work facing me in the morning."

Tomaz smiled as he stood, and leaned over, and shook Renart's hand. "You've been a good friend."

"How could I be otherwise? You are good people." Renart gave a crooked smile before pulling his coat about him, fading into the evening crowd, and disappearing.

Tomaz scooped up the crystal, frowning then, as its

glow had been nearly extinguished. He tossed the small object from one palm to another, pondering it before pocketing it. It should not have dimmed in the time they were there. He would have to stow away that knowledge with other, equally odd, observations.

Crossing town by the back ways, of which there were many, steeply shadowed in what was now the deepest part of the evening, Tomaz felt a prickling across the back of his shoulders. Without seeming to, he angled toward the buildings and looked around when he could, but nothing met his keen glance. Still, his senses told him that it was too quiet about the alleys. The small critters of the dark that always frequented such places, to catch what bits and pieces of food they could, were gone. There was something that startled them besides himself. Tomaz did not like the idea he was being followed.

He knew ways to confound whoever it was, though, and changed his pattern of movement only a little, headed toward the forger and arena where Stefan learned his sword work. The coyote had given him many lessons in stealth and trickery and Tomaz did not worry.

Torchlight flickered at the edge of the arena despite the time of night, and he could see Stef's big, square body, sword in hand, as he went through a series of positions and strike exercises, a slender girl watching him with the keen eyes of a hawk and barking out corrections as Stef took advantage of every moment of his time. Tomaz let himself grin at the sight, an expression which he would smooth away when Stef could actually see him as well. The boy who was not quite a man was sensitive and might misunderstand the humor in seeing someone so large carefully mind the orders of someone so slight. Yet it was true that the most slender of daggers was often also the most deadly.

Looking at the swordsmith's daughter, Tomaz could also easily understand why Stefan wanted his lessons. She was handsome more than beautiful, her expres-

sion intent as she watched, her jaw set, a large, heavy
sword swinging easily from one hand as if it held little
weight at all. Her long hair was pulled back by a
beaded headband, and she wore an armored vest cut
away from her shoulders to leave her arms free. Her
leather breeches showed scuff marks and scarring
from the impact of dulled blades.

He swept the shadows behind him one last time,
then brushed his fingertips across his crystal, checking
for presences he might have missed as he began to
step out into the open. She sensed his movement as
he did so, raising a hand to her in welcome. Stef swung
about with a grunt of effort, as Tomaz let the grin
drop from his face and searched for a more appropriate smile.

Something moved behind him even as his crystal
flickered in meager warning. He started to swing
about . . . too late, as heaviness crashed down on his
head, and everything went dark.

Stef saw Beryl's intense gaze move away from him,
and across the dirt arena to the darkened city behind
the pole fencing. He wondered if her father had come
to get them, declaring an end to the long night of
lessons. Every muscle he had and a few he must have
borrowed ached beyond reason and he felt thankful
for a short break in her attention. Rich, legs stretched
out in front of him and crossed at the ankle, had gone
to sleep long ago in the shed at the arena's back which
connected to the forge. The forge itself was banked
for the night, fires down to a glow, but always present,
never cold. He took a deep breath, then swung about
to see what had attracted Beryl's attention.

Tomaz moved into the barest of illumination from
a still bright moon though the Hunter's Moon was
now days ago. Hand raised in greeting to them, he did
not see the shadow rising from behind him, cloaked
in billowing darkness, nor the sliver of silver that cut
through it.

"Hey!" bellowed Stef. He ran toward the arena

fencing as Tomaz dropped with a heavy thud into the street.

The cloaked figure stood over the fallen Magicker a moment, then turned toward Stef. He dropped the hood to his shoulders, revealing Jonnard's cruelly smiling face, and gave an ironic salute with his saber.

Stef launched himself over the fence with a roar and went after Jonnard. He could feel the bear cub rippling through his muscles as he yelled. "Rich! Rich, get out here, Tomaz is hurt!" He didn't know if he could be heard as he lowered his head and charged toward Jonnard. Alley dirt felt gritty under his feet.

Jon turned to face him with an ironic laugh. "And what do you think you can do?"

Stef bared his teeth as he brought up his blade, into a move Beryl had drilled into him only hours before, and it felt good. Without answering, he parried, then thrust at the other.

Jon met his blow, and stepped back, gathering himself. "You'll have to do better than that. A lot better!" He turned slightly and began his attack, the swords ringing off each other, even as the sound of people running toward them punctuated it. With a harsh laugh, Jon pivoted around and sprang away down the alley.

Stef followed without a second thought. Hot blood steamed through his tired body, and nothing mattered but catching Jonnard. Catching him and wiping that snotty expression off his face. Behind him, both Rich and Beryl called, and he heard it though his ears rang with the trumpeting of his own pulse and anger. The bear cub struggled inside of him to burst free.

No bear! A bear couldn't hold a sword blade or run the streets after Jon. He fought back, zigzagging after Jon's path. He turned a sharp corner into a smelly, dank mouth of an alley, and Jon sprang at him.

He accidentally parried the blow, and the vibration of it stung his forearm, but he forced Jon back onto his heels with a grunt. Stef righted himself and tried a jab which nearly got through the other's guard. A

look flickered over Jonnard's face, quickly replaced by
a curl of his lip.

"Think you've learned a bit?" Jon laughed sharply.
He swung his blade easily and countered Stef with a
series of moves that clashed heavily between them.
Stef couldn't touch Jon, but neither could Jon break
through Stef's defense. Jon tossed his head. "You are
tired and your sweat stinks of bear."

Stef growled in response. He charged, not quite
ready to attack, but his body flung itself forward and
he had to go with it, fighting himself as well as the
other. His body rumbled with the need to change. His
crystal rested on a thick leather choker about his neck,
a collar even the bear couldn't burst, and he dropped
his chin to touch it better, reaching for aid.

His senses skittered away and then latched onto a
Magicker, but not the Rich he expected, the Rich
who'd always been there to help him. Rich had his
hands full tending Tomaz. He only caught the barest
glimpse of his friend. In need, his mind filled with
another Magicker, surprising him. Instead, he found
Jason. He reached out, pleading silently for help to
stay himself in his own skin, to be centered. It was as
if they had clasped hands. Without hesitation, Jason
poured strength into him, steadying, his own anger
fueling him, but with a cool concentration, as if he
had . . . well, opened a Gate into Stefan. He let himself
be filled with the other's confidence and encouragement.

He snarled as Jon saw him hesitate in that connecting moment and darted out of the blind alley, out of
the stink and the fight. Stef went after him. He could
feel Jason's pulse drumming inside his. He pounded
after the dark billowing cloud of Jonnard's cloak,
drawing nearer and nearer. *Go, go, go, get him!* Not
built for speed, never built for speed, he lowered his
head as he neared, and flung himself after Jon in a
diving tackle.

They hit. Jon went down, sliding across the rough
and broken paving of the alleyway under him, both

grunting, and their blades shining like lightning bolts in the darkness. Stef rolled off the other and hauled him to his feet, panting, resisting a howl of triumph. Jon's foot lashed out, and pain shot through Stef s knee. Reeling back, he lost his grip on the other, and Jon shoved him back farther, bringing up his saber.

"Now," he said. "Face a master."

"Gladly!" Stef brought his guard up, feeling Jason still with him, anchoring him, and filling his mind with the moves that Madame Qi had taught him, as she'd tried to teach Stefan. No longer afraid the bear would rule him, he tapped into its strength as well, and a blend of himself and Magicker, he faced Jonnard.

Blades slashed and met one another, struck and countered, parried and stung the air. They rang and clashed off each other's blows, and Jonnard frowned as Stef met him cut for cut. It wasn't pretty or smooth, but neither did Jon outmatch him as he'd intended. Stef found himself grinning in a kind of fierce joy. Right blow, left, up, down, his blade answered Jon's.

He knew a lot of the flow came from Jason. He could feel it running through his mind and memory, Jason in Ninjalike combat with the Dark Hand, flowing through hand and feet and sword. He did not mind. This was what his body was meant to do, had been training to do. He couldn't master it yet, but he *would,* someday and when he did, this was how he would fight!

Stef threw his head back in a gleeful roar as Jonnard stepped back, sword arm trembling with effort.

"Freak," snarled Jon.

"And proud of it!" He raised his sword for another blow, strength still in his arms, and fury coursing through him for what Jon had done, and intended to do.

Jon broke. He grasped his crystal and disappeared in a flash of light.

Stef stood for a moment, anger still at high tide in him, and faced nothingness. He lowered his blade reluctantly. Jason's presence inside him began to fade away, leaving only the softest touch inside him, a congratulation for doing well, and then the other Magicker was gone as well.

Stef took a deep breath. He swung about, getting his bearings in the city, and then trotted back to the forge. Tiredness hit him like a falling tree, and he shook it off with a bearlike growl. By the time he found the streets he needed, he was staggering and laughing at himself.

Rich and Beryl met him.

"How's Tomaz?"

"Thickheaded, like you. Jon clubbed him with the sword hilt. How are you?" Rich swept his hands over him quickly.

"Nothing a good night's sleep won't cure."

Beryl eyed him, her face hiding its concern after a quick look. "Then I suggest you get that sleep. Tomorrow's lesson will be on gauging your opponent and knowing when to retreat!" She slapped his sword arm, not lightly, before walking away.

Rich said, "I think I agree. That was stupid going after him."

"Oh, yeah? Well I caught him and guess what? Bear and I made him run!" Stef let out a growling laugh. The night might be late, but it was good!

"Are you sorry we didn't get to go anywhere?" Ting spoke softly into the darkness of their room.

"There's time. I'm just glad Stef got to go. I mean, there's not much he asks for, you know? So, it's his turn to be Cinderella."

"Only he doesn't turn into a pumpkin at midnight, he turns into a bear!" Ting giggled softly, her voice almost like a wind chime.

Bailey grinned into the night. "Besides," she said. "We still have that map."

"True! We'll have to plan that out very carefully."

"Do you think our theory is correct?"

"I think that we are definitely losing power quicker

than we did at home, and we're slower getting it back. That's not good."

"It sure isn't." Bailey turned onto her side. As her eyes adjusted to the gloom, she could almost see Ting's slender figure curled on her cot across the room. "We can't prove anything yet."

"I'm not sure if it's the kind of thing we *can* prove."

"It's likely," Bailey said quietly, "they already know and have decided not to tell us."

"You think?"

"It wouldn't be the first time. The question is . . . will it be really important at just the wrong time?"

"Yeah," breathed Ting.

Neither said another word, and after a long moment, Bailey realized Ting had slipped into sleep. She pulled her blankets closer about her, one of them brand new from Laura Squibb, and snuggled in as well. Just before she drifted off, she felt the tentative, tiny movements of Lacey climbing in as well and curling up close to her ear. Bailey fell asleep smiling.

"Good morning," Rich said cheerfully as he slid into the hot mineral waters, and sank down with a blissful look on his face. His fair, pale skin immediately pinked from the heat, his freckles standing out, and his red hair began to curl into a mat of frizz, but it was obvious he could care less.

"Isn't morning. Still night from what I can see."

"That's what you get for all the gallivanting around. And wait till Tomaz gets up. Even with that headache of his, I think you're going to catch it from him." Rich peered at Stef. About all of Stef that showed was the top half of his head, his nose barely clearing the bubbling pool of water. "If you can see anything through the steam."

"I can see." Stef jammed a thumb up at the shed's roof, where the sky could still be seen as dark. "Nighttime."

"The sun is on the horizon and Tomaz will be here

any minute." Rich paused. "I'm sorry we have to go home early. At least you got some sword work in last night. Urmmmm . . ." He reached out and touched Stef's shoulder under the water. "Wow. That's some welt. She must pack a punch."

Stef emerged a bit and gave a proud grin. "Yeah, she's good with that sword, dull or not. Really good."

"Maybe we can convince Gavan to let us come back regularly, like we were doing before."

"I hope so! She says," and Stefan cleared his throat, "she says her dad is forging a real sword for me. Special one. The hilt is this rearing bear, like."

Rich whistled. "You're kidding."

"Nope."

"That's, wow, that's some sword."

Stef looked intently at his friend. "You know I don't talk about myself, right?"

"Yeah, I know, buddy."

"Beryl thinks I could be, well, like a hero. Her father says, the lands are gonna need a few. He says the Spirit is getting weak. No one wants to talk about it or admit it, but he can't protect them like he did. If he could, the Dark Hand wouldn't have done what they've done. Jonnard coming into the city last night like he did just reinforced that."

"So the old guy believes in this Spirit, huh?"

"They all do. From what I heard, Rich, it exists. The Warlord existed, and he left this mighty Spirit behind to keep his people safe. But he's a Spirit, see, and he's not meant to go on forever. The other side is pulling on him, wants to make his soul whole. He's thinning out, and some day, the Spirit will be gone."

"What then?"

"Heroes." Stef nodded grimly. "They're going to need warriors to stand up for 'em. I'm not saying I fit into that, you know. I think I could help, though. That, I could do. This strength I get from the bear, this fearlessness. Sometimes that's what it takes."

"Stef—" For a moment, Rich felt very cold, in spite of the hot water of the pool.

"Don't worry, I'm not going to do anything stupid like I did last night. I met Jon, okay? But he's far better and I know it. Still, I like learning the sword. It makes my muscles work, like football used to, and my mind work in a different way. Magick stuff drives me kinda crazy sometimes, you know? I miss football. If I got mad at anything, I could just push it into there. Now, it's got no place to go and that isn't good for me."

"Gavan's just looking out for all of us."

"I know that. Doesn't mean he's doing the right thing, though, for everyone." Stefan stood up, water cascading off his stocky body, and wrapped a towel about himself. Rich could see three good-sized welts on his torso and a couple of purpling bruises on his legs. He wouldn't ask whether the training or the encounter with Jon had made them.

Rich had been a trainer for the football team, and he'd seen Stefan all bruised up any number of times. That had never bothered the big guy. What had bothered him was trying to do his best for the team.

His best for this team, Stef seemed to feel, did not lie in his Magick. Rich began to understand that. He made up his mind to talk with Gavan and Tomaz and the other elders and see if he could make them understand that, as well.

Stef had dressed completely and Rich had gotten most of his clothes on when Tomaz appeared at the shed door.

"Good. It looks as if you are ready." Tomaz nodded in approval, even as he lifted a finger and scratched the small white diamond on the chest of the otherwise glossy black crow on his shoulder.

"Who's that?"

"Snowheart," Tomaz told him. "She came back with me, as did her mate. I do not know if this world will accept them, but I needed them. We must hurry.

After last night's retreat, I don't want Jon coming back to test our weakness." He rubbed the back of his neck ruefully. "He might have tried more if it hadn't been for Stefan."

"I'm ready for more!"

Rich thumped his shoulder. "This ain't the time, big guy. You yourself said you weren't quite ready yet."

"Yeah, yeah." Stef's face wrinkled up in disappointment, but he stepped back in agreement. Instead, he gathered up his things and Rich's herb bags.

"There will be a time," Tomaz told them both. "And let us hope it is a time we can be prepared for." Snowheart cawed sharply at his words, punctuating them.

24

Ghostwalking

JASON WOKE IN THE EARLY dawn, warmer than usual, and feeling it was darker than usual as he looked up and saw the roof overhead. He reached over and touched a fingertip to the crystal lantern, setting off its glow, and the reflector behind it broadcast light throughout the room. Trent's deep breathing indicated he wasn't even close to waking yet, and Jason wondered what it was that had awakened him.

A sensation prickled over him, something unfamiliar and possibly unpleasant, but he wasn't quite sure. Gooseflesh rose on his arms and the back of his neck, and he looked about without seeing anything. He rubbed his arms. He didn't like feeling spooked. What could intrude, with all the wards they had laid into the very wood and stone of the academy?

Jason shifted uneasily, then got up and dressed. Downstairs, in the kitchen, he found no one about but Madame Qi, leaning on her bamboo cane while shaking tea leaves into a china pot. She smiled as she poured steaming water into it.

"Henry brought back some truly excellent Chinese tea." She smiled, her seamed face breaking into many wrinkles, as she took a deep breath and inhaled the aroma. "Have some with me?"

"That would be great." He sat down on one of the three-legged stools, leaving a sturdy chair for her. She said nothing, and he said little more, as she busied herself fixing their drinks and putting biscuits with jam out on a plate. The biscuits had to be from yesterday, but that was all right; they'd be good dunked. Jason waited politely for Ting's grandmother to sit and pour him a cup. It was then he noticed the goose bumps had slowly gone away, although the feeling that something had been watching him was still there.

"Jason, my student, always the quiet one and yet even quieter today. What brings you so early in the morning?"

He pulled the delicate, handleless cup close to him, the heat of the tea warming his fingers through the china. She had not been trained as a Magicker, yet she had told all of them stories of her grandfather who was a Chinese magician in his time, and who had undoubtedly had some kind of Talent as did she, and certainly Ting, her granddaughter.

She did not watch him as she gathered her own drink and biscuit, as if giving him a break from her sharp eyes. Otherwise, she always seemed to see more than others.

"Did you feel it," he asked then. "Something odd."

"We live in a world other than our own, where a dragon comes to talk with you, and someone offers you a six-fingered hand in welcome . . . and you ask if I feel something odd?" She sat back with a chuckle.

He cleared his throat, feeling very awkward. "I don't know how else to put it. It's as though I woke up and something had been watching me."

She nodded then, holding her teacup at chin level. "That, young man, is precisely what woke me. Whatever it is, the wards do not seem to bother it."

"Then I'm not the only one who felt it!"

"Even if you were, would you doubt it had happened?"

He thought a moment before shaking his head. "No.

No, something was stirring. I don't know what, but I felt it."

"Like a ghost walking over your grave."

"Exactly!"

"And then, perhaps it was. Here, they speak of the Spirit often enough."

Jason sipped his tea. It was strong and slightly smoky flavored, with a bite. He wished he'd had some sugar for it, but they used sugar sparingly. It was hard to store and had become a luxury. "The Spirit. Looking us all over? I wonder."

"Wonder more if Gavan and Tomaz did not feel it. Has it cloaked itself against them? Will it test us? What is it looking for in us, and will we pass? Many questions to wonder about."

"I'm the one to ask them?"

"So it seems. Do you mind?"

He thought about it. "Well, I'm not happy about it, but—I guess not."

"Good. You have been a good student." She pushed the jam jar toward him and continued with her breakfast, silent now, her wizened face curved in a pleased expression.

Things like this always seemed to start so simply and end up so complicated, he thought to himself, as he measured some strawberry preserves onto a biscuit gone stiff as a hockey puck, and then dunked it in his tea until it was soft enough to eat. Messy, but good, and on the whole, worth getting up earlier than usual for. When he was done, he cleaned up the fixings briskly but couldn't avoid Madame Qi as she tapped her cane and sent him out on a long, early morning training run, just when he'd hoped she'd forgotten about his exercises.

The sound of his running had barely faded from her hearing when the quieter, softer steps of her granddaughter entering the kitchen stirred Madame Qi from her thoughts. Ting fixed her own cup of tea before sitting with a natural grace that warmed Madame Qi

to watch. So much her mother's daughter, so much of
her own family she could see in Ting. Life did indeed
circle, if one only knew where to look. But Ting
looked far from content that morning, an uncharacter-
istic frown settled on her face.

"There is trouble in you today?" Madame Qi
probed gently, sitting back a little on her stool, and
preparing to listen.

Ting stared into her teacup. "Not trouble," she answered slowly. "Exactly. But something." She looked
up. "Everyone else seems to have a real idea of where
their Talent might lead them. Jason is a Gatekeeper,
Rich a healer, Stef a shapeshifter."

"Everyone?" echoed Qi. "Even Trent?"

"Well." Ting shifted. "Not Trent, no. And not me.
I mean, I make nice little enchantments that last
maybe a few hours or a few days or weeks, but I can't
see that it's really, well . . . a Talent." She looked at
her grandmother with questioning eyes. "Do you
understand?"

"I do. I have no answer for that except to say that
the world turns slowly, and in its own way, under the
revealing light of the sun. What is hidden on one side,
will eventually be revealed, as it turns."

Unhappiness winged across Ting's face.

Madame Qi stretched out her hand and patted her
granddaughter's shoulder. "Because it is something
from within you, it has to be discovered that way, too,
I fear."

Ting nodded slowly. She turned her cup in her slender, agile fingers. "I also dreamed about home last
night."

"Ah." Madame Qi nodded. "Missing everyone?"

"Not that home. Yours. And the house dragon."

"Indeed." Sudden intent interest flared inside Madame Qi, even more interest than that of helping Ting
through a difficult day. "What of my house dragon?"

She missed her home in the San Francisco Bay area,
with its bronze weather vane of a Chinese dragon

upon it, the guardian of her family for many many years now. That bronze sculpture had been forged in their ancestral China and brought over to reign over their homes in America. Of all things in her old life she'd given up without regret, that was perhaps the only irreplaceable object. The Chrysanthemum Dragon, with its brilliant coat of enamel paint, and its long sinuously curling body, moving about slowly in occasional gusts of wind, had always been more than just a weather vane.

"I dreamed it was unhappy at being left behind, and that it wished to be here, with you. Upon the academy roof." Ting's gaze flickered up briefly as if mentally picturing it there.

Madame Qi smiled slowly. "It has its own duties for others, now. Yet it spoke to you, Granddaughter?"

"It did." Ting finished her tea and put her cup down carefully on the table. "Remember when it spoke? Remember when it hissed 'Jason' at us?"

"I do indeed."

"I didn't just imagine that."

"I don't think either of us did." Madame Qi leaned forward on her elbows, quilted jacket rustling about her wizened frame. "Many, many years ago, my grandfather was a magician in old China."

Ting's face took on a faint glow as she leaned forward in anticipation. "I remember."

Qi nodded. "I have told you some of the old tales. Not, however, all." She laid a finger alongside her nose, indicating that Ting should listen. "In the old tradition, a Chinese magician was a master of many things. An acrobat, an actor, singer, performer, with tricks of voice and illusion, and in my grandfather's case, tricks of Magick. Nothing remains from those days. The letters and journals he left were destroyed by war and purging, but there are still memories." She tapped her finger to her temple. "He could make paper chrysanthemums appear from thin air, while tumbling through burning hoops of fire. And he could make a dragon appear, from smoke and mist, as if bidden by his very call. It is that dragon that was cast in bronze, as a symbol and guardian for our home.

"A traveling magician, in those days, could earn much money from the families and weddings he entertained, but there were always bandits on the road eager to obtain his earnings. Sometimes my grandfather traveled with the family, oftentimes alone. I remember, however, the stories told of the dragon who would appear to chase away would-be robbers. A dragon whose strength would pull the wagon out of muddy ditches or rivers swollen with floodwaters. A dragon whose breath would be like the most reassuring campfire on wintry mornings. A dragon who . . . strangely enough . . . was there to help my grandfather even when my grandfather had mysteriously disappeared from the scene."

Ting blinked. "What?"

Madame Qi nodded slowly. "One never saw my grandfather and the dragon at the same time."

"But. . . what did that mean?"

Qi leaned forward, smiling softly, and whispered, "We were never sure. I always thought my grandfather *was* the dragon. He had the same long curling mustache, thin and sinuous as a river eel. Nothing ever frightened him, not even the Boxer Rebellion or the great wars which followed. When I knew him, of course, age had bowed and molded him, as it does me now, and his mustache had turned snowy white, instead of the glossy ebony in old posters he used to show me. He always wore a great pearl about his neck, not jewelry, but a beautiful object he prized. One day, he told me, it would be mine."

Ting had never seen that pearl. "Did you leave it behind?"

Madame Qi shook her head. "It disappeared when he grew ill and we all knew he had begun to die."

Ting gasped. "Someone took it?"

"In our family? Never!" Qi shook her finger at Ting for suggesting such a terrible thing. "No. It was thought he hid it somewhere. No one knows where. He was a clever man, my grandfather."

Ting looked at her grandmother with an expression of admiration. "I wish I could have known him, too."

"He would have been most proud. Many generations have passed without his magic showing, but it does reside in you, and you will discover more and more. You will not be an echo of him, but a fine magician in your own right." Qi reached out again and squeezed her hand tightly. "Never doubt that. Impatience will only slow you down."

Ting sighed. "I know, Grandmother." She stood, and flipped her hair back over her shoulder. "I'd better go wake Bailey. Lots to do today. Leave the dishes, I will clear them." She kissed her grandmother's brow and left.

Madame Qi gazed after her. Yes, her grandfather would have been most proud to see his blood still ran strong in his family. She poured herself a second cup of tea and warmed her hands about it, lost in memories.

Jonnard woke at the first touch of dawn and got up quietly, knowing that Isabella would sleep late. She slept later and later each day as her activities and the turning of the season took its toll. She was old, he knew, far older than he who had slept when thrown through the centuries after the battle of Brennard and Gregory the Gray, while she had lived, and even her own magic and that of the Leucators now seemed to be losing ground in keeping back the natural tides of Time. Still, he had hopes of not waking her.

He'd learned much in Naria, and she would be eagerly after him when she did awake. He would be able to tell her then that Fremmler had done as hoped, and more. The trade would make them wealthy as well as feared, and the first holds she wanted to establish over the cities and provinces of Haven had begun to be well anchored. All this, and more, would please her greatly later. Now was his time for himself.

He drew his father's journals out of their warded safekeeping, and laid them out. So many hints he had read over the days since finding them. To think that this man had raised and taught him, and never said a word about what he'd found in the journals.

Jonnard put a fingertip to one page. It crackled faintly under his touch, not with aging of paper, but with power, an energy he recognized well. He traced the words inked there.

I have found the place of repose of Gregory the Gray. He sleeps a sleep from which none of us could awaken him, nor would I wish to. He did all that he could to kill me, as I did all I could in kind. I could kill him yet; however, his mind walks on planes which none of us could see otherwise and when he awakens, he may be of use to me. So I will leave him be and let the guardian who watches over him think the secret well kept.

Jon lifted his hand. Well kept, indeed, for that information had gone to the grave with Brennard. He inhaled slowly. Even if he had it, he would be wise to think as his father had, and that Gregory might know something useful when he did awaken, and how vulnerable he would be in such a weakened state. When he had first read those words, he'd done the only thing he could, which was to focus a crystal and target it toward the sensing of Gregory if and when he ever rose from his Magick-driven sleep. Then Jon would be upon him.

The journals held other treasures in them. It was rather like sitting in front of a jewelry box and being able to dip his outspread hands deep into the contents, letting each gem shift and play upon his fingers. But what he desired most to know, how Brennard had come to Haven and why, could not be found.

It had to be written within. It had to be!

Jon sat back, puzzling over it, biting his lower lip in thought until the sudden sting and taste of blood filled his mouth. He then sucked a moment at the smarting wound.

He picked up the books and studied the embossed leather, but the pattern imprinted seemed to be only a pretty design and totally at random. Suns and stars and moons in their phases studded the covers. Nice but nothing helpful. Jon closed each journal, holding it tightly in his hand. His ears buzzed with faint power.

"Damn."

He dropped the books and stared at them. His morning time was nearly spent, and he'd learned nothing useful. Perhaps he should turn them over to Isabella and let her work at them.

That idea stuck in him, though. This was *his* heritage and almost all he had, and the thought of giving it to her to shred in her pursuit of knowledge that would benefit her made him dig in his heels against doing it. The journals stared upward at him from the desktop. Years buried in the ground in the casket had done little to them, although the cover of the first book had suffered some damage, its fine-grained leather thickening and bubbling a bit.

Jon picked it up. He rubbed his hand upon it, feeling again the buzz of energy. Then he shut his eyes tightly. "Jonnard Albrite, you are an idiot." His eyes snapped open, and he slid a long thin knife from his boot. Working it carefully around the cover, he separated the leather from the book itself, and it fell off in his hands as though he'd skinned an animal.

Power blazed up at him, revealed, inscribed carefully on the hidden true cover of the journal, and it took his breath away. He read it slowly, whispering the words to himself, and it seemed as if the very room danced in the blaze, like the sun shimmering in a mirage off boiling desert sands. It filled him with a heady energy. "Gatekeeper," he breathed outwardly, and drew it nearer to read and learn it better.

Deep in the stronghold, in the dungeon of golems, the Leucators stirred in their chains, their graying flesh feeling the touch of warmth filtering down to them, as if someone had unleashed a summer sun. They rattled their chains and shackles and stood, with heads thrown back, and sucked in the feeling with a soft, keening moan. About them, in the very stone foundation of the fortress, another being moved through the earth as if it did not exist. It touched each of the Leucators, a fleeting shadow, then passed through wood and rock to other layers of the fortress, searching.

FireAnn woke. She felt a prickling over her skin, and she threw up her hand, crabbed from arthritis, and she moved to lean over the still sleeping Eleanora, to protect her however meagerly she could. She swatted at the prickling, the searcher, the irritant, cursing in the Irish tongue of her youth. Like bees stirred angrily from a hive, the thing stung at her. Here, there, here again, darting off to another place, then buzzing back in. FireAnn's eyes filled with angry tears.

"Off with you, foul Banshee! Ye'll not have my Eleanora this day!" She gestured as if she could still hold a crystal and send power shooting in attack, and the buzzing stopped a moment.

It crept back, and her whole body quivered as something unseen seemed to take their measure. The sting marks became fiery hot, as did the tears of frustration on her cheek, and Eleanora's body twitched under her, as the stings marked her as well.

"No! Git, bully lad. Ye'll not have her today or any other day, as long as I've breath in my lungs!" FireAnn leaped to her feet then, swinging about blindly at bees of power she was unable to see but could feel. She howled with frustration and her body jerked with each bolt from the attacker, and she wept with the pain and fear of it, a torture she could not prevent or answer . . . and worse, she feared, withstand.

After long moments, it withdrew, and FireAnn sank to her knees, hugged herself, and wept softly. Eleanora in her exhausted sleep, wept in echo.

25

Myths of Time

WHEN DO YOU find time to read all this stuff, anyway?" Jason paused to wipe his hands on his pants, then eyed the wall sconce he had just fastened to the inner passage. Trent had been regaling him with information since they'd gone to work, throughout lunch hour, and now the evening dinner seemed to be approaching fast. Not that Jason minded listening to Trent, but he'd only been half listening this time.

"Whenever I can. Sometimes I wake up and read after you're asleep, so the lantern won't bother you." Trent flashed him a grin and went back to assembling the sconces they had yet to install. His nimble fingers worked to fit the metal parts together quickly, with the oil reservoir and reflector and other pieces. "So, anyway, the point is, there are hundreds of creation myths from home. Every tribe has a story explaining where they came from. Some have several and argue about them; it's the beginning of religion, so they would, but anyway . . . not here. Everyone agrees on one thing. They fell in."

"Fell in?"

"Yup. They fell into Haven. Well, not everyone today, there are families and they had children, and *they* got here the normal way, but I'm talking way back when everything started. They fell in."

Jason turned the yardstick in his hands as he prepared to mark off the next placement. "No wonder they didn't think it was too odd we all showed up. You think they . . . what . . . came through a Gate, too?"

"Most of the houses that have a record, or a storyteller to tell the tale . . . even the wanderers agree on this . . . talk about a great war on their lands before they fell. It's been different wars, not everyone got here at once, it's been over centuries and centuries, though." Trent finished assembling a sconce lantern and stacked it next to the other two he had done. "It's as if the energy of a war punches them through."

"A hole in the fabric of time?"

"More like a hole through the universes, I think."

"Not ours, though, we don't have six fingers. Or, it's very very rare."

Trent nodded. He stood, dusted off his hands, and came over to help Jason mark the wall. "There are a few tales about boats of sleepers being found, way, way back in the early times. They had six fingers. Must be a strong genetic trait."

"What do you think they meant about sleepers?"

"Boats of people asleep? Refugees maybe? People in some sort of hibernation? Lifeboats? I couldn't say, but it makes me wonder about the old science fiction thing, is there life on other planets, 'cause these people came from somewhere, and I don't think they came from Earth. But this world is used to taking in the survivors of disasters, so they didn't view us harshly. I think, though . . ." Trent drummed his fingers on the wall, a bit uneasy. "Those holes. I think they're Chaos related."

"Hmmmm. But we don't have stories like that at home, right, people appearing?"

"Nothing too close to it. People disappear mysteriously, but whole families don't just appear."

"Trent . . ." Jason paused, trying to put his question

together. "When you go through the rest of that stuff, look and see if wolfjackals are mentioned."

Trent raised an eyebrow, and Jason knew he'd connected on the Gate energy thought running, through his own head. "Which came first, the chicken or the egg?"

He shrugged. "Something like that. I'm just curious."

"Sure thing." Trent bent over to grab a wall sconce. "Don't we need to get this passage finished before dinner?"

"Four and we're done." Jason dodged around Trent, letting him finish the one he held, while he moved to the next measured location. There was a logic to Trent's interests, and his knowledge of mythology had gotten them out of fixes before. What if his study on Haven were right? What if every one of them had fallen through a hole in the universe to get here? What did that say about Gates, and Gatekeeping . . . and universes?

A chill ran down the back of his neck. What did it say about Chaos and wolfjackals, as well? Is that what the wolfjackal who'd scarred him so very long ago before he even knew he was a Magicker meant when it had growled at him, "You are mine?" It had marked him because of his Talent to Gate, bringing Chaos, which in turn fed the wolfjackals. Or had it meant something even darker?

"Jase? Jason? Wohoo? Watching videos in your head?"

He shook his head vigorously. "Just thinking. I know, I know, why start now?" He bumped his shoulder into Trent before Trent could tease him, and went back to work, trying to chase away disturbing thoughts.

Lacey scrabbled along the windowed wall, something shiny in her grasp as she hopped up to Bailey's toe and then made her awkward way up to the cuff. Bailey leaned down and took the nail from her, as she lifted her up. The little pack rat immediately dove into the pocket in the soft golden-brown suede bodice Bailey wore, and made a little chirruping noise as she groomed her whiskers. Bailey gently massaged the back of the creature's head. "She's sleepy," Bailey said to Ting. "Good Lacey, good girl, look what you found!"

"Why don't you put her back in the room to sleep?" Ting paused, and opened and shut the inner shutters carefully, making sure they swung smoothly. Her face creased with proud joy as they worked perfectly.

Bailey shrugged. "She says it's too noisy with everyone pounding. I think when the school is finished, she's probably going to sleep a whole week!"

Ting laughed. "Must be rough on a day sleeper, huh?" She stood back, with her hands on her hips. "I think we're done in here, Bailey."

"Great. Only . . . twenty more rooms to go!"

Ting nudged her. "Don't be like that! Look at what we've done."

Bailey's pony tail swung as she looked around, then nodded. "I know, I know. Somehow, it's almost all built." She stroked Lacey one last time, before tucking the pack rat's tail into the pocket with the rest of her, and saying, "Mom wants to go home."

"Both of you?"

"No. Just her. For a while." A troubled expression settled on her face.

"She'd leave you alone? She can't do that! She's like . . . like . . . like your best friend!"

"I know."

"Did she say why?"

Bailey shook her head again. "Parents are like that, you know? They have these reasons for things that they never tell you about till later when it's all said and done, and you think . . . I could have helped, but they never asked. Or explained."

"It's a parent thing," Ting said in understanding.

"Exactly. Plus, I don't think she figured the Gate would be closed all the time. I think she thought it would be open and we would go to school here and go home at night or something. I don't know." Bailey finished with a shrug that elicited a sleepy cheep from within her bodice. That made both of them giggle a bit. They picked up their work tools and buckets and headed to the next room where sunlight slanted low and faintly through shutterless windows, and they knew their workday was almost done.

Ting pulled her hair over her shoulder, braiding its long blue-black strands thoughtfully. "I've been watching everyone's crystals," she noted. "And I think our conclusion is right. We're losing more power than ever before, and by day's end, Gavan seems nearly exhausted. This can't be good."

"I know. The question is why hasn't he told us or warned us?" Bailey dropped her work bucket, nails rattling, and picked up a set of shutters leaning against the wall, waiting to be nailed and hinged into place. "I can't believe he hasn't noticed."

"Maybe he's maintaining so much, he expects the drain. But not the rest of us."

"I think we should talk to him tonight."

Ting came to mark the window frame, leaning in and around Bailey. "Not yet. I just want to be sure, you know? Another day or two."

"All right. We should watch Tomaz if we can, although he's hardly around."

"Good idea!" Ting brightened. She lowered her pencil. "Ready for you."

Heads together, sometimes giggling and sometimes yelling because of bruised thumbs, they went back to work.

At dinner, Gavan and Tomaz finished their meal quickly and retired to a crystal-lit corner, where they pored over a chart rolled out onto their table and weighed down carefully with crystals. The opportunity to look couldn't possibly have been better as both Ting and Bailey took them mugs of tea and coffee but did not linger as both men waved them off quickly.

Bailey nibbled on her lower lip. As they drew away, she whispered to Ting, "Even the crystal on Tomaz's bracelet looked dim. We need to know about Jason."

"But Jason's been Gating and we know that takes a lot out of him."

"A day or two more rest, then. We're going to have to ask somebody soon." She rubbed Ting's shoulder. "Look, remember what they told us when we first started learning. There's no such thing as a stupid question, all right?"

"Right." After all, if Bailey had asked one when she first became a Magicker, she wouldn't have been locked in her own crystal for days, almost to the point of never getting free.

Lacey poked her head out, nose twitching, and Bailey fed her a crumb of bread. The little beast took it and dove back in, making her bodice pocket ripple and move about busily.

Trent leaned in. "What're they looking at over there?"

"Some kind of map. Looks like Havenite work," Bailey offered, then shut her mouth firmly, not wanting to reveal that she had a Haven map of her own.

"No kidding?" Trent looked interested, nudged Jason, and the two drifted toward the elder Magickers.

Tomaz looked up as they came near the table, but Gavan barely noticed their presence. Jason and Trent peered down at the paper pinned to the table. "Fortress locations?" Jason ventured, hoping he recognized what he thought he did.

"Aye," muttered Gavan. He tapped the yellowing paper. "The Trader Guild keeps a good record of the boundary, because a main trading route developed along here."

"Makes sense. They'd have military protection, then," Trent said.

"Exactly. So one of these is likely to be Isabella's stronghold. This one," and Gavan pointed, "is the ruins near Mantor's village, where we went and had a look."

"But it doesn't look like ruins to us."

"Right." Gavan nodded to Jason. "Smoke and mirrors, magickal illusion at its best."

Trent leaned over closer, gaze narrowing intently. He put out a hand, as one might stretch a palm to a warming fire. Jason watched him and held his next words, afraid to break the trance his friend seemed to be slipping into. The dull and opaque crystal clipped to Trent's belt seemed to glow briefly. Tomaz also noticed and put his hand on Gavan's, stilling the other's indrawn breath, and everyone at the table went very quiet for a few moments.

Trent breathed. He put his hand down, covering an inky sketch. "Here," he said. "It feels like here. I can't tell you why or how, but the map is warm, right here."

Tomaz and Gavan traded looks as Trent lifted his hand. Gavan stared down at the mountainous spot. A little farther away, but well within range of all the villages which had been raided. Tomaz grunted faintly.

"It looks logical."

"It does indeed." Gavan appraised Trent. "Nothing more than a feeling. A vision, perhaps?"

Trent shifted uneasily. "I can't do that, and you know it."

"I know you couldn't. I also know that your Talent is a very difficult and stubborn one and is unfolding with agonizing slowness." Gavan smiled to take the edge off his words. "We'll take a look here first, then. Tomaz and I have found two other forts which they may have seized, but I have to admit this may be the best possibility." He frowned then. "I overlooked it. You, Tomaz?"

Tomaz nodded. He put out his own hand, turquoise-and-silver bracelet rattling a little. "My eyes slid right over it. I'd say there is an aversion warding to it, powerful enough that it even reflects on maps. Isabella is stronger than we feared."

"Not her. She uses the Leucators. She may even be drawing off Eleanora." Gavan swallowed hard. He reached out and briskly rolled up the map. "We'll let you know," he said to Trent, "when we scout it."

"Can we come with you?"

"Not for scouting. Later, yes." Gavan stored the map in its oilskin tube and tucked it away inside his cape.

Jason hid a fidget, hoping that later would not be too late.

A shout outside from the wanderers at the back of the kitchen door drew everyone out as a bonfire blazed and the workers gave a cry for dancers and stories, while night settled darkly about the academy and the Magickers. Trent and Jason followed the others out slowly.

Trent could not hide the gleam in his eyes, nor could Jason hide the heaviness in his heart. Isabella touched everywhere, like a black plague on Haven, and it was he who had brought her in.

It would have to be he who took her out again. The dragon had asked him if he were a guardian or a warrior and he'd chosen guardian in order to open the Dragon Gate. Now, he realized, he had chosen wrongly.

Only a warrior could cut through the tangle he'd made.

26

Oops

"HOW COULD YOU let this happen? How? Did I give no idea that it was important not to let the others get a foothold here? Everything we've striven for, gone, worthless!"

Saying nothing in retaliation, Jonnard stared at Isabella as she paced the floor angrily in front of him, her long gown swishing and sounding like the sea driven by a high and maddened wind. He had expected nothing less than having to bear the brunt of her displeasure when he delivered the news he'd gathered while trailing Fremmler at Naria. He'd waited a day or so to tell her, knowing that she would explode in fury. He knew word of the Magickers and their academy would distress her beyond measure. He could only stand quietly until it passed. She had been raging for the better part of thirty minutes, however, and he had begun to tire of it.

"All our devices will be for nothing. Our work. We cut off their supplies, I thought! You were to see to that. The building was never to have been begun, let alone finished, and now you bring me this news." Her eyes flashed as she looked at him, her dark hair tangled about her face as it had fallen from the gem-studded combs holding it.

He waited.

"Our bribes were in place at the Trader Guild?"

He nodded.

"Useless. Absolutely useless to me!" Isabella glared at Jonnard. He felt a muscle along his jawline jump as he kept his teeth clenched. Another moment or two of anger, and he would break, and both of them would likely to be sorry. His fingers twitched as he fought not to curl them into a fist.

She took a deep breath. "How did this happen?" Then, lifting the hem of her skirt slightly, she sat down, her back ramrod stiff, and let the elegant folds of material fall into place about her ankles. "Talk."

"Our influence got Renart disbarred temporarily, as planned, and he was unable to procure supplies for them, as we agreed. We were also given access to the libraries for my studies, and I took advantage of warding the maps, as directed. Our locations remain undetectable. I hardly call that useless. As for the building of the academy, it appears that they hired wanderers, Gypsies if you will, who needed the work desperately. No matter what disbarment from the guilds, what whispers they heard, the wanderers are independent sorts and would judge for themselves, and evidently found a bargain to their liking. As for how they gathered their supplies, there is a black market, an underground, for almost any need, anywhere. If anyone could have tapped into it, it would have been the wanderers." He shrugged at that. "We planned well, Mother, and I see no fault in it. The use of the wanderers can be twisted to our advantage, for the people here are suspicious of the Spirit and those who disbelieve. The wanderers are outcast for their disbelief, and the Magickers, too. I think we can still turn it to our advantage."

"I haven't time." Isabella raised her hands and quickly upswept her hair, replacing her combs. She looked tired, and for the most fleeting of movements, well, old. He turned his gaze away before she could catch him staring.

"I'm not saying we must restructure. Our contacts are in place, and they're doing what we hoped. The Magickers have no idea what has been working against them. It is sheer luck they've countered us despite the hostages we hold. I suggest we consider a more direct strike as well."

Isabella lifted her chin. "Such as?"

"Wood burns."

A hungry realization flared in her eyes. "And winter draws near."

"A delay which even luck cannot put off."

She lifted a hand. "Very well, then. See to it. I will not need you when we take the caravan to Naria. Fremmler can handle that."

Jonnard gave a slight bow. He left her apartments then, and not until he was downstairs did he take a long, slow, steadying breath. Did she know how close she'd come to his answering her challenge? Did she even care?

He was not quite ready to battle her for leadership. Not quite yet.

Downstairs, he assembled a group of five, veterans used to being Crystaled to a destination on horseback, and then raiding from there. He gave them their instructions, and told them when to prepare, before leaving them. They would be ready. He'd seen the hard lights in their eyes. They lived for mayhem. It served him now, but he made note of their names. It was never too late to plan or be wary for the future.

He would not examine the journals this night, for he had a feeling Isabella was watching him. His day would come.

Jason stirred restlessly on his cot, with the feeling of whispering inside his head, like an annoying insect. He got up quietly, observing Trent to see if his roommate were reading late, but the bundle of blankets suggested that his friend had burrowed into a sound sleep. He stood, shivered a bit with the cold seeping through the building, and pulled a blanket off the cot to wrap it about himself. The fireplace and chimney structures would be operating soon, yet not soon enough for those Magickers with thin blood unused to winters that could bring frost and even snow soon. He padded out of the room, thinking a bit of food might help drop him back into sleep. He always seemed to be a bit hungry these days. Growing spurts, he thought. When he crept downstairs, the buzz in his head grew louder, and Jason went outside in search of it, hearing hushed words. He drew back against the side of the building.

Peeking around it, he saw Rainwater and Crowfeather, and he sensed the tension then, as well as the quiet. He started to pull back, then held very still to listen, instead.

"You should be resting," Tomaz remarked quietly.

"I know. The days should be getting shorter, but they feel longer and longer." Gavan shrugged into his cape and rubbed his palm over the pewter wolfhead of his cane, as if settling in his mind what he wanted to say next. "I wanted to do this now, when everyone is asleep, in case there are problems."

Tomaz squatted by the fire which had burned to gray ashes and red glowing undercoals. He stirred it up a bit, setting flames to licking upward from within the broken stone ring. The orange illumination gave his face the look of ancient gold. He did not try to hide his worry. "I do not think this a wise thing."

"We can do it this way, or we can spend days, weeks, combing the countryside by horseback." Gavan scrubbed a hand wearily over his face. "I don't think Eleanora can last weeks longer."

"We know nothing for sure. Let me send Snowheart after her."

Gavan shook his head. "I know you can sometimes see through the eyes of your crows, Tomaz, but I need to know for certain what we find, what we can expect."

"You cannot Crystal to a place none of us has actually seen."

Gavan put his hand on the map tube inside his cape. "I think I can find it by the landmarks."

"Even stone changes, given enough time." Tomaz stood. His silver-disk belt flashed as he hooked his thumbs in it and stood, legs balanced. "Even anchored to me, I cannot help if you materialize locked in granite."

"I know." He fetched out the tube, handing it to Tomaz. "Each fortress had a distinctive guard tower. The one we want is studded with obsidian and the picture of it is fairly good. I should be able to Crystal near it."

"If the fortress is manned the way its illusion showed it, you could appear in a tent camp of armed men, Gavan."

"Let's hope I don't Crystal that close."

Tomaz took the map with a sigh. "I shouldn't let you go, but I agree that time is no longer on our side." He put his other hand on Gavan's shoulder. "Don't let the coyote blind you."

Gavan gave Tomaz a lopsided smile. He rubbed his cane again, and the Herkimer diamond inside the wolf's jaws sparkled dully. He grasped it in his palm, and then was gone.

Jason lost his breath at the suddenness of it, and clenched his teeth hoping the noise hadn't been heard, but Tomaz seemed very intent as if he listened to the absence of the other. Jason wondered if he would ever see Gavan again.

As a lad, he'd grown up knowing how to Crystal almost from the moment he could walk. He had memories of using it to cross the moors when frigid howling winds seemed to chase him, and of Crystaling down the Thames to where the grand country estates near Windsor Castle held docks on the water, and of jumping across the London bridge in wild games of crystal tag, back in the days when getting caught might mean being prosecuted for being a witch. He had never known fear. Gavan reflected there were times when he probably should have, although none more than now.

He kept the image of the obsidian tower in his head, flint-edged rock studding a gray stone tower, overlooking the rills of a rocky pass with a verdant valley down below. The pass and valley were unimportant now, and with autumn hard upon them, might already be browned by frost, but it was the tower upon which he needed to keep his inner focus. The tower and Eleanora, for he hadn't told Tomaz that she would be his anchor there, even as Crowfeather would anchor him to the academy, holding his soulstrings if he himself should fail.

Crystaling should be near instantaneous, but he hung in the coldness of *between* for many heartbeats until his bones felt the absence of the life of the world and he wondered if he had emerged already and been sunk into the stone as Tomaz warned. Yet he lived. His heart struggled to beat one more time, his lungs ached for air, and the crimson veil of blood behind his eyes fluttered as if reminding him he could look inward as well as outward.

When his body screamed silently for a breath of air, then and only then, he tumbled outward, onto the ground, hard stone smacking into his knees and palms, and he gasped, trying to breathe. He threw his head back and looked up, and saw the sharp tower not far away, as he'd pictured it but . . . in the thin gray dawn of morning.

Gavan got to his feet slowly, dusting off his hands and stowing his cane away. What had he done? He'd left at night. Now it was dawn. The inference made him shiver. He'd passed through time as well as distance. No wonder he'd nearly died *between.* He'd never known anyone who'd done it and lived. Was it the day before or the day after? No way to tell. He focused inward, felt the thread of Tomaz tied to him, and tugged it gently to let Tomaz know he lived. His only answering response was a faint warm glow inside himself, but he knew it was an acknowledgment from the other.

Thin plumes of smoke from morning fires drifted into the air from the fortress across from him. No doubt filled him now. Trent had identified this as the stronghold, and he had been right. This was the rebuilt and fully manned fortification whose image they had seen. How Trent had known it, Gavan could not say. No one in his history of Magicking had the Talent, or lack of it, or confusion of it, that that boy had. There was no naming of it, and no way to depend upon it except through blind trust.

He sank back to the ground, finding a broken boulder to shelter him, and tried to commit all that he saw to memory. He could see the trade road below, running through a pass cut by a river, for it was fringed with trees and brush, all glowing red and yellow and orange with color, thinning branches showing through as the leaf fall had already begun. The Dark Hand would take that road to Naria, and he traced the route in his mind. Waylaying the caravan too close to the fortress would be foolhardy; taking on the Dark Hand could be dangerous at best and murderous at worse. He would have to send Tomaz's crows over the trade road to get a better look at the terrain.

Gavan felt his nose and ears grow cold as he watched the fortress. He wanted to be closer. His heart and soul ached to be closer. The morning seemed so new that few walked yet, and sound seemed all muffled and hushed. He began to pick his way through prickly shrubs and broken rock, a hardscrabble of a hilltop upon which this stronghold had been built. He moved slowly, foxlike, across the ground, willing himself to be unseen, unnoticed, unheard.

For once, being chilled gladdened him, for his breath stayed invisible on the early morning air. He pulled his cape close and willed himself still as he crawled ever nearer until he could hear the raiders clearly, the first few up as they tended to the horses and built up the cook fires. His nerves tingled as he sensed the beginning of the ward lines laid down, and he knew he dare not creep closer though his eyes were drawn to a heavily shuttered window on the second floor of the stronghold itself. She had to be there. He could *feel* it.

Gavan lay there for a very long moment. The sensation pulled at him, as it had when as a young sixteen-year-old lad he'd first met the daughter of Gregory the Gray. She'd been five or six years older, a world away from him, it seemed, and all he could ever hope for was an occasional glance from her eyes or a view of her slender body as she passed by the study where her father taught Magick. To listen to her play an instrument was like listening to your own heart being drawn out and made to express itself. He had fallen hopelessly, forever, in love with Eleanora. She had noticed, of course, who wouldn't? She had the grace to neither tease nor flaunt his feelings for her. Gregory had tolerated it, saying little until, near the end, although neither of them had known it was near the end for Gregory and all those in those times, he had said to Gavan that if he had patience, eventually the age difference between them would mean little.

Gavan had taken it as a sign of encouragement, though he needed none. After seeing Eleanora, no one else could even be considered, and as long as she remained single, he'd have hopes. Then the great battle of wills happened between the rogue student Brennard, who by then was a master in his own right, and Gregory, and the power backlash from that encounter had killed many outright, throwing the others into comas and even through time. When they'd awakened, Gregory's prophecy had proved true. Time had equalized them. He'd awakened first, matured, grown, and, upon finding her, was no longer the love-struck youth he'd been. Young still, but someone adept in the modern world, finding and restoring Magickers wherever he could when, miracle of miracles, he'd found her.

He would not lose her again. Not to anything less

than death itself, and even that he was not certain would keep them apart.

On the other hand, dying was something he'd rather avoid. Gavan took a long slow breath. He could see her if he Crystaled in. A whisper of power from this distance, little more. He had skills honed by years of playing hide and seek with his abilities. Sometimes those games had meant his own hide, literally. He wanted to see her. He had to know how she fared. If she could wait till they played their game out with the trading caravan.

He rubbed his crystal out of habit, concentrated on her essence, and with a movement like a silken wind barely stirring the air was *inside*.

His eyelids fluttered as stink and dank air struck him, and he staggered back a step. Chains and moans and a soft wailing greeted him. He pushed at his Crystal and brought the lantern light up, and then saw where he had landed.

A sea of Leucator flesh surrounded him. He was nowhere even close to his beloved Eleanora.

A ghoulish hand locked about his ankle and began to tug at him, icy fingers tightening.

27

Chains

GAVAN FOUGHT A MOMENT of panic as he backed up farther and the Leucator crawled along with him, mewling softly, its hand curling ever tighter upon his ankle. Picking his way among the graying flesh of the other creatures, he found a clear spot where none of the others could get to him, but this one seemed to have a longer lead on its chain than most and began to get up on its knees, free hand clawing the air at him.

It was not his own Leucator or it would have been on his throat in a flash, desperate to meld their bodies and souls and be whole again, although it would kill them both in the effort. Gavan felt a moment of shame that he could not identify this creature. If it had ever resembled a Magicker at one time, he either had never known the person or had forgotten who it could have been. It might have recognized him, for it cooed as it grew closer, but perhaps it just craved contact, warmth, fuel, of a sort. He could not even have said if it were meant to be male or female.

The others only seemed a little aware of him, thankfully. When aroused, they would set off a keening, a wailing, that would alert everyone to his presence in the stronghold, something he most certainly did not wish to give away. Foiled for now, when he returned, he intended it to be a surprise.

He shook his leg, hoping to deter the Leucator. It tilted its head, a few strands of stringy black hair flying into its eyes as it did, its clothing mere scraps of moldy fabric about its gaunt body. Its red gash of a mouth opened and closed. Its fingers kneaded his leg like a cat kneading a favorite blanket. He felt a moment of pity for the construct.

The moment fled as the Leucator struck, snakelike, angling its mouth to his leg, where its grasping hand had forced up his trouser, baring a patch of skin above his boot top. Like a sucker it fastened and he could feel it bite deep into the warmth of his flesh. Blood spurted as the Leucator gave a moan of happiness and latched onto him. He muted a scream of pain and shook with it. He raised his cane like a great sword.

Gavan gestured, brilliant white light from his crystal wavering, then dying out altogether, and with it he felt the total absence of power as the focus went black. Panic chilled him. Then he lowered his cane across the back of the creature, hitting hard, with all the strength he could muster.

The Leucator let out a muffled shriek of pain and fell back. Loose, Gavan lunged back out of its reach, his back to the dungeon wall, pain shooting through his leg. Hot blood trickled down into the boot. The other Leucators would smell it and begin their wailing. Injured and well and truly trapped, he stood in a sea of undead flesh and pondered his options.

Jason stayed around the corner, pressed to the outside of the academy and wondered whether to blunder in or sneak away. Long moments stretched by the campfire, with Tomaz immobile, then he stood and stretched with an impatient mutter. The elder Magicker stared into the evening sky as if he could trace the route Gavan had taken, his shoulders squared back. Jason decided to back away as quietly as he could, knowing that Tomaz and his bottomless

barrel of patience could stand and wait all night if
he had to.

He made no sound, he swore he did not, but Tomaz
spoke quietly.

"Stay, Jason, I think I will need your help."

He swallowed at being caught and moved toward
the fire sheepishly. "I . . . I . . ."

Tomaz waved a hand. "It doesn't matter. I remember your days in camp, when you were often about at
night, curious." Without turning around, he took the
map tube, opened it, and shook the map out. "He's
been gone far too long for a quick look, and yet I
know he arrived safely, because I felt him. So . . . like
you . . . he's gotten curious."

"Trouble?"

"I'm not certain. The contact is not quite right. Yet,
this is Haven, where many things are not quite right."
Turning, then, he drew both Jason and the map to the
last dying light of the fire. "Study that."

Jason did so, his eyes sweeping the well-inked map,
taking in all that he could, most especially the stronghold Trent had picked out. When he knew it well, he
lifted his gaze to Tomaz who quickly rolled up and
put the map away again. "Now we wait."

"Till when?"

"Till he returns or calls for aid, or I decide to go
get him." Tomaz threw his head back and faced into
the night wind, his broad face set into the nonexpression he often wore, his thoughts unknowable.

Jason fought off a shiver and edged closer into the
fading warmth of the fire. He wondered if Gavan had
sensed him also, then decided probably not. Still,
being busted at all embarrassed him. He shoved his
hands into the waistband of his trousers and wished
he'd brought a winter cloak down with him. Coats
were far more sensible, he thought, duster-length if
they could be found, closer to the legs and knees, but
capes and cloaks were the style here, even if the wind
found its way inside most inconveniently. He'd rather
have a good hoodie under a coat any day, and realized

those days might be gone forever. Never going back? He couldn't quite comprehend that. There was too much to see here, though! Places the dragon had hinted about that he itched to see, when the time was right. How far did the land of the Warlord's Spirit stretch? What was beyond the emerald sea?

He rubbed his hands together. The fire stirred and sifted down to little more than hot ashes, yet Tomaz did not move to add fuel to it. They never let a fire burn all night without a watch on it. He came from a land of dry hills and wildfires and knew the danger. Still, Jason wished he could be warmer, or at least, inside.

Curiosity had led him there and, he reminded himself, it wasn't keeping him warm. Another reason to think first next time. He wrapped his arms about himself and tried to remember playing soccer in the mud and rain, where sheer body warmth came from the action itself and the joy of playing. If he thought it would warm him, he was wrong as the edges of his ears began to turn cold.

Tomaz made an impatient movement. "I've waited long enough."

"What can you do?"

"Pull him back whether he wills it or not. If he's trying to find Eleanora," Tomaz grimaced, "he'll be more than angry, so stand clear." Tomaz reached out and gripped his hand in his strong one, and Jason could feel the power surging through both of them. Jason had anchored before, so he knew what to do without Tomaz asking him. Tomaz would be going after Gavan, although not quite . . . what the Magicker had planned was even more dangerous, for he would use himself as a bridge in between, neither here nor there, and with only Jason to bring him back safely, if Gavan were in danger.

"Now," said Tomaz quietly, as he made a gesture and uttered a word of Navajo that Jason thought was probably a blessing because he'd heard it before, though only when Tomaz needed great will or strength. Then, also he held his friend's hand and he felt Tomaz just sort of *go*.

The wind gusted wildly, buffeting them, seeming to blow through Tomaz's insubstantial form. Trent should see this, Jason thought. He'd know where the mythology of spirits came from. He shivered and held tight, more with thoughts and hope than by holding hands to nothingness which threatened to fade from his fingers.

He dug in his heels and clung to the essence of Tomaz. Patience as timeless as the sandy land he grew up in, confidence as strong as the sun beating down on the southwest, faith in his friends about him as far-reaching as the never ending bowl of sky overhead . . . these things beat like wings about Jason's head. Then he inched his head back and looked and saw the two crows gliding about, the black-as-black one, and the other with a patch of snowy white upon her chest. He'd called on them, too.

Wherever Gavan was, whatever he was doing, it would take nothing less than all they had to get him back!

He found himself holding his breath, and forced himself to breathe, even as he took his second hand and clasped it over his other, near empty hold on Tomaz. The figure of the Magicker stretched as little more than a mirage, face frowning in intensity, one hand outstretched to the heavens.

"Hold tight," murmured Tomaz more in his thoughts than aloud. "He is not only somewhere, but somewhen. . . ."

He had only a moment for surprise before gritting his teeth and promising himself that he'd never let go, never, no matter what. No matter if a pack of wolf-jackals growled at his back or if . . .

Leucators!

Jason's mouth dropped open in revulsion and he fought not to jerk back in utter terror. They sensed him even though he was not really there and he heard their screeching begin deep inside his skull. They clawed at his thoughts, their own as slimy as the touch of their decaying flesh and he jerked and twitched as if he could dance away from them, but he fought to hold onto Tomaz. Don't let go! No matter what!

They wanted him. They wailed for the chance to devour him, body and soul, till nothing remained of him, not a thought or memory or drop of blood. He would be as gone as if he'd never existed! No!

Jason clenched his hands tighter to that which he knew was Tomaz. His spine bowed with the effort not to run screaming to save himself. Don't let go!

Tomaz gasped. His spirit image shivered on the air, then began to grow solid, and Jason pulled. He fell back on his butt, pulling slow and steady as if he needed to uproot a stubborn tree from the earth, his arms aching and his ears filled with the crying of the Leucators.

Suddenly, the noise stopped, and he felt weight in his hands. As he yanked, two heavy bodies hurtled out of the night and dog-piled onto him. Jason lay panting for air, flattened, Gavan's gasping in one ear, and Tomaz's deep rumbling chuckle in the other.

They sorted themselves out and sat up, Gavan leaning on Tomaz. He peered at Jason through the night, his rainwater-blue eyes narrowed.

"Up past bedtime, are we?"

Jason flashed a grin. "And you'd better thank your booty I am!"

"Indeed, indeed." Gavan started to get to his feet and fell back, and decided to stay sitting in the ashes of the fire, looking a bit like Cinderella as the soot drifted around him. He rolled up his pants leg over one boot, exposing a nasty looking bite.

"Someone was hungry," Tomaz remarked. "I'll get a paste on that. Looks bad, we don't want infection."

Gavan winced as he poked a finger at it, then nodded. "The wages of curiosity." He glanced at Jason to see if he was listening.

"Find her?"

He shook his head. "Her Leucator called to me,

so I found myself in Isabella's dungeon. Unpleasant surprise, all around. But she's there, upstairs I'd say, and she lives." He smiled ruefully. "At least I've that much."

Tomaz stood and put a hand out, and drew Gavan to his feet. "Now the only question I have is . . . were you there yesterday morning or tomorrow morning?"

Gavan's face twisted a little as he put weight on his leg. "Noticed that, did you?"

"I could hardly not. We've no anchoring through time, Gavan. At least, I wouldn't have said so until to-night."

The other nodded. He pointed at Jason. "This is definitely not for you to try. It nearly killed me." He palmed his cane, and the absence of any response from the crystal Herkimer diamond held there shocked Jason. "If not for the two of you, I would be dead. Or worse."

As the dragon had said, there were worse things than death. Jason thought he might have just glimpsed them, although he wasn't sure. He shivered. He didn't want to know.

Tightrope

DAWN CAME WITH A FLASH of lightning, long before he was ready for it. Jason sat bolt upright in his bed, the cot creaking dangerously under him as if it might collapse . . . as Stef's already had, under the bulk of his weight, so he slept on the floor in a nearby room. Trent let out a muffled curse as he came awake, already on his feet, shrugging off blankets. He pulled on his jeans, torn and ragged but still mostly in one piece, and cursed again as Jason threw a shirt at him.

Boots, pants, shirts on but otherwise unready for the cold morning, they raced down the stairs as thunder shook the academy, its wooden sides booming and reverberating like the bass on the loudest boom box in the world, and they all collided into one another in the kitchen. Rich's pale face stood out as everyone reached for their crystals, but before a single Lantern spell could be focused, the inside of the kitchen lit with a brilliant flash. They all stood revealed in white-hot light. Outside the windows, black shapes on horseback flew by in silhouette.

"That's no storm," Jason cried out. "We're under attack!" He threw the door open, his body illuminated by glaring light, and they could all hear the beat of

231

horses' hooves and the whistles of raiders as they circled the building. The smell of crystal Lightning stung their nostrils and the academy flickered with tongues of flame.

Stef grabbed Ting and Bailey by the elbows. "Out, out," he cried. "Everyone out!" His voice growled ever deeper as his words ended and dropped into a low roar as the bear in him fought to emerge. *"Now!"* and he lost his human voice and body altogether as he pushed the girls out of the burning building.

Bailey linked an elbow with Ting as they ran out, trying to keep their feet under them, propelled by Stefan's berserker strength. The bear loped past them, charging at two horsemen as they rode in, their hands filled with burning torches. The horses screamed in fear, their riders shouting and sawing at the reins to control the plunging beasts as Stefan reared in front of them, bear roars filling the night. His paws boxed at them, horses reeling back under the blows.

"Grandmother!" Ting called out in dismay, as Bailey guided her into the sheltering woods. She struggled and pointed at the school. Bailey narrowed her eyes, peering back at the academy as raiders and flashes of crystal Lightning flashed by again and again. She saw two figures then. "Mom has her," she yelled to Ting, drawing her back under a low branch where they could see but not be seen.

Rebecca Landau made her way around the corner of the building, her arms about Madame Qi who seemed very bent and fragile, hunched over her cane. Horsemen thundered near, and the tiny woman straightened in a heartbeat, her cane lashing out, bashing one rider in the leg. The man wheeled his horse away, yelping in pain and anger. Bailey let out a piercing whistle the way only Bailey could, and her mother's head jerked up, a smile cutting across the worried expression on her face. She guided them both toward safety, the two women scuttling quickly before the raiders decided to make another charge.

Ting's teeth chattered with cold and nerves, but she

managed to say, "You absolutely have to teach me how to do that."

"Tomorrow," promised Bailey. She watched her mother and Ting's grandmother inch across the open ground, dodging raiders and Magickers as Trent and Jason both took up crystal Shields and two by fours, whatever they could wield, as the raiders closed in. Henry's crystal knocked a rider from his seat, tumbling him off his saddle, but he held onto the headstall and managed to drag himself back onto his mount while Henry danced around in excitement.

Dokr and two of his men circled Rebecca and Madame Qi to hustle them in under the trees, before the wanderer's leader said quietly, "I go to make my own people safe," and disappeared in the shadows as silently as he'd appeared.

Ting wrapped her arms about her grandmother to provide some protection against the cold, and held her tightly, while all of them stared at the fight in the courtyard.

The academy danced in flames, and the sting of smoke and fire crackled, as the raiders now ringed about Stefan and Rich, Henry, and Jason and Trent. Bailey could see Jonnard in the foreground as his crystal shot forth another shrieking lightning bolt of fire and damage and the edge of the rooftop splintered, giving way. Wrapped all in dark cloth and cape, only Jonnard's face and hands revealed who he was, but they all knew. Isabella could not be seen. Stefan's bear mumbled and growled, swiping at the horsemen, his eyes white with anger and ursine fear of the fiery torches in their hands.

Gavan and Tomaz emerged from the building last, and as they did, Jonnard pulled his horse into a rear, then pivoted it and shouted out a command that snapped through the air. All retreated then, the horsemen plunging about and galloping off, their taste for conflict gone. Jonnard's cape snapped in the wind as he put his heels to his horse and led the retreat. The night went deadly quiet except for the noise of flames. Gavan spoke a tired word, and the fires licking about the academy went out as if they'd never existed.

Bailey crept out from the trees first and went to one of the sooty spots on the wall where fire had just been. She put a hand out cautiously. Warm, yes, hot to the touch, but the wood barely showed a mark. She let out a whoop.

"We did it!"

Gavan smiled tiredly, and rubbed his hand across his face, leaving a charcoal smear over his eyebrow like a salute. "Good warding."

Tomaz held up his crystal and let its Lantern light spill out as he examined the structure, striding the length of the wall. "Morning will show us how good, but I suspect other than a corner of roofing, we'll see little damage." He shook his crystal in triumph before letting out a howl of victory, sounding rather like a desert coyote.

Dokr emerged from the shadows, too, his face folded into worry and curiosity. He trotted about at Tomaz's heels. "It was burning, was it not?"

"A little. Like green wood, Dokr, some flame, some smoke, but not really catching."

"That is good." He tilted his head. "It is a spell? Magick?"

"It is a treatment of the wood," Gavan answered firmly. He caught up with Tomaz, his expression guarded, and Tomaz nodded in agreement.

"It would be good to know such a thing," the wanderer said.

"Perhaps some day I can teach it to you and your workmen."

Dokr hid his disappointment, bowing. "Some day, then." He waved his crew back to camp. "When the sun rises fully, we shall begin repairs."

Rich sat with Stefan, who slowly began to quiet, his growls muffling as his friend rubbed his ears. His change back might take time. "I've got bear cub for a while," Rich said. He poked his feet under the thickly muscled body for warmth. "I'll sit out here with him."

"Want company?" Henry nervously pushed his glasses back to the bridge of his nose.

"Sure! Hey, you knocked that one guy off his horse!"

Henry's face flushed. "I did, didn't I? Too bad he got right back up."

"We wouldn't know what to do with him anyway," Bailey laughed.

"I would," said Jason quietly, and he did not laugh. He shoved his hands in his pockets, filling each with a crystal, and took another walk around the academy despite the darkness of the night which had barely begun to give way to dawn.

"What's eating him?" Ting looked after Jason, puzzled.

"It's hard to fight back with your hands tied," Trent answered her. "Well, I'm for more sleep unless some-one wants to fix breakfast?" He looked about eagerly, and no one answered. He shrugged good-naturedly then and headed back inside, true to his word.

Jason trotted about slowly, shining his crystal wher-ever he thought he saw smoke stains, but Tomaz and Gavan seemed right. The warding had kept the wood from truly catching and whatever burning had hap-pened, was little more than surface charring which could easily be sanded off. He should be happy about the victory, small as it was. Jonnard had intended heavy damage, perhaps even total destruction of the academy. He'd no doubt about that. What were they supposed to do? Take it? They had no choice.

He stood in the shadows between the Iron Moun-tains and their Academy, his hands shoved deep in his trouser pockets now, cradling his crystals, and staring at the ground in thought.

Part of the mountain's foot seemed to flow toward him, glowing like molten volcanic lava in the night, rising up and wrapping itself close, reflecting the heat of the earth. It took shape with a graceful stretch and arranged its curving bulk about Jason.

"Early morning, is it not?"

Jason wrinkled his nose at the dragon as he opened his eyes wide and then settled down on his forepaws, watching him. "Does dawn come," Jason asked the vast beast, "when the sun rises or when the soul realizes a great truth?"

"My. Early for philosophy!" The dragon stretched a paw out, unsheathed his glittering black talons and admired them. "I'd say you just realized one, Gatekeeper."

"I've lied to you," Jason said simply. "I didn't mean to, but I have, and that's that."

"Oh?"

"When I passed the trial to open the Gate here, you asked me to choose. I chose guardian. I lied. I realize now I should have chosen warrior. I'm fighting back." He gazed down the valley, along the path of the raiders' retreat. "I'm not going to stand by and take this."

"Do you think guardians just stand and watch?"

"I don't know what they do. I only know what I'm going to do. I brought them here, now I'm going to take them out." Jason shifted weight. "Gavan has some plan to get Eleanora and FireAnn back, as a ransom. It might work, but it probably won't."

"And your plan will?"

"If it takes everything I have, it will." Jason stared at the dragon, into his large gold-and-amber eyes, and stood fast.

"I cannot help you."

"I didn't ask you to."

"Yet you apologize?"

"I don't like to lie," Jason answered.

"That, I know well." The dragon sheathed his talons, his orange-red scales rippling. The coming morning light began to dance upon his body, tiny motes of white fire upon molten red. "You may find yourself surprised, Jason Adrian."

Jason took his hands out of his pockets. His clear crystal, laced with bands of gold and lapis filled one, the lavender crystal of Gregory the Gray's was in the other. Both glowed with power. "As long as I don't fail."

29

Chaos and Order

BEFORE JASON COULD SAY more, or even blink, the dragon withdrew into the mountain or wherever it was he disappeared to, with as little noise as he'd made appearing, taking his warmth and smell of copper with him. Jason waited a moment to be polite before leaving, wondering if he had done right or wrong and knowing that he wouldn't know until the end of it all—if even then. That was the way of some decisions, he thought uneasily.

He put his crystals back, and his left hand began to ache and sting across the old scar; he smoothed the puckered skin down. The old Shakespearean quote, "By the pricking of my thumbs, something wicked this way comes" ran through his mind, but it was not through his thumbs, it was always the scar. He twisted about in the dawn where black shadow still streaked heavily, and light had barely started to part the night.

They only howled twice. The first hung in the air like a questioning wail, and the second, sharp and loud, answered. Then the noise of galloping, of paws covering the ground, drawing nearer, and the sound of panting as long-toothed jaws bit at the cold and tongues lolled out to scent what lingered on the air. From the very clouds that hugged the valley wolfjackals spawned, one, two, three, five, seven, a pack, ranging down on the academy, their eyes glowing green. Their silver-and-black fur quivered as they circled the building, snapping at the air, swallowing the traces of the Magick fire that had burst all around.

Drinking Chaos, Tomaz would say. Jason stood still and watched them, the scar on his hand pulsing as they loped by. They took little notice of him save for the last one, a great-shouldered, hulking beast of a wolfjackal who paused and stared at him, black-and-silver mask unreadable even for an animal, save for the showing of sharp ivory fangs. After a long breath or two as if he recognized Jason by look or scent or scar, the beast galloped off after his pack mates and they encircled the academy one last time before disappearing into the woods, much like any wild wolf pack.

It took a few moments longer for his scar to stop throbbing painfully. Then and only then did he enter the school. Upstairs, Trent could not be seen under the hump of blankets. Jason lay down on his cot and took out his lavender crystal, staring at it.

Found on a world seemingly populated by wolfjackals, and sometimes filled with an image of the elder Magicker who'd taught many of them, the crystal was his and yet not his. It had come to him, he supposed, because he was the only one who could carry it back, but carry it to whom? No one else wished it. Why was it where the wolfjackals roamed? Had Gregory been thrown there when Magick exploded? Or had he gone there purposely, and left a clue as to his passage? Was he a Gatekeeper, too, among his many Talents, or was Jason the only one left?

He pulled out the faintly lavender crystal and stared into it, his eyes adjusting to the dark, but his mind carrying the image more than the actual sight. It was a totally transparent gem, unlike his which had a band or two of rock embedded in it, and he could see into and through it. On more than one occasion, he'd seen Gregory the Gray within it. Never had the image acknowledged him, so he did not think it living. But he couldn't know, for sure. He only knew that Gregory was not trapped inside the crystal and that, once, it had been bonded to the great Magicker.

It warmed inside his fingertips. All good crystals did, as if they had a life of their own. Gavan said they vibrated faintly with the energy charged throughout them. Supposedly, that resonance also held the elder Magicker although Jason often thought there was more to it than that. Jason rubbed it. He could feel a hum through the object. The more he rubbed it, the louder the hum got.

Although everyone thought Gregory had died in the great conflict between himself and Brennard, Jason had become more and more certain the man had not. He felt him. Where and how, he did not know, and the crystal certainly wasn't telling him. That didn't keep him from trying, though. It hadn't fallen at his feet by accident!

Something stirred inside the crystal. Jason gripped it tightly. Imagination, or had he felt the humming change, grow more intense? He cupped it, staring into it, trying to delve into its depths. Without pouring himself into it, he tried to reach as far as he could, not wanting his own power to flood the power that seemed to be blossoming in the stone.

The gem crackled with heat. He held it together, fearing that it might fracture from the inside out, shattering itself with the strain. Instead, a white snowflake bloomed inside it, and in a moment or two, the optical illusion rearranged itself into a face he knew as Gregory the Gray. The room glowed with the crystal's power, a soft blue yet somehow a warm light, and he could see the wide-browed, strong visage of the man as clearly as if he stood next to him.

He expected it to speak to him. Gregory seemed to look into his eyes, into him, much as he looked into the crystal. Jason's hand shook a little. The heat of the gem burned but there was not enough heat to force him to drop it.

A thought reached him, slow and quiet as if coming

from the bottom of a great ocean somewhere, as if it took much effort and came out of great depths. *I sleep, and must sleep. If you find me, do not awaken me. I have promises to keep in my sleep. Those promises keep you all safe, and the oath must be met.*

What oath? Jason closed his hands tightly about the searing gemstone. Where . . . why?

Nothing else stirred through his mind. No echo, no sigh, no other feeling of support as though the effort to send that much had cost Gregory dearly.

Jason let out his breath, slowly, and released the crystal. Its warmth fled as he did so. Gregory lived, somewhere, some-when. He knew they were all there, and somehow, he held his energy to ward them. Knowing that would have to be enough. Should he tell the others?

Eleanora should know. It would comfort her, he thought. When Eleanora was freed and she was ready, he would tell her.

The more he learned, the more bewildering questions he seemed to have. For now, though, the only one left to really dig at him was . . . if he attacked the Dark Hand's stronghold, would the wolfjackals fight with or against him? Or would they merely rise for the Chaos which would ensue? He would not know till too late, so he decided to prepare against all possibilities.

Somewhere, deep in his thoughts, he fell back asleep as well, not to awaken till Trent opened their shutters and the full-blown sun's rays glared at him.

"That does it," said Ting firmly. "The crystals are definitely draining much faster than they should. Dormant, charged crystals seemed to be only a little faster, but charged ones in use . . . well, look at this." She waved her hand over the table they had covered with bits and pieces of gemstones and quartzes and other crystals, as well as the larger ones they used every day.

"But what does it mean?"

"It means something outside is drawing on them,

because they lose power even when we're not using
them. And when we do use them, it's as if . . . how
do I say it . . ." Ting wrinkled her nose. "It's like
opening up a can of soda with four or five straws and
everyone having a drink at once. Only, we didn't in-
vite anyone to share."

"Isabella!" Bailey smacked one hand into the other,
sharply, and the retort made little Lacey jump on her
shoulder. She let out a resentful chitter before running
down Bailey's sleeve, leaping to the floor, and scurrying off to her nest for some peace and quiet.

"Maybe. That, I don't know. I can't find a way to
trace where the Magick goes, just that it does. Trent
might be able to; Jason says he can see it."

"He has, a few times. Traps and such. I wouldn't
count on it, though. It seems to be erratic with him.
Jason says they're not even sure if it is a Talent or
just a quirk." Bailey tapped the tabletop, setting the
crystals to dancing slightly. "When are we going to
tell them?"

"Now. We can't wait. Suppose a crystal failed entirely?"

Bailey stood, drawing Ting to her feet as well.
"Let's go face the music and tell them the dancing
slippers have serious holes in them."

"Ummm," Ting answered as she trailed after Bailey. "Right."

The two girls found Gavan outside in a serious discussion with the wanderer Dokr who seemed to be
taking his leave. They hesitated at the fire ring, unsure
if they were intruding or not, but Rainwater gave them
a quick smile before clasping Dokr's hands.

"May your roads be smooth and lead always to
home," he said, and the wanderer beamed at that.

"We will return in the spring," Dokr promised, with
a short bow. "To do repairs and finish other projects
you may wish."

"That is a deal. And, if you need anything through
the winter, you have only to let us know."

Dokr smiled. "We are self-sufficient as we have

learned to depend on ourselves. Not depending on a Spirit to guide us or watch over us, we have had to be." He stepped back, then hesitated. "We are outcast because of our beliefs."

Gavan inclined his head. "As I have known and respected. So are we."

Dokr gestured. "No, that is not what I mean. I know you understand who we are, but not why, perhaps. The Spirit exists. We feel it. Others says we cannot feel it, so we reject it, but that is not our way. We *can* feel it. That is why we do not follow it." Dokr took a deep breath as if trying to keep his words from stumbling. He thumbed the crystal on his belt loop that translated his words for him. "The Warlord was a great man, but his time is gone. Like all of us, there is another place for him now, yet he resists and stays. To stay, Gavan Rainwater, he must take from all of us. I say that giving up a bit of my own soul each day is too big a price to pay for his watching over us. So I say to you, in warning, the Spirit takes. It gives, but it takes." Dokr put his hands together then, and bowed deeply, touching them to his forehead, before disappearing into the grove. After a few moments, the sound of the wagons departing could be heard, wheels rolling as hooves paced steadily pulling the loads, and the soft shouts of the children calling back in farewell.

Gavan looked after them, with a strange expression on his face.

"Whoosh," said Bailey, finally. "Maybe that explains it."

"Explains what?"

"Ting and I have been doing experiments. Our crystals are failing. Kaput. Zip. Null and void."

"Indeed?" Gavan raised one eyebrow. He sat down on a stump, stirring up the morning ashes of a nearly burned out fire. "We all grow tired. If I have taught you one thing, it's that the magic you have, you draw from within you. Crystals are only a focus, and sometimes a reservoir."

"And sometimes a leaky faucet." Bailey and Ting plunked down across from Gavan.

"Pardon me?"

"Maybe that's not what I mean. It's more like . . . there's a hole in the bucket."

Gavan leaned forward, propped on the tree branch he'd been using as a poker. "What are you talking about?"

"It's like this," Ting rushed in. "We've been testing crystals for days. Dormant ones fade a little, even though they're not being used. They shouldn't. Nothing draws on them. Charged crystals lose power at four times the rate they should when being used. So, it's not like we're drawing that much power out by ourselves. It's as if power is rushing out of them, like a full bucket that has a hole in it, when it isn't supposed to."

"Indeed." Gavan sat up, dropped his branch and brought out his cane. The wolfhead cane's crystal looked unfamiliarly dark. "We've all been working very hard. I think it would be normal to need recharging, don't you?"

Ting and Bailey shook their heads. "Not like this!" Bailey shot back. "It's like burning the candle at both ends, but we didn't light the fire to do it."

Ting shot Bailey a look, then said quietly, "Something is drawing the power off besides ourselves. We thought it might be the Dark Hand somehow, that they've learned to tap into us. But after listening to Dokr, could it be something else?"

"And that's not even what matters," Bailey interrupted. "The point is, all of us are going to reach for our crystals sooner or later and find them dead. We're going to need them and they're going to fail us when we need them most, if we're not careful."

Gavan's mouth worked a moment before he said, "I'll take this into consideration. Discuss it with Tomaz, and see if we can find a way to test it ourselves. I appreciate your efforts." He stood then, rubbing his palm over his cane. The crystal nickered as if it tried to warm and could not. He closed his hand over it, hiding it from their sight. "I'll spread the word to conserve until we have a better idea." He left Bailey and Ting at the dwindling fire.

Bailey watched a coal break in two, both halves bright orange and then cooling quickly to gray ashes as she watched. "Think he believed us?"

"Yes and no. If we're right, it could mean a lot of trouble. I don't think we need any more trouble right now," Ting finished miserably.

"The thing about trouble," Bailey said positively, "is that there's always a pot of gold to be found when it's over." She pushed rocks from the fire ring into place with the toe of her boot, banking the last of the fire carefully.

" 'Zat right?"

"Of course it is."

"Oh-kay."

Silently, they watched the fire burn down, and the yard fill with noise as the boys awoke and came out to exercise with Ting's grandmother in military control.

30

Planning

THE ACADEMY SEEMED very still with the
wanderers gone, and the incessant work on the
building slowed considerably without them. It wasn't
finished yet, but the work left they could do themselves over the winter, interior work and, as Bailey
put it, "Hopefully, warm showers." Hot showers
would have been a bit too much to expect.

Tomaz sent them outside to enjoy a warm, bright
autumn day, with baskets of crystals to charge, as well
as their own. They swapped looks at each other in
anticipation, and Jason seemed grimly satisfied.

"Do you think," Henry began in a half whisper to
him, but Jason didn't let him finish, answering, "I sure
hope so."

They worked quickly, exchanging crystals and gemstones among themselves, for they all seemed to have
preferences as to the color and composition of the
crystal that worked best for them. Trent could not
help. Instead he began to sketch a map of the magical
lines as he'd perceived them from dragonback, and
listened to their banter, his mouth twisted in a crooked
almost wistful smile when he looked up every now
and then.

Tomaz came by, Midnight on his forearm. "Good

work. Put the crystals up, and wait inside for a bit. I have to talk to Gavan, and then we'll let you know what's going on."

"Words, words, words," complained Trent, throwing himself at the kitchen table. "They're going to talk themselves to death before anything gets done."

"Plans have to be made."

Trent's fingers drummed on the table. "Talk, talk, talk."

"You're ready, then?"

"I don't know about that, but I know it's time to do *something*. Anyone can see that. Grab a sword and let's go spank these guys!"

"Swinging a sword isn't easy," argued Rich. He pointed at Stef. "Bear boy, here, can tell you that much."

"Sword work," Stefan said gravely, "is complicated and demanding, and is nothing like the swashbuckling movies you've seen. Forget any sword fight you think you've seen. They're faked. Choreographed and with anything but real weapons. Real blades are a lot heavier, for one, and one or two hits can bleed you of the strength you need to keep swinging. The moves might be similar, but the ability to carry them out is different. Beryl says my muscles are too old to remember some of it. Real blade users start when young, just like any athlete."

Rich let out a low whistle. "I think that's the most I've ever heard you say in a lifetime."

Stef reached out and cuffed the top of Rich's head. "Listen up, carrot top, this is serious stuff!"

"Yeah, yeah, big guy, you gash 'em and I'll stitch 'em up." Rich snorted and combed his hair back into place, freckles dancing in animation across his nose and cheekbones as he grimaced at Stef.

Bailey shrugged. "What do we do, then?"

"Run?"

Bailey threw an empty basket at Trent's head. Although he ducked, her aim had accounted for that and it still flew off the side of his face.

"Good shot!" Stef's face lit up in appreciation and Bailey took a bow. Trent rolled on the floor, laughing before sitting up and sticking his tongue out at her.

"I guess you can throw stuff and then run," he said, crossing his legs and leaning back.

"My suggestion is that you fight them with your strength, not theirs. These guys can ride, and they can use a short sword. They're used to crystal attacks around them, but they can't use Magick themselves, so there's a lot you can do to hit them and hit them hard." Stef folded bulky arms. "That's all the advice I have."

"Seriously, bro, I am impressed."

"I just want everybody to know that this ain't a toy." Stefan rubbed at his nose, heavily embarrassed and said not another word but stepped back, holding his sword.

"That's all right by you guys," Trent spoke into the silence. "I'd like to swing a light saber myself like the rest of you, but there's no way I can manage that, and it looks like the real thing is out for me. So where do I fit in?"

"You will probably be the guy who keeps the rest of us from getting killed. You can see the wards as they're laying them. You can spot the spells as they throw them at us. Anything Magick that comes through the air to hit, hamper, or hurt us, you're going to see. If this works at all, Trent, it'll be because of you," Jason told him.

Bailey swung her head. "And some of us have to stay home, probably, whether we can throw and run or not."

"We might not have any way of getting back if you three can't pull us, you know that." Jason looked at her.

She sighed heavily. "I know, I know, but I wanted to have fun, too."

Rich patted her on the arm. "You can have fun with me after we get back, putting all the bandages on."

"Not *that* kind of fun."

"Why not? It's fun to me."

"Well, you're strange." Bailey edged away from him.

Rich put his hands on his chest. "Wounded! And mortally, too, I think."

Ting giggled as Rich staggered back and leaned dramatically against a kitchen counter before adding breathlessly, "I agree with Bailey, though. I hate being left behind."

Heavy footsteps sounded in the hallway. "There's a reason for that," Gavan told her, as he and Tomaz entered. "They already have two of our more precious Magickers. We don't intend to hand them two more."

"I can take care of myself!" Bailey tossed her head again, ponytail swinging from side to side.

"We don't want to take that chance, and our lives are going to depend on the three of you. I don't see Henry complaining."

Henry looked up, round face emphasized by his round glasses. "It—it's just that I goof up, and I know I do. I'm better off here, out of the way." He gestured, and his brown hair seemed to go in every direction as he did.

"You don't goof up, but your Talent of Fire is pretty powerful and still needs training. None of us wants to go up in a puff of smoke." He patted Henry's shoulder. "Be that as it may," Gavan said. "Tomaz and I are finished talking. And this is what we've decided. The pieces we've been waiting for are in place, Midnight carried a message from Renart." He paused, looking over the table at each of them, one by one. "We move tomorrow. I've already sent to Avenha, asking for mounts, and they should arrive in the morning."

Stef let out a whoop. He jabbed a fist at the air. Gavan shook his head slowly at them.

"This is a dangerous situation. It may be a pitched battle like we fought at the opening of the Dragon Gate."

"And we're more ready for it than ever," Trent

said evenly. "We've all been training. We know what Jonnard and the crew are capable of. Besides," and he flashed a grin. "Madame Qi has been running our butts off."

That drew a chuckle from Tomaz despite his solemn expression. He hooked his thumb in his turquoise-and-silver belt. "You are all nearly as tall as I am now," he said, glancing at all of them. "But that does not mean I'm ready to let you take shots I should be taking. That being said, Gavan and I have talked. If anything happens, our primary instruction is to fall back to the academy and have Jason reach Khalil. We know the other Council members, we know that of all of them, even Aunt Freyah, Khalil is the most capable of handling matters here. So, protect yourselves, protect Jason. If we lose our Gatekeeper, we are trapped here."

"We all go in," stated Stefan, "we all come out."

"Hopefully." Gavan took out his map tube, and unrolled his map, laying it out in front of them. "Look it over, memorize what you can of it, so you can Crystal safely. Remember the basic rules so that no one ends up where they don't want to be." He tapped the map. "The obsidian-marked tower is the basic landmark and it's not changed much, but we don't want the fortress. We want this valley pass here, about a quarter of a day's travel from the fortress. This outcropping of rock and grove are fairly visual, plus they have an advantage of being good cover for an ambush. Midnight and Snowheart have scouted it, so Tomaz has a good mental picture of it. He'll be leading us in, but you have to remember it on your own, just in case." Gavan tapped another corner of the map. "They'll be out of reach from their own horsemen for immediate aid, and not so far that we can't regroup and get the caravan to the warehouse Renart has secured for us. It's not going to be a hand-to-hand combat, it's going to be crystal to crystal." He lifted his chin to Ting and Bailey. "On that note, let me warn you. Our young ladies here have been looking into some matters and have some statistics which indicate that crystals being used are drained of their focusing power and any magic we have charged into them about four times faster than they should be. We don't know why or, more importantly, how, but someone's tapped into the energy. Be careful. Don't overextend yourself or depend on a reservoir of charge that may not be there. Back each other up and stay in communication." He lifted his hands and let the map roll up naturally, restoring it to its tube. "Any questions?"

"Just one." Jason shifted his weight. "What if it fails?"

"If it fails, we go after Eleanora and FireAnn. And we don't look back."

"You're sure?"

Something undefinable passed through Gavan's clear blue eyes. "I've never been more sure of anything in my life."

"Good enough." He put his hand out. "Team shake."

The Magickers pushed close around the table to slap their hands on his. Jason felt the briefest moment of knowing something he had never realized before, of the unity of all of them, something he told himself time and again, but for the first time really *felt* as they all touched. Their hands dipped down on his and rose upward, as they shouted, "Magickers!"

He could not answer for anyone but himself, but he was ready.

31

Sting Like a Bee

IF ANY OF THEM SLEPT AT ALL, the before-dawn pounding at the front doors, accompanied by the wailing of the alarms woke them. Jason and Trent threw themselves downstairs, having slept in all but their boots, but they didn't beat Gavan who threw the door open in welcome. The others stampeded in behind them, crowding the threshold as it opened.

Pyra stood at the academy steps, her face tilted up toward them, her father's second-in-command Flameg at her flank. Both looked armed to the teeth and ready for anything, as she said quietly, "My father sent me in response to your call for aid."

"That can't be good," Rich muttered, then blushed to the roots of his red hair as she fixed a stare at his forehead.

"Do you question my ability?"

"No, no," Gavan interjected smoothly. "Your father does us much honor by sending his best. Rich means, I think, that . . . well, knowing of Renart's . . . hmmm . . . feelings for you, we are obliged to take good care of you."

Pyra's face glowed for a moment, and she swapped the longbow from one hand to another. "It is I who shall take care of you." She gestured a hand behind her. "We brought horses, as requested. I know only that you have a raid planned?"

"Indeed, we do. Come, sit, have tea with us, and Tomaz will sketch out the plans."

Tomaz had been standing quietly with the others, listening, but as his name was mentioned, he cast the crow he carried on his wrist skyward, freeing it for the moment, and nodded gravely in the direction of the Avenhans. "We have a plan," he said. "Any thoughts you have regarding it will be appreciated as we make ready."

"And haste is needed. The sun is barely up, but the convoy should be sent out soon."

Pyra's eyebrow lifted. "Convoy?"

"Come and we'll tell you."

In the end, it was all of them putting in suggestions, hurriedly, even as they dressed in the gear they'd put together, and Pyra left off sitting and drinking tea to help Stef affix his weapons belt and to show Rich how to tie his herb bags so they would not affect his movements. Tomaz had Jason and Trent outside going over the horses to check the length of the stirrups and the tightness of the girths, and then inspecting the hooves for small stones.

Flameg nodded at Gavan. "A bold move, but one that should set them back." A man trained for such action, his eyes shone with approval and the anticipation of a fight. This was why Mantor had sent for the Magickers. This was the reckoning for the damage to his village and others. He tightened his baldric as he spoke, in readiness.

"So we determine."

He stood, eying Pyra with the same approval. "Your women fight as ours do?"

Bailey put her chin up. "Sometimes! Today we fight from here."

Pyra said softly, "Magic has different boundaries," as if defending that decision.

Flameg gave a curt bow. "Well enough, then."

Gavan touched Ting's and Bailey's hands, and re-

peated his words of the evening, as if to take the sting
out of leaving them behind. "The moment you feel
the crystals going, reach us. Without time to test your
ideas, all we can do is rely on you two. You five here
are our anchors, our backup." His gaze swept Rebecca, Madame Qi, and Henry as well as the girls.

They nodded solemnly.

"Let's go, then."

"I hope you've got a horse big enough for me,"
muttered Stefan as they headed out the door.

"Oh, we do. I made sure I brought the fattest, stur-
diest pony in the herd." Pyra's mouth twitched.

Stef grunted, and the Avenhan gave in to the laughter shaking her shoulders as he stomped past, and she
threw Bailey and Ting a merry wink before following him.

Bailey reached for Ting's hand as she watched the
last of them go out the door. As it shut, and she heard
the muffled sounds of horses being mounted and then
ridden off, leaving them behind, she noted, "I must
be growing up. This is the first time ever I've been
truly afraid to see anyone go . . . worried that they
might not come back."

Ting squeezed her hand. "Me, too."

Ting's grandmother spoke from the other side of
the kitchen where her presence had not been noted,
and her voice startled them a little. "With age and
experience comes the ability to know sorrow and regret. It is our hope that, with our help, every generation knows less and less of it."

Rebecca entered then, holding Lacey by the scruff
of the little rodent's neck. Lacey's tufted tail hung
down dejectedly.

"This little pack rat is going to highly regret coming
into my room if she's not careful!"

"Oh! You found her! I wondered where she'd scampered off to."

"She was pillaging my jewelry box."

"Lacey!" scolded Bailey, as she liberated her from
her mother's hold. "That's a bad rodent!" Lacey man-

aged an indignant chirp as if protesting her innocence as Bailey stuffed her in her pocket.

Rebecca sat down at the table and poured a cup of tea, making a face as she drank it. "Lukewarm," she explained. "Everyone is gone, then?"

Ting nodded as she seated her grandmother at the table.

"Then," said Bailey's mom, looking eerily like an adult echo of her daughter, with her golden-brown hair in a ponytail. "Our real work begins."

"Mom?"

She looked at all of them. "Madame Qi has been teaching me a little of the Hidden Ways, and I'm here to help as well. I can do much more than be a den mother to all of you." She reached out and tweaked Bailey's nose. "Do you think that Talent in your veins just sprang up out of nowhere? I think it's run in our family for a long time, and although you got the lion's share, I am here to offer whatever I can."

Henry looked at her with unabashed admiration in his round face. "Wish my mom could say something like that."

"She probably has, Henry. You just have to know when to listen."

"Each generation builds on the other." Madame Qi nodded in agreement to her own words. "Nothing flowers that does not come from the seed of another blossom, sometime, somewhere." She laid her bamboo cane down on the table. "Now. We need to organize." In a few short moments, she had assigned watchers for the crystals, Henry to keep an eye on the academy and the Iron Mountains, and herself and Rebecca to boil water and make other preparations for wounded and to keep an eye on Bailey and Ting as they anchored. "And now," she finished. "We wait."

The Havenites from Avenha proved to have quite a sense of humor. Rich's borrowed horse was as tall and skinny and bony as Stef's was short, broad, and sturdy. He frowned at Pyra's back as she rode in front of him, her own mount sleek, well-groomed, and trained, while his seemed to jolt with every step, and even the saddle could not keep from bruising him. It was a good thing they would Crystal most of the ride. He said as much to Stef.

"At least you don't have to ride with your legs looking like a turkey wishbone being pulled in two directions!" His legs stuck out from his pony's girth, one foot headed west, the other east.

Rich shot him a wide grin. "Don't be falling off!"

"The head handles are the only things I have to hold onto." And, true to his words, Stef held one hand tightly wrapped in his pony's black wiry mane as he bounced along and the other in the reins, unable to bend his legs well enough to grip with them. He glared at Pyra's back as she rode ahead of them, her head bowed in serious discussion with Gavan and Tomaz, but he could swear her shoulders still shook now and then with laughter.

They rode just far enough to get out of the valley, beyond their own warding system, to avoid any backlash from the magical energies they planned, then Gavan circled them up, and they linked. Tomaz thought of the lands his crows had scouted. Jason got a swooping vision of dark green trees springing abundantly beside a deeply cut brook that must swell with rainwater in the early spring, the rock bed holding it was so deeply etched. He drew the crows' eye view of the site deeply inside of him to be his own guide should either Gavan or Tomaz fail to Crystal the journey.

He thought of Bailey's and Ting's warnings, tightened his own grip on his mount's reins, and then they were *between*. Frightened, the horses thrashed a bit, and around him, he could hear the very, very faint calls of each rider to calm them, and then the *between* opened into the grove, and the sound of rushing water filled his ears.

"Very good," murmured Tomaz. He dismounted immediately and led his horse around a bit to steady him. He glanced up at Gavan, adding, "We may have to fight on foot. These horses aren't used to it, while the Dark Hand has been raiding for months."

"That's a thought. We don't need to fight the horses as well. Everyone dismount, and we'll tie them off."

"I'll show you how to do breakaway ties. If anything happens to us, or the wolfjackals hit, the horse can slip the knot with enough pulling and free itself." Tomaz held up one creased hand, and they followed him, watching how he twisted the reins into a clever knot about a fallen sapling.

Then Pyra led them to the edge of the small grove, pointing down the pass, and they crouched, waiting for their prey. Above them came a low caw. Jason tilted his head back and saw a dark crow in the treetops above Tomaz, its own eyes sharply scanning the pass.

They would see the trading caravan long before it spotted them.

Unless, of course, there was magic at work.

Jonnard woke to the sounds of the harness jingling and shouts at stubborn horses and the creak of wagons being rolled into position. He lay on his bed, contemplating the day. With Isabella gone, he could delve into his father's journals again. He thought he had the full sense of what his father had done and what he could duplicate. The only problem seemed to be the draw of power. He had no wish to burn himself out, which meant he would have to steal. Nor would his uncertain ties to Henry Squibb serve the purpose. No, he would have to consider how to get the magic he needed, because it would have to be done deftly and ruthlessly.

He stood and had just finished dressing when his mother's voice rang down the hall. "Jonnard! Are you up and awake?"

He left his room, calling back, "Both, Isabella."

"Good. I've changed my mind. You're to come with us."

He shoved the disappointment out of his mind and

expression, giving a short bow from the waist. "As you wish."

Isabella straightened as he joined her, and he could not help but notice the drawn look on her face and the heavy dark circles under her eyes. More aging. Every day now seemed to wear on her, and he knew she was no closer to finding the answer. Would she escalate every moment until she became a white-haired crone, as befit her actual age? Was Magick holding her back or hurtling her forward? He could not answer any more than she could, but he saw the fear in her eyes, an emotion she quickly shuttered away as she raised her chin firmly.

"I think both of us may be needed to keep the drivers in line. I would not put it past Fremmler and the others to think of hijacking these wagons for themselves. If only one of us is there it may tempt them to think they can actually do it."

"Understood. I'll be ready to leave when you are, then." He took her hand and kissed the back of it, in the old European way, and she smiled faintly, pleased, as he took his leave.

When the time came, Jon saw that Fremmler had dressed in finer clothes, as befit the trader he'd once been, and found a razor to scrape over his face, reducing his looks from grizzled to merely scraggly. He made a note to himself of the man's reaction to being promoted somewhat, as it could be useful to both reward and keep him in line, in the future.

He mounted the bay he used for a second horse, and his mother took the wagon seat on the first, lighter caravan. Then, at her gesture, the fortress gates swung open and they set out into the early day. Dew sparkled the grass and rock rills heavily, and a coldness lay upon the earth that the sun would have to work hard to dispel later. Seasons turned here, as they did at home. Jon put up the hood on his cape, seeking a bit more warmth until that selfsame sun rose higher in the sky.

The road to Naria led down off the butte where the fortress held high ground over the river valley, and wound its way beside that river. Wagon wheel ruts lay heavily grooved into the road of dirt, and Isabella sat, jolted side to side, as the caravans made their ungainly way forward. Jon rode his horse with a grim satisfaction that he had the easy going of it from the saddle as opposed to the wagon. They were nearly two hours out of the fortress, and with the sun finally high enough he paused to drop his hood.

Isabella crooked her hand, motioning for him to come and ride by her. She squinted across the landscape.

He recognized that alert look of hers, almost hawkish. "What is it, Mother?"

"Too quiet. Altogether too quiet." She unfastened the lacy cuff of her blouse, releasing her crystal bracelet to her touch.

"Shall I ride ahead and scout?"

"I am not sure." Her fingertips ran lightly over her crystals, brilliant gemstones of incomparable worth, as well as worth their weight in Magick.

Trees lined the nearby river here, and crowded the road through the passes ahead. He saw nothing suspicious nor did he feel anything, but he readied himself to put heels to his horse's flanks to calm her worry.

A caw rang out over the quiet morning air.

"Crow!" Isabella flung up her hand, startling Jon's horse. He wheeled it in a tight circle to keep it in hand as she added, "There are no crows in Haven!"

Crystal light flared, white-hot against the brilliantly blue autumn sky. It shattered as it met lances of light from the groves, and with shouts, the Magickers attacked.

Jon's eyes picked them out. Grown from the boys he'd first met at summer camp years ago, he still knew them. He kicked his horse forward, his own crystal blade coming up as Isabella shouted orders to the raiders driving the caravan behind him. He knew the Magickers well enough to know the weaknesses that would get them killed. He bore down on the big-shouldered Stefan. Frighten the bear out of him and the animal would flee, uncontrollable. Stefan would be the first to go.

Divide and conquer.

32

Power!

STEF SAW HIM COMING. Words from Beryl ran through his head. *The best way to meet a blade on horseback is to unhorse him or go for the legs.* Reluctance to cut down an animal made him hesitate, as he felt his friends group at his back, Rich off to his right side, putting up a Shield for both of them. Jon shouted something, beckoning at a raider, even as he drew his sword clear, riding down hard at Stef.

The other rode without hands. Steel shone in his right hand and crystal flared in his left. It took Stefan aback for a second to see that, to see the mastery in the dark-cloaked figure. He knew how difficult it would be to face him on foot, now this! His bear self roared inside of him in challenge as his crystal Shield shattered under the first blow. Rich fell to one knee with a grunt, but cried out to Stef, "I'm okay, I'll have it up in a second!"

He had, but in that second, as horse hooves drummed down on him. Jon swerved at Stef, steel swinging low. He parried. The blows met, with the blades singing out in a low, hard *Thrummm!* Stef stepped back into position, and brought his blade into guard, his shoulders aching with the vibration. Jon dug a heel hard into his horse's flank, pivoting around on

one hoof and charging right at him. Stef stood his
ground. He bit his cheek until he could taste the blood
seeping out, trying to keep the bear down, but his
chest swelled with a contained roar of fury.

Something thwoshed through the air, so near it
would have sliced him if he'd so much as flinched, and
Jon veered his horse with a curse as arrows—one, two,
three—slashed past. They hit the ground, burying
themselves deeply, their shafts quivering. Jon glanced
over one shoulder, then looked back at Stefan.

Then he laughed.

A cold, chilling laughter that infuriated Stefan.

"Archers! Return fire!" Jon waved his blade, wheeling his horse about.

Stefan realized he was about as big a target as he
could be. He swiped his hand across his crystal to call
up his own Shield. It came up and settled about him
like a mirage over the desert sand, a shimmering of
light. He heard the thunk, thunk of two arrows hitting
close by, and a muffled cry.

Rich toppled over, doubled in pain, an arrow shaft
buried deeply in his thigh as Stefan turned to look.
Pyra grabbed Rich by the collar and dragged him back
as Stef stood in absolute confusion for a moment.
"Keep fighting!" she ordered. "I've got him!"

Keep fighting! He roared, and with that poured out
all his anger and frustration, and the bear prepared to
charge through after.

Jon bared his teeth in a humorless grin. "Send your
bearskin after me, boy. He's more of a coward than
you are!"

Stefan threw his head back, bellowing in anger. He
charged after Jon. He would pull him down from that
horse and pull him limb from limb! His head nearly
exploded with the beating of his heart and his skin
pulled, and pulled, until he knew it would split apart,
and the bear would come roaring out.

In mid-stride, Jason's cool voice caught him. From
the inside, not the out. The Magick coursed through

him. *Center on me, Stefan. Keep the bear asleep. Focus on me!*

Stef let the voice sink through him. It cooled the fiery-hot lava of the blood drumming through him, and his skin stopped tearing. He wrapped both hands about his sword hilt and leaped at Jon with all his might. His heavy body arced into the air as if weight meant nothing. He swung.

His blade met Magick. The air shrieked with the clash of it, steel against crystal. The shrill keening sound of it tore at his ears. He came down, all his weight on the blow, felt it sliding away noisily, even as Jon let out an *ooof* and gave way.

As Stefan hit the ground with both feet again, knees bent, pulling his sword back to parry, he saw Jon with one arm out, flailing to stay aboard his mount. Unbalanced, he began to slowly topple to the ground, and he took his horse with him, pulling it about awkwardly as he grabbed its neck with one arm. Stefan scrambled back as the horse fell with a terrified whinny, legs thrashing as it immediately tried to right itself. Before Stefan could blink or gather himself to go after Jonnard, the crystal winked and both Jon and the fallen mount disappeared, to reappear on the far side of the caravan.

Stef let loose a howl of both triumph and disappointment. He fell back to the edge of the trees, searching for Rich and Pyra. He found them where the horses were tied, Rich lying on his back, propped up on one elbow, a shred of shirt wrapped about his upper thigh, his herb bag on the ground and lying open next to him.

A frown marred Pyra's oval face. She shook her head slightly at Stefan. "He won't bleed much, but that's not the worry here." She pointed at the arrow lying on the ground beside them. "That greenish tinge on the arrowhead . . . it's blackmarrow poison."

Rich threw Stefan a slight grin. "Not to worry, big guy. It's only a little poison."

Stefan wiped his forehead with the back of his hand. He seemed to be seeing everything with a red veil over it, his heart still pounding loudly in his ears. It faded slowly. He stood over Rich, not quite understanding.

"The arrow's out, right."

"Yes, but don't touch it. There's still poison on it." Pyra pulled a small vial from her own herb pouch, tapping it into the water cup Rich held. She had to lean over and hold Rich's hand to keep it steady. "Drink that. It will stave off the worst effects for a while."

Rich drained the wooden cup in three gulps and shuddered, making a horrible face. Stef could only imagine how bad the stuff must taste. "How long a while?" Rich's red hair was the only thing of color about him. Shock had sent him as pale as Stef had ever seen him.

"Long enough," Pyra answered tersely. She closed her herb pouch and picked up her bow. "Stay awake and don't let anyone handle that," she ordered. "Stefan. They're still fighting out there."

"But, Rich—"

"I'll be right here. You'll have to come to me when ya get hurt, I can't crawl all that fast." Rich tried to screw his face into a smile, but he just looked all the more pained.

"Not funny."

"Yeah." Rich met his eyes. He nodded slowly. "They need you, big guy. Get out of here. I'll be waiting and I want to know what's happening!"

"Okay," said Stefan slowly. Something knotted in his stomach.

Rich put his hand up. "I'll link my crystal to yours, give you an extra kick."

Stefan didn't intend to let Jonnard get far, Magick or not. "That's a deal." He broke into a lumbering run, heading back to the righting field.

Jason felt and heard Stefan nearing the edge, but he could not spare a look. The touch he'd braided into

Stef grew fainter and fainter, like an insubstantial rope drawn thinner and thinner until nothing was left but a slight wisp. Reality replaced touch as Stef thumped him on the shoulder, saying, "Thanks."

"How's Rich?"

"Okay, but not good." Stef gave a bewildered grunt as if to emphasize his words, but Jason had no time to ask him for more. The Dark Hand hit him with all their considerable might and he reeled back into the other's arms. He shook the stun off as he straightened.

"Just keep hitting 'em. They'll break, there's only two, and then we've got the caravan! But watch your crystal, don't drain it out."

Stef rubbed his nose. He sheathed his sword. "Gotcha."

Jason narrowed his eyes and brought up both hands, each filled with his crystals. The lavender one seemed warmer than ever, and he wondered if it was because it had already been through a war of wizards and magic. It knew the devastation.

Trent wiggled his way next to Jason. He rubbed his eyes. "They've got Tomaz and Gavan pinned down, but I think I got them out of the webbing."

"Pretty bad?"

"It was." Trent scanned the trampled meadow in front of them. "I'd say they're trying the same on you." He traced lines only he could see through thin air. "Net isn't closed yet, but they're trying."

"Show me where, one string at a time, and I'll cut it." Jason's eyes sparkled with the idea. "The game here is to run their defenses into the ground, and then take the wagons. Once the crystals are gone, they haven't much chance if ours hold out."

"Let's play follow the leader, then." Trent sketched across the sky. Jason followed the movement of his hand, and swept a crystal blade through it, like trying to cut an invisible thread. A triumphant whoop from Trent told him he'd done it.

Trent's hands hopscotched across his field of vision, plucking and pulling at lines of magic Jason could only barely sense. Sometimes it took four or five attempts to bring down one casting, but more often he could get it in one or two tries. The fighting around him seemed to retreat to slow-moving visions that he barely saw as he concentrated. A look to one side showed Stefan with Shield up, and crystal in his knobby fist, blond face streaked with dirt and frown, growling at raiders as they attempted to close on them, and he drove them back.

A knot of fighters bore down on Gavan. He stood in a swirl of his cape, crystal Lightning in his hand. Flameg nocked an arrow to his bow and moved in on his flank protectively. Gavan loosened his Lightning and two men dropped. The third one he met hand to hand, while the fourth went after Flameg. He got his arrow off and it hit deep into the raider's leg, but even the cry of pain as it hit did not slow the swing of the outlaw's blade. It hit Flameg square, and the Avenhan fell to his knees, then sagged to the ground in a spray of blood. Jason looked aside, afraid of being sick. He barely caught the sense of what Trent said, flustered, and managed to focus on the last of the web about him.

The last thread of magic ensnarement cut, Jason rose to his feet, and grabbed Trent by the arm.

"We're going after Jonnard."

"Now?"

Jason looked at him. "There's a better time? We press him; either he'll drain his power or she will trying to save him. We haven't much left ourselves."

Thwoosh. Trent dodged an arrow, spun about on one heel, and shrugged. "I guess not!"

Jason threw up a Shield and locked arms with Trent. He gestured at Tomaz, indicating which way they were heading. The elder Magicker hesitated, then gave an agreeing nod. They zigzagged their way through the fighting. Raiders had fallen and lay silent, their bodies stunned by crystal shock or pierced by arrows. Jonnard saw them coming. He reined his horse back sharply, and the horse went back on his haunches, one hoof pawing the air in protest.

Jason struck. He did not wait for fairness or for Jon to acknowledge the duel or anything else. Their fight had started long before this one.

Crystal stroke met crystal in a blaze of sparks, the air sizzling with the noise and sheer impact of it. Jason did not wait to take a breath before striking again, hard, and again the Magicks met in an explosion of energy. Let the Dark Hand think he would kill Jonnard if he could. He knew the other had no such doubts.

His crystals cooled slightly in his hands. Ruthlessly, he reached back along their anchors, back to Ting and Bailey and Henry to tap their resources.

"Jason." Trent put his hand on his arm. "Jason! I can see it . . . Jon is tied into Henry again. He's draining him. You can't do it, too. You'll kill him."

"Show me!"

Trent gulped. His hands swung about aimlessly in front of him, as though signing an impossible message, then, "Here! I've got it!" He held his hands out as though the string were woven through them.

Jason reached out with one crystal, blading it, and swung the edge through Trent's hands. A zzzzt and then a sense of letting go as the strand parted. He had it! He knew it without Trent telling him. Poor Henry, ensnared again, and without even knowing it!

Jonnard let out a curse of frustration and savagely reined his horse around, wheeling to the far side of the first wagon, leaving Jason to look up into Isabella's haughty and furious expression. The rubies and other gemstones at her wrists and neck blazed with her anger. Here and there, a blackened stone hung in its setting, ruined and lost to her Magick. She raised her hand and pointed at Jason.

"Uh-oh," said Trent in his ear. "Incoming!"

Jason pulled Trent to his knees, and dropped himself, shifting all his energy to a defensive Shield. Fire

and rage poured down on them as though dragonfire
spewed from her hands, beating down until Jason's
whole body trembled in the effort to keep the Shield
up to protect them. He held the shimmering buckler
up out of sheer will, and watched her drain herself.
Then she cried out harsh words, and in the blink of
an eye, Jonnard disappeared.

Jonnard stood inside the threshold to the dungeon.
The air stank of the Leucators, filling his lungs for a
moment, his pulse racing with the adrenaline of the
fight and Isabella's hoarse cry in his ears to do something. A weakness tremored through his body. His link
to Henry severed, that mongrel pup Jason sapping
him . . . He palmed his crystal, centering his thoughts.
If he did nothing, they would lose the caravan and the
defeat alone might set the raiders against them.

Now or never, and if it were to be done, it would
be better to be done quickly. Jonnard smiled grimly
at the words of the old Bard of Avon running through
his head. His father had told him, once, that Shakespeare had seen him do Magick and often wondered
if Oberon were based on that sight.

The Leucators got to their feet, chains and shackles
rattling eerily, like a crashing wave of metal upon
metal. They eyed him hungrily. If they only knew what
he had planned for them. They alone had the reservoir
he needed.

He grasped their essence with his mind. He pulled
on the magickal energies they held within themselves,
mere shadows of the people from whom they'd been
cloned, but still potent to a degree. They filled him
with a fiery glow. Like the rush of water from a broken dam, they poured into him. He'd miscalculated
how much they had to offer. He felt the power growing inside of him until his own skin felt too tight, and
he thought he must burst with the sheer frenetic energy of it. His hand about the crystal shook as he
fought to contain what he took from them.

This, then, was their secret. Spawned by Brennard

and Isabella, they were themselves what he sought. As
he held them, he knew them.

He mastered them. The Leucators sank to their
knees as he drained them, pulled all he wanted from
them, and left them with precious little. Magick foun-
tained inside of him, and he raised both hands then,
reaching for what he wanted, seeing it, placing it.

Then, with a deep breath, Jonnard summoned it.
He felt the sudden, shocking emptiness of Magick ex-
ploding out of it, the icy coldness of its absence, the
harsh shock wave lashing back at him. It slammed him
back on his heels, throwing him into the wooden
frame of the dungeon door. He let out a gasp of pain
as his shoulder crunched, but the doorjamb kept him
from falling entirely, as his body went limp.

His mind reeled. It tumbled over and over with
emptiness, with thoughts that bloomed and fled too
quickly for him to comprehend them. They tore
through his mind, a thousand possibilities and more,
and he felt as helpless as a leaf in a hurricane. Then
all came to a halt. Quiet, and trembling. In that moment, he felt as weak as a newborn, as though he'd
touched time itself.

Jonnard straightened. He dropped his hands. His
skin, always pale, seemed ashen. He flipped one hand
through his hair, pushing it off his brow.

Had he done what he thought? If not . . . what had
he done? He took an unsteady step forward, realizing
the fortress walls were gone. The sound of the river
and the wind washed over him, but the battlefield was
gone, left behind or left ahead, he could not be certain
where. The wagons creaked in restless movement, and
the living watched him fearfully.

He had moved the caravan. That much, he'd accomplished. The horses whinnied and shuddered in their
harnesses, eyes rolling whitely, as the drivers held onto
their headstalls and tried to calm them. Isabella dismounted, her eyes narrowing. "What have you done?"
She gestured across the field.

His gaze followed her hand wave. There, in a hollow

of ground, a maelstrom of darkness and fog boiled up. He'd brought the whole scene with him, bodies and all, and the dead slid across the ground and disappeared into the pit. It pulled at him, and he took a step closer, even as Isabella grabbed his elbow with a warning cry. "Don't."

"Look. Look at that!"

"What have you done?" She toyed with the necklace about her throat, unaware that most of the priceless gems upon it were now blackened and useless. She stared at him.

"It's a Gate. I've opened you a Gate." And he shook her off impatiently, eager to see the handiwork he'd wrought. A wind wailed down through the small valley, carrying what seemed to be voices on it. He neared it. It knew him, as he knew it. Where it went, he did not know. The sheer force of opening it had drawn the convoy to its mouth, and it yearned for them, yawned for them. Even as he neared it, he felt instinctively what Isabella had. The veil over it parted, torn by its seething inner action, and he saw it clearly then, a dark gash into the earth filled with bones and skulls, tumbling about as if caught in a maelstrom. The Leucators thrashed inside of it, disappearing and re-forming. He stared at it in fascination, unsure of it.

Chaos poured out of it. "Drink of that, my mother," he said to Isabella. "And our power here will never pale."

"Only if I dare."

"I dare," he said. He put his hand out, palm outward and drew upon that which he had made. Just a touch of it jolted him, and he shut off the contact quickly, composing himself. It held a Magick unlike any he'd ever felt before, and he was wise enough to know he might not be the master of it. Caution, then, until he learned the Gate well. He stepped back to Isabella's side.

She stared at the Gate of Bones for a long moment, then caught the hem of her skirt in one hand.

"I want the Magickers punished for their impudence."

"Of course." Jonnard bowed in her direction. "I will see to it."

She mounted a free horse and reined him off eastward after a moment's contemplation of her crystal. The convoy bumped and jolted into movement after her.

Jonnard's mouth twitched.

She had not dared to drink of the power as he had. She could sense it as he could, and she'd been afraid she could not master it at all.

His time was nearing.

33

Aftershock

THE BLAST SLAMMED Jason on his back, knock-ing the wind clean out of him. He lay gasping, staring up at the sky, feeling the Magick roar around him in utter Chaos, then it was sucked back and ... Gone. He rolled to his side, clawing for air, his body frozen, not breathing and screaming for it. All around him was ... nothing. Every shrub or tree, every blade of grass for a hundred-yard radius about him lay flattened.

Not a wagon, horse, or person, dead or alive, could be seen except for Trent at his feet who lay making guppy noises. What had happened? His body fought to breathe, chasing thoughts away except for the weakness that seeped through him, and the wonder of it. Opening a Gate could feel like this. But he hadn't done it. So why? And why had the Magick smacked him down? And what had it done with the Dark Hand? Were they ... gone?

Jason finally squeaked down a sliver of air and sat up. He nudged Trent's shoulder with his boot toe. "Relax." He couldn't say much more than that, but he'd had the wind knocked out of him before and knew that once the solar plexus relaxed, they'd both be breathing again. It was the hit, the shock of it, that sent the body into temporary paralysis.

That didn't make it any more fun. He hung his head over, whooped a few times, and finally got the circulation going. Jason wobbled to his feet. Trent flopped over like a hooked fish. After a splutter, he managed a long gasp of air.

"Smackdown," he muttered. "What the hell was that?"

"I don't know. Yet." Jason looked around, unable to believe what he could not see. Perhaps the whole convoy had been Crystaled, but it would never have created a backlash like the one they'd felt. It was as if Jonnard or Isabella had loosed a magickal atomic bomb or something. Or they had. Did Gavan dare to use resources the others never suspected? He scrubbed a hand through his hair, and resettled his headband into place.

A wail of mourning sounded behind him and Jason turned about. Figures rising slowly from beside the river and the band of trees along it where they had begun their ambush. The devastation ended there, as if the countryside had withstood it, or perhaps the Magickers' presence inside it had protected it. Pyra went to one knee, gathering up the shattered remains of Flameg's longbow from the autumn-burned grasses. Her voice wailed with primal grief. She clutched the broken weapon to her chest and stifled her cry to one soft murmur, then silence. She looked up, her face streaked with tears.

"Not even his body! How can I bury him? How can we honor him?"

"We will make sure he is remembered. We can do no less for a friend and ally!" Gavan's voice rang out reassuringly across the devastation. He and Tomaz emerged from the grove, each with a fistful of reins, leading nervous horses onto the battlefield. Though no bodies remained, their nostrils widened at the smell of blood and ruin. "We'd best get out of here before the wolfjackals show. I don't want another fight, just yet," Gavan added, weariness wavering his voice slightly.

"Eleanora? They're gone, right? They whacked

themselves." Trent rubbed the flat of his stomach ruefully as he found words.

"What did happen?"

Gavan looked at Jason, then shook his head slightly. "We don't know what happened here. If they'd destroyed themselves, I would feel Eleanora immediately, and I can't. Whatever that was that happened, we didn't do it, so I have to assume they did. I can't, I *won't,* leave her. If it's to be war here, regardless of the price to be paid, I'll free her first. We need to go in with full power, and surprise. If they retreated, then they still have their deal to carry out. They have a day or two to get that caravan into Naria, and negotiate and sell. We have a day, then, to act." He swung up.

Stefan approached them, half carrying, half supporting Rich who limped heavily and seemed to find each step a painful, gasping effort. His face looked deadly pale.

Pyra stowed the only remains she had of her old friend and teacher. "He needs to see Kektl, as soon as possible. That's blackmarrow poison in him, and what I gave him will help, but—" she paused. Then she repeated emphatically, "He must see Kektl as soon as possible."

"How bad is it?"

"Arrow wound," said Rich through pinched lips. "I'd like to say, 'tis but a flesh wound, but it feels like my blood's on fire."

"Tomaz, you can get him to Kektl? I have to meet with Renart and get Pyra back to Avenha."

Stefan said stoutly, "Rich isn't going anywhere without me." He shot an accusing glance at Pyra. "He isn't going to die, is he?"

"No," she answered. "Not yet." She would not meet anyone's glance at that, looking aside. Stef grunted.

"Nothing is gonna happen to you, Rich. I'm like . . . like Samwise."

Rich managed a chuckle. "Big guy, you look like almost anything but a hobbit gardener." He sucked his breath in sharply then, both hands going to his leg and knotting, as if he could grip the pain away.

"No time to waste." Gavan motioned Jason and Trent to his side. "Stay with me." Then, in a shimmering of crystal fire, the two groups went their separate ways.

Every bone in Rich's body ached and throbbed, and he could feel every single pulse of his heartbeat, for it swelled and exploded in pain, and he knew he must be sweating like Niagara Falls. Every movement, jolt, thought, touch echoed violently through his tall, thin frame. Even Stefan's hold keeping him upright was almost more than he could bear. Blackmarrow poison—what Pyra had called it—sounded bad. Really bad. Ironic. All his life he'd been taught to be afraid of getting sick and having allergies, and it was a poison that had gotten him.

They touched down in Kektl's Narian backyard, where the shed and pool rested, and Stefan gently put him down on one of the stump chairs, while he and Tomaz went to find the healer. Rich stared at the bloody tear in his pants, thinking that it hadn't really been much of a wound. Luckily it wasn't deep enough to sever anything major or bleed him to death, and nothing that muscle couldn't heal later. He wondered if he poured a bottle of hydrogen peroxide on it, how badly it would fizz. He wasn't sure if poison would set off the peroxide. It seemed to react mainly to surface contamination, but it was fun to watch.

Rich sighed and immediately groaned. There wasn't a spot inside or outside of his body that didn't ache fiercely. He leaned back against the small fence that surrounded Kektl's little home and garden and wished that Stef would hurry back.

Quickly.

The little garden grew blurry and danced about him, and then slowly he sagged down on the tree stump and everything slipped away.

He came to, sputtering, as someone poured the

most disgusting drink he'd ever tasted in his life down his throat.

"Easy, easy now," came Kektl's stern but soft voice. "Drink it, and to the last drop."

Rich found he had little choice as Kektl's hand closed upon his mouth and insistently poured in the awful goo. He swallowed it all and waved both hands in protest as he did, unable to see much beyond the healer's face, although he could hear Stefan's low rumbling protest off to the side somewhere and Tomaz's dry laugh.

Kektl let go.

"Gah!" Rich sat up like a drowning man breaking the surface of the water that tried to claim him. "What *is* that stuff?"

"An acquired taste, and, I fear, what will keep you alive the rest of your days. Three times a day, I prescribe."

Rich shuddered over and over as the cold, sickeningly sweet thick stuff penetrated his body. "Ugh. I think I'd rather die."

"Don't say that!" Stefan thumped the side of his head.

Rich gave one last, hard shudder. "You taste it, then see if you agree." He blinked several times. The pain and burning in his body began to recede as if nothing could stand up to the awful taste of the potion. Kektl eyed him curiously. "Feeling any better?"

"Well. . . ah . . . actually. Yes."

"Good." Kektl sat, putting his hands on his bony knees, and staring into Rich's face. "There isn't any cure for blackmarrow poison that I am aware of. All I can do is keep it at bay, make sure it does as little damage every day as I can. You take that potion regularly, and you will live a long life yet. In the meantime, herbalists such as I will dabble and test, and perhaps come up with something better."

"I say we take him home."

Kektl sat back. "If you can return to such a place, perhaps. I am not one for the crossing of worlds, so I cannot tell you if the poison will get better or worse elsewhere. I can only tell you what I can do here."

Tomaz shifted his weight and approached Rich. He put his thick, callused hand on his forehead, checking for temperature. He nodded to Rich. "You look better. How difficult is it to make this potion up?"

"Not difficult. Few of us know the ingredients, but as I am the one who devised it—" Kektl grinned slyly. "I think we can make accommodations. The herbs are easily gathered, although an unlikely brew. You, Rich, show much skill and aptitude. I hate to lose a student untimely."

"He can't just drink something all the time to stay alive!"

Kektl gave Stefan a mild look. "And why not? I do."

"But . . . but . . ."

Kektl inclined his head. "Who should know black-marrow poison better than one who carries it within him?" He leaned forward and patted Rich on the knee. "From time to time, you may have to take more of the potion, or less. Your body will tell you. And, if the spirit graces us, we'll find a better antidote." He stood. "For now, I'll leave you with your friends, while I make up a batch and ready a scroll for you on how to prepare it yourself."

Tomaz murmured, "We thank you, healer," as Kektl moved past him. The Havenite smiled and shook Tomaz's hand in encouragement.

Stefan sputtered in barely contained frustration. "Are you going to put up with that?"

"I feel better. Why should I argue?" Rich slowly got to his feet. His leg sent a sharp pain through him, reminding him that there was a wound there, even if the poison had receded greatly. He leaned on Stef's stout, square frame. "See this house? The gardens? The pool? Kektl has this nice little place because he's a good healer. He can help when no one else can."

"I still think we should get you home."

Rich nodded. "We will. Just remember what can

happen when: one—my body is tested for an absolutely unknown poison induced by an obvious wound suffered in some kind of warfare, and two—my body also tests for odd mental powers which can't be accounted for."

"Unfortunately, he's right," noted Tomaz.

"But, Rich—"

"No buts, big guy. Going home could be more lethal than drinking that awful stuff a few times a day." Rich poked him in the ribs. "I don't want to be anybody's lab experiment, do you?"

"No, but still . . ." Stef took a big breath, and shut his mouth, his expression screwed into a grumpy mask.

Rich scooped up the empty mug. "Here . . . try a drop."

Stef's nose wrinkled. "No way."

Rich laughed. "Sometimes you're just no fun!"

"Me?" Stef started to protest, then looked up and saw Kektl headed toward them from the rear of his cottage, his hands filled with what appeared to be a doctoring kit. "Looks like the fun is about to start again."

Kektl gestured at him. "That wound has to be cleansed and stitched. Let's get started."

Rich paled again and sat down abruptly at the sight of needles and thread. Stef crossed his arms over his broad chest in satisfaction.

"Pyra!" Renart darted out of the warehouse door, his face glowing with surprise and happiness, and he caught up the girl in an immense hug and swung her around. Protesting faintly, her face all a-blush, she pushed him away, saying, "Renart! Custom, please!"

"Ah." He cleared his throat and dusted himself off, straightening his dignity, reminding Jason ever so much of an embarrassed cat grooming itself to regain composure. "It's just that it's so good to see you." He took a second look, and then saw the dirt streaks and grime and disarray on them all. "Pyra?" He shot a worried look at her. She turned her face away. "No caravan, and it does not look like it went well."

"It did not," Gavan told him.

He wrung his hands once. "What happened?"

"They slipped our grasp. We are not sure how, but they're bound to come looking for revenge."

"Understood. Losses?"

"Six raiders." Pyra's voice choked slightly. "Flameg. And one of the boys, poisoned."

Renart frowned heavily. "Flameg? Dead?"

She nodded.

"I'll arrange a cart for the body."

"There is no body."

His eyebrows fluttered. "But—" He paced. "All right, then. I'll make sure you've an escort to Avenha, Pyra. I won't let you travel alone at a time like this."

She clenched her jaw. "I will see them dead for this!"

"No. No, a sight like that is too awful for any of us to see. There will be vengeance in its own time. In the meanwhile, you have to make sure Flameg is remembered in the village." He touched her wrist briefly.

She put a hand to her bag, where the shattered remains of Flameg's longbow had been stowed. "He won't be forgotten."

Gavan shifted his weight. "You need to cover your own tracks, Renart. Isabella is shrewd. Once she has gotten her deal, she will begin to sift for any who've helped us. She'll know the ambush was planned. You didn't rent this warehouse openly?"

"No, of course not. Tomaz and I discussed that. I should not be implicated." Renart took his eyes from Pyra and looked at Jason and Trent, then Gavan. "You're the ones who will feel her anger."

"I'm prepared for that. You'll get Pyra home?"

Renart touched her hand again. "If she allows me."

Pyra tried to smile. "Some company would be good."

"Done, then. Go with the Spirit watching, Gavan friend, and I will ask him to keep the Dark Hand from your door."

Gavan made a wry face. "If only it were that easy." He lifted his hand, as he nodded to the boys.

34

No, Henry!

THE MOMENTS CREPT by, and sitting at the table helping Ting make crystal jewelry didn't seem to help, even with Henry telling them both tales of home—good and bad—and trying to ease the waiting. All of them could sense the slow drag on their own Talents as the others tapped them for a bit of oomph now and then, but they couldn't tell what was happening! Bailey kicked an impatient foot against the table leg.

"I feel like the blind man with a racehorse!" Bailey complained.

Henry pushed up his glasses to consider her. "I think that's the blind men with the elephant," he said slowly. "If you're talking about perceptions and how deceiving they can be. You know, one of them feels the tail and thinks the elephant is thin as a rope, another feels a leg and says, no, he's big as a tree, and the other feels the trunk and says, no, he's wiggly as a snake . . ."

She tossed her head. "I'm talking about being ready to ride off, but I can't see where I'm going!"

"Oh. Okay, then." Henry reached down and exchanged a wire cutter for a long-nosed pair of pliers, so he could imitate Ting's quick movements and twist a wire cage into place about the crystal shard he held.

"I just don't think it's fair to get left behind," Ting said. She put a bracelet down in front of her and jangled the crystals, making a pleasant chime. They warmed at her slight touch. "I feel like I never get to help."

"These are helping." Henry swept his hand over the table at all the translucent stones they had imbued with power. "They need us to anchor, too."

"They were already charged. We're just sitting here doing monkey work! We should be out there, helping."

Henry shifted uneasily. "I don't know. I mean, Gavan's right, he doesn't want everyone out there, he doesn't want Isabella to have any more hostages. And . . . and . . . well, for myself . . . I don't trust myself."

Ting's almond-shaped eyes fixed on him. "What do you mean?"

"I mean that sometimes, I think . . . I'm afraid that Jonnard can still link with me. Sometimes I get this awful feeling. It's like getting slimed. I worry that he can get to me again, and know everything we're doing, and I won't be able to stop him."

"Henry, we'd never let that happen to you again."

"I don't think it's anything we can stop," he said sadly. He put the final twist on a cage holding a gemstone and examined it.

"We might not be able to stop his trying, but the minute you know he's doing it, we can stop that. We can." Ting folded her hand over the top of his and squeezed.

Henry turned bright red—from her words and touch—and blinked hard once or twice before sliding his hand away from hers.

Bailey opened her mouth as if to say something, then shut it. Instead, she swung her head, bouncing her ponytail from side to side. She stopped abruptly. "They're pulling on my power," she announced quietly.

Ting and Henry nodded. They began to sort through other objects and start a new bracelet to assemble, their fingers busy even as their minds dealt with the feeling of something at the edges nibbling away at them. Suddenly, Ting dropped everything.

"It's just so not fair. Jason has his dragon. We ought to have something, too."

"Or at least be able to have the dragon when he doesn't. If we had the dragon here, helping us defend the academy, no one would dare try anything. He wouldn't even have to do anything, just sit up and look dragonish."

"He would be awesome, wouldn't he?" Ting stood up on hearing Henry's words. "I'm going to go find him."

"Ting, we're on duty here."

"By the time something awful happens, it'll be too late to go get help. Why wait? We know he's around somewhere."

"I don't know," answered Bailey slowly. "I'm always the one who gets in trouble, but I don't think this is a good idea."

Ting looked stubborn. "I can't ignore it. I've been dreaming of our house dragon, and he's long gone, away in another world, but I know we've a dragon here, and that must mean something. It could be important, Bailey, as important as anything you're always going after."

"This is true." Henry looked from Ting to Bailey and back again.

Bailey sighed. "I know. But . . ." She shook her head. "It just feels *wrong*."

"You won't go with me to help look?"

"Nope."

"I'll go!" Henry jumped to his feet. His glasses slid almost off his nose as he did, and he hastily rearranged them.

"I can't believe you won't come."

The two girls stared at each other a long moment. Bailey shifted uneasily in her chair. "I can't either," she said finally, "but I won't. I'll stay here."

"If I find him, and he agrees to help, can I call you a big wuss?"

Bailey gave a lopsided grin at that. "Sure! As long as you're okay."

"Deal, then." Ting turned to Henry. "Come on. I know just where Jason climbs up on the Iron Mountain, sometimes. We should find him there."

Henry shadowed her out the door, saying, "What are you going to do?"

"Not sure yet, but I'll think of something!"

Their voices got faint as they disappeared outside, around a corner of the academy. Bailey stared out the kitchen door, then bit her lip thoughtfully. She had to go with her gut feeling, and that told her to stay put. She shuffled her boots under the kitchen table, and bent her head over the crystals, arranging them back and forth, feeling rather odd.

Outside, gray clouds scuttled in and hung close about the Iron Mountains and the academy. It would rain in a day or two or maybe even late that evening. Ting and Henry could feel the pressure building in the air. Tilting her face up, she pointed out the area of the mountain range where Jason often climbed, and started up. Henry, puffing a bit and paling more every moment, took a deep breath before following after her. Halfway up, she realized that Henry was nowhere near her. Ting looked under her elbow. He clung to a small boulder a good half a city block behind her, panting for breath.

"Are you all right?"

"I'm really tired." His face stayed pale, though she could see his chest heaving as he struggled to breathe.

"Stay there, then. It's just a tiny bit farther. I can shout if I need help."

He nodded and brought up the edge of his shirt to pat his face dry of sweat. Poor Henry. They must be tapping his power faster than hers. Still, by the time she gained the flat top of the hill, she was breathing hard, too, and had to stand for a moment to catch her own breath. Then she wondered how she planned to catch the dragon's attention.

It seemed undignified to shout, "Here, dragon!" nor did she think he'd respond to it. And, after all, it was Jason's dragon, if a dragon could truly be said to belong to anyone at all. This one couldn't. He came and went as he pleased and, if anything, Jason belonged to him, rather than the other way around. She tucked a long, dark wing of hair behind her ear. What to do?

"How does one call a dragon?" she said aloud, to no one but herself, and wished she'd insisted on Bailey coming along. Bailey would be full of ideas, even if most of them would be wrong, she was bound to have the right one stuffed in there somewhere. Bailey was like that.

"That depends on how polite you are," rumbled a deep voice behind her.

Ting turned around with a gasp, caught her heel on a stubborn bit of rock, and went down on her rump. The dragon lay down on his stomach to look at her closer, asking, "All right, are you? Did I scare you?"

"Of course you scared me! How can someone so . . . large . . . sneak up so quietly?"

The dragon chuckled. It sounded like faraway thunder on a hot summer night, and rather smelled like it, too. Faraway lightning, or something. He wiggled his whiskers at her. "Jason told you I considered young adventurers as appetizers, I see."

"He's mentioned it once or twice. In case he never comes back."

"I am astounded." The dragon, however, looked far from astounded, although he did look a wee bit curious as Ting clambered to her feet and dusted herself off. "If he did, then you must have risked a lot to climb up looking for me. What is the occasion, may I ask?"

"Help. Defense, actually," and Ting pointed down off the plateau at the academy below them.

"Are you under attack? I rather got the impression it was the other way around, that your lot was off attacking someone else."

"No, and yes, and well, they deserved it."

"Mmmmmm." The dragon let out a long, rumbling purr of thought. Then he said flatly, "No."

"No what?"

"No, I will not come to your defense."

Ting stared at him. "Why not?"

"First of all, it should be obvious that you're not under attack. At the moment, anyway. Secondly, and this is a bit more difficult to explain, I have a truce with this world. I come and go as I please, but I do not meddle. I rarely allow myself to be seen, and I do not use my powers in any way at all, if I can help it."

"But you're our friend! Jason's friend. How can you do this?"

The dragon sat up, and laced his long claws together. He said mildly, in his very deep bass voice, "I do not need to explain myself to you."

"Yes! Yes, you do!" Ting cried. "The Dark Hand is a terrible, awful group of people. They've been raiding and killing for months, and we're the only ones who can stand up to them, and if that doesn't deserve your help, then I don't know what does!"

"Ting," called a raspy voice behind her. "Please don't shout at the dragon." Henry staggered onto the edge of the plateau, his face absolutely gray with effort.

"Very good advice," observed the beast in question. "But, here, I feel obligated to explain myself although I normally do not have to. It's a matter of treaty, and negotiation, and tradition. I am not the Power of the world, so I am here by sufferance. I am friends with the Powers that be here, but I neither help nor hinder them. Surely you have friends like that in your old world?"

Ting's mouth worked soundlessly for a moment or two, trying to understand just what the dragon meant, when Henry said, "Switzerland."

"Switzerland?" Ting repeated incredulously.

"Yeah. They've been neutral for centuries. Everyone respects that." Henry staggered up to stand with her. He fought for breath as he did so, and wiped his face with his hand.

"So . . . Jason's dragon is like Switzerland?"

"He is, if he says he is." Henry nodded emphatically.

"There," said the dragon. "I do hope that explanation is satisfactory."

Ting stared at one and then the other, and realized she was getting no place. "Not really," she answered him. "But I guess it will have to do. It doesn't explain at all why I keep dreaming about my house dragon, and what it all has to do with me. I was so sure it meant I was supposed to talk you into helping." Ting gestured in frustration and bewilderment.

"Ahhhhh," rumbled the dragon. "You dream, do you?"

"We all dream. Just sometimes it seems really important, and it's nearly impossible to understand."

"Well," the dragon murmured, dipping his snout close to Ting, and lowering his great voice as if talking to her and her alone, although Henry plainly stood at her elbow. "These things come from within, don't you think?"

"I think—" Ting began, just as Henry let out a loud whimper and crashed to the ground at her feet. "Henry? Henry!"

He gasped, "Jonnard," as his eyes rolled up in his head and he passed out cold. Ting screamed.

35

Gate of Dread

IT FIGURES," mourned Bailey. "The one time I don't go with you, and something really interesting happens. I've always wanted to travel by dragon. It seems so much faster."

Ting was hanging from one claw, and Henry's limp body from the other, while Bailey looked up at them, hands on her hips, the dragon treading air as though he were in a swimming pool, his wings fluttering above them. Ting thought she was going to hurl from the bouncing, the uneven bobbing up and down. "That's not helping any," she moaned.

Bailey spread her hands out. "I can't catch you both. I say jump, and we'll both catch Henry."

Ting moved around inside the dragon's clutch and he loosened his grip a little. She crouched, looking at the ground which seemed a lot farther away than she wanted it to be. "Okay. Ready." She swallowed. The dragon opened his claws and she jumped.

He released Henry at nearly the same time, his limp body tumbling through the air, and both of them collided with Bailey. The three of them went down with an ooof and a grunt and a groan. For a moment, Ting wasn't sure where she ended and the other two began.

Bailey began to laugh as she tried to crawl out from under them.

"What . . . is . . . so . . . funny?" Ting pulled her long hair away from her face with both hands.

"I'm not sure," Bailey told her. "It just *is*. It's about time someone else got in trouble!" She dug Henry out as well. "He's out like a light. What happened?"

"I'm not sure. He seemed weaker and weaker, and then he collapsed, talking about Jonnard." Gently, Ting took Henry's glasses off his face. "Think Jon got to him again?"

"Maybe." Bailey put two fingers to her mouth and let out a piercing whistle. "We've got to do something. The crystals are all muddied, though." She frowned as the dragon landed nearby, following Ting's lead.

"Dragon," Ting stated as she felt Henry's too cold face. "This is the kind of thing they do. They take over your thoughts, your mind. They don't care what they do to anyone!"

"I can see that," the great beast said. His voice sounded a bit sorrowful amidst its low boom. "That does not change the pact I have agreed to. I will not interfere."

"If you're not with us, then you're against us," Bailey said harshly. She flipped her ponytail back and tried to haul Henry's limp body into a more comfortable position.

The dragon considered Bailey closely, and Bailey had the grace to blush a little. "Well," she said defensively, "you know what I mean."

"Unfortunately, I do. I leave you with this, then . . ." And he put out a talon that sizzled as if hot and etched Ting's open hand. "A key to be used for that you need most, Ting, if you've the courage to use it. As they like to say in those epic stories Jason talks about, use it when things seem darkest."

Ting jumped as if burned or branded, and closed her hand tightly, staring at the great dragon. Rebecca and Madame Qi hurried out of the academy in answer to Bailey's piercing whistle, both women letting out sounds of worry as they saw Henry lying on the ground.

"What happened?"

"He collapsed. He was being drained, and he just . . . fell over."

Rebecca knelt beside him, her hand on the boy's neck. "He seems all right now, though very weak. I can't believe Gavan would let anyone draw off Henry like this."

"Jonnard would," Bailey said bitterly.

Madame Qi knelt by Rebecca and Henry's still form. "There are many forces at work here," she said in her quiet way. "Not to hurry to a decision." She lifted Henry by the ankles. "Help me, Ting, and you two get the heavy end." She paused, and gave the dragon a respectful bow.

The dragon inclined his snout back. Then, with a great leap, and a powerful beat of his wings, he flew skyward.

Henry seemed far heavier than he looked, as the four of them wrestled him inside, and then up to the dorm wing where the boys slept. He had his own room, a pie-shaped place at the edge of the dorm, and it seemed to fit him in more ways than one. They laid him on his cot as gently as they could, although it was almost more of a case of all four of them losing their grip at once. Ting flexed her hand a few times where the dragon had touched her, as if in a little pain, but she kept her hand hidden every time Bailey tried to catch a glimpse.

"I shall stay with him," Madame Qi announced, and plunked herself down on a stool. She leaned forward to rest her chin on her cane.

Bailey's mom made a frustrated motion. "You two girls are better off downstairs, watching those crystals. Everything seems to be dimming. Any word on what's happening?"

Ting and Bailey shook their heads in unison. "They're fighting. More than that I can't tell," Bailey added.

Rebecca Landau made a face that emphasized the small lines at the corners of her eyes. "I don't like not knowing!"

As they went downstairs, Ting nudged Bailey. "So like you!"

Bailey muttered. "I know, it's scary." She waited till they got around a corner before grabbing Ting's hand and opening it.

A jagged red mark met her eyes, a fiery mark looking like a flying snake dragon, remarkably like the red enamel weather vane dragon that rested on Ting's grandmother's home, or at least the way she'd described it to Bailey many times. "Whoa," she breathed. "That must hurt."

"It does." Ting snatched her hand back. "And I have no idea what to do about it!"

"Then things can't be that dark. Yet." Bailey finished ominously.

They limped back to the academy. Trent referred to it as leapfrogging, since neither Gavan nor Jason could Crystal a significant distance. They relied on small landmarks from memory, viewed by dragonback or horseback from days ago. It took time as they shared their vision among the three of them, to make sure that they had details correct, and then rested, and then tried to decide on the next hop. Jason relied as little as possible on his lavender crystal, counting on his main crystal, the one he'd bonded to first, although its warmth and light seemed to waver badly every time he focused. Twice, Trent helped him find a ley line of natural energy that boosted his own weak energy, and still they staggered home as though tied together in a three-legged race.

Gavan made a fist about his watch fob crystal, the one in his cane still not having recovered, and they jumped. They landed on grass slick with dew as evening grew close, and they all grabbed each other to stay upright.

Jason felt a cold chill start down the back of his

neck and on down his spine. He chafed his arms. "We've doubled back. We're near the Dark Hand fortress."

Gavan swore and rubbed his eyes. "My fault. I'm tired." As the two of them cast about for their bearings, Trent stared at the ground. He said quietly, "I know I don't feel things the way you two do, but . . . did you feel pulled here? Somehow?"

"Pulled?" Gavan arched an eyebrow. He rubbed his crystal fob.

"We're nearly exhausted. I can feel it, clearly. And while we were Crystaling, I could feel something, I don't know, tugging at us." Trent shrugged. "Can't explain it better than that."

"I feel," Jason added slowly, "watched." Slowly, he turned about in a circle, looking into the late afternoon light, when the sun slanted low across the land and shadows seemed to be multiplying everywhere. It felt damp, too, as though the skies would be gathering storm clouds when nightfall truly hit.

Trent danced his fingers through the air. "It feels like something over there." He found an invisible string and turned to tug on it.

"Watch it, lads." Gavan frowned.

"Think it's a ward or trap?"

"More than likely. Even likelier, if it is, it could be lethal."

"I need to look."

Gavan and Jason stared at each other a moment. Then Gavan sighed. "I suppose we all do."

"You felt it, too, then?"

"I did. What it was, I didn't know." He signaled to them. "Be quiet, and stay close. Trent, keep that Sight of yours alert."

They moved through the edge of a forested land, thin because they were already in the highlands, wiry shrubs with stubborn barbed thorns grabbing at them from time to time. The land opened up into a canyon or cove, and they all came to a sudden halt.

Shadows had a life of their own here. A gash in the

ground opened like a yawning mouth, biting at the world about it. Darkness boiled around it. Jason caught a glimpse of a skull being tossed back and forth through the ebony chasm. Dry clinks and rattles issued forth, along with a low moaning as though wind escaped from the fissure as well, accompanied by the clatter of bones.

"What is that?"

"I don't know, and I don't want us getting any closer."

But Jason said, "I'm not sure," echoing Gavan. The gaping hole both drew him and repelled him.

"We need to get out of here. We'll talk about this later, but I don't want either of you coming back to take a look. Is that clear?"

"No argument here," Trent agreed.

Jason only nodded his head, as the elder Magicker took their arms and pulled them away from whatever it was. The one thing he could be certain of was that he did not believe it had existed before that morning.

In the clear, Gavan took a deep breath. "Home, then, however long it takes us."

They linked and Crystaled again, the moments *between* growing colder and longer as their powers faded.

Lanterns hung from the academy's corner eaves glowed as they touched down in the yard. Gavan staggered and almost fell over. Trent caught him by one elbow and Jason by the other. Looking down, Jason saw the cuff of Rainwater's trousers soaked in dark liquid that must have been blood.

"You're hurt! Help me get him inside!"

"No, no, it's nothing." Gavan hastily pulled the edges of his cloak together, trying to hide his legs from view. "That's not from today. A little bleeding is good. It'll help clean it out."

Trent looked at the shadow pooling around Gavan's boot heel. "Then I'd say a major leak like that must be fantastic." He rolled his eyes. "C'mon, man." He

put his shoulder under Gavan's arm and with Jason's
help, muscled the headmaster into the kitchen doorway. Once inside, Jason propped Gavan's leg on a
stool while Trent stuck his head into the corridor, letting out a cheerful, "Halllloooo, we're home."

Great kettles of hot water steamed in the fire pit,
and Jason grabbed up a torn rag from a waiting pile.
"Looks like they were ready to bandage an army."

"Either that or they took up mummification while
we were gone." Trent pulled a stool up next to Gavan
and looked at the ankle wound in fascination as
Gavan gingerly peeled his trousers away from it.
"That is a bite, and a nasty looking one. Not
from . . . there?"

"Indeed it is, and no. I didn't get any closer than
you two did."

Trent nodded at Jason as he lowered rags and a
bowl of hot water onto the table. "He's going to need
a rabies shot."

"I most certainly am not!"

Trent sat back with a wicked laugh as Gavan, frowning, grabbed a rag and made a hot compress from it,
laying it over the green-and-purple, jagged wound.

"That does look bad."

"It festered, but now it's bleeding cleanly and it will
be fine."

Jason rubbed his left hand. "That's not a wolfjackal bite."

"No. It's from a Leucator."

Both boys whistled sharply at that. Then both spoke
at once, Trent saying, "When'd you get that?" while
Jason said, "That came the other night, then. You
were looking for Eleanora."

Gavan closed his mouth stubbornly and answered
neither, wincing as the heat settled into tender flesh.
"Without success," he said finally. "And I don't want
any discussion on the other until I've talked with
Tomaz and others first. Agreed?"

Trent drummed his hand on the table, nodding, but

Bailey and Ting, and the older women burst into the kitchen before he could say anything.

"What other," demanded Bailey.

"Nothing important. Is Tomaz back yet?"

"No, but he sent to us. They're staying the night in Naria." Bailey plunked herself down on a stool next to Gavan. "Ew!" She eyed his ankle.

"Ugly, isn't it? Good thing FireAnn can't see it. She'd have my hide." Gavan took up a clean cloth and wrapped it tightly, then tied it into place. "All right. How about a cup of hot tea and stories all around? Who wants to know what happened today?"

"We do! And we have something of our own to tell you."

"Good enough. Where's Henry?"

"He's upstairs resting," Ting said softly. "And he's part of it."

"Hmmm. Well. Rome wasn't built in a day, nor the Dark Hand defeated in one, it seems." Gavan tried a smile that did not quite work.

"What he means is, back to the drawing board, I think," Bailey said smugly, and laced her fingers around one knee as she drew close to listen. That brought fond laughter from everyone else much to her puzzlement. "What? I thought I got that one right!"

Rebecca kissed her daughter's forehead. "Yes, dear, you did. You got it absolutely right."

36

Aunt Freyah

HE WAS TIRED ENOUGH to sleep like a log, but he couldn't. Trying not to think about Rich and the blackmarrow poison and Tomaz's warnings of it didn't help. The more you tried not to think of something, the more you thought of it. Logic told him that it wasn't his fault. He hadn't invented Haven or the raiders or the poison one of them had decided to use—and that didn't help either. Tomaz said the healer Kektl told him the rare poison came from a very difficult to grow flower and very few people could prepare it. Yet someone had and now Rich would have it infecting his system for the rest of his life, however long that might be!

Jason turned and thumped his flat pillow. Not his fault!

Still. He buried his nose in the rough sheeting of the bed and squinched his eyes shut. That was when he felt it.

He'd felt it before, but the strangeness of it chased the very last edge of sleepiness from him as it tickled along every nerve in his body. Very quietly he pulled out his crystals from under the makeshift pillow. They glowed faintly in answer to his touch, the clear gold-and-lapis banded quartz and the lavender gemstone.

As he did so, he could feel the immediate attention of whatever it was that walked unseen, unheard through the academy. A shivering like a pool of water passed over him and as it did, both crystals dimmed. He could feel and see them growing cooler, weaker, in his hands.

Whatever passed over him was sucking off the reservoir of energy he'd put in them and, from the prickling of his skin, from himself as well! What the—

Jason rolled over angrily. He stared into the dim room, sweeping it for sight of something, anything— Jonnard in his black cloak, Isabella in one of her extravagant European dance gowns sweeping past—anything at all. The thing shivered away from him as he reached for it.

Trent murmured something in his sleep and kicked a bare foot out from under the homespun blankets.

Jason tilted his head, listening, feeling, searching with senses he hardly knew he had, for something magickal stalking the academy halls. He found it, and it evaporated from his grasp almost the moment he touched it.

Jason recoiled. He didn't know what it was, but he knew it wasn't the Dark Hand. Still unseen and unstoppable, it passed beyond the walls and his ability to reach for it again, and then was gone.

The lavender crystal cut into his palm. He looked down at it, its glow flickering like an ember trying to stay lit and alive. For a moment, he saw Gregory's countenance, so familiar and yet not, and then, he saw Aunt Freyah's. The vision looked distressed, but it reached out for him.

So independent and defiant and now utterly alone, she held a hand out to him. He had to go to her.

He dressed silently and slipped out of the room, leaving Trent behind. Halfway down the main stairs, a step groaned behind him. He turned and saw Bailey, rubbing an eye sleepily, Lacey tucked away in her other hand.

"Going somewhere?"

"You know me. I always seem to take a walk in the middle of the night."

Bailey had dressed, too. She yawned. He hesitated. "I think . . . I think I have a rescue mission or something."

She grew alert. "Really? Where?"

"Aunt Freyah."

"I'm going with you!"

It seemed like a good idea. He took her hand, and then thought of Aunt Freyah's little kingdom and her cozy cottage, and they Crystaled there.

Time always changed when they went to Freyah's. Jason anticipated that. What he never expected was the sight that greeted him. Her country cottage looked as if a bomb had struck it. Only two walls stood and a third of the roof still clung to them. The picket fence had fallen like loose sticks to the ground and the lawn and gardens were rampant with weeds and unruly thorn-bushes. The place was wrecked.

"It's falling down," breathed Bailey as if one loud word might add to the disaster. She moved cautiously across the weed-infested lawn.

"No kidding." He was surprised, and not surprised. He'd expected to see worse, but had hoped he wouldn't see anything like this at all. He was often wrong and wished this had been one of those times. He held out a warning hand. "Don't touch anything."

"No way." Bailey put her hand up to her bodice pocket and repeated the caution to Lacey. "Not even with a whisker," she added. "No wine cellar trips this time either. I don't know what you find so fascinating in her wine cellar, but you stay with me!" Her pocket squeaked back at her.

They approached the cottage door hesitantly, and Jason raised a hand to knock, stopping, because it looked like the only thing that wasn't falling over. Two walls and a door . . . surely she heard or saw them coming? He made a fist.

The door swung open. Aunt Freyah looked out, eyes snapping, silvery hair in bouncy ringlets. "Well, well! Come in, come in, have lunch or breakfast or whatever time it is out there."

"Midnight snack," supplied Bailey helpfully.

"Mmm. A challenge! Come in, then, before something falls on your head." Freyah turned away briskly and snapped her fingers, calling for her picnic hamper. It shuffled in with a grunt and a moan, as she led them to the parlor. Bits of plaster and roofing drifted down from above like a tree shedding brown-and-red leaves. Bailey sneezed and rubbed at her nose. "I apologize for the dust, dear, but it seems inevitable."

George, the serving tray, came galloping around the corner and skidded to a halt in front of them. It shook in delight to see them, or perhaps it was in terror. Jason studied the long-legged tray. Difficult to tell with an animated inanimate object, frankly. George could have been either.

"George," said Freyah. "Do a good job. These are likely to be our last guests." She sat back with a sigh and looked about the ruins of her comfortable abode, her own bit of a haven. George sidled up between Bailey and Jason, its tray filled with a steaming pot of hot chocolate and two big empty mugs waiting to be filled and a small bowl of marshmallows. The hamper, pouting a bit, bumped Jason's knee as it popped its lid, releasing delicious smells of freshly baked muffins.

He did as expected, dishing out the muffins to everyone while Bailey poured the hot chocolate. Freyah had a steaming cup of café au lait by her chair, which she'd evidently been drinking before they'd arrived. Time sometimes got muddled that way in Freyah's home. As politely as he could, he bolted the blueberry muffin down to its last crumb before starting on business. Bailey was at least half a muffin behind him, even with Lacey's help, when he said, "Aunt Freyah, you can't stay here. It's why we came. I thought something might be wrong."

A ceiling tile hanging by one corner crashed down at his feet, covering his boots in dust and debris. Jason looked down at it and cleared his throat.

"Whatever makes you say that, dear?" asked Aunt Freyah.

Bailey finished her muffin, folding the paper cup it had come in, and dusting the last crumbs onto her knee for Lacey. "We really want you to come to the academy. It's dangerous here for you and George and everybody."

Freyah gave her a piercing but not unkind look. "I am touched that you both have come. But I can't leave. This is, or was, my life. As you two are keenly aware, I've been at odds for many years with Gavan about finding and educating you younger Magickers. It's left me out here, alone and isolated. It's only fair that I'm hoist with my own petard, isn't it?"

Bailey's mouth opened and she looked sideways at Jason. "She means," he interpreted, "she's suffering the consequences of her action."

"Aha. And people think *I* talk funny."

Freyah laughed, and waved a hand at the two of them, but her smile faded, and she looked as if she were almost in tears. "I can't come with you. I'd ask you how you knew I was in trouble, Jason, dear boy, but since you are responsible, we both know how—"

"Me? Responsible? I couldn't have done this!"

"It's all right. I don't blame you. It's all in the training." Freyah sat up straighter, holding her coffee cup and saucer on her knee. George tiptoed back to her side as if worried. "You've done very well, all things considering."

"I would never, could never . . ." He stopped in mid sentence, thinking of how his Dragon Gate had brought disaster to Haven. "Not on purpose, anyway," he finished lamely.

"You really don't know, do you?" Freyah tilted her plump face at him curiously.

"Not really."

"When you manipulate great energies, Jason, there

can be great backlashes. For every action there is an opposite and equal reaction."

"Elementary physics," put in Bailey.

"Exactly." Freyah pointed her chin at Jason. "This . . ." and she glanced around at the wreckage of her cottage, "began about a day and a half ago, by my reckoning."

He drew in his breath sharply. The attack on the convoy and Jonnard's actions! "That wasn't me, but that was Magick. Jonnard did something, we're still not sure what. It was like a bomb blast."

She looked sharply at him. "No other effects?"

"One we're investigating. Like an abyss or something that opened, we don't know if it's related yet or not, but it feels like it."

Freyah shuddered. She dropped her coffee cup onto George, his tray ringing as he caught it. "So it begins." She stood. "You absolutely can't stay, then, children. Not for another moment. There won't be but a smidgen left of this place soon, and I . . . have things to do."

"You're coming with us. You and George and the hamper and anything else we can carry!" Bailey leaped to her feet.

Freyah shook her head. "No, dear. It's too late for that."

"We've lots of room. There is no way the academy couldn't use you for a teacher, and if you disagree with Gavan, so much the better. We're all different, and we need a lot of different teachers," Jason told her.

"It's not just that." She hesitated. "If you didn't cause this power surge, then how did you wonder about me?"

"This." Jason lifted his lavender crystal.

Freyah's mouth lighted into a sad curve, for she knew her brother's magical gemstone well. "I see."

"It's not just etched with his likeness. Sometimes I get feelings from it."

"It sent you this way?"

"It made me think I should see you, yes."

Freyah let her breath out, then shook her head. "What's done is done."

The far wall of the cottage began to creak and groan. It leaned away from them all, slowly, and then began to topple as if some great weight pushed it over, and it crashed to the garden grounds. They all stood in amazement for a moment. Only one exterior wall and the door remained at the front. Jason had never seen anything like it outside of his stepfather's construction business. He had seen something remotely similar with a great demolition down to one last wall which would be kept so that, technically, the new building could be called a "remodel." McIntire didn't like bending rules like that, but he'd done it that time because the remaining wall had a hand-painted mural on it that was irreplaceable by any means, and worth saving. The wall then had been propped up to keep it in place. There was no way a few timbers could prop up what was left of Freyah's cottage.

He picked up George under one arm, and the hamper under the other. "Freyah," he said firmly, in his deep-sounding new voice. "You are coming with us. There's no time to take no for an answer."

Freyah raised her hand, ring sparkling, her chin up. "Jason. Put my things down, and step away, or I will send you away, and with as much power as I have left, I am not exactly sure where you'll end up."

"Aunt Freyah!" Bailey took a step toward her, hands outstretched to block any crystal beam, and Lacey took off squeaking, across the floor, through the rubble and down the hall, headed toward Freyah's wine cellar. "Not again!" Bailey twisted about.

"Leave her." Jason stood rooted in place, determination running through every fiber of his being. The last remaining wall groaned and shivered a bit. "Please come with us."

"I can't." Freyah's voice dropped to a strained whisper, and she swayed as well, as if time and strength were a wind that moved her body, at last.

"What is it?"

Bailey let out a yip. "It's not a what. . . it's a who! Jason!" She grabbed at his hands, enveloping the lavender crystal. "Isn't it, Aunt Freyah? Tell him!"

The elder Magicker swayed again, and her shoulders drooped. "I'm so tired." She fell into her chair and gestured weakly.

"Come with me!" Bailey tugged on Jason. "Drop that."

He set George and the hamper down carefully, and shot a glance at Freyah. "Don't move."

"As if I could."

"Well, if something is going to fall on you, move then, but wait for us!"

Freyah nodded slowly.

Bailey shot through the dusty inner hallway, after the little rodent hopping and making running tracks in the plaster dust. She pointed. "There . . . the wine cellar stairs."

"And . . ."

"Look for yourself. You'll never believe me. I saw it last time she ran away, but it didn't hit home. And then I kind of forgot about it, although I imagine Freyah made me forget, I don't know. But go down and look. That's why Freyah won't leave."

Carefully, Jason moved down the old, worn wooden stairs. It would have been rather dark, but with most of the ground floor above it disintegrating, light from the crystal sconces above found its way through in streaks and rays. There, in the corner behind a nearly empty wine rack, was a long, long heavy wooden table and on top of it, a sarcophagus. A crystal window revealed the face of the occupant, and Jason came to a halt, wordless.

He looked at Gregory the Gray.

Footsteps paused behind him. "When Lacey finds a treasure, she finds a treasure," Bailey commented.

"I don't think he's dead," whispered Jason.

She shook her head. "If he were, I don't think Freyah would insist on staying. She means to move him somewhere safe."

"He can't be awakened. He's told me that. I don't know why, but he can't be. Not yet." He looked around the wine cellar and thought of the cottage and its gardens, the pocket of safety Freyah had spent an entire lifetime guarding. He took Bailey by the elbow and guided her back upstairs. She paused long enough to sweep up Lacey who had found something in a corner and stuffed it in her cheek pouch, instead of eluding capture.

Freyah had her face in her hands as they approached. She looked up.

"So," Jason said cheerfully. "We'll have more to move than I thought we would." He glanced at the hamper. "How much can you pack in that?"

"Almost everything important."

"And I can get the sleeper downstairs, and between the three of us, we should be able to Crystal out of here easily."

"I'd be bringing Gavan a world of trouble." Freyah stood and dusted herself off. A window frame off the front wall had gone while they were in the cellar, its paint flakes falling like snow.

"As if he doesn't already have one!" Bailey scoffed. "Besides. We need you, Aunt Freyah."

"You need me."

"You bet we do," Jason reinforced Bailey's statement. "We always have."

"Well, then. George and I never refuse a challenge." She fluffed out her hair. "Quickly, then! Pack up the essentials." She tapped George and the hamper. "You know who to gather. I'll get a satchel for my clothes. You two. Finish the muffins."

The hamper spit out a plate of muffins which Jason leaped for and caught in midair, George's job usually, but the tray was scampering off to the corners of the ruined cottage, doing Freyah's bidding.

Before the two of them had finished their cherry crisp muffins, everyone had come back. The hamper waddled laboriously as if weighed down, and George's surface was stacked with books and picture frames. His legs bowed under the burden.

"All right. You two be ready. I'll be downstairs with Gregory. On the count of twenty, we're headed for the academy kitchen. Right?" He stared at Bailey.

"Absolutely."

As Jason made his way down the creaking wine cellar stairs a second time, he could hear Bailey saying, "Now the main thing you have to do is convince my mom it's okay to have a casket with an almost-dead-looking man in it lying around. Other than that, it'll be a piece of cake."

It struck him as funny and he was still laughing when they landed in the academy.

37

Isabella's Fury

THE SHRILL SCREAM echoed throughout the fortress, beating at his eardrums. Jonnard took the dungeon stairs at breakneck pace, letting gravity give him speed that his tired, aching body could not. Every fiber of his being screamed in echo as he skidded to a halt, the dungeon doors thrown open, framing Isabella by torchlight.

She swung on him, her hand clawing the air. "The Leucators! My Leucators, gone, all gone. What have you done?"

Jonnard stared into the filthy, stinking depths of the cavern. Not a being could be seen, although the debris of their presence littered the area. Scraps of bone and food here and there, dirty strands of clothing. But the Leucators had vanished, their chains and shackles with them, and he shut his jaw quickly lest his mother see his own surprise.

He leaned a shoulder against the wall. "Well, of course. Did you expect anything different?"

"You fool. You idiot. Do you have any idea what you've condemned me to?"

"Mother." He kept his voice mild, even as hers strained higher and higher in rage and despair, while his thoughts raced ahead for an answer. He thought he found one. "I've condemned you to nothing. I showed you the Gate, did you not see?"

"I saw a miasma of Chaos." Isabella turned her head then, away from him, away from the stink of the dungeon. Her shoulders slumped. Her voice lowered to a hoarse whisper. "Oh, Jonnard. What have you done?"

"Nothing." He reached out and took her hand. "Nothing but good in the long run. Come upstairs, and sit."

She shook her head.

"You must," he said firmly. "Listen to me. You formed the Leucators out of the Chaos of a would-be Gate. It is a Gate my father almost dared open, but could never quite finish, but he taught you how to manipulate its energies and create the soul hunters we call Leucators. Now the Gate is opened, and the Leucators have returned to their elements. You can still draw on them. Even better," and he stroked her hand in his as he began to lead her upstairs, although she shrank back from him a little. "Even better, you can draw on the stuff of the Gate itself. This place has been draining us, slowly, and now we're invincible."

She stared up at him, the torches on the stone walls reflecting her face in harsh, strong planes. "You don't know what you dare."

"No, I don't. Not yet." He spoke not another word till he had her in her apartments, where the walls had been soundproofed, and no one could hear their voices. He sat her down at her desk, her place of power.

She seemed to regain her composure in the brightly lit room, its paneled walls and furniture a world away from the dungeon. "The Leucators are no longer bound, and we're all in danger here."

"Not all of us."

"They hunger for flesh, soul, and Magick, and we, above all, have to fear that."

"For right now, I can hold them. That's all that counts."

"For now? For now?" Isabella looked down her nose at him. Jonnard fought the instinct to grit his teeth. His intention of reassuring her evolved into one of withstanding her recovering scorn and outrage. "What about later?"

"Now is all that counts."

"How can you say that? How can you even *think* it?" She slapped a hand down on her writing desk. The furniture shivered under the blow, but he did not move a muscle except to answer her.

"How can I not? Did you think any further when you created the Leucators?"

She met his stare. Long moments passed in which he said nothing more, silently daring her to answer. Then, finally, her gaze flicked away. "It came out of necessity."

"We have an advantage. This Gate generates a Magick we can bend to our uses. It also creates fear, and we can use that as well. The obvious, you don't seem to have grasped. I am a Gatekeeper, Isabella." Jon leaned forward intently. "I've done it once, I can do it again."

"That is a Gate we dare not pass."

"Perhaps. We haven't tried yet, have we?" He sat back in his chair, stretching his long legs out in front of him, crossing his boots at the ankles.

"You can't be serious!"

"Can't I? You asked me for a bloody miracle, and you got one! But am I given credit? No. When did you get old, Mother? When did you grow so cautious?"

"Silence!"

Jonnard held back his next words, watching Isabella's face. Handsome rather than pretty, strong features, strong nose, lustrous dark hair that now showed a single strand here and there of silvery cast. But she'd lived centuries longer than he, and he knew she hadn't done it by accident. She'd done it by sheer power of her will and her intelligence as well as her Magick, even though the toll had begun to catch up with her.

She stirred, with a rustle of the fine satin of her

gown. He wondered how many gowns she'd packed away when they'd fled to Haven, and how long her finery would last her on this rustic world. She tapped one fingertip upon the highly polished sheen of her desk. "What you have done is remarkable, Jonnard, I give you that."

He inclined his head at her acknowledgment. "But . . ."

"Yes, but. That is the crux of it. We have no idea of the consequences of what you've done, other than the initial outcome, and I'm not inclined to want to investigate. It may take resources we don't have, and it may bring to pass things we cannot handle."

"Or it may not. Look here. I am not forgetting who you are or what you've accomplished, and I know you are speaking from experience. Still, we have an opportunity here, and I am excited by it. I will be cautious, but I expect to be able to use this to consolidate our position here as well as elsewhere."

"Then study it, but cautiously. You are of no use to me dead, Jonnard."

He sprang to his feet and then paused in her doorway. "Thank you for both the permission and concern, Isabella." Hiding his grin, he left her stewing in her study.

38

Who's Been Sleeping in My Coffin?

THERE'S A BODY in my kitchen!" Rebecca Landau let out a shriek, and her voice wailed throughout the academy, from floor to floor, waking anyone who wasn't already awake and drifting down wondering what might be happening this morning.

It was, Bailey would say later, a scream loud enough to wake the dead, except, of course, it wasn't, for Gregory the Gray continued to sleep peacefully right through it, even as Magickers stampeded down to the kitchen in response to Rebecca's terrified yell. Bailey and Jason stumbled down to the kitchen last, her hair looking a wee bit like a pack rat's nest, and his eyes all bleary as he rubbed them and looked upon the sight. Even stiff-legged Rich made it to the scene of the crime before they did.

All Gavan could say was, "Good lord," and he sat down abruptly on a nearby stool, staring through the translucent part of the coffin at the face of his old teacher long thought to be dead and gone in the mists of time.

Rebecca took a deep breath. "Gavan Rainwater.

I've put up with a lot. You came to me and said, 'May we teach your daughter sorcery,' and I said, 'Well, okay, if that's what she really wants.' You say, 'She has to go to another world to be safe,' and I say, 'Well, all right.' You say, 'You've got to come, too,' and I say, 'Well, if I have to,' and you say, 'There's nothing for you to do here but be a glorified kitchen maid,' and I say, 'Well, as long as I'm helping,' but This! This!" And she pointed a trembling hand at the sarcophagus. "I draw the line at this!"

"Mom," said Bailey, catching her hand. "Chill."

Jason shot a look at her. "I thought you were going to sit with him."

"I did. He didn't do anything, and I got sleepy, so I went to bed." Bailey wrinkled her nose at Jason. "I planned on being up before anyone else." She shrugged.

Gavan swiveled around on his stool, his clear blue eyes staring at them. "You two knew about this?"

"We found him," Bailey stated proudly.

Jason shook his head. "We knew, but we didn't really find him. That is, he's never actually been lost. He, ummm," and Jason cleared his throat uncertainly. He always found it difficult to tell anything remotely like an untruth. Rich, still pale and a little uneasy on his leg, watched him, while Stef paced back and forth, rolling an eye now and then at the seemingly dead man. He looked as though his grip on his bear self had reached the breaking point.

"I had him, Gavan," snapped Freyah from the doorway. She looked at him from her tiny height, silver hair practically sparking about her face. "I will leave immediately if we're not wanted."

"Not wanted? How could you be not wanted?" Gavan's mouth moved a few more times, soundlessly, and he turned to Tomaz whose solid body filled the doorway to the outside, a crow perched on each shoulder. He waved soundlessly at Tomaz.

"I think he means we're honored and moved at the sacrifice you've made all these years to keep watch on

Gregory. It is a burden we'll gladly share with you now," Tomaz said humbly.

Freyah's indignant expression immediately melted, and she gathered her robes about her, with a sniffle.

Gavan cleared his throat. "Right. Exactly that." He reached out and touched the coffin. "This looks familiar."

Freyah colored slightly. "Hmm. Well, um. It might. I do believe that was the ancestral coffin meant for you someday, Gavan. I, hmmm, borrowed it, rather."

Gavan blinked. He stroked the side of the chiseled artifact. "Well done."

"Do you think so? Your family didn't mind. I paid them well for it. I suppose they thought it was for you, after all, having lost you so young to Magicking."

Gavan nodded. In those days, Magickers walked away from their families to avoid political and religious troubles. He'd been little more than an orphan, studying under Gregory. He stood up slowly. His fingers went to the latches covering the translucent part of the coffin.

"No!" Jason leaped forward. He charged toward Gavan. "You can't wake him. Not yet. I don't know why, I just know you can't."

Freyah crossed the room swiftly, backing up Jason. "The lad is right. My brother left specific instructions no one was to wake him. He sleeps, but it is a part of some bargain, and he'll wake when his time is due."

"Bargains," muttered Gavan. "Some good, some bad. Who is to know? But I gather waking a sleeping wizard is even more unwise than waking a sleeping dog. So." He patted the latches back down firmly into place. "He stays."

"That is good." Madame Qi, who'd been standing quietly, leaning a little on Ting, tapped her cane. "One less mouth to feed at the moment."

"What kind of bargain could he have made? And with whom?"

Freyah shook her head. "Even if I knew, Rainwater, I couldn't tell you. It is his wish. Not even Eleanora is to know." She frowned, dark eyes snapping. "Not got her back yet?"

"No. Not yet." Gavan ran his hand through his hair.

"What's keeping you?"

"At the moment? Finding someone sleeping in my coffin, in my kitchen." He made a distracted gesture. "We'll have to find someplace to put you, someplace that Isabella with all her wiles can't detect." His brow arched. "Ah, and I might have just the spot."

"Ooooh," breathed Bailey, in recognition. "Just don't trip the trapdoor!"

"I do not like small places," Freyah stated. "Cozy, yes, small and confining, no."

Tomaz shook his crows off into the morning sky, and came fully into the kitchen. "It is best."

She eyed him. Then Freyah gave a little sigh. "All right, but only until I find another cottage. You, and you, accompany me. You have Talent and absolutely no schooling or discipline," Freyah pointed at Rebecca whose only response was to stutter a denial, and then she pointed at Madame Qi, "while you have discipline but not much flexibility. If I'm going to be bored, I might as well be teaching."

Madame Qi bowed from her waist. "I shall be honored."

The men and boys took up the weight of the sarcophagus and followed Gavan through the academy to the silent hallway where Bailey had found herself imprisoned. They left the doors standing open, and took their breakfast in there, and let Freyah know of the plans to attack the Dark Hand fortress and all that had happened to each of them since she saw them last. George trotted from Magicker to Magicker like a happy pup, just to nudge them and say hello. So the day began.

High Noon.

They crouched at the foot of the inner stair, Gavan gesturing warningly behind him to Jason and Trent, stilling them. Not that they needed that. The fortress was not empty as they'd hoped. Worse, Jonnard and Isabella seemed to be about.

"It's not now or never," Jason whispered. "But now is better."

They'd split into two groups, Tomaz taking Stef and Rich as a decoy from their movements inside the fortress. Henry stayed, frowning, with Freyah and the others at the academy. His job was to distract Jonnard if Jon should try to draw from him again, giving him false ideas of what might be going on. The look on his face had been one of extreme unhappiness as they'd Crystaled out.

Now he might be one of their only hopes to Crystal back safely. None of them alone could anchor; all were too tapped out, just as none of them dared attack alone. They would succeed together or not at all, but only failure would meet those acting alone.

Jason felt his pulse pound in his throat as he waited for Gavan to signal their progress upstairs. Behind him, Trent put a hand on his back, fingers drumming to an unheard tempo. He could feel the tension in Trent as easily as he felt it in himself. Gavan looked over his shoulder, making a motion that looked as if he were plucking harp strings in the air with his hand. He was asking Trent if he saw any sign of magic streaming their way.

Trent shook his head slowly, but held his hand up, and indicated an invisible line down the stairway. Not for them specifically but built into the fortress, much as they'd warded the academy. Gavan made a sign that he understood, and beckoned them up the stair, staying well away from the warding. As near as Jason could tell, it would act like a laser beam on an alarm system . . . touch it and it would trip. What sort of trap, exactly, it could spring, they had no idea. Knowing Jonnard, it was bound to be nasty.

Gavan paused. In a whisper pitched so low that they could barely catch it, he said, "That way are Leucators. Stay here. I'm going to check something."

Jason sat down on the step, his back to the safe

wall. His body shook slightly, with eagerness and adrenaline, and he could feel the same emotions running through Trent. Trent looked at him, then checked back the way they'd come. He motioned with his hands at the web of enchantments they'd crept through, indicating the holes were getting bigger and bigger.

Jason decided it was because they approached the living floors of the fort and they couldn't have people setting off alarms all the time, could they? He mimicked foot traffic by walking his fingers about, and Trent grinned. He either agreed with Jason or thought he'd suddenly gone crazy. Jason laughed silently back, ducking his head.

Gavan returned after long moments. He drew the boys close, his face grave. "The Leucators are gone."

"What?

"Nothing left but their stench. Stay close to me. I don't dare leave anyone behind."

Trent shook his head emphatically at Jason. Isabella drew energy from Leucators like vampires drink blood from their victims. As despicable as Leucators were, they held great value to Isabella. Where were they, then, and why? The two got to their feet, and followed on Gavan's heels.

On the second landing, he slowed, casting about for any sign of Eleanora that he could catch. Boot steps thudded down the hall, and he pulled both Trent and Jason to him, throwing a dark shadow over the three of them. They held their breaths as Jason watched the raiders disappear into the stairwell. Trent blinked. He stepped out of the cloak and saluted Gavan. Then he leaned over as if picking a piece of lint off the ground. He held it between his thumb and forefinger.

"Music," he said quietly. "It's a strand of music. Don't ask me how."

"Eleanora!" Gavan said fiercely, his voice pitched low but intense. "They've got her blocked, but they couldn't block that. Lead on!"

Trent took up that which only he could see. Jason

stayed at the rear, alert, ready to fight or do whatever else was necessary.

They entered a dank, dark wing, one built where the sunlight would never filter, its walls and doors old and stout and scarred. It spoke of misery, much as a dungeon would, telling of prisoners from the past that were treated a little bit better than those shackled down in the stony cellars, but not much. Gavan put his hands to the wood of one massive double door. There, guided by Trent's quick gestures, he cut the cords of enchantment holding the door shut, one crystal knife edge at a time, while Jason listened for interruptions headed their way.

The door fell open. Gavan stood for a moment on the threshold as if uncertain whether to enter. Trent leaned in and waved a hand signifying all clear. The three entered an ill-lit room that smelled like an old attic, musty and closed up. Slowly, Trent turned in a circle, indicating all the walls. Indeed, rather like the closed-in corridor and Magick-proofed room in the academy, Magick here was meant to neither enter nor leave. Nor were its occupants.

The entry room looked sparse and worn, almost devoid of all furniture and heat and warmth. A broken lute sat in the corner, as if leaned there with as much care as could be given an instrument with missing strings and a soundboard punched out far more than it should be. Somehow Jason thought she might have played it anyway, setting it across her lap, and trying to coax some sort of music from its remaining strings. Eleanora was like that. Gavan caught him looking at the instruments, and his mouth quirked bitterly. He must have thought nearly the same thing.

"Tormentors!" A low, hoarse whisper came from the dark room beyond. "Banshees!"

"FireAnn." Gavan stepped into the second room carefully, his eyes narrowed, peering into the permanent twilight. A rustle of clothing, and then he fell back, with a wild woman howling and clawing at his throat. Gavan wrestled with her. Jason kicked the outer door shut, muffling the noise, while Trent jumped in, calling the redhead's name, over and over.

Gavan wrestled her down to her knees, his hands on her wrists. FireAnn growled in disappointment, hot tears welling in her eyes. Her hands, misshapen from arthritis, curled into claws as if she would fight him yet. "Now, now," he murmured softly. "It's Gavan, FireAnn. It's me, finally. We've come to get you."

"She doesn't know us," Trent said numbly.

Jason bit his lip. In the long weeks, her hair had gone from copper-red to silvery-red though a kerchief still tamed her unruly natural curls, and her eyes of emerald green glared dully at them. He took one arm from Gavan and signaled for Trent to hold the other. "Go find Eleanora."

The other did not hesitate. He bolted past them, his cloak sweeping over them as he did. FireAnn threw back her head and looked around, owllike, if totally dazed. Jason stroked her wrist soothingly, but kept a firm grip as he felt muscles still wiry and strong.

She squinted at him. "Jason, lad, is that ye?"

"Nobody else but."

The camp cook and chief Magicker herbalist stared hard and long at him. "And how do I know this, lad? There's nobody but tricksters around."

Jason leaned close. "I'll eat anything you cook but red Jello." He shuddered a little at that, having had all he could stomach of the red fruity flavor when very young.

She gasped. "Lad! But ye canna stay! There's traps everywhere. Take your friends and flee whilst ye can. Do ye hear me? Afore the banshees and others know ye're here."

"We know," he said softly, quietly, firmly. "It'll be all right."

"No, no, no." She shook her head vigorously, curls bouncing under her faded scarf. "The boy is as mean as the devil himself and he'll come for ye, he'll come for Eleanora. The lass can't take much more. She thought she felt Gavan the other day, thought he'd come for us, and it near broke her heart."

"FireAnn. He has come for you, and this time we won't leave without you. But you must be quiet, and help us."

"Hist! Quiet, he says. All right, then, quiet I'll be." FireAnn twisted her arm in his grasp. "She did this. Her and her Leucators, taking the very life out of my bones. And that other, the watcher, he drinks of what we hold all the time, small sips, and thinks I canna tell!"

"I know." It hurt him to see her half-crazed and twisted as she was. Jason heard heavy steps and looked up. Gavan stood, a slender figure bundled in a wretched-looking blanket in his arms, but she wept, and held her arms about his neck, and it was indeed Eleanora. He straightened his shoulders. "Get us out of here, *now*."

Trent and Jason drew FireAnn to her feet, and they linked together, Jason cupping his crystal, as Trent kicked the outside door open. It was then the scream hit, a wailing of banshees woven together, piercing their eardrums with anger and dismay. Rebecca's scream of terror from that morning couldn't hold a candle to this decibel-challenging screech.

They shrank back, discovered.

Webs

"RUN!"

"Run?" Jason looked at Gavan.

"We can't Crystal out from here without Tomaz and the others. I haven't enough strength to jump to him and then out. We have to get to him on foot. So, *run.*"

"No!" Trent threw his free arm out, blocking them. "It's like a spiderweb down there. We'll be caught for sure. We can't run. Creep out, maybe, the way we came in."

Gavan stood stock-still, listening, cradling Eleanora tightly to his chest. He tilted his chin to Jason. "Find out if that was his diversion and if not, tell Tomaz to stay low and quiet."

Jason ran his hand over his crystal of quartz and gold and lapis, and made the link. Tomaz seemed as baffled as they were about the screaming, but agreed to lay low for the moment although he indicated urgently that they should get out. Jason repeated that to Gavan.

The fortress fell silent. Gavan shifted his weight. "It is possible that was no alarm. Isabella is known for her temper. We've no way of knowing what set it off."

"Then I say we get to Tomaz, link up, and get out."

Trent tapped his feet on the hallway floor in impatience.

"Trent in front. Jason, behind me." Gavan took a slow breath. "I am counting on you both, lads."

Trent led FireAnn behind him, saying, "Not far to go."

She put a crooked finger to her lips in answer. Told to be quiet, it seemed she would. She stumbled along behind Trent, trying to pick her way as he did. Jason watched anxiously. Gavan followed, moving as though carrying Eleanora was no burden at all to him, and perhaps she wasn't.

Jason raised a Shield for the rear and tried to keep track of Trent in front. The stairs sounded with every one of their steps upon it. No matter how quiet and cautious they tried to be, the old wood complained. Every slow step they took was with Trent guiding them through it as if they were climbing through barbed wire. It looked odd. He unwove webs they could not see, although they sensed the magic all about them, malevolent and harsh, a mirror image of the power they used, and as they went farther, the more tangled it got. Jason felt the shivering of the power as it shrugged past, seeking and missing him time after time. It gave him the same creepy crawlies as bugs did.

At last they reached a door to the outside compound, and it swung open invitingly, the haze of afternoon struggling to shine through it.

At the sight of daylight, cloudy though it was, Fire-Ann broke away from Trent. She staggered out of the fort and into the compound yard with her hands in the air, and did a wobbling Irish jig of joy. "Free," she cried in a cracking voice and then sank to the ground. Trent grabbed her up, shushing her. She nodded and began to cry, softly, brokenly.

It pierced Jason's heart to hear her. A murmur came from Gavan's bundle. Gavan dipped slightly in answer so that Eleanora could put her hand out and comfort FireAnn. Little could be seen of her but the frayed blanket and one terribly thin arm. His eyes and heart filled with the drama of the scene, but his ears heard a noise behind him. He turned.

Jonnard smiled thinly from the fortress door. "I thought I heard mice scurrying about."

"Difficult to hear with Isabella ranting."

"Sad but true." He came out of the doorway.

Jason raised his Shield between them. He called Tomaz to them, his hand over his crystal and added, "Now," to Gavan and Trent. "Or never, I think." He could feel the power welling up in Jonnard. They had gambled the Dark Hand would be as drained as they.

Gambled, and lost.

Tomaz, Stef, and Rich appeared in a shimmer. Jonnard dropped his shoulder and Jason instantly sensed the gathering and focusing. He charged forward, dropping into a sliding tackle, Shield up, and drove Jonnard off his feet gasping. Trent was the one who linked them all, as Gavan stood, dazed, and tried to protest, and Trent told Tomaz, "Now, now, go now!" amid the dazzle of crystal energy. The last thing Jason heard was Trent's thin voice from out of the nothingness vow, "I'll be back!" Then they were gone.

For one quick moment, he cursed himself for not going with them. All would stand or all would fall, but he knew better. They had a good chance of getting out, and he had a good chance of keeping Jonnard from blocking them.

Jason rolled and got up. "That," he said, "was soccer."

Jon spat dirt from his mouth. He dredged his crystal out of the ground behind him, and did not even try to stand before focusing a blade and slinging it at Jason, intent on cutting him in two. Jason danced away as blade hit Shield, and sparks flew, and Magick hummed angrily like a hornet's nest greatly disturbed.

Jonnard leaped to his feet. He wiped the back of his hand over his mouth, then spit aside one last time. "You never cease to amaze me," the young man said, circling Jason warily. "Although I would rather you just *cease*."

"Oh, I can't do that." Jason kept his power up, just as cautious. "I have friends who depend on me."

Jonnard swapped hands, crystal blade sparkling, and then he had a blade in each, and dropped into a stance the other recognized all too well. Jason took half a step back, turning his foot on a large rock on the stony fort courtyard. It saved his head, as he bobbed suddenly, and the blade cut through the air so close, the ends of his hair sizzled.

Jason spun away. "Another duel?" he said as he straightened up, dancing a little from foot to foot, loosening himself up, just as he would before a soccer match. His boots weren't as limber, but his muscles felt good. Not all of him was mind and Magick! Madame Qi's long runs, and hard work and exercises, had seen to that. "I don't always win, but I seldom lose."

Jon showed white teeth in a wolfjackal snarl. "I will see you finished off."

"Not if I can help it." Jason dodged again, as Jon's hands moved in a slash of light, crisscrossing. He went to the ground, rolled, and came up, not knowing how close it had been, only knowing he hadn't been hit. That was what counted. He laughed. "How about a bet? If I win this time, you and the rest of the Dark Hand go back."

"Go back? Back there? You must be kidding. If there is one thing that you and I agree upon, it is that going back means becoming someone's laboratory experiment. Going back will never be an option." Jonnard moved with dangerous grace. Magick fire seemed to outline his entire form, dazzling Jason's sight of him. His name, after all, was Jonnard Albrite, despite the dark nature and every intent of his birthright. "And you have nothing to wager that I value. Anything you have, I can take from you."

Jason hesitated. Just for a moment, his mind taking stock of what he had that he valued, the faces of his friends and family flickering through his thoughts, and in that instant, his foe struck.

The blade sank deep. He reeled back in white-hot

pain, his arm on fire with the hurt of it, wrenching away, feeling the blood fountain up. He put his hand to it, still holding the crystal, and as blood washed over the quartz, it seared him a second time. Jason cried out. He held the gaping wound shut, still moving, not giving Jon a chance to hit him again, and wondering if he could get the blood to stop.

He gasped with the torture of it, once, twice, narrowing his eyes, trying not to howl or cry, shaking with the effort. His crystal hummed loudly and grew searingly warm and he pulled it away to see . . .

Nothing.

Yet, not nothing, but an angry white seam of a scar showing through his torn sleeve where before there had been a gash of bloody flesh. It ached and throbbed in fresh pain still, every pulsing ebbing a little as though his body could not realize it had just been healed, nerves still yowling with being freshly cut. His finger traced the ropy scar.

He'd done that. But how?

"Well, well. Blooded your crystal." Jon made a *tsking* noise, circling around him. "Not a good thing to do."

Jason shook it off, gathering his scattered thoughts. "What are you talking about?"

"Blooding your crystal. They didn't tell you? Alas, your education is sorely lacking. It might be the death of you." Jon slashed again, lightning quick, but Jason saw it coming this time.

Arm still sore, it was his feet that reacted. He kicked out, curved instep meeting that round rock that had nearly tripped him earlier, half the size and probably twice the weight of a soccer ball. His foot met it squarely. It felt like one of the best kicks he'd ever taken as a forward. The rock shot through the air, arcing like a cannonball at Jonnard's head. The young man ducked away, and it caromed off his shoulder with a solid, sickening thump of rock against flesh. Jon let out a cry, going to his knees.

"Someone," Jason observed, "is going to be very

upset you let her captives get loose." He gripped both crystals tightly and felt them answer to him. Shield or flee, and he decided that fleeing would be best for now. Home, he thought, picturing the academy, and felt the chill of *between* take him. Jonnard's shout of pure hatred and anger pieced the void as he went.

Even then, he wouldn't have made it. He stayed *between* long enough to know that, the chill creeping into his bones, when he should have Crystaled here to there in the twinkling of an eye. Nothingness numbed him and the longer he stayed, the more paralyzed he would become, until the end. He wrapped his arms about himself and felt a webbing of power in the abyss, tiny threads of those he loved and who had been in his last thoughts. He clung to them, Bailey's amethyst thread and Ting's of vibrant pink, and Trent's punk blue and Gavan's pewter gray, and Henry's flaming red, and all the others, a rainbow of strands that he could knot around his hand and pull himself. . . .

Home.

Sanctuary

I'M MAD AS a hatter," FireAnn remarked cheerfully. "Yes, dear," Aunt Freyah told her, patting her on the shoulder as she passed by, steaming teapot in hand. "We all know that. Hopefully we'll know even more, in time."

FireAnn cackled to herself and sat back in her chair, near the cooking fire pit, enjoying the warmth of the banked fire. Dancing flames reflected in her wild copper hair. The promise of rain was finally fulfilled at nightfall and the sound of drizzle could be heard against the academy walls.

Rich held Jason's arm across one knee and looked at it for the tenth time or so. "I'd say it's healed," he finally said, reluctantly. "Not neatly, and there may be some nerve regeneration needs to be done. That was quite a slice. It's numb here and there?"

"Part of it still stings and, yes, part of it's numb. Weird."

"You're lucky you've got full mobility." Rich shook his head in wonderment. "I don't know how you did it."

"Neither do I." Jason rolled down his sleeve, watching Gavan, still waiting for an answer on his earlier question of, "What did Jonnard mean by blooding a crystal." Gavan hadn't responded yet, but stirred as he sensed Jason's attention.

The Magicker flicked a finger against his mug. "As for your question, I haven't a clue," he said, reading Jason's mind.

"Doesn't ring a bell? Nothing? Even something Brennard or the Dark Hand might have done that we think is forbidden?"

Gavan shook his head, adding, "Although it sounds as if you have the right of it there. Any kind of blood ritual sounds like their portion rather than ours." He stood. "It's been an exceedingly long day. I'm going to check on Eleanora and turn in."

Freyah perched on one of the stools. "Wait a moment, Gavan."

He paused.

"I can't stay here. I think we need to discuss moving Eleanora, FireAnn, me, and my brother."

"And where would you suggest?" Although weary, his voice took on an edge. Jason didn't blame him. He'd just gotten Eleanora back; now Freyah wanted to move her away. "And how would you protect yourselves?"

"I'd go with her," Rebecca said quietly.

"And I." Madame Qi tapped her cane firmly on the floor. "She cannot take care of everyone by herself, and I would not lose a good teacher. At my age," and she flashed a wrinkled grin, "classes are not to be wasted."

"Grandmother," said Ting, moving close to her, and putting an arm over her shoulders affectionately.

"This earth is good to me. Yet my days do not stretch forever in front of me." Madame Qi nodded.

"That does not answer my concern. Where would I send you? Where could you be safe?" Gavan frowned and his jaw tightened before he could say more.

"We have drawn attention here," Tomaz said mildly. "You know that. Freyah is right, they should be moved. The where of it, we'll have to consider."

"Avenha? It's almost rebuilt for the winter."

"Perhaps," Tomaz replied to Henry. "Much to think about." He stood. "Isabella won't be happy."

"Even more reason for us all to rest well, while we can." Gavan tipped his fingers to his brow in a wry salute and went up the stairs to the rooms given to Eleanora and FireAnn. Freyah watched him leave, then released a tiny sigh.

She stared into the fire's flames for such a very long time, she did not seem to notice as everyone else, even FireAnn, said good night and drifted away. George stirred then, and came to her side and butted her, as her drooping fingers nearly dropped her teacup and saucer. She patted the tray. "Thank you, George. Deep thoughts on a deep subject nearly put me into a very deep sleep." She rose and followed after.

"I have killed people for lesser failures," Isabella intoned.

"As I have, for lesser insults and reprimands." Jon raised a defiant eyebrow. He stood his ground.

"The Leucators are gone, now the hostages. How do you expect me to make a stand on this world?"

"I don't think I need to point out that your coin purses are quite full now."

"But my fortress is empty." Isabella paced angrily, turning her back on him, another insult. If she respected him at all, she'd be afraid to show him her back. Jon stared at her, his eyes gone steely hard. His shoulder ached, marked deeply black and blue from the rock blow, and his anger grew icy deep inside him. He would take out the Magickers, one by one or all at once. He no longer cared if they had power they could contribute or if they could be subverted by him. They would be his and regret the moment they became so. Fools with Magick were still just fools.

"Your fortress stands, as does your Gate."

"The Gate. Where would an abyss like that lead?"

"It doesn't matter."

She swung on him. "Doesn't matter! Listen to yourself."

"No, listen to you." Jonnard leaned forward. "I opened one Gate, I can open another. Did that possibility escape you? Or did you think it a fluke? Did you think I tripped and flicked a finger, and a Gate flew open by accident?"

An expression glanced across her face that he couldn't read. Had that indeed been what she thought of him? Jon contained himself though he wanted to shake in anger and continue shaking till the building dropped in rubble about them, but he did not let himself. He clenched a fist until the sore wound of his shoulder throbbed with the force of it. He moved for the door.

"Where are you going?"

"Out," he grated through clenched teeth. "In case you've forgotten, someone knew we were moving our goods for sale. Someone in the Trader Guild betrayed us, and I intend to find out who. They won't do it again." He left before she could deny him the right to go although he almost hoped she would try to stop him.

He rode the bay. The horse took to Crystaling well, and did not mind being ridden in the light rain, although both were soaked by the time they reached Naria's outskirts. Smoldering lights tried to brighten the night when he dismounted at the Trader Guild and turned the horse's reins over to a stammering stableboy who may or may not have recognized him. An apprentice let him in the front door, immediately bowing and bolting off for one of the senior guildsmen. Jon did not care who answered his call, as long as someone did. He stripped off his riding gloves and stamped his boots, shedding drops of rain.

"Master Jonnard! I am honored, honored." Presumptuous, overdressed as much as his flesh was overstuffed, and smelling of vinegary wine, Guild Leader Shmor himself came to press his hand. He still had a cloth napkin stuffed in his waistband, obviously interrupted at dinner. "What can I do for you? The deal is done? Problems?" Shmor shifted uneasily, and his body wobbled.

"Done, yes." Jonnard released the sweating hand as Shmor let out a long breath of relief. "Well done, no. Part of our negotiation concerned the need for utmost secrecy. I thought we had your assurance on that." Jonnard drew his gloves slowly between his fingers.

"You had! You have!" Shmor rumbled indignantly. "I don't understand."

"Let me make you understand, then." Jon stepped in, neat and clean, his hand to the trader's throat. Loose skin and wattle pooled about his fingers as he began to close them. "We were compromised, Shmor. Compromised badly enough that we almost had no deal to make, and I know that no one on my end was foolish enough to wag his tongue. That leaves your end."

Shmor began to turn red. "No, no, no! None of my people." He gargled a bit for breath and Jon loosed his hand just a touch. "I assure you. In the old days, I would have pointed to your man Fremmler, but I doubt that now. He seems quite loyal to you. Believe me, Master Jonnard, I know of no one who would be stupid enough to go against the guild or Isabella of the Dark Hand." He panted, his fat throat undulating against Jon's grip. "Our deal stands, and we hope to make many more. No one in the Trader Guild would run afoul of that."

"Someone did."

The trader gestured wildly. "I will make inquiries! I will leave no stone unturned finding out what I may!" Shmor gargled again.

Unpleasant as the man was, Jonnard believed him. He let go. Shmor hastily took a step back, rubbing at his throat. "I will not rest until I find out who, and turn him over to your tender mercies." He bowed heavily at the waist.

"Don't throw me a crumb," Jonnard warned.

"Don't set up some poor fool to make me happy. I want the truth, and I'll know it when I see it."

"Understood, Master Jonnard. Well understood!" Shmor cleared his throat with a fruity noise. "Have you, ermm, dined yet?"

The last thing he wanted to do was share a table with the man. "I'll find an inn."

Relief flooded Shmor's face. "Well, then. May I recommend The Hot Spit? It's a block over. Clean, plain food, good brewery."

"I look forward to hearing from you soon."

Shmor brought his napkin up to his mouth. He looked as if he might be trying to stifle tears. "And I, I look forward to answering your inquiry." He bowed but did not leave till Jonnard himself did.

He thought he heard a muffled sob as the door closed on his heels.

Unheeding, Jon made his way inside the establishment which smelled of straw and the wetness being tracked inside, beer, and sausages crackling on spits. The beer tasted like beer of old, thick and rich, not the swill served in many modern-day bars, and the sausages were not quite like any he'd ever had before, but he did not care, they filled his stomach. He sat at the table by himself, his five-fingered hands wrapped about a crude mug and endured the stares of passersby who marked him for his difference.

After two mugs of the beer, he decided he was ready to go home. He'd rattled the traders enough, something would shake out or not, although he wanted someone he could settle the score against now. The beer soothed his temper a bit. He'd have to bide his time. He dropped a coin on the table, a hand-stamped metal of unknown origin that passed for precious on Haven and drew his feet under him to stand. A sopping wet bundle of rags dashed up against him.

"Sir! Sir! A coin for a street lad? I'll clean yer boots, sir!"

Jon grabbed the small boy by the scruff of the neck.

Muddy and stinking, the child struggled a bit, then went limp. "How did you get in here?"

"They let me in, sir. I clean boots. I sing, sometimes. And I draw pictures. Look, look!" Dangling from Jon's fist, the urchin still managed to open his cloak and from within his shirt, he took out a fistful of papers. He scattered them on the table's edge.

They caught Jon's eye. Drawn in firestick charcoal, they showed a bit of talent. He recognized streets of Naria, peopled by various characters, going about their lives. He picked out one. It showed fat Shmor on the Trader Guild steps, thumb in his vest, talking with a hapless apprentice. Jon peered closely. Upstairs, on the second story, a crow perched at a window. Plainly, a crow.

But crows did not inhabit Haven.

"What's this?"

"Oh, that one, sir. The Head Trader, sir."

"I know who he is. This," and Jon stabbed a finger at the crow.

"A great dark bird, sir. Ne'er seen anything like it, I have. It comes and goes sometimes."

"From that window?"

The boy looked at him shrewdly and pressed his lips firmly together. Jon let him drop. He flipped him a coin. "From that window?"

"Always, sir. None other."

Jon took the sketch and put it in his own pocket. "You know nothing."

"Never did, sir. It's why I'm poor." The lad scrambled together his other art, and dashed off, stowing them away, zigzagging through the inn and off into the rain.

He had to fetch his horse from the guild stables anyway. Jon put up his cloak hood against the rain which had tailed off to a fine mist, and slowed as he came upon the building. He paced the street till he saw the unusual window from the urchin's sketch. He thought he had an idea where it might be on the second floor.

The apprentice let him inside again, and hesitated. Jonnard pressed a few coins in his palm. "No need to disturb Shmor again. I think I left something up on the second floor. I'll just be a moment."

"Well and good, Master Jonnard. Shall I wait for you here?"

"Good idea." Jonnard took the steps cat-quick, before the apprentice could decide the bribe was too little and told someone of his presence anyway. The small offices upstairs all seemed to be dark. He lit a crystal, passing door by door. He nearly missed the one he wanted, and back stepped. Lantern light from his hand filled the small office. Stacks of papers met his gaze, an unremarkable clerk's office. Racks of books, scrolls, and maps lined the wall. The one window seemed high, but a small ladder to reach the bookshelves stood in the corner. Jonnard paused at the desk, and sifted through the top layer, trying to determine who sat there and who signed the documents.

He did not know the written language yet, but he recognized the signature, nonetheless. Renart.

Of course. He should have known.

Jon tilted his head at the window again. He knew where the crows had come from, and now he knew who they'd come for. He no longer needed Shmor's help, although he would give the trader credit if he confirmed it. Jon shuttered his Lantern spell and withdrew. A knit scarf hung on a chair by the door. He took it with him.

A little something for the wolfjackals to remember Renart by.

Warm with accomplishment, he Crystaled to his Gate instead of going directly to the fort. He dismounted a distance away, as the animal became skittish at the turmoil of energy, and left the horse tied to a shrub. He would go to bed full, in more ways than one, he decided. Jon approached it, the moon lowered in the sky and barely illuminating the night, and he could hear the skeletons rattling about in an ever circling movement of Chaos. He extended his hand to drink of the Magick it contained. It drew him closer. It held everything he wanted or needed. It flowed into him, warmer than sunlight, more bracing than any drink, and it *knew* him. He swore that as it filled him to overflowing. Jonnard broke it off at the moment when it seemed he would become more it than he was himself, and the Gate seemed to sigh as he did.

He pulled his hand back, wiping it on his pants leg. Shadows boiled. Figures began to emerge, watching him with baleful eyes as they solidified. They took a step toward him. He should have felt fear, but did not.

A whisper in the night. *Let usssss hunt.*

Jonnard considered that. What would they hunt? Dare he ask? Did he want to know? Leucators had come from this stuff combined with some human essence, and now they'd returned to it. He knew how Leucators hunted.

On the other hand, he had a lesson to be taught.

Jonnard withdrew the scarf from his cloak and dropped it on the ground. "Hunt that one, then," he said.

Shadows rippled and whirled about the scarf and in moments it was shredded into nothing more than bits of yarn as if devoured. The Gate shimmied. Jonnard backed up a step.

"Hunt no other," he commanded.

Yessss.

He did not turn his back on the Gate and the fiends as he left. He would find out soon how much a master of it he was. It could be useful.

Or it could be disaster.

Hunting

THE REPAIR WORK is going well," Renart said, pulling back the reins and drawing his cart to a halt. Avenha was absolutely bursting with construction as they drove in past the new gates. He jumped down to put a hand out to Pyra, but she had already vaulted over the seat, two strides ahead of him.

"Many hands," she shouted back at him, before dashing off to her father's gatehouse.

Fresh wood gleamed in the afternoon air, and the sound of industry filled the morning. The stench of burned wood and death was gone, cleaned out by wind and rain and hard work as the villagers had hauled out the past. He knew the proverb she quoted, about many hands making a village, and indeed it did, whether building from the ground up or in day-to-day living. He steadied the carriage horse with a pat to the neck before following after Pyra. He would give her a decent amount of time to break the ill news to her father.

The horse, on the other hand, puzzled him. The beast, one of the fine Trader Guild stock, had been skittish the whole trip, as though something trailed them. Once or twice, Renart thought he had seen something loping off the road behind them as well,

but few animals could keep up with the sustained trot
of a carriage horse bred for stamina. They'd camped
overnight, with a bright fire, just to keep the horse
quiet although the animal had slept fitfully, ears flick-
ing back and forth and whickering nervously now and
then. They'd taken the road slower this morning because the horse had seemed tired. The horse roiled an
eye at him now, before dipping his head and shifting
his weight and relaxing a bit. A stabling lass approached them, and Renart handed her the reins, and
a coin. She bobbed in thanks and led the animal and
cart off, chatting cheerfully to the horse in the way
that good hands with livestock do, and the horse
rubbed his muzzle on her sleeve looking for a treat.

Pyra had not seemed to notice either his nerves or
the horse's, her mind filled with worry and grief. Mantor and Flameg had been close, she'd told him on the
ride. It would be like losing a brother, and worse, she
could not even bring his body back so his bones and
ashes could be blended in with the dirt of the village
which would mourn him. Renart straightened his
clothing, and set off after her.

He entered the gatehouse to hear Mantor let out a
guttural sound, the deep-throated noise a man makes
who seldom cries and cannot do it even though he
needs to. Renart hung back a step or two, hearing
that, and feeling his own throat tighten. They all dealt
with loss. Some came shockingly quick, some in its
own good time, and some never in time enough to
prevent suffering. It was the way of all life, but it did
not make it any easier to realize that. He straightened
his jacket a second time before rounding the threshold.

· Mantor sat, his great, scarred hands holding the
leather pouch with the only remains of his guardsman.
His fingers tightened as he stood. "What is done, is
done. He lived well and died well. We will burn his
remains with honor and till them into the soil, to return to the living. The Spirit knows his name and will
not forget it."

Pyra looked down quietly. Her shoulders shook a few times. Renart stepped immediately to her side and slipped an arm about her as Mantor looked at him. "Thank you for bringing them home."

"I couldn't do any less," he told the chieftain.

The smallest corner of Mantor's mouth quirked slightly, as he observed Renart, and the trader felt himself warm a bit, as though the chieftain could see right through him and how he felt about Pyra. Mantor said nothing, however, except to slap him heartily on the shoulder as he strode past with Flameg's remains. He wondered if the chieftain's daughter was as perceptive. He waited till she stopped crying silently, then stepped away a little, giving her space. She cleared her throat and composed herself, giving thought to the business of the future.

"You will stay the night? To rest the horse, if nothing else."

He bowed his head. "Of course."

"Good. We'll be putting Flameg to rest at sunset. It would be nice . . ." She paused, as if searching for words. "It would be nice to have you there."

His heart soared. Did his feet leave the ground? He hoped not. She had quiet ways and he had no wish to scare her off even though he now wanted to shout from the rooftops. She brushed past him, saying, "Let me show you where you can rest."

Pyra halted in the doorway, her eyes sparkling. "You're quite flushed, Renart. Perhaps you should wear a hat more often, the sun seems to have burned you a bit." She ducked out then, and he thought he heard her chuckle as she led him on.

He dozed after lunch, though he meant not to, but having stood watch during the night left him drowsy and he slipped into a light sleep despite his intentions. He woke to the sound of voices raised in greeting.

Jason poked his face around the corner. "Hey, sleepyhead! Pyra said I'd find you here."

"Jason! You are well, then?" Renart sat up hastily, and grabbed for his boots, tugging them on.

"We're wonderful. We've got Eleanora and Fire-Ann back."

Renart beamed at the Magicker. "Incredible news! But I thought our endeavor went badly?"

"That part did, but we don't give up easily."

He joined Jason in the gatehouse hall and noticed that the boy had grown again, and now stood a bit taller than he was. Jason jostled him good-naturedly before wincing slightly, and gripping his right forearm with his left hand.

"Something wrong?"

"Nah. It's healing, just smarted a bit. Tomaz wants me to bring you in. We may have some negotiating to do."

"Oh? What about?" Renart's eyebrows raised, intrigued.

"You'll see."

Tomaz sat opposite Mantor who had reined in his emotions of the morning and now sat with his customary, stoic expression. Pyra was dipping out cups of cooled cider and passing them around. The air smelled of the pressing, crisp and sweet like the apples it came from, and Renart took a cup eagerly. Was it his imagination or did her fingers linger on his hand as he did?

His thoughts whirled as he seated himself at the other end of the table, neither with nor against either of the two men already sitting, his trader training working even before his conscious thoughts could gather.

"You ask a lot of us, even as you honor us," Mantor noted. "I will return Flameg to the ground which birthed him tonight."

Tomaz inclined his head. "We know this. There aren't enough words to thank you for his help, or comfort you for his loss." Jason slipped up to the table and sat quietly next to the elder Magicker, his glance darting about, placing and weighing everyone. Renart had a quick thought of what a trader that one would make, before turning his own mind to the negotiations at hand.

Mantor said to him, "Tomaz has asked us to take in a group and keep them secured, quiet, hidden from the Dark Hand."

"Who?"

"The rescued hostages, and a few caretakers. Such a thing could be done. However, it would not be secret within the village. That could not be kept. Knowing this, then, every Avenhan would be opposing the Dark Hand and the risk is shared by all. We've already paid a price, but I also know that the Dark Hand won't consider that."

"We wouldn't ask, Mantor, but we know that our academy will be the main target. I'd like to see Eleanora and FireAnn get the rest and care they need without facing that hazard," Tomaz said evenly.

Jason looked to the outside wall, restlessly, and this time his right hand went to his left hand and rubbed it without his seeming aware of it. Renart, trained to note the movements of everyone at a negotiating table, did. However, it seemed to have nothing to do with the current matter.

"What are the compensations for such a risk?" he asked.

"We can offer lanterns that require no flame to keep lit. Our aid when needed. Training in certain technologies that you might find useful."

Mantor looked at Tomaz, then at Renart, before commenting, "We need your aid because of your very presence. This would only compound it."

"You had no bandits before the Dark Hand?"

"The world has always known bandits." The chieftain smiled wryly, indicating he understood Tomaz's point. He nodded to Renart. "I'm not inclined to say yes or no, understand this. I am only asking if there is a way to conceal this, for the sakes of my people."

Tomaz tapped his finger on the table. "The Dark Hand won't know of this. I'll ensure that."

Mantor gave a low laugh. "Spies and greed are as old as bandits. You can't keep an entire village quiet."

Leaning forward, Tomaz said softly, "I could, but my methods would be no less despicable than those we call enemy, and I won't do it. Have you suggestions, then?"

"I can perhaps find kinsmen who would consider it, outlying farmers or shepherds, that we can support quietly."

Jason twitched again. His hand rubbed the other once more, a glancing movement that he scarcely seemed to note.

"Hmmmm." Tomaz scratched a thumbnail along the edge of his jaw. "A possibility."

Jason opened his mouth and shut it. Renart looked toward him. "Something to add?"

"Kind of. I think I know where to place them, but they'd need Avenha's help."

"Put it on the table, then," Renart told him.

"The wanderers would take them in. But, through the winter, having extra people around and stuff might be a hardship. They'd need supplies and things like that, help."

"The wanderers have chosen their own course." Mantor's gaze rested lightly on Jason.

"Oh, I know. I understand, and all that. But they're good people, too, and they'd be eager for the lantern lights and such, and I bet the Dark Hand wouldn't even know where to find them."

"For that matter, where would we?" Pyra set down her cider cup, tilting her head slightly with interest.

"I can find them," Jason told her confidently.

From anyone else, Renart would have thought it a ploy to shame the Avenhans to take in the Magickers, but from Jason, he knew it was a sincere communication. Mantor shoved back from the table a little, his brows lowering in consideration.

"It might be done."

"Father?"

"It might be done," the chieftain repeated, "without

breaking their self-imposed exile. We would be aiding
the others, not the wanderers, and the Spirit has always guided us to help where we can. This one world
is like a great ship on a voyage, and we are all but
passengers. To not aid is to impede the voyage for
everyone."

"Right. So it's a deal?" Jason asked eagerly.

Renart coughed. Tomaz leaned slightly, pressing his
heavy shoulder into Jason as if to squelch him a bit.

"There are details to work out, not the least of
which is finding the wanderers and asking Dokr if he
wishes to do this." Renart began making mental notes.

Jason's head turned away from them, and he
frowned, as if noticing his fidgeting for the first time.
He got to his feet, still awkward in his lanky body and
height. "I'm not sure," he said, "we have much time."

"What's wrong?"

"Something . . . is coming."

"Show me!" Pyra grabbed up her longbow from the
rack on the opposite wall, and the two sprinted out
of the gatehouse meeting room. The men scrambled
to their feet, close on their heels, Renart last of all
despite his youth, his fighting instincts not quite as
sharp as his trading ones.

The guardswoman let out a piercing whistle. Heads
jerked around, and then people rushed to the gates,
preparing to close them, as she led Jason up onto the
catwalk so they could look down the valley and the
approach to the village. Workers on the outside
streamed inward quickly, slipping through the gates
before they slammed shut and the great bar dropped
into place.

Pyra nocked an arrow in the longbow as the others
joined the two of them on the catwalk. "What do
you see?"

"Nothing, yet."

Mantor laid his hands on the top of the wall which
surrounded Avenha. His nostrils flared slightly as if
he could scent an invader. He shook his head.

"It doesn't matter," Jason said tersely. "I know it's coming."

Tomaz rubbed his crystals. "Not far away either," he said. As if in answer to him, two crows arrowed through the sky toward them from the trees lining the valley's edge, their caws demanding shrill attention. Midnight and Snowheart dove at his head, before circling and taking up a post on the gatehouse roof.

"There." Jason pointed at the under shadows of the faraway grove. Something loped to a stop, and melted behind a tree trunk, but they all saw the movement.

"Wild animal." Renart tried to sound hopeful.

"Not a wolfjackal. It looks to be standing upright."

"Bandits would ride in, would they not?" Pyra sighted down her arrow at the trees, far too distant for a shot, but keeping ready.

"Aye, Daughter, that they would. Quickly in, damage what they can, grab what they can, quickly out."

"What, then?"

No one had an answer. Mantor drew his own bow, and readied it. They stared along the cleared ground and down the road. After long moments, the shadow separated itself from the tree and began to cross the expanse. Other shadows grouped behind it, staying half hidden.

Mantor stared. "Hold your fire! Hold it!"

Pyra breathed in disbelief, "It's Flameg."

Renart blinked as he stared down. The figure moved in an oddly fluid way that seemed wrong somehow.

"No, it's not," said Jason.

"Hold your peace, boy. I know that man like my own brother. He's managed to get home." Mantor turned away from him. "Open the gates!"

Jason swung on Tomaz, grabbing his arm. "It's not him, believe me. He's dead, think about it. Don't let him in!"

Tomaz stared down at Jason, but it was Renart who moved. He leaped off the catwalk, and flung himself against the gate, as they unlatched the great bar and began to tug it open. It inched wider despite his efforts. Jason jumped to the ground next to him, straightening, his hands filling with a white fire.

"Don't let it in!"

Renart swung about. He could hear the snarling. He turned and saw the . . . thing . . . running at him, charging at the gap between the gateposts. If it had been Flameg once, it wasn't now. He didn't know what he faced if it wasn't the living dead. His heart froze.

Jason shouldered him aside. The air sizzled with white heat, and the thing stumbled, then rolled to its knees. It got up with a growling noise from a throat that had been ripped open. It kept coming.

"It's a Leucator! Or . . . something," Jason shouted up. Villagers jostled him, hurrying to close the gate again, as the terrible thing threw itself toward them, and other things began to break out of the forest, howling.

They got the gates closed. They fought from the catwalk. Some of the attackers had flesh, but some were little more than bone and gore. They pounded at the walls, mewling and howling. They took blows from arrows, reeling back, and then coming on again.

Only fire seemed to deter them. Three of the fiends fell in crystal fire and flame, and the pack fell back to the forests and disappeared.

Renart helped stand the watch until late in the evening, but the things did not return. They burned Flameg's longbow anyway, although the thing that might have been him had run off, and none of them knew if their neighbor and friend would have peace or not.

When it was done, Mantor turned to Tomaz. "Whatever needs to be done, will be. If the wanderers agree." He walked away without waiting for an answer, his heavy shoulders bowed.

42

Desperate Times

"IF I NEVER HEAR the words, 'Are you the Magickers and are you going to help us?' again, it will be too soon," Stefan said wearily before collapsing onto the floor, his legs folded up under him. He scrubbed at reddened eyes, not caring that he'd missed a chair entirely.

"Well, it *is* our fault," Henry said mildly. He leaned on the table, his head propped in his hands as if he couldn't hold it up any other way. His glasses sat askew on his face, one of the lenses sooty and smeared.

"How do we know that? How?" Rich pulled himself up a stool, got his flask out and measured a draught of his medicine. He quaffed it quickly, making a terrible face, then closed his flask.

"Okay, guys, listen up." Trent leaned over the group. "Bailey, give me that map tube I gave you earlier."

With a smothered yawn, she fetched it out of her ragged backpack and handed it over. With a quick twist, he liberated the map inside. He unrolled it and smoothed it out on the table. He grabbed one of Henry's hands and slapped it down on a corner, took one of Rich's and did the same, and Ting put her own down, taking the hint.

"This is how they used to do it in big city police departments. Watch closely." Trent fished a pencil out of the billowing sleeve of his shirt. "Attacks have been here, here, here, and tonight, here." He marked the map starting with Avenha and going to the different villages, including the city of Naria. "Now. We know these things don't ride, animals can't stand the sight or smell of 'em. They move on foot. They're faster than we are, 'cause they don't need to rest or eat or breathe, but they're still on foot. So . . ." He drew a circle connecting the targets. "It suggests that they radiate from somewhere within this circle. Look familiar? I think it does."

They all stared at Trent's map. "The Dark Hand."

"Has to be."

"The abyss they opened."

Trent nodded. "A given, I think."

"That confirms it." Jason took a deep breath, shaking his head slowly. "I didn't think Jonnard could be that stupid."

Gavan and Tomaz came in, their steps heavy. "Jonnard is far from stupid, give him that," Crowfeather stated.

Rich snorted. "I wouldn't give him the time of day."

"Underestimating your foe gives him the first strike against you. Remember."

Jason stared at the map until the lines blurred. "If he's directing the bone fiends, what's he got in mind? It's no longer looting. It just seems to be terrorizing."

"It has to be more than that, he wouldn't waste resources. What do the villages have in common? And what about Naria? That's a pretty big city to attack."

Tomaz tapped the bright star that indicated Naria. "My understanding is that the Trader Guild was hit. There weren't enough fiends to infiltrate more than that."

"Renart was here." Jason put his finger on Avenha.

"Here." He touched Naria. "And here, I think," indicating the small village of Missail. The hills beyond Missail was where Jason's dragon told him the wanderers often wintered, and Renart had gone there in search of Dokr. "Coincidence?"

"Probably not, but the other two, then?"

Gavan said quietly, "Who says Jonnard is in complete control? These are more than Leucators. They're taking dead with them."

"He's opened something he doesn't know how to deal with?"

"Possibly."

"Then how can we expect to?"

"That, lad, is something I don't know. Yet." He slapped Jason on the back. "You all need a shower and sleep, I think."

Ting shivered. "No hot water!"

"Someday," Gavan promised. "In the meantime . . ."

"We know, we know." They got to their feet, the kitchen filled with the sounds of chairs and stools scraping. Sleep while they could, while it was still peaceful.

"I promise you, it will be exhilarating. You will feel omnipotent when you're done." Jonnard patted Isabella's hand as he led her over the landscape carefully, darkness masking her face and eyes from him, but her ragged breathing betraying her fear. That and the coldness of her hands in his. "It'll be fine."

"I have little choice." She faltered a step, and he righted her. He could feel a frailness in her body that he'd never felt before, Isabella of the iron will and temper. He wasn't sure that he didn't enjoy the weakness, but he shuttered that feeling away. He needed her, for now. He tightened his hand on her elbow.

A pack of wolfjackals circled uneasily about the Gate as they neared it. Their eyes caught the light from the sickle moon overhead, and glowed an eerie green as they trotted around the two of them. They growled, low and nearly muted, but still defiant.

"There was a time," Isabella said bitterly, "when they didn't dare snarl at me."

"That will return. All things will bow to you."

"Even you, Jonnard?"

He did not answer. She cursed in French, then laughed. He recognized only the word serpent in her fluid muttering, and decided not to answer. Instead he tugged her forward faster, harshly, over the foreign ground, uncaring if she stumbled, making their way to the Gate. The wolfjackals slunk away, looking back over their shoulders, eyes flashing like hot emeralds in the dark as they did.

He stopped. Isabella said quietly, "What do I do?"

"Hold your hand out, dip it into the shadow, and drink of the energy. Stay wary of getting any closer, though. It is an abyss and a fall."

"We wouldn't want that, would we?"

"Actually, no," he answered flatly.

That seemed to mollify her a bit. She brushed her hair from her face, resetting her jeweled combs, and then put her long-fingered hand out, just touching the swirling edge of darkness. The Gate immediately let out a low moan, as ghastly as any haunted house could issue, and she shivered but did not stir. He could see in the dim light, the bones tumbling about, and the black aura of the power within.

Isabella hissed a long breath inward. "How powerful!"

"Drink deeply. You'll see."

"Jonnard," she murmured softly, entranced, not seeing him, her whole concentration fixed now on the Gate. She almost glowed with it as it filled her. He knew what she felt, and he smiled to himself.

When she was done, he could feel the iron in her again. She drew herself up, and turned to look at him. "Now," she said. "For the price."

"Price?"

"There is always a price to be paid."

He could never put anything past her. He drew her aside. "Not by us." It took but a moment, and then

ghouls began to spill out of the Gate. Whole flesh and
broken flesh, bone linked by sinew and little else, and
the bone fiends gathered.

We hunt.

No longer a question asking permission of him.
They told him they were going. Jonnard gave a bow,
and the hunters went forth, their feet whispering
swiftly across frost-burned ground.

"What do they hunt?"

"Whatever they wish. Not us."

She waited until they stood alone. Then, she said,
"This cannot be."

"For a while, Mother. Only for a while. It has its
purposes. How long has it been since you felt this
good?"

"Do you control them?"

Jonnard thought of several answers, discarded them,
and answered, "No."

"Then it cannot be. If you're a Gatekeeper, open
us another Gate. We'll drink of purer, safer energy.
Escape to another world if this one is corrupted by
them."

He shifted weight. He'd been studying in the days
since he'd opened this Gate.

Isabella arched an eyebrow.

"I can't open a Gate as long as this one is open.
One at a time, it seems."

"Then shut this one."

"It won't be shut."

"No?"

"Not without every ounce of power I have. It would
consume me."

She considered him for a very long time. Then she
said, "It needs to devour a Gatekeeper to close?"

"So it seems," he said reluctantly.

"Why, Jonnard, the answer is simple. Give it a
Gatekeeper. Give it the Magicker Jason Adrian."

"He has one weakness he can't protect from me,"
Jon stated. "His friends. Even Jason cannot be everywhere, all the time."

43

Desperate Measures

A TAP, TAP, TAP DREW Rich's attention as he huddled in a blanket, teeth chattering and sweating off some of what he'd come to call blackmarrow fever. It came and went, and he knew it was his body trying to throw off the poison. It gave him some hope that he might do it someday, that his constitution was different enough that a cure could happen.

Tap, tap, tap. Rich blinked. That was definitely not his teeth. He shrugged off the wrap and got to his feet. A black crow fluttered by the window, and he quickly opened it for Tomaz's Midnight. The creature cawed at him and swiped his beak across Rich's hand as if chiding him for taking so long. It took two tries with shaking hands for him to untie the message scroll. As soon as the weight left his leg, the crow hopped off the table and winged outside, in search of whatever crows went in search of. He supposed roadkill could be found just about anywhere.

He decided the object of search ought to be Tomaz and found him giving Stef a lesson in bear lore, which the big guy seemed to be only half absorbing. Both seemed relieved when Rich interrupted by handing Tomaz the scroll. Tomaz shook it at Stef's nose. "Think about what I told you. The bear is a powerful creature but an unthinking one. You need to learn to use the power without letting the animal take over."

Without waiting for an answer, he unfastened the scroll.

"Where's it from?"

"I left Midnight at Avenha, so it should be from Mantor or Pyra." Tomaz unrolled the small bit of paper. He ran a crystal over it, frowning, deciphering what he could of the writing. Talker crystals worked much better, although Renart had been giving them books from which to try to build a Writer crystal. "It's from Pyra. Renart is missing. Another attack while . . . I think she means the wanderers . . . trying to finish his mission with them. The wording is not exact, but that seems to be what she's trying to get across."

"No! Not Renart."

Tomaz ran his crystal over the scroll again. "Missing," he repeated, although his voice sounded disheartened.

"Not as bad as dead."

"Bad enough." He twisted the scroll in his hands. "I need to find Gavan." Without another word, he walked off, and Rich and Stef traded looks.

"Not good."

"Definitely not good," Rich agreed. He shuddered, and his teeth chattered violently.

"You don't look good either."

"Thanks." Rich stomped off, headed back inside in search of his blanket and solitude. Stef made a puzzled snuffling noise as he went.

He felt no warmer despite the fever boiling off him and not much better when Bailey came strolling by the door. She poked her head in. "Rich?"

He nodded miserably.

She took a hesitant step in. "You want me to get someone?"

"N–no. My fault. I didn't take enough stuff yesterday." He clenched his jaw shut for a minute.

"Take more?"

"I did." He looked down at the floor miserably. He'd dropped his waterskin, and the thick liquid pooled around his feet.

"Oh, Rich."

"I've got s—some more. Somewhere."

Bailey picked up an old shirt in the corner and tried to wipe the mess up. "Ugh. This just smells sickly sweet."

"Tastes good, too," he said sarcastically. "I'll brew more up tomorrow."

"Ting and I can help. What do you need?"

"Dried keffelberries and thane grass. I've got the berries. Thane grass is that stinging, needlelike grass down by the river. It grows here and there. And water, gotta boil it all day."

"That's easy enough." She bounced to her feet. "You go ahead and drink what you need, we'll brew up more, okay?"

Rich heaved a sigh. "Thanks, Bailey."

"Don't be so stubborn. If you need help, ask for it."

"I have to learn how to deal with this." He shook again.

"We all do," Bailey told him solemnly. "Today it's you, tomorrow it could be any one of us, okay?"

It chilled him even more to realize she could be right. He watched her miserably as she ran out to find Ting.

Ting got gathering pouches for both of them, while Bailey tried to explain what it was they were looking for. Finally Ting said, "Ooohhh! Those awful grass things by the rocks."

"Right. Thane grass, looks like a blade, and if you're not careful, you'll slice your fingers up good on 'em, and they sting like crazy."

"Gotcha. I haven't seen any by the pool lately. I think we're going to have to follow the river down a little."

"He says it boils down so if we both get a bagful, that should make at least one batch, don't you think?"

"It should." Ting fretted.

"What?"

"Let's stay close, just in case."

"No problem. I don't want to go outside the wards anyhow. You start here, and I'll walk down the river. Any problems, go for the crystal."

Ting nodded and began to search the edge of the deep water pool. Bailey followed the river, skirting the rocky shore carefully.

Having been there once, it was no problem to get inside the wards a second time. Rainwater lacked a certain finesse and strategy for subterfuge, Jon thought, as he guided his horse through the intricacies of the alarms. He wanted to get close enough to observe, though not close enough to be observed. The key to Jason was the sense of obligation he felt to others, and if he was going to trap Jason, that would be the way. They'd taken the wrong person in taking Eleanora, he thought. One of the girls would have been better. The slender, almond-eyed Ting or the vibrant Bailey. Gavan had stayed cool over Eleanora despite his feelings for her. But the younger ones, they did not have the experience or the maturity. He could have broken them over the girls. He knew each of them well enough to know how they would react to one of their own being in trouble.

The sound of running water covered his movement through the woods as he let the horse pick a cautious way closer to the academy building. He sensed it, more than saw it, for it had its own aura and he knew that Gavan and Tomaz had imbued the place with a great deal of energy.

The bay put his ears forward in curiosity, listening. Jon reined him back, and pitched his senses as well.

When he recognized her voice, he thought it must be a moment of wishful thinking.

"All right, all right, down you go. You see if you can find the stupid grass." And there was a Bailey laugh when a series of indignant squeaks and chirps answered.

Jon leaned forward, peering keenly through the foliage. A slow smile broke across his face. If it was an illusion, it was the one he most hoped to see. And alone, although no Magick worker was ever alone, if they used their senses properly. No, he would have to isolate her. He'd lost one chance to do that, he wouldn't do it again. Coax her to come with him willingly. He sat for long moments, considering, remembering, sifting through the times he'd lived among them and they'd not known him for what he was. Then he thought he had it.

Bailey watched Lacey scurry off, whiskers flattened to her cheek pouches, little tufted tail snapping now and then in irritation. She let the rodent scamper across the mossy rocks, picking up glistening pebbles here and there that shone prettily in the partial sunlight of a day where there were as many clouds as not. The thought of thane grass flitted through the kangaroo rat's mind and left, but Bailey let her go. Lacey had been, after all, a wild thing, and sometimes Bailey wondered if she should ever have bonded with the small creature. It had happened suddenly, though, without either really knowing.

Lacey ran right through a patch of brilliantly green blades, her body barely bending them as she twisted through, intent on something she saw and coveted with her pack rat mind.

"You found it!" Bailey went to her knees. A saw-like edge whipped through her touch. "Ow!" If she'd had any doubt this was the stuff, it fled. Wryly, she pulled out a pocket knife and began cutting the blades down, cautiously putting each one in the pouch as though it were a thorny rose stem. Even so, she found herself sucking on a cut finger every few minutes. She'd quit, but this patch was a treasure trove, enough to fill her gathering pouch and more, and she could get back to Ting. Next time, gloves!

Faintly. "Bailey."

She looked around. "Mom?"

"Where are you, hon? Bailey?"

Anyone else could Crystal for her. She got to her feet, wondering where Ting had gotten to.

"Bailey, I need you."

She sounded hurt. Fear rushed through Bailey. "Mom?" She whirled about, trying to catch the direction. "Where are you?"

"Here. This way . . ."

Bailey walked toward the overhanging trees. She left the pouch and Lacey behind.

She stopped dead in her tracks. "You!"

"Not another word. To anyone, by any way. Think on it carefully."

She stared at Jonnard. "What are you doing here?"

"I came to help, actually. I need you for that, though, Bailey." He crossed his hands on his horse's neck, his clothing all in black like the shadows he stayed half hidden in.

"Like I believe that."

"If you want to or not, it's of little matter to me." Jon leaned forward, the expression on his pale but handsome face very intent. "Warfare between us will destroy Haven. It opened the abyss, and it will spread the contamination until that chasm devours all of us."

Bailey shivered. "You're lying."

"Am I? I was alive when Gregory and Brennard fought. I know what Magick, when it explodes, can do. You, of all people, should know that as well. You're a Magicker. Why do you think Gavan and I don't just go toe to toe and end it all, for once? Because after that once, it became the single, unthinkable thing to do. Our hatred for each other is great, but not great enough to destroy an entire world for it."

Bailey breathed out. "You are serious."

"I am."

"Then what are you doing here?"

"I came for help. It will take two of us to close the abyss. Myself and one of you."

"You're sneaking in."

Jonnard gave a crooked, dry smile. "I think my reception probably warrants that, don't you? The need to avoid conflict is great, however. With every attack between us, the abyss widens, and gets more powerful."

"My mother—"

"A trick, one I apologize for. I wanted to draw you close enough to have a chance to tell you the truth, to convince you . . . I need help." Jon's voice trailed off. "Desperate times mean desperate measures." He leaned forward, extending a gloved hand. "Will you come with me, Bailey, and mend the abyss?"

How could she not? She took his hand reluctantly. "All right. But if you're lying to me, Jonnard, there'll be hell to pay."

He laughed as he pulled her up on horseback. "How could I doubt that?"

The thing was as gruesome as she'd heard. It made her sick to look at it. Jonnard reined to a halt, putting away his crystal, and dismounting. He put his hands to her waist and helped her down as well. They'd ridden and Crystaled, so she knew they'd come a distance, but she also had a good idea where they must be.

"What do we do?"

"We get as close as we dare," Jonnard said. He took her hand reassuringly. "You'll feel it, Bailey, it has an energy all its own. It'll fill you as much as you let it."

Bailey took a step closer, but Jonnard's hand was tight on her and pulled her even nearer. Then, his other hand whipped out and he began tracing his crystal through the air. She saw lines of light falling about her, caging her, disappearing almost before she even realized she saw them. Her feet froze to the ground. Her arms would not work. She looked at Jonnard, stricken. Words failed her.

"Yes," he said. "It is a trap. I have you where I want you." He ran a gloved finger through a strand of hair that had fallen loose across her forehead. "If he doesn't come in time, then the bones will take you, and you'll still be mine. If he comes in time, then I'll have him. Either way, it's a win-win for me."

He hesitated, his fingers on her cheek. "Of course, it doesn't have to be that way. I have been watching you grow. Blossom. I can wait for you a little longer, if I knew you would join with me."

She glared at him. "You must be crazy!"

Jon sighed sadly. "Not yet. Although that day is probably coming. I take it your answer is no."

He traced his hand across her mouth then. "One scream I'll give you, then silence." Jonnard smiled thinly.

It burst from her throat. She heard it ring through the air and through her crystal. "Jason! Help me please!" Then her mouth sealed shut and it was all she could do to even breathe. The ground began to sink under her feet as the abyss yawned wider to swallow her.

Jon backed away from her slowly, still smiling, swung aboard his horse and began to ride away. She saw him pull it into shadow and sit there to watch her, his pale face an oval moon, just out of reach.

She struggled. Every slight movement pulled the cage closer and tighter about her. She could feel hot tears of fear sliding down her face. She could sense the abyss aching for her and she thought her heart was going to jump right out of her chest.

Wolfjackals came. Their howling filled the air, joining in chorus with the howling of the Gate of Bones. Their green eyes caught the light, flashing, as they circled, tails lowered, teeth gleaming. Watching her, they came nearer and nearer. Bailey fought just to breathe. Swallowed by the abyss or torn by wolfjackals? What was her fate?

A wolfjackal broke away from the pack, all silvery and black, with a white throat. It paced near, nostrils flared, sniffing, voice in a low warning snarl. Then it reached for her hand with ivory fangs. Closed its mouth upon her wrist, gently, and pulled. A second wolfjackal trotted up, licked her other hand, its tongue hot as flame, grasped her in its massive jaws and pulled as well.

Their gentle tugs did not move her, and the wolf-jackals whined anxiously. They milled around, talking to one another in low growls and yips. Two or three pawed at her boots, digging, and then yelped as the shadow and fog rolling out of the Gate touched them.

Jonnard raised his arm. He spoke a harsh word, and whipped the air with crystal Fire, lashing the pack with ropes of power. They snapped at him, backed away, tails down, eyes slitted. Then the leader gave a yipping howl as the pack formed about him, and they raced off.

Bailey knew something important had happened, but she was not quite sure what. She took a very careful, long slow breath, as if sipping the air, for it was the only way she could breathe now, as the cage of power tightened again, and the abyss began to pull her feet out from under her.

Jason! Anyone, please!

Tomaz frowned over the scroll. "It doesn't mean we've lost Renart, only that Renart is lost."

"We should have given him Snowheart. A crystal. Anything he could have relied on if there were trouble." Gavan paced back and forth. Henry, Trent, and Jason watched.

"I think we don't give him enough credit," Henry said, pulling his glasses into place.

The two men stopped arguing.

"I mean," Henry said apologetically. "He's done a lot of trading. You should hear his stories about caravanning through flash floods, and clan wars, and stuff. He's a resourceful guy."

Gavan flicked the edge of his cape back. "True enough." He took a deep breath. "Pyra will undoubtedly be scouting the area."

"Undoubtedly."

"She could use help."

Tomaz nodded. "I'll offer."

"All right. And the rest of you. We're going to have to watch each other's backs from here on, carefully. The attacks are spreading. We have to be a target, sooner or later. Stay close. No one wander off."

Doing laundry could hardly be called wandering off, Jason told Trent, as they hiked down to the pool. "Although if you wear those jeans one more day, I think they could stand on their own."

"Hey, hey! These are vintage jeans. Holes and all."

"Henry's offered to buy you new ones."

"They take time to break in." Trent's expression looked serious. "Do you think I want to wear stiff, scratchy new denim? Give me soft, old, worn denim any day!"

"I think you just don't want to let go."

"Maybe not. Just like Bailey wears that old watch of hers, even though it's never kept time here." Trent dumped his bag on a rock ledge. "Looks like Ting beat us down here."

Ting rounded the water, a muddy smear across her nose, and a full pouch of greenery bulging on one hip. "Either of you seen Bailey?"

"No. Better watch yourself going in, Gavan's put the word out no one is to go off alone."

"Too little too late, I think." Ting stood on one foot and then the other. "I can't find Bailey."

Jason dropped his laundry bag next to Trent's. "Leave that, we'll find her, you go on."

"Okay. Don't get her in trouble, all right? We're gathering Rich's potion stuff for him. She said she'd go downriver."

"Understood. I'll give you a holler when we find her."

Trent matched Jason's long strides down the stream. "Think she's in trouble? Fell in or something?"

"Bailey is so stubborn if she fell in, she'd float upstream. She just got involved, probably. Or Lacey ran off again." They ducked under the cooling overhang of the forest's edge. Trent picked out a fresh boot print in the soft shore of the river. "She went this way."

They had gotten deep into the forest when the shout hit Jason and drove him to his knees. He doubled over, gasping with Bailey's pain and terror.

"Jason! Jeez, man, what is it?"

"Trouble. Big trouble." He grabbed Trent's hand and Crystaled without warning or thinking. Cold *between* rushed past them both.

He felt it the moment they touched ground. He jumped to his feet, still linked with Trent. Bailey's mouth opened in a silent scream and she reached for them as the Bone Gate roared wide open behind her. He could feel its pull, its yearning for him, for her, for Trent.

"She's caged!" Trent yelled over the moaning and wailing of the Gate.

"Show me!"

He reached for Bailey, tracing the bonds that held her, and Jason's crystal flared about his neck as he grabbed her hand and held on. The Gate pulled her and she hung in the air between them. He cut her loose strand by strand, but the Gate sucked all three in. Bones crackled underfoot and he gagged at the stench of rotting things. It glowed as if it could feed off them, its darkness lightening to the color of gangrene.

"Don't. Let. Go." Bailey mouthed to them.

"Hang on!" Jason yelled at her. He dug in his heels. The Gate promised him things, whispering in his ear of undying life, power. He wanted nothing but the three of them out and safe.

Trent cried out, "That's the last rope!"

Jason lifted his hand, crystal Fire streaming from his fingers, the pendant on his chest so hot it felt as if it could burn through his shirt.

And then they had her, pulling her toward them, out of the abyss, out of the Gate of Bones, and it wailed in frustration and grief at losing its prey.

44

Frying Pans and Fire

WHAT WERE YOU thinking?" Rebecca waved a hand. "If we had a dungeon, I'd throw you in it for a few days." She paced in front of the girls. Bailey opened her mouth, and her mother jabbed a finger in the air. "I'm not done talking, young lady!"

Gavan said aside to Tomaz, "I'd punish them myself, but I think a mother's wrath is probably worse." Tomaz chuckled, his hand covering his face. Both men cleared their throats and quieted when Rebecca gave them a look as well.

She swung back on Ting and Bailey. "I could have—we could have—lost you. There's no excuse for going off alone. Latrine duty for a month. Darning duty. Laundry duty."

Bailey shuffled her feet. Finally, spent, Rebecca dropped her hands, eyes red, and she said, "Don't ever, ever, ever do that again!"

"Yes, ma'am," both girls echoed each other.

Rebecca gathered them up in a massive hug, hiding her face against them for a moment. Tomaz stirred, and dropped a leather gathering pouch in Bailey's lap. It fell open, to reveal not only the harvest of thane grass, but a tightly curled up furball who woke from sleep long enough to twitch her tufted tail. Bailey beamed at Tomaz, and hugged the pouch to her chest.

Gavan waited respectfully for a few minutes before saying quietly, "Be that as it may. We need to know what you can tell us. All three of you."

Rebecca let go, retreating to the corner, where Madame Qi sat, her back straight, her face lined not only with her age but great worry. She took Rebecca's hand and held it for a few moments.

Bailey said defensively, "He told me the abyss was caused by our Magick warring, like what happened between Gregory and Brennard. He said we were all creating it, and it would take two of us, one from each side, to heal it. That's why I went."

"Did you not think of who he was?"

"Of course I did!" Bailey looked up defiantly. "But if something could be done, we'd do it, wouldn't we? We'd do what we could to stop that thing. I thought he meant what he said. Even if he didn't mean to heal it, he could still be right."

Gavan leaned on his cane, wolfhead gleaming. Bailey looked at it and thought of the wolfjackals. "Even the wolfjackals are afraid of it."

Tomaz took a step forward. "You saw them?"

"A pack. They ran in, and circled me."

"Chaos draws them, we know that. They need it."

She shook her head at Tomaz. "It wasn't like that. I thought I was going to die, one way or the other. But then, one of them crept close and took my hand and tried to pull me free. A few of the others came to help. They dug at my boots, but nothing they did could move me. Jonnard drove them away."

Tomaz inclined his head slowly. "They are not tied to the Dark Hand, though they serve it sometimes. They are like what they sprang from, Chaos. I can't predict them."

"Sounds like they were just saving dinner, to me." Trent waved a hand.

Gavan faced him. "What did you feel?"

"Jonnard had her all spun up. It took us a bit to

cut her free. The thing itself—" He shrugged, his face tightening. "It is like a nasty pit of slime. I can't explain it better than that."

"Negative energy?"

"The most negative energy I could imagine." Trent crossed his arms over his chest, as if protecting himself.

"Jason?"

Jason had been studying the floor, listening. He looked up. "It's definitely a Gate. How it opened, I don't know, but it knew me, knew my powers." He rubbed his hands together lightly.

"Could Jonnard have spoken truly?"

Jason shifted uneasily. "There's a lot I don't know about Gates, but I don't think so. I do know, it's opening still. It's devouring. It could take everything with it and still be hungry." *And it wanted him. It wanted him the most.*

"Could you close it?" Gavan looked him in the eyes, and Jason met it, unflinching.

"Maybe."

"Did you Open it? Somehow, without knowing?"

Jason shook his head violently. "Never! Not something like that!"

"I had to ask."

"Did you?" He stared back, and after a moment, Gavan did look away.

Rich took out his flask and took a drink, shuddered, and capped it, putting it away. "What do we do now? Is anybody but me bothered that the only one who heard Bailey through the crystal was Jason?" He swept his red hair from his forehead. "Has Jonnard got that kind of power?"

Gavan cursed. Words spilled from his mouth that would have made Shakespeare blush, and he stamped his cane into the floor, driving a dent into the wooden boards. "Is this true? No one else heard?" He pointed the cane at all of them, sweeping about the room.

Trent spread his hands. "I'm deaf to those things, I never hear anyone."

"N-not a thing," answered Henry. He took his glasses off, cleaned them, and set them back on.

Everyone else just shook their heads.

Tomaz tapped his fingers on his silver-and-turquoise belt. "If he had that kind of power to tap, we wouldn't be in this struggle. We'd have been swept away already."

"Maybe he's just learning. Maybe the Gate feeds him."

"If it does, then we've no choice but to do everything we can to stop him, and close the Gate." Gavan stamped his cane again. "We can't afford any weaknesses if we're going to strike at the Dark Hand." He pointed at the boys one by one. "Search party. Ting and Bailey will hold the academy."

"What are we looking for?"

"Renart. Safety. An answer to the Gate of Bones. Whatever it takes," Gavan answered.

The academy went deathly quiet after the search party left. Ting dragged her feet as they started their chores and finally Bailey nudged her, hard. "We got off easy."

"Maybe. But at least you got to do something, even if it was wrong." Ting sighed. "I feel absolutely useless."

"Don't. I think that's why Jonnard keeps failing. He's picking on us one at a time. Henry. Stefan. Jason. But we're more than that, we're all of us. You can't bring us down one at a time."

Ting considered her. "I don't know. Maybe you're right, maybe not."

Bailey hugged her. "Of course I am! I'm always right except when I'm wrong."

Ting laughed in spite of herself. She pushed Bailey away gently, about to say something else, when the academy lanterns flickered. One by one, the crystals dimmed to the lowest of lights and even though the sun shone outside, the great building grew dark.

From upstairs came a shriek. "Death! Death and disaster! Banshees!"

FireAnn appeared at the top of the stairs, her hair unbound, red-and-silver curls wild about her head, her hands upraised. "The banshees come!" Cackling, she tottered down the stairs, grasping the banister for dear life.

"Jonnard's back!" Bailey swung around wildly, dashing to the front door to drop the guard bolts in place.

Madame Qi came out of the kitchen, the wooden spoon she was holding fragrant with the aroma of Rich's potion, its sweetness permeating the air. "Something is here." She gestured. "Feel it, Ting?"

"I've felt it before," Ting answered slowly. "It's settled over the whole place."

"Demon."

"Banshee!" FireAnn reached the landing and grabbed for Bailey. "Protect Eleanora! Go to her, lass!"

Bailey unwrapped FireAnn's twisted hands from her arm carefully, saying, "Stay here." She took the stairs two at a time, leaping upward to the third floor where Eleanora rested. The door was thrown open, and a coverlet lay on the floor. Eleanora swayed by the side of her father's coffin. She turned to Bailey.

"It's come for Father."

"What has?"

"I'm not sure. Can you feel it?"

Bailey spun on one heel. Defeated, she shook her head.

From the doorway, Ting said quietly, "I can. It's dampening everything. I can't reach Gavan or Jason or anyone."

"It's Jonnard!"

"No," breathed Eleanora. "It's not Jonnard." She looked up. "It's not one of us, it's something beyond."

"We need to get out." Bailey took Ting's and Eleanora's hands, pulling them from the room.

"Gregory!"

Freyah burst in. "Get her away from here." Her voice snapped briskly. "I'm staying with him. I've kept him this long, I can keep him a bit longer."

Bailey looked at the sarcophagus and the feisty silver-haired woman as she sat on it, and crossed her arms. "I think he's probably as safe as he's gonna get. Come on!"

She and Ting had to draw Eleanora with them. Still weakened, she struggled gamely to keep up with the girls, her breathing growing ragged. Madame Qi and Rebecca were trying to soothe FireAnn as they arrived downstairs.

"Is it an attack?"

"Only one way to tell. I'm taking a look." Bailey took a deep breath, stepping to the front door. She unbolted it, then drew it back. Or tried to. The door stayed firmly shut in its frame. She braced her heels, pulling on the handle with all of her might. It wouldn't open.

"Kitchen door." Ting raced Bailey to the side door, reaching it first. She tried to yank it open, and nearly fell, as it refused to yield.

Every window in the kitchen refused to open as if hammered close. She and Bailey rounded the big room, pounding on the frames.

They tried every exit they could think of, one by one. The academy stayed shut. They returned to the others.

"We're locked in."

"Is it the Gate? What's happened to the others?"

Bailey shook her head. "I don't know." She shivered. "I don't know!"

Madame Qi drew herself up. "My grandfather fought demons," she said. She looked at Ting. Ting swallowed. She opened her hand and looked at her palm. The fiery red dragon mark seemed to wink at her.

"This may be our only way out." She traced the mark.

A hot wind swept the room, filling it. Ting jumped back, startled, her hair streaming behind her. FireAnn fell to the floor weeping in fear, and Eleanora went to her knees to comfort her. As Ting and Bailey stared, a fiery ring opened up, like a great eye.

"Go," urged Madame Qi. "Hurry!"

Ting gulped. She tugged on Bailey. "After you!"

45

Pearls of Wisdom

"ARE YOU SURE this is the darkest time?" Bailey asked, wrinkling her nose. "I mean, it's desperate all right, but somehow things always turn out and I really wonder if one bad Gate a day isn't enough—"

"If you don't move, I'm going to kick you in the rump myself," Ting said firmly. "Now go!"

"Jeez. When did you get so bossy?"

"Since . . . since I met you! Now move!" Ting waved her arms wildly, startling Bailey into jumping through the fiery aperture, Ting on her heels. The fire ring hung in midair a moment with the roar of flames, then disappeared.

Instantly, the world changed. The silence of Haven disappeared and they could hear the once familiar sounds of auto traffic, the buzz of electricity in the air, the drone of an airplane passing by, although all seemed muffled in silvery fog. From far away, a fog-horn sounded forlornly.

"Where are we?"

"Home, I think." Ting brushed her hair from one eye, looking about. "Grandmother's home, that is. I think we're in San Francisco."

"So it really is foggy." Bailey peered through the

soft, billowing ground-hugging clouds, unable to see almost anything except Ting as she flashed an embarrassed smile.

"Only sometimes. I like it, though." Ting took a deep breath. For a moment, all her troubles seemed to drop away. "The funny thing is, if you're on one of the hills, often only some areas have fog. It's like part of the city is gift-wrapped. I like to sit in Grandmother's courtyard and watch it drape the house." Ting tilted her face up. She took a few steps forward across short-trimmed grass that was as wet with the fog as heavy rain, her shoes making whispery sounds as she crossed it. "Bailey," she said softly. "I *am* home. Look." And she pointed at the house beginning to emerge, walkway by corner by roof eave from the silvery fog, and the proud enamel red Chinese dragon gracing its roof tiles.

Bailey looked up. "So you think your great grandfather really enchanted that."

"It seems logical. It could be our only help now. I have to bring it back!"

Bailey stared at her friend. "Nothing about Magick is logical. It's all wondrously improbable but possible. So. How do we get this dragon down? Climb a rain gutter?"

"I was thinking garden ladder."

"What if someone sees us?"

"That," Ting said solemnly, "is an excellent question, and I have no idea. Family still lives here, but I'm not sure I want to wake anyone up. I think it's early morning."

"Very early." Bailey stumbled. "Streetlights are still on, if anyone can see them. Note to self: try not to walk into one, they are tall and solid and hurt." She rubbed her kneecap ruefully. "Where is that ladder?"

"This way." Ting slipped through a side courtyard, opening the gate latch as quietly as she could, and guiding Bailey past a koi pond where brightly colored fish slithered lazily through the water, themselves looking as if they were only half awake.

"No alarms?"

"We've never needed any." Ting looked guilty. "They might now, if we take the house dragon. I should leave them a note."

Bailey put a hand on the back of her wrist. "I think someone stealing it is probably enough of a hint."

"Oh. True."

Fog had barely filtered into the back courtyard, although its dampness dappled the flagstone and left rainlike drops on the many flowers and plants. Ting found the ladder and she and Bailey managed to somewhat quietly carry it to the mostly likely corner and place it. By silent agreement, Bailey held the foot of the ladder while Ting climbed up. It was, after all, her dragon.

The fog seemed to follow her up as she climbed. It curled about the ladder rung by rung until when she emerged, she could see the roof but not the street or anywhere else around. She stepped cautiously upon the red-clay tiles curving like ocean waves under her feet. The Chrysanthemum Dragon stayed motionless on its weather vane, facing her, metalwork even more beautiful and fantastical than she'd always seen from the ground.

The long and sinuous body of a Chinese dragon was accented by the large head with wire whiskers, and a curling tail. It ran on three feet, the fourth one curled with a reaching step, as though the artisan had caught the dragon in a gallop or perhaps frisking through midair. The vane was made to turn in the wind, but she had never seen it do more than circle gracefully no matter how forceful the breeze, as though it was beyond a dragon's dignity to whirl crazily about. Up close, she could tell it was half as long as she was tall, or maybe even slightly bigger than that. She hoped it wasn't too heavy for her to carry, at least as far as the ladder and Bailey's aid.

She reached it in three more cautious steps. It slowly swung about to face her, although she couldn't feel a breeze. The fog did not stir at all.

She put her hand on it. "We need you," she explained, "at Haven. I need you, and Grandmother Qi, and Eleanora and Freyah and FireAnn. I know it's been your job to guard here, but I'm hoping you'll come with me, at least for a little while."

The enameled metal felt warm to her touch, surprising her, for the San Francisco morning seemed very cold yet. She bent over, examining the structure. It appeared all she had to do was lift the dragon from its post, the one sleeve slipped into the other. The rest of the dragon would rotate and swing freely about the post. If she could lift it, that is. She reached down.

The dragon swung away.

Ting frowned. She moved into a better position and reached again to grasp and lift it. It spun in the other direction, coming about so quickly it knocked her off her feet. Ting ducked and dug her hands into the tiles suddenly afraid of slipping, as the dragon swung about.

"What are you doing up there?"

She could hear but not see Bailey. "I'm trying," she said, "to get it loose."

"I think somebody is awake down here. I hear a teakettle whistling."

That was the last thing she wanted to hear. Ting carefully stood up, balancing on the curved tiles. Did she remember a story her mother used to tell, about a workman come to paint the dragon once? A high wind spun it around and around, eluding every stroke of the paintbrush until he finally came down off the roof, ranting in rapid Chinese about demons and tricks and refused to do the work. Grandmother Qi finally hired an art student to enamel the vane, and he had sat patiently, day after day, doing a true craftsman's job and never once did the dragon move.

"Please," pleaded Ting. "I need your help!" She grasped the dragon along its spine with both hands and pulled up.

It snapped its head around with a hiss. "Sssssstaying!" As it exhaled, fire and smoke spewed out, swirling away into a huge ring, just like the one that had brought them there. Its free paw uncurled to swipe at her hand, and as it spun about, it knocked Ting clean off the roof toward the fiery portal. Her ears roared with the lick of flames, and as she flew past Bailey toward it, she reached out and caught her friend by the sleeve. Together they went tumbling through air and fire.

She landed on her back, Bailey across her legs. The impact hurt, as if she had fallen from the roof and she didn't move for a while. She wiggled a foot first. Then an arm. Nothing seemed to be broken, just squished.

"I can't believe it."

Bailey groaned and crawled off Ting's other leg, sitting up. "It didn't work."

"It wouldn't come. What did I do wrong?" Ting put her hand to her face in dismay and something fell out. She stared at the ground. A great opalescent pink pearl rolled to a stop near her knee, a delicate gold chain trailing behind it.

"Wow," breathed Bailey. "Where did that come from?"

"I don't know!" But she did. Ting sat up. The house dragon had had that front paw curled up tightly for decades since being cast. Had the pearl been in its clutch all that time? It must have been. She picked it up reverently. "This is great grandfather's pearl. It has to be!"

"The one you told me about? The one he wore?"

"I had the wrong dragon. This must be the one." Ting cupped the huge pearl, its colors swirled from creamy white to blushing pink. "He summoned it with this. Or this became it."

"Either way. What are you waiting for?" Bailey gave her a hand up.

"I don't know what I'm doing, that's what."

"That's never stopped me!" declared Bailey.

Ting laughed at her, wrinkling her nose a little, then looked down at the pearl in concentration. "I should ask Grandmother."

"But she'd never seen the pearl either, right?"

"No, just heard stories of it." Ting cradled the object. "If I focus on it, I should be able to tell if it has any Magick at all. Then we can figure out what to do."

"That sounds like a plan."

Ting felt the pearl warm in her hands, the gold chain dangling from it. It was not made as a showpiece of jewelry, although the object could be worth a king's ransom. It had been worn as a pendant, perhaps, or a talisman. She let her eyes and attention be drawn into its richness of color, the play of the opalescent sheen over it, the essence of the pearl itself, a seed of possibility held within an oyster once upon a time before being worn about the neck of her ancestor—

POOF!

Pink smoke exploded everywhere. "Holy moly!" Bailey jumped and let out a shriek. Magick slammed through her, knocking her off her feet and onto her duff. It had been that kind of day, she decided, and just sat where she was rather than get up again. When the smoke cleared, she began to laugh and looked around for Ting.

"Ting! Ting? Here's your dragon. Well, I think it's a dragon. I don't know if we can use it for a guardian, though. It . . . it's kinda small." Bailey got on her knees and looked at the beast, Chinese in every aspect, like the weather vane creature, but this one was a blushing pink from tiny whiskers to sinuous tail. "It's not really a dragon, I think. About the size of your average cat. Smallish."

"I know," said Ting, very muffled.

"Where are you? Come see this. It seems a little . . . frightened." Bailey looked about, bewildered, then held a finger out to the dragon. It hissed. "Heh. It's spunky, though. Okay, I can't call anything this small a dragon. I mean, it's like . . . garden-sized. It would get lost in a hedge. That's it. There's hedge wizards. This is a hedgedragon."

Ting sighed. The hedgedragon let out a long, corresponding steamy *sssssss*.

Bailey peered at it. It stared back at her, whiskers drooping.

"Oh, no." She leaned down. "Ting?"

The hedgedragon sniffled.

"Oh. My."

46

Face-to-Face

I'M NOT RESPONSIBLE for this mess."

Hedgedragon and Magicker stared at each other. The beast wiggled its nose, fine kitteny whiskers waving as it sniffled again. A big golden tear formed on a lower eyelid and ran down the delicately scaled face. "Okay, okay." Bailey reached out and gathered the hedgedragon into a hug. "We'll do something. I don't know what, but something." The pearl bumped against her chin. The hedgedragon now wore the object around its neck. Her neck. The dragon was Ting. "You'll change back."

"But when?" Ting's voice sounded very, very far away, and wrapped in tissue paper. "We have to do something *now*."

Bailey looked around, having been far too busy and bewildered to note where they had returned. They sat in the academy courtyard. "At least we're outside," she pointed out.

"I don't think I can face any demons like this!" And the hedgedragon wailed pitifully. Not only was it a pitiful sound, but a pretty poor attempt at wailing, Bailey thought. It was more like a squeaky yodel. She reached down and scratched the hedgedragon's floppy ear to comfort her.

"Oooh," murmured Ting. "That feels *good*. No wonder cats like it." Her eyes closed to slits.

Bailey looked up. And up. She stopped scratching, saying in a distracted voice, "That's good. I'll do more later. After."

"After what?"

"After we find out what that is." Bailey stretched an arm out, pointing at the huge apparition that stood over the academy, vaguely man-shaped, draped in body armor, with a helmet on, reminding Bailey of an ancient warrior knight or maybe a shogun. She thought of standing, and decided it wouldn't make her tall enough to make any difference, nor would getting to her feet help running away any. She touched her crystal, but it remained cold and mute. "We're face-to-face . . . um . . . snout . . . with the demon."

The hedgedragon turned about in Bailey's lap and then froze. A string of sounds burst from her that sounded Chinese, although Bailey had never really heard Ting speak it. She didn't know if Ting even actually knew Chinese. The hedgedragon put up a curled paw, then flexed it, and talons snapped out, like a cat putting out claws. It might have been impressive if the hedgedragon was anywhere near the size of the other.

The thing leaned down to peer at them. "Who are you?" it said, the man's voice as thin and hard to describe as the wind. "You who throw ancient curses at me?"

"I am Ting!"

"You guard this house and all who dwell inside?"

"I do!" The hedgedragon punctuated that with another few words in Chinese.

"Do you know who I am?"

The hedgedragon let out a low hiss. Stalling, Bailey thought, or bluffing. Ting whipped her curling tail about, looking fierce. "Is that wise?" Bailey asked in a low whisper.

"I protect," Ting declared, "what is mine."

"As do I." The being, which had been leaning over

peering at them, now stood and stretched. It raised its arms and looked as if it could hold up the sky with them even as insubstantial a ghost as it seemed to be. "This is mine." With a gesture, the being indicated everywhere about them. Its eyes gazed down at them again to see if they understood.

A terrible idea struck Bailey. She pulled on one of Ting's wings to get her attention. "Ting. Ting, I think that's—"

The hedgedragon let out a boiling hiss of warning as the being reached toward them. It paused, and its body moved as if it might have been shaking with laughter, though not a sound reached them.

"Ting, do you think that could be—"

The hedgedragon swung her tail around, whapping Bailey right in the mouth. "Ow!" Startled, she put her hand to her lips.

Ting put her ears flat, and uncurled all her talons, arching her back. "Touch us if you dare."

"A dragon is a dragon is a dragon, it seems." The hand that had begun to extend downward withdrew.

"A pact is a pact. We are both guardians in this place."

"So you know me, then."

"I do. You take from all so that you can protect all."

"A balance is reached."

Ting's whiskers wiggled. Her ears flicked up alertly. "You've overstepped here."

The being crossed his arms. "You mistake my powers, small dragon. I take a little, to guard a little, to guide. That is all I can do now." It made a sad noise, like waves crashing upon a seashore, and then withdrawing. "The one who takes much now lies inside, asleep."

"Gregory!" muttered Bailey, then immediately clapped her hands over her face again, wary of the hedgedragon's snappy tail.

"It is disturbed. There is much imbalance here," and the being looked across the valley, toward the faraway hills and the Dark Hand's fortress. "I have calmed the sleeper, but know this. We are entangled, he and I, from centuries ago when we walked together in this land, and we learned much from each other. He draws from you to live, as I draw from my people to stay in this existence, and we learned this together. There is nothing that exists without balance or it ceases altogether." It inhaled, a great sucking in of air, and the very forest moved and shivered with it. "He tried to awaken, but there is not enough power he can draw to do so without harming you. He wanted to defend you against that which has opened, but he is helpless. As I am helpless."

Ting made a sound in her throat.

"You are not helpless. Yet. Time is running out . . ." The apparition began to grow wispy and shred, like an insubstantial cloud on a windy day, and then it was gone.

Bailey leaped to her feet, dumping the hedgedragon to the ground. "That," she said, "was the Warlord Spirit!"

Ting shook herself off, scales making a fine, chiming noise. "I know."

"You knew?"

"Inside me. Something dragonisssssssh."

Bailey's crystal bracelet began to warm, very slightly. She sighed in relief. "It's coming back."

"Good. I think." Ting scrubbed a paw at her whiskered snout. "I can't go in like this. I can't!"

A roar sounded from the Iron Mountains, a roar that carried the scent of hot copper and magic with it. Bailey cringed. "We may not have to. I think we've been summoned."

47

Dragons and Dungeons

"EXPLAIN TO ME AGAIN why I'm carrying you up this mountain."

"Becaussssse," hissed Ting, "I hafffft to meet Jason's dragon to find out what'ssss going on."

"No, no. I've got that part," Bailey said, as she shifted the hedgedragon from arm to arm. "I meant, why do I have to *carry* you. You may be as small as the average cat, but you weigh as much as a big dog. Why aren't you flying? Dragons do fly, don't they?"

The hedgedragon ruffled its wings, then said sadly, "I don't know howwwww."

"Oh, sure, like that's a good excuse that's gonna hold. I think I'll try that at home. I don't know how to make my bed or wash the dishes. How long is that going to work, hmmmm?" A little out of breath, Bailey paused, swapping Ting from side to side again, as climbing took all her attention. For long moments she clambered up the side of the Iron Mountain until she reached a plateau.

Ting let out a hissing sigh. "Do you think this is eassssy?"

"Look, sister, I don't know how you cut it, but being carried up this mountain has got to be easier than climbing it one-handed with a heavy reptile in the other!'' Bailey put the hedgedragon down. "All right, call up the big guy.''

The hedgedragon curled up and ducked its head inside its wings. "Don't want to,'' Ting said sulkily.

Bailey looked around. Besides the slope they had climbed, leading down to the academy and the pool of water of the small valley, and the grove, the other side of the plateau had a steep drop-off. "I wonder how dragons learn to fly,'' she observed. "I wonder if they have that 'kicked out of the nest' first lesson, like falling off the side of a cliff.'' She leaned her head to look off the steep side, then looked back at Ting.

"Nooooo!'' The hedgedragon scuttled away from her, and Ting's words evaporated into high-pitched dragon squeals.

"Oh, jeez, I was just kidding. Lighten up, Ting. This isn't easy for anybody. It's not every day your best friend turns into a dragon, you know?'' Bailey sat down and crossed her legs, and made a coaxing sound like she made to Lacey whenever the pack rat was being stubborn.

A great shadow fell over the two of them. "Well. And well, well. I didn't believe it when I sensed it.''

Jason's dragon hunkered down on his forelegs, and looked the two of them over curiously. "Yet, here you are. We don't have a cutoff to qualify for dragons, but if we did, I'm not sure you'd make it.'' The large beast rumbled in gentle laughter.

"Both of you!'' Ting huffed and puffed, and a tiny bit of blue-gray smoke came out her nostrils. "Ewwww! That ssstings.''

"What is it you called her?''

"A hedgedragon,'' said Bailey firmly.

"Yes, indeed. Most appropriate, I think.'' The dragon put out a claw to poke Ting. "I am not an expert, but I think it could grow to some size, given enough time.''

"I'm . . . sssstuck like thissss?'' Ting curled up again, wings over her whiskered face, and wailed.

"No, no, little one. And do show some dragon dignity. We do not wail in public. Or," the dragon coughed. "Ever." He shook himself. "You'll return to yourself when ready. With enough lessons, you'll become adept at going back and forth."

"Like Stefan-bear!"

"Yes, well, rather like that, although one hopes with a bit more aplomb and less angst."

"Whatever." Bailey reached out and gathered up Ting, scratching behind one scaly ear. "See?"

"Will I fly?"

"Eventually. Think of it as swimming, that will help." Jason's dragon pulled back to sit on his haunches. "You have a great deal to learn about yourself, young Ting."

"So it seemsssss." Ting rested her chin on Bailey's shoulder.

"Let me say this. A guardian's ability is not always in its size or its fierceness. You learned that earlier, however, did you not?" The dragon looked her over. "I think you'll do."

"I will?"

"Let us hope. Now off with you two." Jason's dragon curved his talon and gave Bailey a nudge back the way they had come.

"But—but . . . we're not done," Bailey spluttered.

"Of course you are."

"We have more questions."

"But I," the dragon intoned deeply, bass voice rolling out of his chest, "have no more answers."

"One more, one more, pleassssse!" Ting fluttered anxiously.

"Perhaps one."

"How do I change back?"

"By the pearl, naturally, although why you would want to, I can't begin to guess. Being a dragon is so much better."

"But I'm not a dragon."

"Only sometimes. One last word of advice. Never eat a friend. It can cause all sorts of disconcerting trouble you can't imagine, and simply isn't worth it."

Bailey paled. Ting dipped her head saying, "I'll remember."

"Now off with you. There is some worrying going on downhill, and you've some explaining to do."

Bailey picked Ting up. Both of them called out thank yous to the dragon, even as it lay back and melded into the great mountains, its brilliant red-orange color dulling until it became one with its background and they could not tell where the dragon ended and the mountain began.

As for the dungeon, Bailey expected they were both going to end up in one after all, for the trouble they'd put everyone through.

Freyah was stunned when they told her about Gregory. They finally went upstairs to tell her, after watching Ting POOF in and out of dragon form a few times, to everyone else's amazement and delight. She grew tired of it, though, and hungry.

The hedgedragon beat Lacey to a cricket and gobbled it up. Then, POOF! As the pink smoke cleared, Ting put her hand to her stomach. "I can't believe I did that! Ew! Bailey! You let me eat a bug."

"Not only did you eat it, but you beat a famished pack rat to it. There was no one here going to stop you." Bailey coaxed Lacey over and gave the little rodent a bit of very stale biscuit.

"Grandfather used to carry a sign with him," Madame Qi said. "It read, Don't Feed the Dragon. He kept it for many, many years after he retired. I used to ask him why. He told me, it was a reminder that the dragon must feed him, not he the dragon. It was a matter of discipline and control. You may be very wise to remember that, Ting, and not feed as the dragon lest its instincts overcome your own."

"That sounds like a good idea. Plus, I'm not sure I can handle any weird meals."

Bailey glanced at Ting. "Are you stable now?"

"Stable?"

"No more POOFing?"

"I hope so."

"Good." Bailey looked upstairs. "We need to talk to her."

Freyah had moved to a chair, sitting near the sarcophagus, knitting needles and something made of fluffy yarn in her lap, with George patiently at her side holding the ball of yarn on his tray. "I can't believe my brother would draw on us like that, jeopardize all of us."

"I don't think he meant to. From what I can tell, he absorbed most of the explosive energy of the war between himself and Brennard. He expended that, keeping everyone safe, but it left him no reserves. You've been keeping him alive and asleep, Aunt Freyah, ever since. Now he feels the imbalance, the jeopardy, and wanted to awaken to help, but he needs that energy back just to do it." Ting held her hands like scales. "Energy in, energy out, energy in. He had to draw from us and yet, when he realized it could damage us all, he couldn't stop. The Warlord felt the imbalance and stepped in. He can't awaken yet. We just don't have the input to give him."

"That makes sense, in the magickal equation, for our side." Freyah told her. "And it seems the Warlord's Spirit has been tapping all of us a little, capping our abilities, to keep his own world in balance, but he's failed with the Dark Hand."

"There's nobody to stop the Dark Hand but us, and I'm not so sure about us." Bailey rubbed her eyes in worry.

Freyah started knitting again, needles clicking quickly. "Sometimes great sacrifices have to be made." Smiling wistfully, her gaze fell on her brother's motionless face and stayed there.

The girls left quietly.

The search party came home in the middle of the night. While they ate and rested, Stef wouldn't be satisfied till Ting had POOFed for him in and out of hedgedragon form at least three times. His hand wrapped about a huge sandwich, which he then consumed in three bites, he managed to say, "Wow. Does that hurt? It does me, sometimes. Not like they show werewolves in movies or anything, but my bones and muscles ache."

"I get heartburn." Ting coughed, and a little puff of pink smoke came out. She blinked in surprise.

Trent and Stefan nearly fell down laughing, and she shrank back, her mouth in a small pout.

"Be that as it may, we had as busy a day as you did."

"Did you find Renart?"

"Possibly. Packs of wolfjackals are roaming the countryside. We've identified at least three. Some attacks have been quite hostile, and some are merely coming in after bone fiends, as we know wolfjackals will do. Renart appears to be one step ahead of one of the packs. As Henry said, give him credit. He seems to be quite resourceful and hmmm . . ." Gavan grinned tiredly. "Fleet."

"So we have much hope in him yet," Tomaz added. He stood. "I'll see you all in the morning."

Slowly, they all drew away. Bailey and Ting went up the stairs last. At the top, Bailey turned around and looked down.

"What is it?"

"Did you ever look at something and realize it'll never be the same again?"

She'd felt that in the moments she stood in the fog. She nodded solemnly. They hooked arms together.

"Things change. They always do."

"Sometimes they change too fast."

A Helping Hand

"IF A TRAP WON'T work," Isabella mused, "then perhaps the direct approach."

"You would recommend what?" Jonnard sat, charging a handful of crystals on the table in front of him, their gemstone transparency gleaming with an inner fire, bursting with the power he put into them. Eyes still dazzled a bit, he narrowed them as she caught his attention.

"I think we need to talk to the Council. Convince them we can be quite helpful."

"I'm not following you, Isabella."

"That, my son, is why I still lead." She rose. "Get a carriage ready. We have a trip to make. Naria, I believe, before the storms move in and the roads get muddy. I don't know how long it will take these people to make a decision and do something, so we had better make haste now."

Jonnard swept up his crystals and pocketed them in his cape, his mouth twisted in a swallowed word. His failure with Bailey and Jason had not earned him any respect from her. The day would come. Soon.

"Rich doesn't look good again."

"Did he take his medicine?"

"Yup." Stefan shifted his weight uncomfortably. "I think we should take him to see Kektl. I know you think it's 'cause I want to see Beryl, and I do, but that's not it."

"I know it's not," said Gavan, not unkindly. "Let me take a look at him." He let Stef lead the way, noting that despite his lumbering size, the young man had developed a kind of grace. Most certainly his body had gone to muscle now, instead of just largeness, and it was obvious the sword work had done him a lot of good.

Rich huddled on his cot, covered with all of his blankets and most of Stefan's. Still, he shivered and shook, and a cold film pooled over his forehead. Gavan let out a deep breath. "All right, then. You take Rich. I'll get Jason and let the others know, and we're off."

Rich rolled an eye at them. "I'll be fine. Really. Once the Ice Age goes away."

Stef pulled him out of bed and hoisted him over his shoulders. "Nice sense of humor. Don't give up your day job."

"Shivering *is* my day job."

Jason joined them outside. "He's really that sick?"

"I don't know. Yes, he's feeling badly, but if it's the blackmarrow or if he's picked up something, I can't tell. It's a new world, we could all be exposed to something we have no immunity to."

"Oh, joy," Rich mumbled from somewhere around Stef's armpit. "A hypochondriac's paradise."

"Then you should be happy."

"I'm giving it up," he said. "It takes too much of my time." He stopped talking to shiver and groan as Gavan took them *between*.

Kektl looked a little startled as they all appeared before the outer doorway of his home and practice. He looked up from the leg and ankle of his young patient, eyes widened at the sight of Rich, and motioned to them. "Please. I won't make you wait long."

Stef rolled Rich onto a chair. He promptly drew his

knees up under his chin and tucked all the blankets
he had brought with him around himself. The young
lad Kektl bandaged shot him a wide-eyed look.

"I had ten stitches," the boy told Rich. "I didn't
cry once."

"I cry all the time," Rich fired back. "It gets me
attention."

The boy edged away, drawing a curt word from
Kektl who calmly straightened his bandaging out and
then finished. To Rich, he said, "Don't tease the lad."

"Right. I'm sorry." Rich sat up, shedding his blankets. "That was pretty brave, actually. And keep it
clean!" He called after the lad who sprinted away as
soon as Kektl said, "You're finished."

The healer washed his hands in a minty smelling
basin, then came over. "Let's have a look at you."

Anticipating the question, Rich muttered, "Yes, I've
been taking my medicine." His teeth chattered and he
gritted them between every word.

"How much and how often?"

"Four times a day. A swig from the flask."

Kektl pursed his lips critically. "Actually, I told you
three. Four if three didn't work, and I said to take a
ladling spoonful. A swig can be more or less, and in
your case," Kektl took Rich's hand in his and eyed
the thumbnails and then looked at his eyelids. "I'd
say you took even more than that. The good news is
he's overmedicating."

"But he looks worse than ever," Gavan responded.

"Because thane grass is, in itself, a poison. That's
why the doses have to be worked out and carefully
administered. I'll give you a spoon, and I want it
used." Kektl turned to a small, carved bureau, with
legs like paws, opened a drawer and fished out a flat-
bottomed spoon with a hole in the handle. "I suggest
you tie it to the flask. Three times a day, absolutely
no more. Two times tomorrow and no more today at
all. You need to work that out of your system."

"You're giving him a poison?"

"Thane grass is much milder, really an irritant, but

it counteracts the blackmarrow. It's the best I can do, for now." Kektl smiled sympathetically. He went to the basin and washed his hands again. "How is everyone else?"

"Fine."

"That bite?"

"Clean and healing well." Gavan bent over and rubbed his ankle as if checking. He nodded. He dropped a few coins in the dish on the bureau provided for payment, and Kektl gave a deep bow.

"Would you care to stay the day and night?"

Stef looked hopeful, and his face fell as Gavan shook his head. "Much to do before winter sets in."

"I remember those days well." Kektl made a sign of gratitude, his six-fingered hand flashing gracefully. A commotion in the street outside drew everyone's attention.

Kektl bowed and went out to see who hailed him. He returned, a little drawn, and made another bow. "It is discovered you are here. The Council has sent for you. You may leave if you wish, but . . ."

"Council? Is that the same one that meets with the guidance of the Spirit?" Jason had been quietly watching, brought along only to help Gavan in case of fatigue, but the words went through him with a disturbing ripple.

Kektl nodded at him. He started to tell Gavan no, but the headmaster had already begun answering, "Perhaps we should meet them."

"I will tell them you'll be along, but you have a sick member who needs to remain in my care." Kektl glanced at Rich. "He should stay quiet for a while."

"All right. Then it's the three of us, and I suggest you two listen and learn."

Jason murmured a vague word of agreement. When the escort came for them, and took them to a great house, with tall arched doors, the sinking feeling of a dream come true hit him.

The Council stood in robes at the far end of the hall. Most of the finer details didn't match his foreboding at all, except a group of people waiting for them, and to the side stood Isabella and Jonnard. If he had felt better about that for a moment, it fled.

"We are here at the Council's behest," Isabella said. "Come to give them a helping hand, as it were. How fortunate to find you here today, although we've been here several days, in discussion. Troubles have beset our lands."

"And ours. Strange that the trouble seems to be quite close to your borders."

"It comes, brethren dear, from strikes made against us. I've told the Council of everything that falls between us. We're all agreed." She reached out and put her hands on the railing before her. "The warring must stop."

Stef made a low growl in his throat, only to find Gavan striking his cane across his chest as if to hold him back from anything further. Gavan tilted his head toward the speaker of the Council. "Are you mediating, then?"

"We will if we have to, but we prefer you make your own terms with each other."

Gavan absorbed that. "Very well." He faced Isabella. "Close the Gate. It is an abomination."

"Of that, we're also agreed. However," and her glance flickered. "We didn't open it, so we have no control over it. There is only one we know of who can be called Gatekeeper." She looked past Gavan to Jason. "It is a Gate of the dead. The only thing that can close it is . . . a life."

Jason only half heard her. His dream played loudly in his mind, muting the sounds around him. He heard Gavan make an exclamation, then a denial, and then, with a flash of his hand, he Crystaled them out of there, before Jason could blink and Isabella's words could sink in.

Gavan paused at Kektl's to gather up Rich and then brought them home, so angry he said scarcely a word to anyone.

If it was a dream, it was a very bad one.

They gathered at the worktables, and Ting's quick fingers braided a thong for Rich's spoon and attached it to the flask while Jason related as much as he remembered of the Council meeting.

Trent frowned. His fingers drummed the table in agitation. "You couldn't have heard her right."

"Well, I'm baffled." Stef scrubbed a hand over the top of his head. "Isabella got snotty, Gavan got angry, and we got yanked out of there. That's all I know."

Jason's mouth drew tight. "Think about it, Stef. That Gate is rogue. It will take everything a Gatekeeper has to close it. Everything." He shoved away from the table and left them all sitting there.

Ting looked after the disappearing back of Jason, her forehead creasing in bewilderment. She swung around to Trent. "What is he talking about?"

Trent said nothing. He looked down at an invisible spot on the table and appeared to study it intently.

Stefan slapped his heavy hand over the imaginary target. "Come on, you know, so give it up!"

They traded looks all the way around the table. The sound of Rich scuffling his boots filled the otherwise quiet room.

Stef frowned heavily. "Come on, guys. I may not be the sharpest knife in the drawer—" He paused. "Well, actually, now with all my training, I *might* be that, but you know what I mean! What's Jason talking about?"

Trent cleared his throat, then took a long, slow breath, and sat back with a squaring of his shoulders. "He hasn't said it directly, no one has, but everything seems to point toward it. Closing the Bone Gate will require a sacrifice. Not just any sacrifice, but the ultimate one."

"Oh, no." Bailey paled. She reached out and took Ting's hand in her own, and both girls trembled slightly.

Stefan kept his steady gaze fixed on Trent's face, waiting for more.

"That's all I think I know. It'll take a life to close the Gate."

"You have to tell someone!"

Trent shook his head. "I think almost everyone knows, they're just not talking about it. And neither should we."

"I almost . . . I was *there* . . ." Bailey gulped. "If you two hadn't pulled me out, who knows. . ."

"And that's probably how he knows. He felt it. He knows what lies in there." Trent's words fell heavily among them.

49

Stuck on You

HEAVY RAINS BROUGHT a few days of rest and peace. The bone fiends quieted as if even the undead could not face nature's fury. The Magickers all concentrated on patching the roof, which inevitably had a few leaks, or tossing Ting off the stairwell banister in her hedgedragon form to teach her how to fly and a myriad of other duties and classes. Some assignments seemed a lot more fun than others.

Jason grew increasingly restless. He woke early on a gray morning which found the sun breaking through again, and had barely dressed when alarms began to shrill. He roused Trent and ran outside to find the valley awash with wolfjackals and two crows.

Snowheart swooped through the air, her shrill cries ahead of the alarms, sharp beak and talons plucking at the invaders with a nip here and a rip there, attacking as only a crow can do, with speed and agility. All she could do was harass and tease the wolfjackals, but she kept them dodging and yowling from her, distracting the beasts as they circled the academy. Midnight joined her, his smaller, more muscular body weaving patterns in and out with hers, the two birds turning an entire pack of wolfjackals despite their flashing jaws. Yet for all their effort, the wolfjackals only altered their course to another path, bearing down on the academy.

For all their help, the crows of Tomaz also hindered. No one dared send a crystal flash at the wolfjackal pack for fear of hitting one of the birds. Instead, they concentrated on circling the academy as Gavan and Tomaz shouted orders, and the Magickers ran to their posts. Blushing, Ting poofed into her hedgedragon form, pearlescent scales glittering in the late afternoon light, flying not nearly as well as the crows. Twice she bumped into either Bailey or the corner of the academy eaves, letting out a tiny cloud of pink smoke as she did, her tiny dragonish ouch of pain. She flitted and darted at the wolfjackals as they circled past Bailey, her little dragonish talons extended, her Chinese body curling and uncurling as she hissed and spit in hedgedragon fierceness at them.

Bailey bit her lip to keep from laughing, for Ting was hardly as fierce as she thought she was, although the wolfjackals swerved away from them as they galloped past, their howls on the air. Bailey kept ducking away from her as she bopped up and down, still trying to get the hang of flying in hedgedragon form.

Stef stepped out boldly, his sword in hand, and Rich took up a position at his back, crystals in his. Stef's big square body dwarfed Rich's in width, but both were of a height, and the wolfjackals slowed as they neared them, foam splashing from their teeth as they gnashed and snarled at the boys. Stef turned his broadsword slowly hand over hand. "Come and get me," he said.

Jason and Trent nodded at each other and took up similar stances, although Trent's weapon was more of a basher than a blade. He hooked one elbow with Jason, as the crystals in Jason's hands flared, and Gavan spoke to all of them through their gems.

Stay close to the building, use it to guard your back. Take them out as they come through.

Jason repeated it aloud for Trent who set his jaw in answer. The pack circling them was huge, the biggest he'd ever seen, and the first time he'd noted young cubs running with them, wolfjackals probably still young enough to be nursing. He frowned.

Bailey let out a shriek. Jason peered around the corner of the building to see the hedgedragon caught in Bailey's hair. Well, no, not caught—Ting seemed to be determinedly yanking at Bailey's golden ponytail with all of her hedgedragon strength, all the while spitting and hissing. Bailey bounced on one foot.

"Get her off, get her off!" She stopped bouncing for a moment, frowned, then yelled, "Get Madame Qi! I can't understand a word she's saying, it's all in Chinese, I think!"

The hedgedragon let go of Bailey's ponytail and let out a teakettle whistle and began to fly around Bailey in excited circles, tail lashing.

Jason gestured to the academy, alerting Henry inside, asking for his aid. Eyes nearly as round as his face, Henry darted out, helping Madame Qi through the makeshift barricade. She put her palms in the air.

"Granddaughter, Granddaughter, slow down. I have not heard this dialect in many a decade." Qi tilted her wizened head and listened intently as the hedgedragon perched on her wrist, rather like a dragonish bird of prey. The exchange had gone silent, mind-to-mind. Qi's face frowned in concentration, and then she put her chin up. "Everyone stop! Ting says the wolf-jackals are here to help, not harm! Please note, she says, wolfjackals have always come after an attack before, to absorb the Chaos. Or they have attacked with the Dark Hand. But this is a family pack, see the cubs? They are here to help."

Tomaz loped from the far end of the academy, the silver roundels at his wrist and belt flashing in the late afternoon sun. The wolfjackals stopped circling and came to a halt, still growling, teeth bared, enough of them to ring the building. The ones facing them lowered their heads warily, tails stiff behind them. The elder Magicker paced toward an enormous male wolfjackal, likely to be an alpha member in any pack, his hand held out.

"He's gonna lose that hand," muttered Stefan.

The hedgedragon swam clumsily through the air and made a slow circle about Tomaz as Tomaz continued to approach. The wolfjackal peeled his lips back in a long, slow, continuous snarl. But he did not snap nor did he back up as Tomaz drew within range.

"She's sensed something," Tomaz said calmly. "This pack is different. I have run with one or two, not all are savage."

The wolfjackal male scratched at the ground. He looked over his shoulder with brilliant green eyes, as if he could see into the distance.

Gavan's voice flared from Jason's crystal, and he could hear a dim echo from other nearby crystals. *Are they here to help? If so, aid against what?*

Snowheart flew overhead, diving down and then drawing away, her white diamond chest skimming the trees leading from the valley. Tomaz tilted his head as he followed her flight with his mind.

"Raiders," he said. "Raiders riding hard."

The wolfjackal growled low in his throat and shifted restlessly. Then, as if making up his mind, he put his muzzle to Tomaz's hand in canine entreaty.

Jason had never seen a wolfjackal act like that. Ting made a giddy circle about Tomaz, whistling in delight. Tomaz said, "I think we have allies. Asked for or not."

The circle of wolfjackals drew close. Jason felt the hair on the back of his neck and his arms rise, as one of the beasts brushed by him, fur grazing his leg. He'd never been so close to one not focused on killing him. He swallowed tightly. Before he had much more time to think on the strange partners, war whoops filled the air, with the thunder of hooves, and the crackle of crystal energy, as raiders charged through the grove.

Henry took Madame Qi by the elbow as she brandished her cane with her free arm, her voice ringing out in a high-pitched Chinese phrase that sent the blood drumming through all of them. Reluctantly, Ting's grandmother returned inside the more secure academy, Henry Crystaling the doorframe as he moved through it, restoring the door's strength and locks. Sparkles danced along the wood before sinking into its very fiber.

Jason turned to face the raiders, and as soon as he saw them, his stomach clenched and shrank inside him, and he let out a wordless sound.

Trent shuddered beside him, and the two backed up a step in disbelief. These riders bearing down on them now came from the jaws of the Gate of Bones itself. With ashen-gray faces, bloodless wounds still gaping open on them, the raiders were echoes of all the battles they'd fought in other villages over the last weeks. Stef let out a low rumbling in disbelief, "I killed that lead rider last week."

Fiends from the Gate of Bones rode down on them as if seeking the very life inside them. They whipped and spurred the horses under them, and the poor beasts trembled with every jump as if they could not bear to carry the riders on their backs, their flanks heaving with ragged breaths and foam. No longer afoot, the undead could range as far as a horse could go before it dropped.

Tomaz made a gesture with his hand as if warding himself. He sent both his crows back into the air with a shout, and his hand came down with a blade of crystal light, slicing across the horde of fiends.

Jason raised his own hands, feeling Gregory's crystal as well as his own grow heated in answer to his need. Let them last, let them give until the fight was over. . . .

And he understood why the wolfjackals had come. Chaos drew them, they fed on it as if it were air itself, and the fiends of the Gate of Bones were Chaos itself. Yet their corruption roiled about them like filthy boiling water, and it stank, and he realized that the aura they gave off was as deadly to the wolfjackals as poison. They had come as much to save themselves as to save the Magickers.

He had no more time for thought than that as the raiders closed on them, and they fought for their lives. What he could not get with crystal, Trent got with his shovel, and what they could not get with either, wolfjackals tore from their sides, growling and snarling and pawing at their muzzles after as if the touch of the bone fiends disgusted them.

Gavan set flash fires on the cleared ground about the academy. The wolfjackals and horses sprang over them, but Stef and Rich dragged raiders' bodies into them as soon as one could be unhorsed. The stench of burning filled the air. The afternoon sun nearly spent, Jason found himself fighting shadows as often as a dead raider in dark shrouds.

He swung his crystal blade and Shielded until his arms ached and he did not think he could stand, and he backed up, leaning on an object for strength. The object, a panting wolfjackal, leaned back on him and for a moment they drew power from each other.

A horse veered past, eyes wild, rearing at the scent of fire and smell of death. Its rider bailed, landing on his feet, and he bared his teeth at Jason in a grin. "You are mine," the dead man said. "Gatekeeper." He gave a low hoarse sound that might have been meant for laughter. He stalked toward Jason. He bore himself with the ease of a fighter, and Jason recognized a man who in life had been the second headman of Avenha. Pyra had mourned Flameg, but this . . . thing . . . resembled him only vaguely.

Trent swung around, shovel in hand. The raider grabbed it and pulled Trent to his knees, then clubbed him with the back of his hand. Trent went down, stone cold.

Stef growled, but he and Rich struggled with their own fight, too far away to help. It was just Jason and the wolfjackal as the dead man stalked closer. Flameg drew a short, curved blade from his waistband. The last, lowering rays of the sun glinted off it. The old, crescent-shaped scar on the back of Jason's left hand throbbed with a painful stabbing.

The wolfjackal sprang. Jason stumbled as the beast launched past him, with a growl and a snarl. He did not stop growling even as the sword blade impaled his body, and the heaviness of his weight brought the raider to his knees. Jason blinked. He brought his crystal up, and took the dead man's head off before he could think about it twice.

For a moment, the raider's body stayed upright, on his knees, and Jason wondered if there was a way the things could be killed. Then it toppled, taking the wolfjackal with it.

Pain creased Jason as the animal let out a low groan, and then, a gasping whine. He went to it, but he could see nothing could be done. The beast whimpered a moment, then put his muzzle to the back of Jason's hand and his tongue gave a slow, hot lick. The light of knowing fled from his bright green eyes, and the wolfjackal died.

Wetness stung Jason's eyes. He swung about, with a remembered cry. "Trent!"

Trent lay on his back, staring upward, but his chest moved and then he kicked a foot out with a moan. He sat up, with Jason's help. "What hit me?"

"Never mind. Are you . . . you're all right, right?"

"Sure. My head is probably the best place on my whole body to get hit." Nonetheless, Trent wobbled as he stood, face pale.

It took Jason a moment to realize they stood in relative quiet. The fiends, or what was left of them, had fled into the shadows, their weary mounts stumbling off. Wolfjackals, what was left of the pack, lay on the ground, panting. Magickers, all of them, took a step back, exhausted, their crystals going dim one by one.

Gavan came out, as did Henry. Henry lifted his crystal solemnly after all the bodies had been rolled into the front fires. His Talent of Fire roared as he raised his crystal high and the flames answered, shooting skyward with a brilliant hot fury that almost instantly seemed to burn away the dead raiders. When the fires died down, no one spoke for a long moment.

Jason didn't see Bailey. He swung around on one heel, in the smoke, feeling panicked for a moment.

"Bailey? Bailey!"

Had they lost her somehow? But how?

A whimper answered him. Frowning across the fires and haze, he saw her seated at the corner of the academy, a fur bundle across her knees. She looked up, tears streaking her face. A wolfjackal pup huddled in her arms. "His mom . . . his dad . . ." she said, slowly.

Jason nodded then, understanding. Tomaz moved across the ground, and stood with Jason, hand on his shoulder, watching Bailey.

"He's . . . he's stuck," she said.

"Hurt? I mean . . ." Jason tried not to think of the wolfjackal who'd saved him, impaled on a sword blade.

"No. In my head. We're—" Bailey took a deep breath. "I think we're bonded."

The pup let out another whimper and laid his head on her shoulder, shoving his snout into the curve of her neck. An outraged squeak greeted him, as Lacey pushed her way out of Bailey's pocket and glared at the newcomer. The wolfjackal turned his silver-streaked mask quickly, snuffling at the rodent who chirped and dove headfirst back into the safety of Bailey's pocket. The interested pup tried to shove his nose after, but Bailey thumped him. "Stop that!"

The pup chuffed and buried his face on her shoulder again. Bailey stood, holding the animal in her arms, its legs dangling. Ting, still in hedgedragon form, came to ground.

"I think we won," Trent remarked.

"This time," Gavan replied. He signaled to Henry to snuff the fires. "Only this time."

The wolfjackals got to their feet, put their noses to the sky, and let out a series of mournful wails. Then they faded into the forest as well, not a one of them looking back after the orphan Bailey carried. "Hey!" she called. "Hey! Hey! You can't just leave him."

"I think they already have," Tomaz told her.

She hugged the furry pup closer.

In quiet time, Trent worked on his maps of what he'd seen on dragonback, using a purloined copy of one of Renart's maps to help him. Jason came into the study after him.

"Bedtime."

"I'm almost ready. I'll be able to give this to Gavan soon." Trent raised an eyebrow at him. "You're up late."

"Been thinking."

"Gate raiders?"

"I think I was their target."

"Couldn't prove it by me, I think I was out cold at the time." Trent's voice trailed off, as he saw the serious look on Jason's face.

Jason said quietly, "I've looked at this from all the angles I can think of, and there's only one way I can be sure will close the Gate of Bones."

Trent paused in his sketching, and flicked a look at Jason in disbelief to which Jason shrugged, adding, "I think the Dark Hand is correct about this one."

"You're kidding me, right?"

"Wish I were. Think about it. In all your beloved myths and legends, this boils down to it . . . someone's gotta go slay that dragon, so to speak."

"No. I refuse to believe that. The only solution they've come up with is a human sacrifice. And not just any human, they've elected you, Jason. I don't think they care whether or not it *works,* they just want you out of the way."

"I know."

Trent dropped his drawing pencil and lifted both hands. The sheet of paper he'd been mapping upon began to roll up slowly, as if cringing and hiding. "This is crazy. You're walking right into their trap. Without a fight?"

"No. I've been thinking and thinking." Jason dropped onto the stool next to Trent so he could look eye to eye with his friend. "Jonnard isn't a real Gatekeeper, but he opened that one. It doesn't swing open and shut like a normal Gate, and as near as I can tell, it doesn't portal like a normal Gate. It doesn't lead from place to place. I think it . . . well, I'm not sure, but I think it leads from existence to existence. From life to death, from good to evil, or something like that. Whatever it is, it doesn't belong here, and it's corrupting everything every moment it stays open."

"And your point is . . ."

"I can't allow it to stay open, and I think it will take all of a Gatekeeper's power to shut it."

"All of their power?"

"All."

Trent shoved back from the table as if rejecting everything he said. "No way!"

"I need you to trust me on this."

"Trust you? When you've gone insane or something?"

Jason took a short breath. "If I've learned one thing—make that two things—since becoming a Magicker, it's to trust when I look inside myself, and to trust in my friends when I reach out to them. I can do this, Trent, but I can't do it without you. I don't want anyone else to know what I'm planning, but if you think you can help, then let me know. Either way, I know what it is I have to do." He stood. Without another word, he left the study, and behind him he could hear muffled words that sounded like Trent muttering, "Oh, maaaaaan."

Trent watched Jason walk out of the study and rocked his stool back on two stubby rear feet, balancing himself precariously. His fingers drummed the edge of the tabletop in time with his thoughts as they galloped through his mind. Although he'd come to the same conclusion, he hadn't voiced it to Jason, and he hadn't thought Jason would ever come to believe in it, too. No way would Jason say, all right, Jonnard is the big kahuna and he's right, and I'm gonna go throw myself in the volcano for everyone's sake. No way.

But he just had, in so many words.

Trent syncopated his tapping fingers and mind through every myth he could think of, without finding a way out, and finally let his stool sink back to the floor on all fours. He needed ammo if he was going to talk Jason out of anything, and he couldn't come up with it. If anything, old stories and tales and religions tended to reinforce what Jason intended to do.

There was no way Trent would let that happen. And he couldn't think that Jason would just give up that easily, not the Jason he knew, not the friend he'd come to depend upon.

For that matter, why had Jason come to him, and not to all of them? They were all in this together, always had been. There was no doubt the two of them, though, had shared thoughts with each other that no one else knew. Jason had opened up to him about things Trent knew he would never tell another soul, unwilling to vent anything that could hurt anyone else. Trent had listened to him when Jason feared he could tell no one else. Then, why his cryptic last words? Why would Jason possibly think he'd help do something so rash?

Trent blinked.

Because . . . possibly . . . Trent was the only one who *could* help.

"I'm an idiot," he said, and got to his feet. He reached for his crystal. He couldn't find Jason through it the way the others seemed to find each other by talking and seeing, but there was no way he was going to run through the academy yelling at the top of his lungs. If, as Gavan had hinted, the walls might well have unfriendly ears, there was ample reason Jason hadn't come right out and said what he meant.

But he had his own ways of finding people, and as he held his crystal, his mind cleared a bit and he could see through the doorway a faint aura-colored pathway trailing after the way Jason had gone. Magick leads Magick, he thought, and went in search of the other.

50

The Decision

A HEAVY HAND THUMPED on the academy's front door. Gavan opened it, Jason at his elbow. Rain had come and gone again, but more clouds threatened on the horizon. It did not, however, dampen their pleasure at seeing who stood there, as the other Magickers raced downstairs and crowded around.

Dokr stood there, hat off. "A bargain has been made," he said. "I have come to help." A faint smile creased the man's face.

Henry whooped behind them. "Renart did it!"

The wanderer gave a slight bow. "He has given us seed for fields and seedlings for orchards, and land for us to hold. We would make him king for that, but he tells us it is your doing. I'm here for fulfilling the bargain."

They hurried to get everyone packed and ready, while the wanderers stood by with the same uncurious, patient look they had held while building the academy. Gavan brought them all together.

He held Eleanora in his arms, but she sat up, smiling, looking far better than she had days ago, her hair brushed softly about her face. He kissed her temple lightly before saying, "We're never alone, as Mag-

ickers, you all know that. But we can't use the crystals
to stay in touch, not right now. There is a chance,
however slight, that the Dark Hand might overhear
us at these distances. So, our correspondence will be
as the crow flies. Snowheart or Midnight will be taking
small messages back and forth when needed. We
won't be far apart, or for long."

Tomaz held up a forefinger. "Small messages," he
repeated. "And only as absolutely necessary. Crows
are not jet planes."

"Everyone ready?"

"I am staying," Madame Qi stated firmly. "Otherwise, I think all are ready."

"Staying?"

She nodded at Gavan and said nothing more.

"Then let's go. I don't want to attract attention to
wanderers on the road this late in the year." Gavan
carried Eleanora out first, murmuring something none
of the others could hear in her ear. She laughed and
pinched his ear back lightly, bringing a flush to his
face.

Dokr seemed unfazed by the invalid Eleanora being
loaded onto the first wagon, or even FireAnn who
cackled and either blessed or hexed in her Irish
brogue the teams of horses hitched to the wagons, but
he did give pause as they loaded Gregory in his
sarcophagus.

"He is dead, no?"

"He is dead, no. I mean, no, he's not dead. Just
sleeping. For a very, very long time." Jason faltered
in his explanation.

The wanderer stared as they stowed the coffin in
the cargo bin of the wagon. "Very well," he said to
Jason finally, with a shrug. "I have seen stranger
things, I believe."

Freyah tapped him on the shoulder. "We're all in,
young man. Time to move out."

Ting leaned against her grandmother. "Are you
sorry you're not going?"

Her grandmother smiled, her face breaking into a

thousand wise wrinkles. "There is something here I must finish first. Let Rebecca get the first lessons, she has much more to learn."

Jason watched as Rebecca and Bailey hugged each other fiercely.

"Stay out of trouble," mother told daughter as daughter burst out, "I'll try to stay out of trouble!" They laughed at each other. Then Dokr gave orders to his drivers and the three wagons pulled out to the slap of harness and sharp whistles urging the horses, leathers creaking and wheels jolting. Eventually, they all turned away but Gavan and Bailey.

Jason watched from the doorway as Gavan leaned over and hugged Bailey tightly. Jason listened as he made her no promises, though. They might be safe for now, they might never be safe, as long as the Dark Hand valued power more than life. He turned away, thinking that this was as good a time as any. He and Trent exchanged looks, and he gave a nod.

Trent frowned and nodded back.

He tidied his bed and few things. He took his crystals, the one in his pocket, and the one he often wore on the chain about his neck, his old soccer shirt twisted into a headband, and sundry other items that meant something to him. His other things he left in a neat bundle at the foot of the bed. He did not say goodbye to anyone, not until he Crystaled to the edge of Dark Hand holdings.

Wolf jackals surged toward him, snarling and yipping, a wave of fur and flashing eyes, the first alarm of intruders on the land. He waved a hand, and they stilled. He rubbed the scar on the back of his left hand, the scar he had carried since before he had even known he was a Magicker, the scar a wolfjackal had marked him with, and he said, "I am yours."

They parted to let him through. He strode across the outer boundary of the hills until he reached the blackened valley where the abyss broke through, and there he waited.

In a few brief moments, Isabella and Jonnard appeared. She was dressed in midnight-blue satin, her gown sweeping the winter grass of brown and sand, while he was all in black, as usual. "What are you doing here, Magicker?"

"I've come to close the Gate."

Jon's eyes flashed in triumph. Isabella raised a hand. "You're agreeing to do whatever is necessary?"

"That's why I'm here. In case you're doubting me, I brought a witness. Someone so there won't be any trouble later, no blame for whatever happens." Jason turned, quirked a finger, and Trent loped up behind him.

Jonnard's mouth curled. "The Magicker without Magick."

Isabella put her hand on his, stilling him, saying, "I think that's wise. A witness is an excellent idea."

Jason looked at the Gate, and took a deep breath. It sensed him, its voices growing louder, calling incoherently for him, for the power he carried. A moment of regret filled him. He wouldn't see his families again, either one. He hadn't told the dragon what he intended to do. And he'd dragged Trent into this. He turned around. "You don't have to stay," he said to his friend.

"There is no way you're getting me to leave."

He put his hand out. "Whatever happens, then." Trent took his handshake, then pulled him in for a hug. In his ear, fiercely, Trent whispered, "Never alone!" before letting go and moving back.

"The Gate is quiet," Jonnard pointed out. "It would be wise to do whatever you're going to do before the fiends start emerging. Their taste for flesh is . . . not pleasant."

"I don't need encouragement," he answered flatly. He took Gregory's crystal, warm to his touch, out of his pocket. He thought about it a second, then passed it to Trent. "See Eleanora gets that."

"But—"

He shook his head quickly. "I won't need it."

Trent whistled softly. "All right." He tucked it away, his own crystal swinging from its chain on his belt loop.

Without any more thoughts, he stepped into the whirling edge of the Gate, into the mists at the lip of its abyss, bones snapping underfoot, and a skull caught in the maelstrom of its movement bobbing around in vacant-eyed mockery of him. Power licked at him like cold green flame. It wanted to crawl inside of him, but he thrust it away. He didn't want any part of it or its false promises. He looked up and saw Trent's tense face, watching him, and he smiled. With a hand to his crystal, he began to do that which he could do best.

He learned the Gate. Without taking its powers, he learned its fury and its weakness, its purposes and its ending, and he began to deny it pulse by pulse. Jonnard leaned close. He had to shout to be heard over the whirlwind and the moaning.

"What are you doing?"

Jason smiled at him. "Closing the Gate. What I came to do."

"Fool. You're doing nothing. Step inside it!"

"It will devour what it wishes," Jason told him calmly. He continued to set up his matrix, and for a moment, he thought he could do it, actually do it, and survive. He drew on himself, and he drew on the Chaos of the wolfjackals circling the Gate, their eyes glittering with hope and anger at the nearness of their freedom.

Then the Gate awoke. Like a great beast that sensed prey within its grasp, it truly awoke. A thousand Magicks erupted inside of it, bathing Jason, dragging him back and down. He thought he felt hands on his ankles, Leucator flesh, grasping him. Jonnard licked his lips.

"Power," he said. He leaned closer.

Jason felt the Gate open him up, atom by atom, tasting him, deciding how it would devour him. Stricken, he stared at Trent, his plans evaporating. He thought he knew it because he'd taken Bailey from it.

He realized now that nothing the Gate truly wanted would ever escape. He lost his grip on the earth. The maelstrom of energy bore him upward and then began to drag him back into the mists and carnage, back into its throat of an abyss.

Jonnard reached out. He grabbed Jason's outflung hand, crying, "Give it to me!"

Jason hung between the two of them, Jonnard and the Gate of Bones, power draining in both directions, his life flowing out, a candle burning wildly at both ends. So quickly! He thought he might have more time. . . .

Trent moved. He reached out and grasped Jason's forearm, his other hand untangling line after line of magical force only he could see. The Gate groaned and wailed as its strands snapped one after another, and Jason could feel himself flowing back. He gripped Trent tightly. Then, he pulled Jonnard in with his right hand.

The Gate seized them both. Jonnard yelled in fury and thrashed about. Jason anchored on Trent and let himself be pulled out, even as he continued to shut down the Gate, its attention fastened on Jonnard. It had him by the throat. His cries ceased, but his thrashing grew wilder.

Isabella flung herself at her son and heir. Whether she intended to push him in, or pull him out, no one could tell. Jonnard grabbed her fiercely, his face in a snarl, even as she screamed at him to let go and just feel the power.

Trent hauled Jason out, hand over hand, and the Gate snapped shut with a tremendous roar. It sucked itself inward, imploding, with a sound and fury that deafened them. Like a land sink, it filled itself in and the two had to scramble for it, dirt collapsing into a tremendous crater and they running to keep from being sucked down into it after all.

No sight could be seen of Isabella or Jonnard whatsoever.

The wolfjackals lifted their heads to the sky in a

long, triumphant howl. They whirled about. Lightning crackled off their silvery-black forms, and the clouds gathering opened up to take them in, as the two stared.

The quiet lasted only a moment. Then their crystals burst with voices, and Jason leaned back, listening to the Magickers, and he laughed.

Emily Drake

The Magickers

A long time ago, two great sorcerers fought a duel to determine the fate of the world. Magick was ripped from our world, its power kept secret by a handful of enchanters. The world of Magick, however, still exists—and whoever controls the Gates controls both worlds.

Book One:
THE MAGICKERS   0-7564-0035-X

Book Two:
THE CURSE OF ARKADY   0-7564-0103-8

Book Three:
THE DRAGON GUARD   0-7564-0141-0
(hardcover)

To Order Call: 1-800-788-6262

DAW 15